C.J. Cherryh

THE FOREIGNER UNIVERSE

FOREIGNER	PRECURSOR
INVADER	DEFENDER
INHERITOR	EXPLORER
DESTROYER	CONSPIRATOR
PRETENDER	DECEIVER
DELIVERER	BETRAYER
INTRUDER	TRACKER
PROTECTOR	VISITOR
PEACEMAKER	CONVERGENCE

EMERGENCE
RESURGENCE
DIVERGENCE

THE ALLIANCE-UNION UNIVERSE
ALLIANCE RISING (by C.J. Cherryh & Jane S. Fancher)
REGENESIS
DOWNBELOW STATION
THE DEEP BEYOND Omnibus:
Serpent's Reach | Cuckoo's Egg
ALLIANCE SPACE Omnibus:
Merchanter's Luck | 40,000 in Gehenna
AT THE EDGE OF SPACE Omnibus:
Brothers of Earth | Hunter of Worlds
THE FADED SUN Omnibus:
Kesrith | Shon'jir | Kutath

THE CHANUR NOVELS
THE CHANUR SAGA Omnibus:
The Pride Of Chanur | Chanur's Venture | The Kif Strike Back
CHANUR'S ENDGAME Omnibus:
Chanur's Homecoming | Chanur's Legacy

THE MORGAINE CYCLE
THE COMPLETE MORGAINE Omnibus:
Gate of Ivrel | Well of Shiuan | Fires of Azeroth | Exile's Gate

OTHER WORKS:
THE DREAMING TREE Omnibus:
The Tree of Swords and Jewels | The Dreamstone
ALTERNATE REALITIES Omnibus:
Port Eternity | Wave Without a Shore | Voyager in Night
THE COLLECTED SHORT FICTION
OF CJ CHERRYH

C. J. CHERRYH

DIVERGENCE

A *Foreigner* Novel

DAW

First Paperback Edition, September 2021
2 3 4 5 6 7 8 9

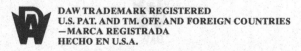

To Scott and Andrea.

DIVERGENCE

DIVERGENCE

Table of Contents

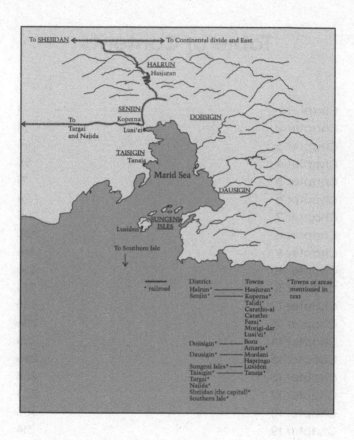

To SHEIIDAN ← → To Continental divide and East

HALRUN
Hasjuran

SENJIN
Koperna
Lusi'ei

To
Targai
and Najida ←

DOIISIGIN

TAISIGIN
Tanaja

Marid Sea

DAUSIGIN

SUNGENI
ISLES
Lusiden

To Southern Isle
↓

District	Towns	
		*Towns or areas mentioned in text
▬▬▬▬		
* railroad		
Halrun* ——————	Hasjuran*	
Senjin* ——————	Koperna*	
	Talidi*	
	Caratho-ai	
	Caratho	
	Farai*	
	Morigi-dar	
	Lusi'ei*	
Doiisigin* ——————	Boru	
	Amaria*	
Dausigin* ——————	Mordani	
	Hapringo	
Sungeni Isles* ———	Lusiden	
Taisigin* ——————	Tanaja*	
Targai*		
Najida*		
Sheiidan (the capital)*		
Southern Isle*		

1

A deep-voiced wail came from up the track: the warning howl of a train's imminent arrival.

Bren waked in utter dark, aware of a violent tremor in the rails—aware that Jago, who had slept next to him, was not in the bed.

A train coming straight for Hasjuran station and their own—stationary—train. Another wail. The train was coming fast and showing no sign of slowing down.

Something was insanely wrong. Will it hit us? was the immediate thought, but no, surely not. *Their* train was sitting on a siding, safe—one hoped—with the switch-lever locked and chained in place. Bren rolled out and onto his feet on ice-cold decking, fumbling in the dark for his nightrobe. His slippers eluded a brief, heart-pounding search. He saw a tiny red flash in the darkness of the windowless sleeping car: Jago's bracelet flashing an urgent signal. She was by the door, and dimmer flashes, partially obscured and reflected, resolved as other staff gathered mid-car, seeking and exchanging what information they could get through the coded Guild system.

The train was on them. The rumbling of the track and the scream of its warning drowned everything. Air-shock rocked them as it passed, roaring by at full throttle on the neighboring track. Its warning dopplered off and died in its passage into the night.

The usual warning signals for track conditions were all dead, taken out with the station transformer. A replacement was on its way, but had some train failed to realize that lack—and was it possibly hellbent past the town with absolutely no awareness that it was headed for the steepest grade on the planet?

Impossible. Every train with any reason to be on this remote route *had* to know that there was only one station and one town, Hasjuran, and that beyond it lay a nasty set of switchbacks. Impossible that the engineer wouldn't know . . . unless . . . unless that train had no legitimate reason to be here.

That racket would have waked the whole town to alarm, but even if some train *had* been hijacked and was headed full tilt for that descent in an act of sabotage—there was absolutely nothing anyone could do about it from here but advise the authorities in the distant capital and report a train wreck imminent on the Hasjuran grade.

Bren shivered, standing barefoot on the numbing cold of the decking, with the shock of that passage still reverberating in the air. He waited. If there was news from the rail system—or anyone else—his bodyguard, with him in the dark, would get it and pass it to him.

In the meanwhile, they *had* electrical power aboard the train, as the station and much of the town did not. That neither his bodyguard nor his staff had turned on the lights said either that they were too busy right now to bother with it or that they were purposely keeping things dark inside the compartment and the passage corridor outside—not because of the windows, because there were none to speak of in this whole train—but because they might have trouble aboard.

Which begged the question—could any outsider have forced a door and gotten aboard in the confusion and the racket? Doors on the Guild cars were all secure far beyond ordinary and currently set to open only from the inside. But they had one man aboard this train under firm arrest, with three partners they were not sure of.

They had no assurance, either, that those were the only problems they had, even granted that all the other personnel on the train were Assassins' Guild, units either absolutely and lifelong attached to specific persons, or teams certified reliable by the central Guild in Shejidan. They had posted sentries *outside* the train tonight despite the cold. Security around the stationary train was beyond tight, but their sentries might be vulnerable, and there was a whole town out there, with mountain trails leading in and out to the villages of the district, a complexity they could not secure.

This tiny province, Halrun, the town of Hasjuran, was the highest point and the southernmost that could be counted on as loyal to the aishidi'tat, the Western Association, which in fact had grown to span the continent. The hostile territory of the Dojisigin, the northeastern province of the Marid, lay at the foot of the pass, where that other train was headed at such ungodly speed. So did the northwestern Marid, Senjin district, with which they had just yesterday arranged an alliance.

"No information as yet," Jago said. The aiji-dowager, Ilisidi, with *her* high-level bodyguard, was rearward of their car, and Ilisidi's several units of bodyguards occupied the car between them. Bren's bodyguard and the dowager's young men, as she called them, were constantly in close contact, and communicated with others further up the train, units on loan from Assassins' Guild Headquarters in the capital.

If they collectively had no idea what was going on, Ilisidi's Guild-senior Cenedi would be asking coded questions of that distant headquarters, and if *they* had no idea, Cenedi would very possibly be rousing Tabini-aiji himself out of bed with news of a burgeoning situation involving the Marid, the Shadow Guild, an attempted assassination, sabotage, and possibly a destabilization of the whole district.

With the aiji-dowager, Tabini-aiji's grandmother, sitting on a train in the middle of it all.

Keep her safe. Tabini's final order to him, hours before he boarded the train.

Safe. God.

Whatever had passed them—quiet returned. The other train was gone, whether to slow down for the grade—or not.

One dim light now came on at the end of the compartment, two dark figures, Narani and Jeladi, domestic staff beginning to dress for duty, as Jago also began to do in haste, snatching clothes from wall hooks near the bed: Guild uniform, in her case—trousers, black tee, boots, holstered pistol and a heavy leather jacket. Her hair was still loose. So was Bren's. And his two staffers being also plainclothes Guild and taking their immediate orders from his four-person bodyguard, Bren decided that their minds were best occupied with security this morning, not his wardrobe or his comfort. He hugged his nightrobe about him, endured bare feet on the icy floor, and kept out of Jago's way as she moved further back to confer with Banichi, Guild-senior in this unit, and with Tano and Algini, the unit's second team. There was no information yet, and one just had to wait and let one's protectors all do what they needed to do.

He was, in fact, the sole human on the whole megacontinent, an official protected by his staff and his guard, who were atevi—native to the world, as humans were not. Atevi were head and shoulders taller than he was, dark-skinned, golden-eyed, seeing far better in the dark, and *far* less bothered by the cold. *He* was blond, pale-skinned, and at the moment, his feet were going quite numb. But it was not a moment or a situation in which the whereabouts of his slippers seemed a pertinent question.

His bodyguard, his aishid, ranked higher than any but Ilisidi's own on this train, so the discussion going on in low tones and coded flashes of light was not only information-seeking, he suspected, but decision-making, the issuance of orders in consultation with Cenedi's team. Sentries, wherever they were posted in this bitter cold night, were likely the only ones in position to have had a wide view of what had passed them—likely no more than a black shape and a headlamp arriving out of the dark and then disappearing into the night. With the station lights out, there might not have been a chance to read a number. If it had communicated with anyone in its passage, the Guild units aboard should have gotten a message by now. The conclusion was, it had not hailed them or passed a message, and up and down their own chain of command, they had no idea what its business was.

Town officials and local Transportation Guild were likely out of their own beds in the adjacent town and asking questions, none of them answerable, either. Lord Topari and his household would be in the dark—literally, since the loss of the transformer had taken out that part of the town—and Lord Topari tended to brim over with anxieties and doubts. There was no prospect of information for him tonight. Ilisidi's bodyguard *might* opt to communicate with the local officials, or vice versa, but that only as a formality. *No,* they would have to say. *We have no idea. No one aboard knows where it came from or what it intends. Yes, one sincerely hopes it will brake before it reaches the descent, but no one can currently swear to that. . . .*

It was not the sort of observation the Assassins' Guild ever liked to give to local officials. But that was the state of affairs.

As far as he knew.

Meanwhile his feet were no longer freezing; not, he feared, a good thing. He could hear the pinging of the small forced-air heater that served the car, now turned on, and trying to take the chill off, but it would take time.

Clearly information was not yet forthcoming, nor appearing to be likely any time soon. Bren sat down on the edge of his bed, and worked the blanket over his lap. In the slight light afforded by his staff's activity at the far end of the car, he thought he spied his slippers. Once he could feel his feet again, he would fetch them. His clothes, court dress and fussy, were not the sort of clothing one could hang on a hook. They were in the closet, and trying to dress himself in the narrow aisle was probably not helpful to anyone.

He caught no sense of further alarm in his bodyguard, more a determination to get at information which no one seemed to have, not even, evidently, the dowager's staff.

And the dowager did not like to be surprised. She liked even less to have significant events unfold which she did not control.

Which is how they came to be waking in the dark, in the Red Train, at the top of a mountain pass, surrounded by snow.

Not too many days before, comfortably sitting in her Eastern estate of Malguri, she had been mightily annoyed by the news of her grandson's apparent settlement of northern issues in her absence, issues involving a candidate for a contested lordship—a candidate she had neither approved nor endorsed—and precarious events involving her precious *great-grandson*—whose endorsement the candidate *had* won.

Not that Ilisidi was emotionally fraught, oh, no. That was not the way Ilisidi expressed her deeper grievances. So what *had* Ilisidi done in that mood of displeasure? She had gone to Bren's estate on the west coast, ostensibly to welcome the paidhi-aiji back from his mission to the human island of Mospheira.

Curiously, she had not been the only one waiting to surprise him, a coincidence he still suspected her of engineering. That night, as she sat in *his* estate, sipping *his* brandy in *his* sitting room, and while *he* was still getting his land legs back from the sea crossing—Lord Machigi had turned up, a putative ally of hers, the strongest lord on the western shore of the Marid, with neither an invitation nor a forewarning. They had shared brandy. She had listened, in apparent ignorance, to Machigi's sudden desire for a railroad to link *his* capital to the rail system in the middle of Lord Bregani's province, just to his north. Machigi had claimed that Bregani's alliance with his eastern neighbor, Tiajo, was in trouble. That there was an opportunity. That time was of the essence.

Ilisidi had promised to think about it.

Think about it? Ilisidi had come to that meeting in Najida with a towering lot of completely unrelated things on her mind, and at the top of that tower was the midlands, where her old ally Tatiseigi sat with vacant lordships on his east and his west, both gone down in a bloody sorting-out that had rattled the aishidi'tat to its core. The lordship of Kadagidi would remain vacant; but a young man had lately shown up claiming to be the heir of Ajuri. And Tatiseigi had believed him. Backed him. And had not consulted Ilisidi. That was the crux of matters.

Central to that bloody sorting-out years back, the outlawed splinter of the Assassins' Guild that was known as the Shadow Guild had found refuge in service to Lord Tiajo in the Dojisigin Marid—the same province that was now, according to Machigi, causing Bregani so much trouble.

Was it coincidence that Machigi arrived with an open invitation to Ilisidi to deal a major blow to that festering wound in the south, just when she had been summarily dealt out of the Northern solution? Possibly.

But that Ilisidi, whose endorsement of a candidate for the lordship of Ajuri had not even been requested—given an opening to deal a major blow to a target the Guild had long wanted to take down—would merely *think* about it . . .

No. In retrospect and considering how rapidly it had all come to pass, Bren would wager she had left his estate with the current mission fully planned and ready to implement.

Now . . . a train passed them in the middle of the night. A train *not* a part of that plan. And very likely coming from the capital, where the choice of agency was her grandson, the Assassins' Guild, or both.

No, Ilisidi would not be pleased.

Keep her safe, had been the sum of Tabini-aiji's instruction to him, when he had informed Bren of this trip into the mountain province of Hasjuran, to *discuss* Machigi's rail link with Hasjuran's minor lord, Topari. Keep her safe, Tabini had said, when she'd demanded Bren's presence as well as that of Nomari, the disputed candidate for Ajuri, and ordered the Red Train to be made ready.

Keep her safe . . . said to *him,* since the aiji-dowager was not currently speaking to her grandson—the hot issue being Nomari's pending appointment.

In point of fact, Tabini had not opposed the move she was making in the Marid, and he had not prevented her taking Nomari with her. Not even Tabini would ratify that lordship without Ilisidi's acceptance, if not wholehearted endorsement of the candidate. Ilisidi was fully capable of making such a young lord's life intolerable— and possibly short—and the aishidi'tat needed unity, not division, where it came to this appointment. A breach between Ilisidi and her old ally Lord Tatiseigi was likewise unthinkable. It needed to be resolved—particularly as Tabini's wife, the aiji-consort, was herself Ajuri, and Lord Tatiseigi's niece: Nomari was, among other things, *family.*

So Nomari was swept up without explanation, apparently with no relationship to the railroad issue—except that he had been, in his years of exile, a worker on the selfsame railroad. A switchman, without higher education, without courtly graces. And Ilisidi was going to consult *Nomari* on technicalities of railway construction? Hardly likely.

That Ilisidi would take the opportunity to grill the unfortunate candidate for Ajuri about his identity and his suitability for connection to the family all the way to Hasjuran and back—provided she let him return—was a foregone conclusion. And recalling his own encounter with Ilisidi's investigative process years ago, Bren had thought his own moderating presence *might* be a good idea.

If a visit to snowy Hasjuran and a diplomatic contact were *all* that was at issue. The Red Train, awaiting them in the Bujavid station, had turned out to be, not the usual two cars, not even the four or five entailed in a transcontinental trip, but a long string consisting of five luxury sleeping cars, windowless, armored, for security; two baggage cars, the antique luxury of the Red Car itself, and three state of the art Guild mobile command cars, as well as one well-worn boxcar tagging oddly behind the Red Car.

Then Machigi himself had shown up at the train station. In Shejidan—which he had never visited. And boarded one of those extra cars.

Keep her safe . . .

Easier said. Far easier said.

They were here in Hasjuran to talk, Ilisidi indicated . . . before she sent the Red Train down to Koperna in Senjin, and invited Bregani to come up, at night, in secret, to join those talks.

Invited.

Bren shifted his feet, tucking the blanket against an insidious draft, and wondered what Bregani and his family were thinking at the moment, five cars away, far less informed than he was about that speeding train.

Bregani had found himself in a vise, no matter whether he boarded that train as the dowager asked, or refused the conference and stayed in Koperna—because either way his neighbor Tiajo would hear that the dowager was communicating with him. Either way, all hell would break loose. And being on the icy heights of Hasjuran when that news broke was the survivable choice.

So Bregani was trapped, snared, netted, and ruined,

so far as his alliance with Tiajo was concerned, leaving Bregani only the dubious safety of the dowager's whim. Bregani had chosen to board the Red Train, but such was his fear of Tiajo's agents, he had left home with precautions. He had set a cousin in charge of his capital, and brought his wife and teenaged daughter with him, intending to put them under the dowager's protection, no matter what happened to him, that being a far safer future for them than remaining in reach of Tiajo's fits of temper.

Bregani certainly had not expected to face his old enemy Machigi in a meeting the night before last—or for Ilisidi and Machigi to propose not his ruin, but alliance, Guild protection, and association with the two of them in a rail link, with the promise of increased trade.

All Bregani had had to do was sign the agreement, officially break relations with Tiajo, in essence—and stay alive—in the interests of which, Ilisidi serenely informed him that the routine freight train currently undergoing service down in his capital was actually hers, a Guild operation, and that if he signed the agreement and asked for Guild protection, those cars would open and a Guild force would immediately deploy to defend his people from whatever elements Tiajo might send in reaction.

Bregani had signed. What choice had he? With the offer of a pen and an inkwell, Ilisidi had taken a province.

Now here they sat—Lord Bregani, his wife and daughter; Lord Machigi of the Taisigin; the aiji-dowager, lord of distant Malguri; himself, Bren Cameron, paidhi-aiji, the chief negotiator for Tabini-aiji *or* his grandmother over the last number of years . . .

And felicitous seventh, a young man who had not expected to be invited to an interview with the aiji-dowager, let alone take part in this historic meeting of lords. Nomari, a railway worker, favored candidate to take on the lordship of Ajuri, the aiji-consort's clan, and become a neighbor to Tatiseigi and a cousin to Tabini-aiji's wife.

That, it turned out, was not all he was. Nomari had worked not only for the railroad, but for Lord Machigi during a brief overthrow of Tabini-aiji's government, spying on the activity in Lord Bregani's railyard. Machigi, it turned out, *knew* him. By one source or another—hers were many—Ilisidi knew Machigi knew him, and characteristic of her dealings, had thrown these two together on this lengthy train trip and just watched the outcome.

Bren had tried to contact a source *he* knew, a former Shadow Guild operative, Homura, a man who, for a life-debt, had turned so far against the Shadow Guild as to swear man'chi to a human. The man had finally made contact with the train *here*, at Hasjuran, this tiny town on the inconvenient roof of the world. Tano and Algini had gone outside to meet with Homura, by no means trusting him. Homura had warned them specifically about Bregani's bodyguard, told them his own partner Momichi was down in Koperna, warned them of changes in Shadow Guild tactics, then appeared suddenly ill at ease, and broke off the meeting.

Before Tano and Algini had quite gotten back onto the train, the station transformer had blown up, taking out power to the station, and to the great house of Hasjuran, and a section of homes and businesses in the town, while doing superficial damage to the train itself. Tano and Algini had caught the edge of the blast—Tano still suffered from it—and Homura had not been seen or heard from since.

Had Tiajo gotten Shadow Guild operatives up here that fast? Or had she gotten a message through to agents already ensconced in Hasjuran? If it was a Shadow Guild action, why had there been no further move? Had Homura then taken out their problem?

Or was *he* the problem?

Bregani's wife's bodyguard *was* indeed compromised. That much had proven true. One man of that unit had turned, not because he was Shadow Guild—but because the Shadow Guild had kidnapped the man's family, exactly the situation and the tactic Homura had warned them about. Tiajo's agents cared nothing about civilized standards, or honor. The threat used to control Homura's unit, two partners held hostage to assure their performance, had now turned on others, and intended to have a man betray his own unit and kill the people he was sworn to protect.

The man had hesitated, and against high-level Guild, he had failed. So *that* had not happened. But the transformer had blown, they had lost track of a known, if former, Shadow Guild agent, and before all was done, Bregani had had to deal with an unthinkable breach of trust, poor man, all attending his signing an agreement with Ilisidi and Machigi. His guard was under detention, replaced with a four-man unit of Ilisidi's choosing. He'd gone to bed in a train now running on internal power, and knew that, though he had authorized the Guild to deploy in Senjin, fighting had broken out down in Senjin and the port city. They had that information through Guild communications, routed God knew how, but likely the message had sped around the lowlands and up to the capital before it got to them.

That was yesterday evening.

And well before the night was done, Bregani, with the rest of them, had waked to that thundering presence in the dark, uninformed as to what had happened, or what might happen, or what worse threat was headed down toward his province.

Bren felt his own heart still recovering, and the memory of that passage still in his bones. He was sorely in want of a cup of strong tea. He had no idea what time it was. But it was unlikely anyone anywhere on the train had slept through that howling passage, and if there was action contemplated, there was no going back to bed. He should, he thought, at least send a reassuring message to Bregani and Nomari.

He wiggled his toes and finding them functional, stood up, walked the few paces to where Jago stood, in a lull in the flurry of communications.

"There is still no word," Jago said, to his implied question. "It is still snowing, with a high wind. One can scarcely see, and the sentries have been on extreme alert. There was no warning of this train at all in the system. We have that from the Transportation Guild."

That in itself was disturbing. The Transportation Guild ran the rail line. The Transportation Guild employed the engineers and mechanics and the people who kept the signals and the switches all over the system. Communications to and from Hasjuran were seasonally chancy, partly because of isolation, partly because of the surrounding peaks and weather. The Assassins' Guild, in force on this train, he understood had communication with their own headquarters back in Shejidan, and they had not expected this train. The Assassins' Guild as well as Transportation monitored the rails wherever the Red Train went, and that *they* might have been caught by surprise was almost unprecedented.

True, the guilds did *not* always inform each other when security on an operation was extreme—and particularly the Assassins' Guild did not use regular communications when the Shadow Guild might be at issue. The Shadow Guild had identical equipment, identical communications—had once had identical codes, one having been part of the other not that long ago, in a scheme that reached back decades. There was also, though lessened now, the possibility of sleeper agents in their own network, so that wherever Shadow Guild interests might be drawn into a situation, the Assassins occasionally sent false messages on their regular networks to try to draw out such persons, operating in constantly changing codes.

That much he knew of their procedures. The Assassins did not generally deploy noisy means—but if somebody was intending to get down from the heights ahead of

Bregani's return, a train was the only way. There were two authorities that *might* make such a move: the Assassins' Guild Council, making its own assault on the Dojisigin Marid, and declining to discuss the move with the aiji-dowager—or Tabini-aiji moving forces, either to protect the dowager—or to restrain her from a move that could set fire to the whole Marid. The Hasjuran grade was not the easiest or safest route from Shejidan to the northern Marid, but it was the fastest.

Granted Ilisidi had not consulted with her grandson nearly as thoroughly as she should have done in advance of this venture.

Granted Tabini might have some reservations about her mood and the outcome of a mistake.

Maybe her sending a trainload of Guild down to hold Bregani's capital had tripped an alarm and set Tiajo to invade Senjin outright.

That would not be good news.

Tano, half of the second team of Bren's bodyguard, left the compartment for the through passage, headed, Bren was sure, for the Guild car forward of theirs. The senior member of that team, Algini, exchanged a hand-signal with Banichi, head of the unit, and went out, likewise on a mission of some kind.

Banichi along with his partner, Jago, stayed with Bren, while Narani and his assistant Jeladi moved quietly to the galley nook and set water to heating. Tea and wafers would be available.

Bren went in search of his slippers, that seeming about all that the paidhi-aiji could do about the situation, besides staying out of everyone's way. If Ilisidi wanted his presence, she would call him, and Bregani and the rest would simply have to wait for information. He found his slippers not where he expected, but close by the rumpled bed, then came back to the little galley to a seat at the adjacent table, a narrow fixture that served them additionally as conference table and office.

"We just do not know, do we?" Bren said to Jeladi as Jeladi set a steaming cup in front of him.

"Not yet, nandi," Jeladi acknowledged.

"But no one will have slept through that." He took a sip of hot tea, enjoying the warmth in his hands as Jeladi stood waiting for orders. The whole car, like the cup, like the seat, was scaled for atevi. His feet did not reach the floor. He tucked one slippered foot behind his knee, to finish thawing it. "We should communicate with our passengers, Ladi-ji, that first. Barring some order from the dowager, or a problem aboard, I shall need messages run in a moment."

"Nandi." Jeladi bowed. "I shall get my coat."

"I should dress," Bren said. "But I shall write the notes first." Another sip of tea. Then he set down the source of warmth and took the writing kit and three sheets of paper from the caddy on the walled side of the little table. A call from the dowager to ask *him* about the train was not likely: *he* had no information to give her. But when the dowager moved on to next questions, in particular anything regarding the possibility of her grandson's actions interfering with *her* operation, he could not be found sipping tea and doing nothing.

Keeping their assorted passengers from attempting moves of their own was a start.

Selecting a sheet, he wrote hurriedly.

Bren paidhi-aiji to Machigi, Lord of the Taisigin Marid.
We were also startled by the passage of the train and as yet have no explanation. We are secure here, we are amply defended, and the aiji-dowager will be seeking an answer. It is possible, though only my own theory, that the aiji may just have put additional forces at the dowager's disposal.

That was the entirely optimistic interpretation. They were days out from the capital. If anything had been launched from there, it was *not* due to recent developments.

Please stay where you are and rest if possible. We have no appearance of local danger and certainly right now the descent to the Marid is unavailable to us, so long as that train's whereabouts and the track conditions are unknown. I shall inform you the moment I have additional information.

It was essentially the same message in all three notes, one to their ally Machigi, one to Bregani, and one to Nomari—the latter being Transportation Guild himself—and likely with a more specific image of what could possibly be going on, at least as regarded the way down to the Marid.

To Nomari, instead of the last paragraph, he wrote: *Advise your bodyguard if you have any insight into the situation of the train that passed us, who it may be, or any technical problem it may cause us if ill-intentioned. Your aishid will relay it where useful.*

And he added, as an afterthought. *At some time this morning, granted my schedule has not yet materialized, I should welcome a conference with you regarding conditions on the descent. I have questions.*

Bregani had been supposed to go down that route last night. Ilisidi had promised him as a condition of his coming up here that, if he came, he would be given safe transport back again, possibly soon enough that no one would have realized his absence. That expedited return had not happened. Prior to the signing of the agreement of association with Ilisidi and with his old enemy Machigi, there had been dinner. There had been further negotiations. Details to work out. By the time the signing was completed, it had been very late. Rumors had spread through Bregani's capital and the repercussions had begun. Bregani's acceptance of Guild assistance had set protections in place and begun a sweep for hidden problems, but Bregani's return had been delayed awaiting an all-clear from the Guild.

Too, there was the matter of courtesy to their host, Topari of Hasjuran. For all Hasjuran and Senjin were neighbors, give or take a hazardous rail link, these two had never met. Topari, lord of Hasjuran, smallest and least of the provinces in the Western Association, of which they all were members, had not been party to the signing of the previous night's agreement. He was not a man used to conference rooms and delicate maneuvering, and being firmly counted as a lord of the aishidi'tat, he could not wish to entangle himself and his people in the politics of the Marid.

Economically, however, his tiny province stood to benefit greatly by the new agreement, and to that end he would soon, if all went well, sign a separate agreement, forming an association with, specifically, Ilisidi and *her* associate, Lord Machigi. That agreement would create an additional felicitously three-way agreement. In it, Topari was promised increased trade—and a large warehouse to handle the increased trade. Machigi's link would bring far more traffic into the system—entailing jobs, and fees and recognition of the district within the aishidi'tat, all of which were very welcome with Topari and Hasjuran.

Of innocents involved in all of this scheming—and there were few—Topari was the central one, and he had wakened to the same uproar this morning, poor man. Now he would be faced with more questions from his town, and was likely wondering whether the whole situation had changed, or whether, which could be the unfortunate case, he had become unwitting host to an attack on the Marid.

He meditated a note to Topari, as well, but risking someone to take it across the square, no; and sending information through the airwaves was a Guild decision, not his.

Bren folded the notes, to have no wax, no cylinders since they were short and straightforward, requiring no reply. He gave them to Jeladi, as Jeladi reported back dressed for the nighttime chill of the passage. "Be particularly sure of the addressee," he said, and knew Jeladi took the cue that they were not identical. "Are we still secure?" he asked Jago, with a glance over his shoulder, not about to send Jeladi out even into the through passages if there was any doubt of his safety.

"At the moment," Jago said. Banichi was still listening to the information flow, standing, a looming black figure, beside the passageway door.

"If anything happens, take the nearest shelter, Ladi-ji. Do not attempt the passage in that case."

"Yes," Jeladi said, took the three notes and left, with a waft of icy air from the passage that communicated up and down the train. Jago and Banichi were meanwhile consulting quietly, and Jago tapped the earpiece she wore, listening to something, but nothing either of them shared. Narani set down a second cup of tea, which Bren sipped slowly, cradling it between his hands to warm them.

"Is it daylight?" Aboard the train, absent a clock, it was impossible to tell.

"An hour before," Narani said. So it was no good trying to rest.

Bren finished the tea and, finally warm enough to trust his feet, visited the accommodation. He blinked into the mirror, shoved his hair back and gave it a twist to keep it there, then shaved in the dim light, an operation he usually did after his hair was in its habitual queue, but nothing on the trip had been in ordinary order. By the time he returned to the common area, Narani had made up the bed, and had clothes ready for him—his best, Narani's own estimation of the day's requirements.

"Is Topari still coming this morning?" he asked.

"We assume so, nandi," Narani said.

And Topari, nervous fellow that he was, was going to have questions when he arrived for the signing, a lot of questions—to which there were no ready answers.

Given a fairly fraught situation, and Topari tending to the sort of nervousness Ilisidi constitutionally abhorred, Ilisidi was going to say—paidhi, *deal* with him. Bren had no doubt of it.

He had had his personal difficulties with the fellow, who did not readily take *wait* for an answer, who had been both forward and over-energetic in the capital in his pursuit of advantages for his district, and who truly had no idea how to deal with a human within the atevi power structure.

But having *seen* Hasjuran, its snowy isolation, its unique wooden buildings, its ways and its character, Bren had acquired an admiration for the courage it had taken for this very rural lord to have faced the social complexities of the Bujavid aristocracy. Hasjuran had a difficult and small-scale economy. In a world increasingly dominated by human science and technology, by strange ideas raining down from a space station owned jointly by humans and atevi, Hasjuran saw none of it, only heard, and hoped for some importance in atevi affairs.

For years, all Topari had wanted was to get consideration for his province, his people, their ancient, traditional ways and crafts, and here it had had its chance, hosting the aiji-dowager, a personage of immense consequence in the aishidi'tat. It wanted to show its very best, and Topari had accommodated the dowager in every respect, had not stinted hospitality to the venture. Beyond question he *hoped* for some sort of substantive gain for his district, but thus far there had been no specificity in his asking or in the dowager's offering.

This morning, that was due to change. This morning, he was scheduled to sign a significant document: an association with a former enemy, Machigi, and, beyond his wildest dreams, the aiji-dowager, an agreement that could bring that long-sought prosperity to his province.

Could.

The problem was, the new arrangement was not going to set well with Tiajo, lord of the Dojisigi province, who had come to power as a teenager without restraint and who had a nest of willing killers at her disposal. Tiajo had used those killers to wreak havoc in the Marid and terrorize her neighbor, Bregani, into compliance with her various schemes. Topari might be naive about the capital and the politics there, but he was not naive about the Marid's potential for problems. He knew that another war in the Marid could cut off *all* through commerce, not a fatal hit, since at least half of Hasjurani trade went north and west to the midlands, but half went south, into the Marid and points westward. Losing that, in potential, would be a heavy blow.

He'd been ready to take that chance—in actual fact, he likely would sign anything the dowager asked him to sign—and the contract was to be Topari's assurance things *would* be to his people's good. But before he could sign, before he had that protection in place, the transformer blew and Hasjuran lost all power to its train station and a third of the town. Accident or sabotage by Tiajo's Shadow Guild, there had been no warning, and they had no reserve equipment. Even now, they were stringing lines out there in the snowy square to bring up power for public safety, and to keep businesses running, but it would be days before a replacement arrived.

At this point, a very nervous Topari likely hoped simply not to be at odds with Lord Machigi *or* Lord Bregani, who were both here now, and who had been bitter enemies, and who were, even now, at least as far as Topari knew, accusing each other of the act. He undoubtedly hoped not to have the wrath of Lord Tiajo come surging up the grade to do sabotage and murder—neither of which was beneath Tiajo.

Indeed, one had sympathy for Lord Topari's situation.

Which was useful, considering it was likely going to be on one Bren Cameron to handle Topari. It would certainly be up to him to inform Topari of the politics aboard the train, where one of Bregani's bodyguard was in detention, a bodyguard whose family was being held hostage by the Shadow Guild, imperiling Bregani's compact with the dowager and Machigi. Meanwhile the dowager herself would be unwilling to admit she had no idea *what* had just run through the station . . . not because Topari would choose any other side than hers, but because Topari's discretion with information was, by past experience, non- existent.

He would have to provide pomp and ceremony enough to keep Topari satisfied, try to organize a brief gesture from Ilisidi to reassure the man—and above all to make sure nothing else untoward happened.

Given the weather, too, if there was trouble still out there, there was every possibility it might try again to disrupt the proceedings. Topari's crossing from the great house to the train station was a worrisome thing, given the weather they had had; and they also had to worry about Topari's situation once they moved on. They had no auxiliary power to heat and light the train if they sent the engine to take Bregani home. They might have to take Bregani to Shejidan instead. And moving on and leaving Topari to deal with whoever had taken out the transformer—that was not an optimum situation, either.

All of which—was his problem, if Ilisidi did not step in to make decisions this morning. And they had no word of her doing that. She *likely* was trying to get information out of Guild Headquarters. Or perhaps just over-tired. She was extremely old. The environment, the thin air, the complications and the decisions that had to be made . . .

She was busy. He told himself that. She was doing something needful. He was apparently in charge, second in authority aboard, God help him, without knowing what precisely she *was* doing, what was happening down in the Marid, what Tabini-aiji thought of the mess, or whether Tiajo had realized that, up atop the longest, steepest grade on earth, Ilisidi had just peeled away her chief ally.

For the immediate future, he had to be sure the sentries expected Topari to cross that open square. He had to weigh how much to tell anyone about Homura's undercover and ill-omened arrival—no way in hell, he thought, that he had just happened to answer his summons *here,* turning up in a place they never could be expected to be. Either Homura had made the world's wildest and luckiest guess where to find them, or had business here—or he was back in the employ of the people who held his partners hostage. The fact he was alone and his remaining partner Momichi was not with him—was worrisome. He had said Momichi was down in Koperna, where a person *would* be if he intended to take the rare train up to Hasjuran.

Of course, it was possible Hasjuran *was* where Homura and Momichi had been operating, all along, unfindable until now. The high mountains and the villages were a place to be lost, and still pick up news out of the Marid.

Trust Homura, under the circumstances?

Bottom line, one was down to that aspect of human-atevi relations that Bren could *not* feel and *not* judge, that emotion that distinguished and often confounded atevi. Man'chi. Homura had given man'chi to *him,* in debt for his life and freedom. To him and to the dowager, in the same moment. Attachment. Loyalty. The psychological willingness to take a bullet for another person.

He felt ashamed to doubt Homura's sincerity in that regard—it was a deep and serious gesture Homura had made, in Lord Tatiseigi's entry hall; but he had to consider that possibility, for the sake of his own aishid, for the dowager, and everybody else. Order Homura found? It could expose an innocent man; or get someone else killed; and they had too many loose ends flying in the wind right now, no surety they would be staying here longer than it took to get Topari's signature and seal on a piece of parchment.

And bottom line right now, *Ilisidi* also held hostage

Bregani's man'chi, his authority over Senjin: his dignity, his lordship, his people's man'chi vested in him. Ilisidi, getting Bregani up here, had told him she would send him back again at his request. She had pledged him her support—but delayed because *they* needed the engine for power; and now replaced his guard with her own because that guard was turned.

Now that other train had passed them, of what nature, they still had no word, and in what intent, they had no word, but the train had not bothered to identify itself or ask a by your leave. With the dowager involved—that said something.

They could not go on delaying their own action. He read that well enough. They would go in some direction, either turn around—the station had that capability—or go down. And his own instinct said they would not turn around, not with Ilisidi having given her word.

Court dress, indeed. Bren dressed his lower half, put on his shirt, and did the buttons himself, his preference. Narani came to assist, and stood ready with the bullet-proof vest, that stiff and unpleasant defensive item recent events made advisable—blue, this one, matching the coat, and for once he was glad of its extra warmth. But he did not fasten it until he had, with Jeladi's assistance, put on his boots.

"Bren-ji," Banichi said quietly. "Regarding the train—we do not yet have a statement, but headquarters has now sent a plain code specifically to us regarding our question. They do not take alarm."

That *was* reassuring. He stood up, and made a half-hearted try at the vest. Jeladi intervened and fastened it under the arm. "The train was theirs, then? Or is its owner higher up?"

Of *higher up* in that chain of command, besides Ilisidi, there was only one.

"Unclear," Banichi said. "That does not answer for its speed going through here, but Transportation would likely have warned the operator that the signals were not working, and likewise affirmed that the track was clear and that the switches were safely chained and locked."

Little snowy Hasjuran offered a clearer *clear track* than one would ever find down in the midlands, where trains wove their way to every village and township and ran tightly interlocked schedules. Up in this lonely little station, trains that came from Shejidan and occasionally from the East picked up and delivered cargo, then reversed and went back down to the transcontinental rail. Two regular trains twenty-three days apart would come here, shed cars in excess of what the switchback descent permitted, and head down to Koperna, the Marid's only rail connection. A freight would shed cars there, pick up others, and head west to Targai and Najida, then head north along the coast to Cobo, again take on cars, and then leave on the transcontinental line. It was rare that any train ran *up* the Hasjuran-Koperna rail.

Excepting the very small railyard here at Hasjuran, it was single track all the way from the transcontinental line up into these mountains, and down the hellish grade to Koperna, where there was another, much larger yard. The plan had been, once, to link the Dojisigin Marid with Senjin, welding the two northern Marid provinces into one trade entity, but decades back, Cosadi's warfare in the Marid had gotten too ambitious, and in the upshot of a brief shooting war, the Transportation Guild had cut the Dojisigin Marid off cold and refused to build their rail, though it maintained the Hasjuran grade and the railyard in Senjin as a useful access to the entire Marid, and as a useful turnaround for trains headed in either direction.

"We cannot get to the Dojisigin by rail," he said to Banichi. It was a question, because things might have changed since the last map he had seen. "That old line was never finished, am I right? We cannot get to them by train and they cannot get to us."

"There is a siding," Banichi said, "and an unfinished

spur at the end of the descent. We are told the siding is maintained useable, and is under Transportation control, as Koperna could cease to cooperate without notice for some reason. The spur, such as there is, is reported impassible. They have not maintained it."

"So that train that passed us could either go on to Koperna, or stop on the siding, if it were so disposed—without blocking our descent."

Banichi gave a little frown and nodded. "Even so."

"Has the dowager given *any* hint of her intention to go down?"

"She has not. But she has promised to get Lord Bregani home."

"One can only hope she will wait for more clarity on the situation in Koperna. And on the track."

Banichi looked at him, assessing, as it seemed. Weighing answers. "Guild Headquarters knows what the train is. We do not."

"It is my guess that the dowager will keep her word, and we are going down to guarantee Lord Bregani's safety."

"If it can be guaranteed," Banichi said. "Which is to say—Cenedi will be very reluctant to move until we have better information."

Narani had prepared his coat. Bren reached back for the sleeves, and Narani settled it on his shoulders.

"How *is* the situation in Koperna at the moment?" Bren asked, letting Narani fuss with his right cuff.

"We do not have details and one would not call it stable. We have sketchy information that sites the government as having moved from the residency area to the broadcast center—we assume this is Bregani's cousin in that location. We are told the situation is moderately stable."

So government was being run, effectively, from the broadcast center: it gave the government a voice and placed key personnel in a fundamentally more secure building. But it did not sound like complete tranquility, and it could get worse without notice. The Guild would secure the railyard first; and the station; and secure avenues from that, with a priority of protecting the broadcast center and being sure of the cousin's safety.

"One would hope they are protecting the records," Bren said, thinking of the Residency dropping to a secondary concern.

"Those and the utilities," Banichi said.

They had hoped for more certainty. But the Guild would secure areas before it moved on, certainly leaving nothing of resistance between them and the railyard, logically moving to relieve any pressure on Bregani's cousin.

Time was when the human from Port Jackson had had a very limited grasp of strategy and tactics, but he had gained something over the years—listening to Banichi.

And staying out of the way. Now—

Now it came to him that Ilisidi might have played this board in a very different fashion. If she had simply sat aboard and not communicated with an increasingly anxious Lord Topari—Topari would have been beyond agitated. But the Dojisigin might have regarded the Red Train's arrival as a bluff. Or a decoy. Or even an uncommon but not unknown routing. The Red Train had occasionally come through here in the past, stopping briefly in Hasjuran, before going down on a non-stop run to Najida.

"One would think," he said to Banichi, "that the dowager need not have made her presence aboard known. We made that excursion, all of us, to Lord Topari's dinner. And if the Dojisigi have agents here, as they surely do— they will have reported it."

"Indeed."

"When the Red Train left half its cars and went down to Koperna, they may have suspected she was going there herself."

"When it turned about and went up again," Banichi expanded on the hypothetical, "they may or may not have realized Bregani was on it. They may not even have realized it as the Guild deployed down there, and it is remotely possible they *still* do not realize he is here— though once the Guild deployed, with a declaration it was at Lord Bregani's request, it would put the mecheita in the dining room, so to speak. And orders *have* been coming from Bregani's cousin, purporting to be from him. Now the Dojisigin see another train coming down the grade. They might move to stop it. They *might* mistake it, in the dark, for the Red Train coming back again, to take control of the action in Koperna—which would be interesting."

"Sabotage?"

"Say that we are not sitting and waiting for them to try it. The first train down to Senjin deployed agents with cold-weather gear along the route, with better equipment *and* insulation than the Shadow Guild will have. That is classified, Bren-ji. We retain all options. Should the Hasjuran grade not be an option, we can reverse here and go all the way around the Southern Range to come into Senjin from the west. But that is a good seven or more days, and the longer Senjin lacks certainty the worse for the situation. We do not want to fight the people of Koperna."

"So we are going down."

"I think that is the conclusion the dowager will reach. There are no barriers down on the coast. One bridge. That also will be under our surveillance by now. Koperna has no defenses on the eastern approach—its defense having rested with the Dojisigin even before the Shadow Guild existed, there are not even the remnants of walls. The land is flat and the marsh drainage, save that one river, is to the south of the railroad. This has been extensively planned. I can say that. Cenedi's briefing covered all points."

"Except that train just now."

"Excepting that," Banichi said. "So we are fairly sure where we will meet it."

"We are wagering a very great deal on that."

"If it surprises us, it very likely surprises the Shadow Guild."

"To our good, in that," Bren said. He stood in court dress. Banichi in the more armored gear the Guild used in combat. "I am to deal with Lord Topari, assuming he keeps the appointment. I do not think the dowager will be in any mood for it."

"She will not," Banichi agreed.

"Do you think Tiajo is not going to survive, this time?"

"I think it was not the dowager's direct intention. I think it likeliest the aiji is simply moving to protect his grandmother against any unforeseen countermove. It would be foolish to make a try at the Red Train with the aiji's forces in place . . . but Tiajo is not known for common sense."

That was true. Tiajo had gotten power as a teenager, and she never could have stayed in power without the Shadow Guild and all its apparatus. They moderated her bad decisions, but they had humored her hates and her tantrums and killed for them with no particular objection. She was manageable and she was feared by her people. That was her function, for them.

Could her recklessness push the Shadow Guild into a desperate move, and into a Guild trap?

On the one hand it was a wonderful prospect—seeing the last of the Shadow Guild go down.

On the other hand one did not want to be a close observer to that event. The Shadow Guild was entrenched in the folded landscape of the inner Dojisigin. They had lost heavily in the last set-to with the Shejidani Guild, who had outfought them in the field. Now Ilisidi had just stripped away the province that was Tiajo's last ally. Ilisidi *was* directly threatening them, daring them to risk more of their assets to come after her.

"Let me know," Bren said, "whatever you can find out. And have breakfast, Nichi-ji. Let us take whatever we can while we can. We are not at all certain about supper."

Narani laid out all the stores of teacakes they had without access to the galley, with toast and preserves, and pots of tea; and they had, at least, breakfast before them, on the inadequate table. It was set as a standing buffet, and Algini poured tea in a row of cups.

Tano came back just then, quietly entered the compartment. "There are messages besides the replies," Tano said, and offered a small, cord-wrapped bundle of four cylinders and a bare paper roll.

One of those cylinders was the dowager's. One had Bregani's colors. The third had Machigi's. The fourth had Topari's. The bare paper roll was likely Nomari's.

It was no question which missive to read first. He took a deep breath and drew out Ilisidi's message.

Your presence is required at breakfast immediately.

Well—that settled the question of his own breakfast. And maybe one not of a flavor he would wish.

Narani had shed the casing of the other notes, and handed them to him in order.

From Nomari, who knew something of trains, to say the least: *If I can be of service please call on me. Thank you for the message, nandi.*

From Bregani: *We are deeply concerned. We appeal to the paidhi's office to inform us what is happening here and down in Senjin.*

From Machigi: *Whose was the train?*

And a formal parchment message from outside, from Topari, in a nervous hand: *Shall I still come to sign the document? Is everything well? Please advise me, nand' paidhi.*

One did not delay about the dowager's summons. But he cleared the edge of the food-laden table and, standing, dashed off a quick note of his own:

Bren, Paidhi-aiji
To Topari lord of Hasjuran.

We hope to have information soon. Expect to come as planned, but be ready to come sooner if called. Take strong security precautions while crossing the square. This message without my seal, as I am in haste. I am about to meet with the aiji-dowager and I shall know more soon. Please be assured the welfare of Hasjuran is equal with all other matters in the dowager's concern and you will be protected as a bastion of the aishidi'tat.

He passed the rolled note to Tano, who was waiting for answers. "Case that. Seal it. Do not leave the train yourself, Tano-ji. Call in a local messenger to carry it, and then come straight back here, sit down, and have breakfast."

"Yes," Tano said, and went off again.

Bren shook back his lace cuff, bent to the table again and wrote, in three rapid instances, *I am about to meet with the dowager and will have some answers shortly. We believe the train in question is ours. Please be patient.*

"The breakfast will await your arrival, nandi," Narani reported. And, more precisely: "The dowager is at table."

"Nadiin-ji," he said. "Have breakfast. All of you. That is an order. I can travel the passage safely enough."

"Bren-ji," Banichi said.

"I shall be in Cenedi's territory in fortunate seven easy strides, nadiin-ji. And I am armed." He had felt the weight in his pocket when Narani had settled the coat about him. "Breakfast. Please."

2

Cajeiri opened his eyes on a windowless dark bedroom, his room, in his father's apartments, in the Bujavid, awake not for the first time in a long and uneasy night, and not wanting to get up—because if he did, his younger bodyguards, asleep in their two rooms opening onto his, might also wake, and once they woke, then Eisi and Liedi, his major d' and his doorman would wake—and then his senior bodyguard, and then everybody, including the new servants. Which was not fair. And it did no good for them to be awake.

It did no good for him, either, and he could not say why he had waked twice before in the dark. Even Boji was asleep—which was a good thing. Boji would be curled on a branch in his filagree cage in the sitting room, a furry blacker knot in a very deep dark. At times he wished he could be Boji, and not wake thinking about things that had no shape and no reality.

Most of all, Boji spent no time in his day worrying about things.

And he once had been like that. But no longer.

He was fortunate nine. He was halfway to decisive ten, that number fraught with choices, two lucky threes, two extremely infelicitous twos, and a number perfectly divisible into an infelicitous two of equally chancy fives, in which lucky three won over the infelicity of two by a perfect unity of one.

Ten was that kind of number, delicately balanced, either to set one on a good course to indivisible eleven, or to become that sort of boy nobody trusted.

Father said, "Regard the truth of the numbers, expect others to believe in them, but do not expect that everybody will believe, and do not be afraid to take a chance. The forces that move the world are not all atevi. But you know that."

He did. Humans had terrified the world when they arrived because the numbers had not foretold their coming. Nobody expected them to have dropped in, as people had once thought, from the moon.

They had actually come from much, much further away, in a great ship that sat now just off the space station. And they had built the Foreign Star in the heavens, when atevi had only just invented railroads. Humans had landed in petal sails, and brought amazing technology with them.

But for a time the Foreign Star had faded into legend and no one had seen it except in telescopes, until it had miraculously reappeared in the heavens. He understood why—he understood a thing that a great many adults did not remotely understand, how the station had moved back into *geostationary orbit*. That was a word most adults did not know. But he did. He was proud of that.

Only a handful of atevi had left the solar system and come back again. And he was one of them. So was Great-grandmother. He was extremely proud of that distinction.

And nand' Bren, of course, had gone with them. He had never been afraid of humans, nand' Bren having been part of the household since he could remember. And on the voyage he had gained human associates besides nand' Bren, associates of his own age who had grown up in faraway space and survived a terrible attack on their space station. They had only just recently been able to come down to the island of Mospheira to live, and learn how other humans lived. Now they were only a plane flight away, living in a building that sat on the grounds of the Mospheiran University, and studying with tutors to learn things they needed to know to be Mospheiran, things they had never known, having been born far off in space. So close—only across the straits from the west coast—and one day . . . soon, he hoped . . . they *would* come to visit him again in Shejidan, or better yet, they would come by boat rather than plane, and he would meet them at nand' Bren's estate of Najida, where they could fish and go out in nand' Bren's boat, and do all sorts of things.

That was now. That was real. And it was a good thing. But sometimes, in bed at night, he dreamed about the ship, and the tunnels where they had used to meet as the great ship raced between stars. And sometimes, too, he dreamed about the station, and about Hakuut an Ti, who was another associate of his, a kyo, and as different from atevi *or* human as one could be. The kyo had almost been enemies. But now they were not.

He had been so many places. Dangerous places.

He had been in such situations, always, with mani, Great-grandmother—and with nand' Bren. And with Cenedi and Banichi, and all the rest. He had been with them in all sorts of dangers, and met his human associates, and the kyo, and learned all sorts of things, things he never would have known, had he not left the world.

But now he was back from the stars, and like his human associates, he had to learn to be something different from what he had been all his life. Someday all those things he had learned in space, all those associates he had made . . . would matter, but in the meantime, he was officially Father's heir, and as such he had to learn things about trade and supply and demand and clan histories and old wars. And because the security of the aishidi'tat would one day, some time in the far future, rest on him, he had to stay in the Bujavid. Where it was safe.

Too safe.

And while he rested here, being safe, mani was off with Lord Machigi, who was scary all on his own; and with Lord Topari, who was *stupid,* and who insulted nand' Bren; and, if Father's information was right, they had met with Lord Bregani, who was a cousin of Lord Tiajo, who was a wicked woman who *murdered* people in her fits of temper, and who was right across the Marid's northern coast from Bregani *and* Lord Machigi.

It was a dangerous place to be in, Lord Topari's Hasjuran, which was a little town at the top of the only pass that went down to the Marid plain. Which was a *stupid* place to build a railroad, but politics made reasons to do stupid things. Wars with the Marid were the reason they had started, and wars were why they had stopped. They had settled those wars, mostly, but only temporarily, and Tiajo would be the reason if they broke out again.

Of course mani, Great-grandmother, had taken nand' Bren, who was going to have to deal face to face and be pleasant to Lord Topari, who was not respectful of him, and deal with these people in the Marid, who had mostly been at war with each other.

Meanwhile mani had kidnapped Mother's cousin, Nomari, apparently because she did not trust Nomari and wanted to have a chance to question him before he made any more bargains with Uncle Tatiseigi, who was *not* stupid, and who was trying to settle peace in the midlands.

It was all complicated. It always was. Mani was Uncle's ally and associate, and mani *knew* Uncle's intentions were good, but mani had never gotten along with Mother, and mani had not gotten to have a voice in the Ajuri succession. Mother had just said Nomari was her cousin, and had a right, and that was that.

Nomari had been respectful of Uncle and he had been very brave, turning up when he did. If he became lord of Ajuri, he would try to be a good one, which would be a great improvement over Grandfather, and particularly over Aunt Geidaro, who had just been murdered—but not murdered by Great-grandmother. He was fairly sure of that. It had almost certainly been Shadow Guild who had killed Aunt Geidaro and set fire to the basement of the great house, trying to destroy records.

The fire had not worked. People had moved quickly enough to put it out, and the Guild was going through the records.

But the politics of who would be lord of Ajuri was all still in confusion. And now mani had dragged Nomari away from the midlands, and he was on the train with her and nand' Bren and Lord Machigi.

It was all a confused mess of people who ought not to be trusted with people who ought not to be put at risk—in Hasjuran, a tiny place which had the poorest communications of anywhere in the whole aishidi'tat. And it was supposedly all because Machigi wanted a railroad, and wanted it right now and right across Lord Bregani's territory.

Right across from Bregani's province of Senjin was the Dojisigin Marid, and Tiajo, who had sent assassins into Uncle Tatiseigi's house with *no* provocation, and who let the Shadow Guild do anything it wanted in her province.

So it was very likely she was going to make trouble when she knew Great-grandmother was sitting up in a little town that had no defenses except its bad weather and thin air. She *would* find it out, Cajeiri had no doubt. Shadow Guild were ex-Guild, and they were good.

He was not getting sleep tonight. A number of people had come to meet with Father today, and given Father's office was right across the hall from his own little suite, and given he had staff and bodyguards to report to him whatever was going on, he knew that Uncle Tatiseigi had come to talk to Father, and so had elder Dur, and a number of western lords, all of them concerned about what was no longer much of a secret, that Great-grandmother's negotiations with Lord Bregani involved moving trainloads of Guild down into Lord Bregani's province and waiting for the Shadow Guild to attack them, while Lord Bregani had been drawn up to wait at the top of the world, in Hasjuran, in the middle of a snowstorm.

Everybody had been afraid of another war with the Marid, sooner or later. And now mani seemed to be touching it off on purpose.

Over a railroad that nobody used much. And another railroad that might never even be built.

He slipped out of bed, walked barefoot across cold marble floors and opened the door to the sitting room, quietly, ever so quietly, so as not to wake Boji, whose cage was in there, against the long wall. He moved cautiously, opened the door to his office and shut it behind him just as carefully before he turned on the light.

It was his place. His books. His notes.

His map, that he had kept from his childhood up, that spanned half the wall. It had three pinhole scars among the colored pins, pins that represented people he knew, people whose man'chi he could rely on. He had used to collect those pins with a cheerful sense of growing up and learning things—until he had lost those three pins, and he had begun to understand the future was not all happiness and gain. One of the scars, Ajuri, was recently refilled . . . meaning that there he had lost Grandfather, but now he had a new ally, or would have if Father and the legislature confirmed Nomari to have Ajuri. He thought Father would. But it was going to be trouble with Great-grandmother.

There were neither pins nor pinholes around Hasjuran, into which he had never set any pin to denote a lord well-disposed to him. Across the map, he used black for a lord whose man'chi he was sure of, like Dur and Uncle Tatiseigi, and of course, Malguri and Najida. He used red for a lord whose man'chi might possibly come to him. Topari had neither black nor red, and because of his insulting nand' Bren, was nowhere on his list of potential allies.

From Topari's Hasjuran, with no pin, the rail went down to the Marid and turned west, running from Koperna in Senjin clear across the south, past Targai—a black pin there, for Haidiri, who was someone favorable to nand' Bren, and a very agreeable fellow, though Cajeiri had no personal contact with the man; over to Najida—*certainly* a black pin there, for nand' Bren, and another on the peninsula just to the south of Najida: that was Lord Geigi's Kajiminda, an estate which nand' Bren was taking care of while Lord Geigi managed the aishidi'tat's operations on the space station. Lord Geigi was extraordinary—one of his very, very favorite people.

After Najida, the train followed the coast, going north to Cobo, which was the main seaport of all the aishidi'tat, and there the main rail turned east again toward Shejidan, completing a huge oblong circle, and starting the transcontinental line, which, ignoring the line going south to Hasjuran, ran on east, over the continental divide, clear to mani's territory of Malguri.

Very few trains ever went up that spur that went to Hasjuran, because it was steep, the weather was always bad, and most trains had to turn around there rather than go down to the Marid, first because most of the Marid trade went north either by ship or by the lowland railroad over to Najida and up. He knew that much. Most times, trains going to Koperna turned around at Koperna rather than climb up the mountain rise to Hasjuran, even though the lowland route to Shejidan was twice as long. They had only used to do it, really, when the Kadagidi had been trading with the Marid.

But now the Kadagidi lordship was vacant, too, which was another of those scars on the map. The lord was banished, and the Guild was managing that clan, whose great house was almost in sight from Uncle Tatiseigi's back lawn. After Kadagidi had gone down, for very good reason, the trains from there to Koperna no longer ran at all. He knew that, the way he was supposed to study trade and regions and clans and know who exported and imported.

The mountains atop which Hasjuran sat, where mani and nand' Bren were at the moment, were the wall that kept the Marid separate from the rest of the aishidi'-tat—which was generally, in his opinion, a good thing. The Marid was always trouble. There had been wars and a lot of skirmishes, and the trouble that had temporarily overthrown his father had come out of the Marid—well, and out of the Marid's allies in the north—particularly Kadagidi.

That had happened while he and mani were off in space—and when they had come back from space, and when Uncle Tatiseigi threw off his pretense of neutrality, Father had just taken a train back to Shejidan and taken back control, well, with a *little* more trouble than that. But it had happened very fast, and with very little fighting.

He had accepted it then as luck, and thought people's common sense had told them this was a good chance to throw out the usurper, Murini, and all his allies. But he was older now—and began to understand that *he* was part of the reason people had thought it was time and why things had turned around so quickly. He had not been Father's appointed heir then, but once people knew that he and mani were both alive, and Father did have an heir, and, as much as any of that, that space was a real place people could venture into and come back from—people decided Father had been right. It was *not* just a waste of all the resources they had poured into matching the humans and getting into space, and humans had *not* betrayed them when they had the chance. So people's thinking had shifted into belief that Father had been right to do what he had done, and that there *was* a future and they *could* work with humans.

Murini, the Kadagidi traitor, had replaced Father, but the whole north had just risen up, shaken Murini and his lot off their backs, supported Father and mani *and* him in their homecoming to Shejidan, and the problems had all flowed out of the aishidi'tat proper like some foul drain emptying.

That had not been quite the end of it. The problems had flowed right down into the Marid, which never had been really attached to the aishidi'tat. The Shadow Guild had pushed people in the Marid around and assassinated the lord of the Taisigin Marid. But that lord's son, *Machigi* of the Taisigin Marid, had not only held out against the Shadow Guild, he had gained the man'chi of the southern two-fifths of the Marid: the Dausigin and the Sungenin.

And now he was allied with mani.

That was not a stupid move on Machigi's part. It had made him safer, but not richer, than the northern two-fifths of the Marid, which consisted of Senjin and the Dojisigin. Tiajo, only infelicitous sixteen, had taken over in the Dojisigin and put her own father in prison with Shadow Guild help. She had let all of Murini's people flow right down that mountain wall into her domain and terrorize her own people.

That was where things had stood when mani had reached out and made an association with Lord Machigi, offering him a way to build ships, steel ships, able to travel the Southern Ocean, guided by the space station, with Lord Geigi's help—ships that could reach mani's own eastern provinces and carry cargo on schedule, despite the storms.

Most everybody thought that was an empty agreement, that it was just a way to explain their alliance to the rest of the world, when mani's real aim was to push the Guild system into the Marid and start to push back at the Shadow Guild—that was what Father said she was really up to. Keeping Machigi alive was a major part of mani's plan. Getting the Assassins' Guild to recognize a Marid state's bodyguards as official and bring them into the Guild system was a major move, too.

And it was true that Tiajo and Bregani would have to think twice now about assassinating Machigi, because of mani.

But mani kept saying the association with Machigi was not an empty agreement, that the ships would be built, that these ships could survive the storms, guided by the space station; and that it would bring industry into the Taisigin Marid. Why not planes? he had wondered. And mani had looked at him in silence for a moment and then said . . . would the aishidi'tat be safer right now with Marid planes coming and going overhead?

No. It would not. That was a scary thought.

But ships—ships made from designs from the human archive, could work, with the station watching over them and guiding them, the Taisigin and their allies would grow accustomed to cooperating with the station, and with Lord Geigi, and eventually they would do something about the Dojisigin Marid—eventually.

Eventually seemed to be sooner than he had thought.

Machigi and mani were up to something that was really dangerous. Lord Tiajo was not going to *like* having Bregani snatched from her association, the Shadow Guild was going to get into it, and something was going to happen. They had already murdered Aunt Geidaro up in Ajuri and tried to burn the house down, to take out records of Ajuri's past dealings. They very likely wanted Nomari dead, and mani had taken him right to their doorstep. Nomari was not even there because he was needful, so far as he could guess. He was there because mani was upset with Mother, because Mother had taken the Red Train and gone to Uncle to settle the problem with Ajuri even while mani was flying back from her own province to deal with it herself. Mother had just left mani stranded, with people watching, which *nobody* dared do.

And Mother and Great-uncle had nominated Nomari, nearly a total stranger, a railroad worker, to head Ajuri, without consulting mani *or* Father or even running security checks.

Which might sound foolish to someone who had not been there. He *had* been there, and his opinion on the matter had been regarded by both Mother and Uncle, and he had been quite certain, before he added his voice, sure of Nomari's man'chi . . . to both Mother and to himself. Nomari was smart. And brave. He'd proved that, and Father would never actually ratify a nomination without running his own security checks, no matter *who* made the nomination.

So, well, that might be in process, Nomari was up for appointment, and mani was mad, truly mad at Mother and upset at Great-uncle. He had thought originally that mani, about to take the train east, was going off to her own district, intending to consult with nand' Bren and find out all she could about Nomari, keeping him away from the capital so it would delay his being appointed to Ajuri. Cajeiri had believed that—until his aishid had reported seeing Lord Machigi down at the train station.

He had been smart for once. He had gone to Father to tell him what his aishid had seen and Father had rewarded him by telling him what was *really* going on. Or at least as much of it as Father had found out himself, which with Great-grandmother was not always everything.

Nomari was with her, that was sure, and mani was promising Machigi a railroad, but Nomari being along was certainly *not* because he knew something about railroads . . . and the train going to Hasjuran was not because they had taken a wrong turn halfway and gone south by mistake. Mani had her own plans underway. She was headed down to the Marid to upset the Shadow Guild, and she did not want Nomari confirmed in the meantime.

Which actually led back to Ajuri in a tangled way: an

old man in Ajuri clan had *created* the Shadow Guild, which had supposedly killed Nomari's whole family. Except Nomari.

Cajeiri believed it. Nomari had the support of hundreds of Ajuri who had had to go into hiding because of the Shadow Guild. He was certain Nomari was *his* cousin, *his* associate, and Nomari had given him his man'chi.

But *Mother* had nominated him for the lordship; and mani and Mother had been at odds forever, and after Mother stealing the train, mani's temper was up.

It was not the nicest side of mani. But it was thoroughly mani. He knew that. People were afraid of her—with reason.

Father stood up to her. Father . . . and sometimes Uncle, and sometimes nand' Bren. They could stand up to her.

He never had tried. He had never had reason. He was only fortunate nine.

He was not even *angry* at mani, because in the end she was generally right, or came to be right, and would settle down and do justice. She always did.

But in the meantime it was not fair that she ran risks, it was certainly not fair that she stirred up something that could get people killed. It was not fair that she treated Nomari badly, and she was risking herself and nand' Bren by going down there. *Machigi* was not a person to trust. He was sure of it.

And that only said to him, because things did not make sense, that there were pieces missing, things he did not understand, and two of the pieces most out of place were cousin Nomari, and Lord Machigi. They just did not make sense, if mani was taking on the Shadow Guild. And he had no way to reach her and ask questions. If Father knew, Father was not saying.

But . . .

His senior bodyguard had access on all levels.

That was a thought.

His senior aishid was new. They had only been with him since the Nomari business, and they were terribly senior in the Guild. They were retired *instructors,* and if anybody had clearance to get Cenedi's attention, or Banichi's, or even find information all the way up to the Guild Council, they could. They had that capability. Maybe nobody had asked them to use it.

Maybe he could mess things up by asking, and let word leak in places that could be dangerous. Not so long ago there *had* been trouble in the Guild, and his body-guard said it was still not certain they had gotten all of it cleared out.

He could not *think* of all of it, he could not reach far enough. He could give orders, and some people would obey, but he was not thoroughly sure where his senior guard might take something he asked.

He wished—he desperately wished he had his human associates with him now, Gene and Irene and Artur. His own thoughts made more sense to him when he had to explain things to them. They thought differently. Their minds went in unexpected directions. What he needed . . .

The office door opened very quietly.

Jegari was there, second-senior of his younger bodyguard—his senior bodyguard, in terms of time served with him. Jegari and his sister Antaro had been with him almost from the day he and mani and nand' Bren had come back from space. They were Taibeni clan, with a man'chi to him beyond any question, ever.

He could escape mani's senior guards. He had done it. But not them, the four . . . counting Veijico and Lucasi . . . who lived with him.

"I was not sleeping well," he said to Jegari. The way he suspected his bodyguard could hear his absence, he could already hear the question that Jegari—standing there in his nightrobe—wanted to ask . . . the question that probably Lucasi and Veijico were back there in the dark with Antaro, waiting to understand.

Jegari asked, then, "Have you heard anything?"

"No," Cajeiri said. "Have you?"

The way Jegari frowned and looked down, prepara-tory to saying anything, told him Jegari had nothing cheerful to say. "Last word, Jeri-ji, is that fighting has broken out in Koperna. It has started. But the Red Train is still in Hasjuran."

The Guild, that meant to say, had engaged. In the city at the foot of the mountain wall. In Lord Bregani's cap-ital. But mani and everybody would be in Hasjuran, still. He was glad to know that.

There is fighting, but no word which way it was going. Jegari had put on more than his nightrobe. The device in his ear was tapped into Guild communications, which had no stand-down hours: through that network Fa-ther's bodyguard, down the hall, kept in touch with all the other guilds and even the station aloft. But not everything came on that network, which the Shadow Guild could tap.

"Is Rieni awake?" he asked. That was the senior of the new bodyguard.

"He said there was nothing they could do here," Jegari said, "so they would be informed in the morn-ing."

Nothing they could do here. He could ask them to try to talk to Cenedi. But it sounded as if an operation was in progress, and since the Shadow Guild had all the old codes and might still have agents in place able to get the new ones—nothing important could come that way.

His senior bodyguard had made their decision to go to bed and let events just happen, far away, beyond their reach. *Do they know about the fighting?* he wondered. *Should we wake them and tell them?*

But what, indeed, *could* they do? What he lacked was the seniors' ability to lie abed and not imagine all the things that could go wrong.

"I want to know," he said quietly, "every detail of everything that the seniors can find out in the morning, and if they think I would not understand, I want to be made to understand. Tell the seniors that, in the morning, I want to know what my father knows." It was in an uncommonly grim humor that he said what he had used to say lightly, and to win childish forbidden things. "Tell them it will be *educational*."

3

It was a breakfast set in the cozy warmth of the dowager's car, not the edge-of-dawn chill of the dowager's breakfasts on her own apartment balcony. The paidhi-aiji could at least appreciate that.

But rarely had a breakfast been more fraught.

It would have been no good showing up and asking questions. Ilisidi had her own agenda. She sat at a somewhat larger let-down table in formal black lace, a darkness from head to foot, gold eyes full of her own thoughts. Silver streaks on her gray-black head glimmered in the Red Car's golden lights. The same light sparked off the rubies of her jewelry, and gilded the dark planes of her face.

She sat on one side of the table, with her Guild-senior, Cenedi, standing, a similar darkness beside her: two of the senior powers of the aishidi'tat, in their separate realms . . . politics and protection.

Bren, unescorted, had the seat on the other side of the table, uncommonly conscious of that same golden light on his own pale hands, on white lace, and modest—pale—brocade. The paidhi's color was, officially, white. No-color. No-clan. As such it was completely impossible to be inconspicuous in court dress, even at times when he earnestly wished to fade into the background. He was the arbitrator, the translator, and quite often the messenger between parties. His role was always, no matter what the distress, to maintain a quiet tone, a quiet manner, and generally to observe in silence unless he was actively representing a position. The dowager was his frequent employer and she was generally his ally, even in the worst situations, but being what he was, he never trespassed recklessly into the dowager's territory or offered unsolicited opinions.

She *could* order him to go to Amarja, capital of the Dojisigi province, and take a message to the Shadow Guild. It would likely be the end of him, the Shadow Guild having no intention of honest negotiation and a great deal of curiosity about things he had witnessed. She could do that . . . but he was relatively sure that was not her intent.

And breakfast came first. No matter the constraints, in atevi etiquette practiced end to end of the continent, one never discussed business over meals, particularly with cutlery in evidence.

Food was extravagant. There were eggs and sauces, with breads. There was seasonal fish, likely from the Mospheiran Straits. Across the little table there was absolutely nothing but small talk—the hope that the new transformer would appear on a train that did *not* rush madly through the town, the weather—the quaintness of the town, the hope that children were staying warm despite the crisis.

One duly observed that the town, most of which did have light and heat, was faring well in the interim, and that the older houses on the square, which shared power with the train station, would be able to heat and light themselves in good order by the old methods, live fire and oil lamps.

Usually by this point in one of the dowager's more stressful breakfasts, a human's teeth were chattering and his muscles locked with cold, but the Red Car was by no means arctic chill despite the lack of power from the station. It was, in fact, a little warm by now, by atevi expectations, and considering their dress.

A condition which in no wise affected the dowager's appetite. A number of eggs disappeared, along with helpings of other dishes. Bren had two small eggs, with a slice of toast, and delayed about it so as to finish somewhat in time with the dowager, who took a cup of tea to finish, savored most of it slowly, as Bren did his, and then abruptly set it down. Click.

"We believe we are shortly to receive Lord Topari," Ilisidi said, "and we are not in a humor to hear his personal apologies for the power outage or his questions about our intentions."

The suggestion was clear and no more than he'd expected. "I might receive him and secure his signature," Bren said. "If you wish, aiji-ma."

"That would be preferable," Ilisidi said.

A silence ensued. And went on.

"Oh, ask it!" Ilisidi snapped.

Bren drew in a deep breath. "Was it, aiji-ma, your grandson or the Guild who waked us this morning?"

Ilisidi stared at him, eyes like molten amber. "Both. I am well sure, *both*. So *you* did not have warning of this."

"None, aiji-ma. Absolutely none. Your grandson spoke to me before we left, and told me I should go with you. Protect her, he said."

Ilisidi snorted.

"But he told me nothing of his view of the agreement, aiji-ma, nor did I have any knowledge from him as to what you meant to do. Nor do I know who sent the train, though I can guess, as may you."

The stare continued for a moment. Then Ilisidi drew a deep breath and blinked. "This has to be settled."

"The business in the Marid, you mean, aiji-ma."

"The business in the Marid, for a start, *yes.*"

"For a start" on *what*, one had to wonder, and declined, at the moment, to ask. Instead, one said, quietly:

"Your grandson's orders were to provide you such assistance as I can, aiji-ma. I shall do that."

"Begin by dealing with our guests and with Lord Topari this morning, as soon as you can stir him forth. We have already signed, so you may have the documents we shall leave for him to send to the capital, and he may know *we* are dealing fairly. But we have no time for extensive festivities. It is very likely, paidhi, that we shall go down to Koperna today, *if* our grandson's addition to the confusion has not fallen off the mountain or stopped to block the tracks. Particularly be careful of Lord Machigi this morning. Be gracious to him."

Gracious and Machigi in the same sentence was a stretch.

"Do we have any notion, aiji-ma, what that train passing us *is* actually about?"

A sharp frown. "There are several possibilities, one of which is that that young fool Tiajo is moving a major force to intervene in Koperna, but that would be a happy event."

Not in everyone's estimation. Not even in hers.

"But that train," Ilisidi continued, "surely came from Shejidan, and had to have left not that many hours behind us. I surmise that *my grandson* cannot keep his fingers off the situation."

"His concern is for your safety."

"We are certain of it," she said. She was smiling, now, an expression which one could hardly call beneficence. "I at least do not think my grandson will have countermanded my specific orders. It would look like indecision. And now he has sent us a train, and means to park it—one does wonder where."

"I have absolutely no knowledge, aiji-ma. I am told there is a siding where it could wait. In all honesty I heard *nothing* from him but to go and advise you as best I could."

"We are attempting to communicate with it. It has been observed by Guild at various critical places along the downward route: it is going down the switchbacks, if one of *my* emplacements does not blow it off the rails by mistake. And where will it stop and make clear its purpose?" Ilisidi drew a deep breath. "We *are* going down to Koperna, paidhi. And if *we* come down, that train will *take* the available siding and get out of our way, or we will both sit, disturbing politics across the northern Marid for as long we must, disputing in public, and I doubt my grandson would care to have such a confrontation viewed by our enemies. Koperna is currently occupied by my forces, so it will be very clear we will not back up. And if that train wishes to sit and wait for the Dojisigin response, I am perfectly content."

"I am at your disposal, aiji-ma. Such service as I can do, I am willing to undertake. I am hopeful that when that train has reached its stopping point it will communicate in whatever way the Guild can manage such things."

"Well, well," Ilisidi said, frowning, "since it has not done the courtesy of dropping off a message in passing, we shall simply carry on as planned, however late. Setting Lord Bregani back securely in charge of Senjin may present some difficulties, if this intervention from Shejidan does delay us in the process. But we shall see." A flick of her fingers. "Go. Go. Deal with Topari. Keep him calm. We have signed the documents. We want his signature. Arrange something. I have every confidence in you."

Arrange something. Locating the document of association, which was in the dowager's staff's possession, was no problem. Narani was able to deal with that, and Jeladi likewise scoured up the requisite waxjack and ribbons of appropriate colors.

The next question was the time—and Ilisidi's intent to move. "Urge Lord Topari to come to the Red Car at his earliest opportunity," Bren said to Narani. "And tell Banichi take whatever measures we can to assure his safety."

So that problem ran through channels.

Meanwhile they were shut in a windowless train, separated from each other in most instances by cars devoted to Guild operations and personnel, with two Marid lords and the candidate for Ajuri each attended by bodyguards, in separate cars. They had had less sense of isolation aboard the starship.

Machigi had ordered breakfast. So he was awake and waiting. But Bregani and his wife and daughter were reported still abed, nor was Nomari stirring in his car. At least *some* of them had managed to get back to sleep this morning.

But the day had to start. The sun must surely be up. There was a damnable scarcity of clocks aboard.

"Wake everybody," was his instruction to staff. "Absent the dowager, we should put on as much formality for Lord Topari as we can manage. Ask our passengers to turn up as for a court appearance and let us give Lord Topari the chance to meet his nearest neighbors in this business. Do we have word on his schedule yet?"

In his apartment in the Bujavid, he would have had an abundance of staff and phone lines to solve such problems. Aboard, now, he had only his bodyguard, whose business was to protect *him;* and only three others—one of them his cook—to arrange the signing and seating and appropriate refreshments, and then arrange to get Topari safely across the square and back again, because he was determined that his aishid would not go out there.

Narani, his major d', rapidly managed to learn, from what source one had no idea, that Topari was ready and only awaiting word . . . that he would gather his guard and be there in short order, under careful attention from the sentry positions that guarded the train.

One had to think sooner was better than later, both for Topari's nerves, and for the unstable situation in general.

"Advise all our guests we have a meeting within the hour," he said to his staff, and things began to move.

Meanwhile there was the other matter that wanted tracking, granted Ilisidi's determination to go down. Leaving with an ex-Shadow Guild assassin on the loose and his situation unresolved meant leaving either a protection or a problem in Topari's capital, and he had no sure knowledge which.

"Homura," Bren said. "One is reluctant to take him, reluctant to leave him, and we have had no word whether he is alive."

"We are still attempting," Banichi said, "to get a response from him. We can add a signal of urgency as well as invitation, which may tell observers that something is afoot, but that is all we can do. We do not know whether he *can* respond. We do not know there are not operatives out there looking for him."

"And Topari's guard may not be adequate protection against his skills, if he has turned."

"Until he moves," Banichi said, "we do not have the means to find him. He is emitting no signals and doing nothing. We cannot even swear that he is alive. He told Tano and Algini he was answering your summons, and that he had come up from Koperna. He said he was uneasy about the meeting, feared that they might be observed, regretted that Tano and Algini would not go with him elsewhere, and he wished us to contact him later, said that he would signal again for a better meeting. Then the explosion. No signal has come. If the train this morning did not rouse him out, I do not know what will. And we cannot verify anything he said—except the problem in Lord Bregani's aishid."

"I take my aishid's advice," Bren said. "Not being a fool. Do not risk any of us in the effort. I hope we have not attracted a problem into this town. Topari's people support him. But they are in no wise able to deal with the dowager's sort of enemies."

"Best to spend our resources protecting those aboard. We cannot search for him."

"No," he said, agreeing. "No. If he sends a message, I will hear it, but if we are to move, we cannot delay about it, and if what passed us this morning has not informed the Dojisigi that something is going on up here—they are not listening."

"They will certainly be listening," Banichi said. "They likely have been listening since Machigi disappeared from his province, and certainly since this train took a turn toward Hasjuran. And given we now know that Lord Bregani's bodyguard was compromised, we are sure he will not have left Koperna in secrecy, either. We have to assume the Dojisigi know exactly where he is, and if Homura is turned, or if there are other agents in Hasjuran, then they will likely know precisely who is here. That will not bring any comfort to Tiajo."

"What are the odds Homura was responsible for the transformer?"

"Someone in this town was. Tano is charitably disposed to believe the man is honest. The others of us, less so."

It was Tano who had been caught in the edge of the explosion. It was Tano who generally took a charitable view.

"At this point," Bren said, "I can only say I am human. I lack both the instincts *and* sufficient information."

"Information is our continuing problem," Banichi said. "If we take Homura with us, we may remove an agent *protecting* Hasjuran from his enemies. But if we fail to take him, we may be leaving an agent capable of taking Lord Topari down. The enemy is holding two of his partners, maybe three: Tano directly asked him about Momichi and had no answer except that he had stayed in Koperna. Hostage-taking may be as old as the machimi . . ." Which was to say, ancient history. "But the Shadow Guild's target is now ignoring the lords and attempting to subvert the Guild with this tactic, and this has to stop. The Guild pointedly has to stop this, by suffering personal losses if need be, even of the innocent. Our enemies may think they have found something new. They may instead rouse something very old. I urge you, turn your back to this man's problems, Bren-ji, and do not ask further."

"We called him here, Banichi. *I* called him."

Banichi returned a flat stare. "Coming here is, Bren-ji, in most sincere regret, *his* decision. And if he does not know what he risks under current circumstances, in approaching you and the aiji-dowager, he is part of a generation that will have to learn late the law these outlaws have invoked by their actions. *I* think he well knows that we can have no tolerance of him in proximity to the dowager and these two lords. I think he is reluctant to answer *because* he knows he has arrived at a critical position, while his man'chi cannot but be engaged with at least two partners he cannot find. We have appointed him one means of contacting us safely. If he does not advantage himself of that, if he does not trust Guild signals from the dowager's *own* bodyguard, there is no more we can give him."

Which said things, in itself. One understood that.

"I shall not argue," Bren said. "I have learned that much. Keep me advised. I shall certainly not try to contact him."

"Meanwhile," Banichi said. "We expect Lord Topari, and the dowager's staff is arranging the Red Car for the second signing. Our guests have responded, Machigi included. It will be complete attendance, except the dowager."

"Do we have a schedule, Nichi-ji?"

"Within half an hour for the signing," Banichi answered, and added: "Within two hours, we expect this train to be moving, with or without word from Homura."

4

Nomari was the first of their passengers to arrive in the Red Car—a good-looking young man with callused hands and a shy demeanor, a habit of caution. Two of his four bodyguards, Guild-assigned, came with him, trustworthy people. Machigi arrived soon after—as different from Nomari as night from noon: Machigi, a lean, scarred young warlord with three provinces at his command; and Nomari a rail worker, who had been a spy *for* Machigi in Bregani's capital.

Bregani was aware of that. And the two had met. Nomari's history might have been an embarrassment for a young man of, as yet, no standing—had Lord Bregani wanted to make an issue of it. But everybody spied on everybody in the aishidi'tat: even allies spied on allies. It was how things were verified, among other social uses. Genteel spying was how word was passed delicately, and how provinces communicated with each other, at times when, say, radio communication with the capital might be intercepted. Servants gossiped. Shopkeepers gossiped. Spies took note.

Bodyguards were another matter, bound by man'chi. And it was that assumption of unbreachable trust which had failed Lord Bregani, corruption of his bodyguard, far more personal and concerning on this trip than an encounter with a former employee of his railyard. Bregani's bodyguard, his aishid, was in protective custody at the moment, relieved of duty, and Guild under the dowager's command now provided Bregani's personal security, not people he knew, not people with connections to him.

So it was no surprise that Lord Bregani brought his wife and his daughter to the signing with him this morning, not leaving them with strangers, no. The wife, Murai, had at least an interest in the proceedings, being of a border clan through whose territory the rail passed; while the daughter . . . well, teenaged Husai was simply caught in the midst of it all, a girl too young to sign anything, but safer here than down in Koperna at the moment, and due to go back with her family today. One even thought of suggesting the young lady stay here in Hasjuran, under Lord Topari's roof, but one could not swear that would be safe, either, if the Shadow Guild was up here, and saw her as a target.

Nomari had left his own house at a young age, when Shadow Guild had killed his older brother and his parents. Maybe it was that memory that had him looking often at Husai, a young woman likewise caught in a situation she could not control. Or maybe it was that Husai had been looking back at moments, and glancing down and pretending not to have looked at all.

But as they moved closer to the table, their gaze collided, at arm's length from Bren, as it happened. One saw—indeed a time-stopped moment, which Husai's parents also might have seen.

Nomari's shyness suddenly evaporated. Nomari looked at Husai, Husai looked at Nomari, nothing to do with politics, treaties, and Nomari's history as a spy—or maybe everything to do with that, in a handful of heartbeats. Nomari looked flustered, which he rarely did, and gave space for Husai to join her parents at tableside. Two gazes met a second time.

Briefly.

It had perhaps begun before this session: last night, during the dinner, Bren had seen a slight exchange of glances here and there, strangers assessing one another. Machigi might have looked with interest, but a young woman of a hostile clan looked at him with, well, apprehension: nothing new for Machigi, who had a dangerous, even piratical, reputation.

But the young candidate for Ajuri, who seldom spoke, but watched everything?

That looking and not-looking had gone on all evening, until a moment ago that two glances intersected, and stayed. Nomari, having recovered some gentility, gave a respectful little nod and let the moment fall.

Husai kept staring for a heartbeat.

Oh, one was not blind. They both were attractive young people, Nomari was a young man who, after a life on the run, stood to gain a province . . . and Husai, a young woman whose family was in danger of the sort Nomari had narrowly escaped.

Bren saw it. And being, himself, more than a little concerned with connections, negotiations, alliances, and powers of the aishidi'tat, he had to ask himself what to do about it, or whether the dowager had noticed it as a possibility at last night's signing.

That was hardly a question at all. Ilisidi loved intrigue and scandal, she was an inveterate matchmaker, and she lived and breathed politics. Had she noticed last evening a prospective lord of Ajuri possibly forming yet one *more* connection of the midlands lords with a troublesome house down in the Marid, kin of Cosadi, the very connection that had created the situation they were going down to the Marid to deal with?

Oh, one would bet that she had noticed.

Whether and how Ilisidi could use that connection was another matter—while plainly enough, this second agreement, her absentee signing of a special agreement with Topari and Machigi, was fortifying an ally, and Bregani's invitation to witness it was making a point with Lord Bregani, that she *intended* protection for the smallest of her allies in the move she was making.

Would another connection of the lords of Ajuri to the troublesome house of the Dojisigin and Senjin lords be any sort of asset in her thinking? Or an absolute disqualification?

Should he do something in Ilisidi's absence? Should he *warn* Nomari on what ground he was treading?

But if Nomari could not see or had not informed himself of the politics behind his family's assassination and some twenty years of his young life on the run, he was little qualified to run Ajuri. That was the whole of it. A provincial lord had requirements to consider, responsibilities far ahead of his personal wishes.

So, absolutely, did that young lady, Bregani having no other heir, and his district being under continual threat from one side or another. Any indiscreet alliance could lead very dangerous places.

And the question was—was Nomari trying to assure connections in the south for his own preservation, should he not be confirmed, or was he simply casting about for *any* favorable link he could make?

One had access to Nomari, at least.

Bren used it, approaching the young man at tableside, in the general serving of drinks before Topari's arrival—mere fruit juice, considering there was official business yet at hand and they were not yet seated. "Nadi," he said very softly—atevi ears were keener than human.

"Nand' paidhi."

"Only bear in mind your future must be in the north, nadi."

Nomari looked down at him, frowning slightly, and said not a thing for a moment. Then, eyes not quite meeting his:

"Is it at all likely I shall be in the north, nandi?"

"It is not at all unlikely, nadi. The dowager is, after all things settle, fair. Be confident of fairness. But do not test it. Or complicate it. Be aware."

There was no answer. Nomari's expression was troubled, and he flashed one look toward the young lady, then back again.

"Nand' paidhi."

Bren walked off, and Nomari found occupation in another direction. "I have advised him," Bren said to Banichi and Jago, who had never been far from him in the encounter. "Too much is uncertain. She is a stranger in a foreign and hostile place, and Nomari is very much the same."

"This may be a ploy of her father's," Banichi said.

"Or just youth," Bren said.

"Or a plan," Jago said. "Bregani and his daughter are Cosadi's line, Bren-ji."

The situation was atevi. A human could read it intellectually, but feel it, no, never. *Love* was assuredly not in it, but certainly attraction was. Biological attraction worked chaos in atevi lives as effectively as it did in human ones. A one-candle night, as Banichi had once put it, creating a hundred-year problem, and a problem for far more than the two young people in question. Cosadi, now deceased, had had blood ties to Kadigidi, and Kadigidi to Atageini and Ajuri in the midlands, as well as to the Dojisigin, and to Senjin in the Marid. Cosadi's alliances and ambition for rule still tangled lines of descent in ways that lay behind a host of current troubles. The north did not want another round of it.

"Lord Topari is on his way," Banichi said quietly. Banichi was, in point of fact, the highest-ranking Guild officer present, Cenedi having opted for absence, along with the dowager, so Banichi was in charge and it was all the paidhi-aiji's ceremony . . . and would be the paidhi-aiji's problem, should anything go wrong.

Narani was likewise in charge of the documents, the waxjack was in place, as were the appropriate ribbons. There were a number of commemorative cards to be signed and ribboned as favors for all present, particularly for little Hasjuran to display along with a copy of the agreement, a memento for local pride in generations to come. They had not done that gracious addendum on the previous signing: it would have been a little strange even to consider congratulatory card-signing, with the threatening undertones of that event.

But Topari's district, Topari's capital, and Topari's house were all innocent of the goings-on down in Senjin district, whatever those might be today, and a little festivity was due.

The mood on the train this morning might be nervous, but it was definitely lighter than had prevailed last evening, when Ilisidi had been forcefully persuading Bregani that she *was* his best ally, and that continuing his hostilities with Machigi was not the best route for his district.

The end result, signed and sealed with a profusion of ribbons, lay on the table with the documents yet to be finished, that copy to be sent back to the archive of the aishidi'tat, the rest kept individually. That document governed the association consisting of the aiji-dowager, Bregani, and Machigi, for the simple purpose of extending the rail line from Bregani's capital, Koperna, down the coast to Machigi's capital, Tanaja, in the Taisigin Marid . . . that was the agreement signed last night.

Awaiting signature this morning was another three-way document of association, that of the dowager and Lord Topari and Machigi, regarding transport and storage for the project. The two documents were interlaced in political effect: breach one, and it triggered the other, not to mention what the dowager could do on her own.

"Lord Topari is on his way," Jago said, "with Guild escort. It is just past sunrise. It is snowing heavily."

The hour, Bren had determined, made some sort of refreshments a good idea, in the likely event no one else had come from a formal breakfast, hence the trays of assorted little cakes: Bindanda had sent those out, his special recipe. They were well-received.

Having just had as much breakfast as he dared, Bren

stayed mostly to tea. Nomari gathered up some small items from the food offering and shared them with Husai. Machigi helped himself to a small plate, and shared with his bodyguard. Bregani and Mirai just sipped tea and looked worried . . . not here to sign, but here to witness, *and* to have breakfast, with a bodyguard not their own. Their presence added to the pomp and circumstance of the affair, a presence that would be particularly significant to Lord Topari, especially given the aiji-dowager's absence.

"He is here," Banichi said quietly, and indeed, with a clang and clatter outside, the outside steps went down, Guild went on alert, and the side door of the Red Car opened to a white world and snowy figures inbound, two Guild security guards first. Beyond was a view of a snowy morning in mountain shadow, the station platform and, beyond it, the town square and its great house of a design unique in the world—interconnected wooden buildings, set on terraces to provide entry in deep snowfall. It was still summer in the lowlands, but fat snow clumps blew in with the fur-clad party, and the shutting and latching of the door against the whiteness threw everything back into shadow, warmth, and golden light.

Lord Topari brought in, besides his Guild escort, his entire personal aishid, four local folk with hunting pieces: no question, even by Guild standards, that the men would be good shots, if not expert in other things. Topari himself swept off his fur cap, with snow quickly beginning to melt on his furs and on his slightly disarranged dark hair. He had come in formal queue and ribbon, and, as he shed the furs, it became clear that he had worn his Shejidani court dress for the occasion, brocade and lace—until one came down to the fur boots—he had contended at some point with snow over his knees, and it clung and melted.

Bren hastened to meet the man, hastened to bow politely and explain the situation.

"The dowager is very pleased, nandi, at your quick

response. She was waked this morning by the passage of that train—"

"It gave us no information, nand' paidhi! If we had remotely expected, one assures you—"

"*Certainly* you would have. The dowager entirely understands. The reason the dowager is not here for the reception is her need to deal with this situation, to be absolutely sure that Hasjuran remains safe, and that we have clear understandings of what actions Tabini-aiji may be taking."

"Tabini-aiji!"

"He will by no means countenance a move from the south to threaten Hasjuran, let all potential enemies understand that. And the presence of Lord Machigi, of the Association of the Southern Marid, cosignatory with yourself and with her, and cosignatory with Lord Bregani of the northern tier in the other document you see displayed, is precisely to make it clear that Hasjuran is becoming a key point, a gateway for peaceful trade with the south, and a barrier to enemies of the aishidi'tat. This agreement will have profound and important effects. The dowager has asked me to welcome you in proper style and extend utmost courtesies, and she has already signed and sealed the agreement which I am to present. She asks you kindly understand, while she attends the matter of identifying the train that passed us, and coordinates next steps. There will quickly *be* next steps, nandi, of that we are sure. And this agreement is an important part of it."

Topari did not look put off. It was an earnest, honest expression on that occasionally confused face, and one felt—not quite ashamed enough. Putting the best face on the dowager's decisions was, in fact, the paidhi's job. But he might have laid just a little too much emphasis on next steps and Hasjuran's connection to them. He hoped he was telling the truth about Hasjuran's safety and future profit.

"She asks me to assure you that by the agreement you

will sign this morning, the integrity and security of Hasjuran will become a matter meriting direct action on her part." That much was true. "And any move against you and yours will now be taken as an attack on her and on lord Machigi as well, entailing defense obligations and fulfillment of treaty obligations across the aishidi'tat. And meriting my own personal concern, nandi, though I am not a signatory in this matter. I take it as a matter of honor, far as my estate may be from Hasjuran." He meant that part sincerely. They owed Topari. He felt personally obliged, and a little aggrieved, now that the dowager had put him in this position; and thoroughly determined not to let this quaint and quiet place and its fairly naive lord suffer harm in consequence of the dowager's actions in the Marid. "This signing places you under her protection, no small assurance, you may count on it. You have met Lord Machigi. But not your immediate neighbor to the south, I believe."

Eyes widened. Topari half-turned to look at the others, apprehension evident. "One has not, nand' paidhi. I am distressed to have walked past . . ."

"Lord Bregani, allow me to present your neighbor to the north. And, Lord Topari, this is Murai-daja, of the Farai, and their daughter Husai-daja."

"Nandiin," Topari said, with a proper little bow, properly reciprocated, and Bren rapidly sorted protocols and mental notes.

"So. Please enjoy light refreshment the dowager has provided us," Bren said, and signaled the head of staff, waiting by the table, to begin tea service all around. "Lord Topari, the others know, and I can inform you, that measures are being taken in Senjin to break association with the Dojisigin, and join Lord Machigi and the Taisigin in creating a new rail connection. We are relatively sure the train that passed us is related to that matter, and seeking to forestall problems."

"Are we at war, nandiin?" Topari asked uneasily.

From serve-the-tea to worst case in a heartbeat. *And*

over tea. That was Topari. But Topari had asked. He had to answer it, etiquette aside.

"Not unless Lord Tiajo attempts to prevent it, nandi. Your agreement with Lord Machigi and the dowager is properly none of Lord Tiajo's business, and rest assured she will be made certain of that if she seeks to interfere. Lord Bregani . . ." Bren paused, as a servant was providing Lord Bregani with a teacup. "Let us assure you, this morning, too, that Guild forces report they are holding steady down in your district and that Koperna is quiet. I have no information as yet when the dowager will make a decision, but I am confident she will not delay too long in getting you back to Koperna."

"You are leaving us," Topari said.

"We are certainly not leaving you to mischief," Bren said quickly. "And we are certain concern for your safety is part of the business that has claimed the dowager's attention this morning. Please, let us proceed to the signing to have that surely done, in the case of any interruption in our business, and then we shall resume a brief refreshment afterward. The dowager is well aware of Lord Tiajo's record, and this document you are about to sign will assure that the rails remain safe and open to the aishidi'tat. Please be assured. And one particularly recommends the little cakes. I believe you remember them, Lord Topari."

"One does, yes." Topari was nervous, justifiably. He swallowed half his cup at one go, ate the other half of a teacake, and licked his fingers afterward. His eyes moved to the signing table and the waxjack, and nervously from detail to detail in this famous car, in this place, with these people, these lords and ladies, these authoritative servants and bodyguards with their procedures, all different than Hasjuran's easy-going court.

"Come," Bren said. "You shall sign first, nandi, right between the dowager's signature and Lord Machigi's. Lord Machigi, do you mind?"

"Not in the least," Machigi said, with a wave of his hand. "I am right behind you."

That he was, the sole other signatory, and one of two reasons for Lord Topari's anxious glances. Neither Machigi nor Bregani had any close dealings with Hasjuran, excepting exchanges between shippers, and trust was a still unexplored territory.

"I promise," Bren said under his breath, for Topari alone, as the documents were being laid out and the ribbons arranged, "I am very certain that you are making the best possible move for Hasjuran. Your isolation will never cease, which I think is your preference, nandi. But your importance as a gateway is only dawning. Let me tell you, I personally have associates in the heavens, aboard the space station, who can provide you with additional benefits—like the same weather warnings Lord Machigi will receive down in the Marid. You can be warned of winter storms from a vantage even your mountains do not reach. And you will see improvement in communications."

Topari stared at him for a moment . . . looking down to do it, but it was a hopeful and respectful stare. "Can you say so, paidhi?"

"It is all one piece, nandi. The weather warnings will come with a system Lord Geigi is setting in place for Machigi's ships. And your elevation and your situation are an asset in establishing a weather station. There will be all manner of advantages to come."

Not to mention—and he did not—that it was not only storms the system could track. When Lord Geigi had shown the dowager the world from space, and casually pointed out the storms of the Southern Ocean, and how they moved   after-dinner conversation that evening had meandered on to proposals some on Earth would call pointless and useless—Lord Geigi's desire, for one thing, to map the whole globe, when everybody knew there was no land to be had but the several great islands and the continent. Ocean, people understood, covered the rest of the world.

Not so, Geigi had said, and showed a very curious view the Ship had gained, and pointed to a series of three parallel clouds. Volcanoes, Geigi said, in a chain of very small islands, which he also showed. So, however small, there *was* land in the Great Ocean.

And, Geigi said, the storms that swept that expanse were massive, and if the rocky headlands of Mospheira and Crescent Island did not help break up the seas and if Mount Adam Thomas and the central ridge did not break up the weather, coastal civilization on the mainland would have had a much harder time of it.

A strange, strange evening, that had been. Geigi had even proposed submarine ships to cross that space and explore the ocean bottoms.

So here he was, standing by a rural lord of the most remote town in the aishidi'tat, telling him about Geigi's weather system, and how it could serve him.

He would never have predicted Geigi's project would result in the dowager proposing a treaty with Machigi, of all people—proposing a sea route and steel ships and an eastern harbor, which no one in their right mind would have expected could ever exist, economically. And here they were about to expand on the concept and link on another piece of the Marid. One *still* doubted it would ever take shape, though the dowager was investing steel and political effort in Machigi's port . . . by doing that, she had convinced Machigi to accept some of the northern guilds, and gotten the northern guilds, notably the Assassins' Guild, oldest of all guilds, not only to acknowledge her *Eastern* branch, which Cenedi headed, but to acknowledge irregular operations such as Machigi's local militia, and personal guard; and Topari's, Topari's little state not seeing the need for professional Assassins . . . well, until now, perhaps, that Ilisidi had brought reasons to Topari's doorstep.

Who knew but what the steel ships *would* work? Who

knew but what submarines were feasible, despite the hazards of the Southern Ocean. Or the Great Ocean itself.

Submarine ships. Irregular guilds. Weather satellites—which Geigi was preparing—and the promise of other wonders.

It was a strange place for the mind to drift, watching first Topari, then Machigi sign and seal a document that, on the surface of things, simply declared Topari might support the dowager's agreement with Machigi, saying nothing of Bregani.

But when added to the document which the dowager had signed with both Machigi and Bregani, the structure, atevi-style, began to appear. Bricks in a wall. One agreement linking here, and there. Topari's non-Guild bodyguards conversing with Banichi and Jago, and Machigi and Bregani talking quietly to each other, with Murai looking on.

And . . . not unpredictably, Husai talking to Nomari, which was a linkage not so desirable, and one he had to discourage . . . two young people as yet unable to affect anything. On one level they had *nothing* in common, and on another, they might feel united in their youth and their status as onlookers.

Well, but it was a brief meeting, not one that they could prolong: there was other business to deal with, and the timing and conduct of the event had devolved totally on *him*, granted the dowager's absence. He signaled the staff to start carrying things away.

"You will be protected as never before," Bren said to Topari, in preparing to send him off. "One is certain among other things that the dowager will have you in mind, whatever her other decisions; and one is equally certain, considering the matter of the transformer, that you post guards and be suspicious of strangers until the matter in the Marid is settled."

"We will be protected," Topari repeated, as if for assurance.`

"The dowager does not permit her allies to suffer

attack. Be assured, you will not lack force should *any* threat materialize here, though I have read, in my own study, that Hasjuran's own people have met threats in their own way and with very good success."

"That is so." Topari nodded emphatically to that. "Indeed we have done, paidhi."

"There is one man in town, too, that you should know about and *somewhat* keep in mind. His name is Homura. He had been in conversation with one of my bodyguard when the transformer blew. We do not yet know the agency that destroyed the transformer, and you should both be aware he *may* be an ally, but do not hesitate to take action if he proves a threat to you. The Guild is concerned about the incident of the transformer, and is looking into it, as is the Transportation Guild, and they will also be investigating this man Homura. I will tell you he *is* Guild, he *has* partners held hostage by the Shadow Guild, who have tried to compel him to hostility against us, and he has since pledged man'chi to me and to the dowager, so his is a very mixed report."

"I do assure the dowager no one of my people would have exploded the transformer."

"I am very sure she knows it, nandi." There was so much simple honesty in the man it was well he had protectors, Bren thought—it was also well he governed a very small region, and God help them, if there was to be a war, they would rely on Topari only to stay where he was and to ask for help if he needed it.

But in command of their own mountain trails and passes, in winter warfare, Hasjuran *had* held its territory. They were not to discount, a force to be reckoned with in their own element.

And without fail, one was sure, in Topari's care the designated copies of both documents would reach Shejidan and be filed in the archive of all such compacts, in the room with the Great Document that had founded the first railroad and set Shejidan as the capital. By such little steps the Great Document had expanded from the earliest railroad to cross a number of clan territories, to lines serving the Padi Valley, to the transcontinental line, to the extension southward, and last of all, and from both directions, to Koperna, in the Senjin Marid, the hope of a time of relative peace to bring the troublesome south and the southern plateaus into the system.

The history of the railroads *was* the history of politics on the continent. So when Ilisidi decided the head of the Taisigin Marid should have his own railroad, and that it should tie on to the system at Koperna, in Senjin ... yes, it was an earthquake. Because of Machigi's own associations, southward, the dowager's signed agreements now embraced four of the five parts of the Marid, and the Dojisigi were suddenly alone on the rock, as the saying went, meaning everybody else had been offered a seat in the boat, and Tiajo was left out.

"I shall do my best," Topari said. "We know the routes trouble could take," Topari said. "We know the back ways and the passes. And we will stop them, nand' paidhi."

The fur-clad, rifle-bearing hunters from the remote villages, the same that had risked avalanche to get here and had never yet gotten a meeting with the dowager—they would safeguard this place, and their lord.

"I shall tell the dowager exactly that, nandi. And I know she will thank you."

"Nandi."

It was a far better sense he had of the man, and he resolved to convey that not only to the dowager, but to Tabini. God help him, he had begun to respect the fellow.

It was not a lengthy festivity they had had. The outer door of the Red Car shut, leaving a dank chill gust with Topari's departure.

It closed. Jago locked it. Staff began clearing the solitary table of refreshments.

Banichi moved close, but Tano and Algini, who had

been there a moment ago, were not there now. The passage door was open, leading forward.

"I suppose that we shall hear," . . . from the dowager, Bren began to say, and then heard the blast of the Red Train's horn, three blasts in succession, drowning all else.

5

They were about to move. That much was evident. And it was going to be a long day and likely an anxious night. There was no information about their schedule or their expectations or whether the dowager had been in contact with Tabini.

Just the warning whistle.

"I have had no word," Bren said to the company still present in the Red Car: Machigi, Bregani and his family, and Nomari. "The dowager has not told me her plans, but surely she will. We all should get to our compartments, I think—to be where we can be contacted, have security constantly around us, and do nothing to distract the Guild from their observations. That would be my advice, if asked. I shall try to get more specific information and deliver it to you."

"We are anxious to return," Lord Bregani said. It was the dowager's promise to him that was being honored, but there was no guarantee for any of them that it was safe to go down to Koperna despite the assurance of the Guild it was now quiet. They had to get down there, on a very chancy route. They *might* be about to turn around— Hasjuran had the means—and go the long way around.

"Has the train that passed us," Machigi asked, "met any difficulty?"

"We have no idea, nandi. The timing suggests that the dowager waited only for the signing this morning. Matters are now proceeding with some plan in mind. It is possible we may uncouple, but since we have had no instruction to return to our respective cars, I do believe it is unlikely. Best, however, for our comfort, that we go back to our appointed places. I do promise that as I receive information the dowager will let me release, I shall send it to you. Let us all go before we get underway."

Machigi looked, if anything, unexpectedly agreeable to the idea of heading down through his neighbor's province. Bregani had outright asked to go home; and Nomari, a railroad worker by training, simply stood there looking concerned—possibly because he had nothing whatever to win, and had seen enough of Marid politics, and possibly because he did hope they were going the long way around.

In that position, the paidhi-aiji was in complete sympathy. The aiji-dowager could choose to sit and wait for events, could communicate her support for Guild forces by radio and then summon the principals to deal with her later, at Najida or at Hasjuran—granted things went well.

But it was not Ilisidi's style and he did not believe she would take the long and cautious route. She would not direct forces in the field when it came to a fight; but Cenedi could; and Banichi could also, before all was said and done.

Had Ilisidi told Banichi what she was up to? Cenedi likely had known—perhaps. But he was reasonably certain Banichi had been left in the dark—about all of it.

He went with his aishid, behind the other parties. He passed by the galley car, where people were at work cleaning up after breakfast or beginning preparation for lunch—one of his own staff was involved there: his personal cook, Bindanda, who had insisted on coming, along with Narani and Jeladi, to take care of him—faithful as his bodyguard, and handling all the details.

He passed by Ilisidi's door, half hoping for some signal to stop there, but the door was shut and sealed against view from the passage; and passed through Cenedi's car, his last hope of information. It had its access open, but guarded, offering still no signal for a conference.

Another horn blast warned of movement imminent, whether because Ilisidi had gotten an answer regarding that other train, or precisely because she had not and she was hellbent on having one.

He reached his own compartment, the rest of the company, with their respective attendance of bodyguards, having gone on through the passage door.

Narani met him at the open door of his compartment, and he and his aishid passed the door just as the train began to roll, still coupled, still the full complement of cars . . . moving forward, not backing up as they would need to do to reach the turnabout.

"Well," he said, "so we are going down, are we not?"

"It would seem so," Banichi said.

"Is there *anything* yet of explanation?"

"Not as yet," Banichi said.

Jeladi helped him shed the formal coat, and Bren reached for the fastenings of the vest, something he routinely shed in privacy.

"Wear the vest," Jago said, and he dropped the hand . . . resigned to the damned thing for the duration of whatever came.

"Your aishid appreciates it," Algini muttered.

"Try," he said, accepting the casual coat Narani held for him, "to get something out of Cenedi."

"Yes," Banichi said, and, as the train rolled, went back out the door. Algini followed.

Bren had time to sit down at his small table in the windowless compartment and accept a cup of tea, trying to arrange his memories of the session in the Red Car, while worrying about where they were going. The train gathered a moderate speed. The click of rail after rail confirmed it.

Jago appeared to receive some communication, and quietly left the compartment. Of his aishid, only Tano remained, sitting quietly on the bench at the end of the car, likely listening to short-range messages. They operated cautiously and in internally-made codes, and ran physical messages for what was not routine. It was the way they had had to function ever since they had restored Tabini to the aijinate, in the likelihood even the purging of the Guild had not rooted out all the problems.

Jago came back, and Tano stood up.

"News?" Bren asked, as they both came near.

Jago slid into the opposing seat. "We have heard from Homura."

That was unexpected. And the timing—was as worrisome as Homura's background.

"So is he coming with us, or have we left him?"

"We have left him. The message, as we began to move, was a short unsecured signal, stating it answers Tano's last question."

Bren looked up at Tano. "Which was?"

"'Where is your partner?'" Tano answered.

"The answer he gave," Jago said, "is 'Koperna.'"

Momichi, the man's name was.

The missing one of the pair they had met—which left two of that four-man unit still missing, presumably in Shadow Guild hands, possibly alive, possibly not.

And Homura *and* Momichi remained as doubtful a question as ever.

"Implying there might be a contact from him?" Bren said. "One hopes—a contact not involving explosives."

This, with a glance at Tano, who, with Algini, had narrowly escaped the transformer explosion.

"One read him then as very anxious," Tano said. "Fearing discovery. And he maintains that mode."

"Anxious," Jago said, not the most forgiving of his

bodyguards. "And not *advising* us of problems in Has-juran. We still do not know whether he set that explosion himself."

"Surely," Tano said, "no one would expect to frighten the dowager. Or you, nandi."

"One is flattered," Bren said, "but it does worry me. They worry me. But they may be an asset."

"If Momichi turns up," Algini said, "we shall not meet him where one of ours can be a target—whether or not he might be the agent."

"Was it set off by remote?" Bren wondered.

"With the weather, the snow, the hazard of searching out there—" Jago said. "No. We are not sure. Transportation investigated it. Cenedi ordered us all back."

"They say it might have been simply a power surge," Tano said. "Or a small device, possibly with a short-range signal. The actual force of the blast would have been a coolant explosion, and the transformer building, being native stone, contained it."

Flying debris had broken many of the train's windows, as one heard, none of which, fortunately were real windows. Had they been . . .

"Homura was likewise at risk," Tano said. "He may have been injured, for what we know. It was his urging to break up the meeting, and it was a sudden change of tone. I think he saw someone."

Tano had said so before, and still spoke for Homura. Algini, who had also been in that meeting, took the more suspicious view.

"So we still cannot say whether we are leaving Lord Topari a protection or a threat."

"We cannot," Tano said, "except—"

"Except," Bren said, "he warned us about Murai-daja's bodyguard."

Had Homura not sent that warning, Bregani and his family, and possibly the dowager herself would have been at risk. One bodyguard's family had been kidnapped—the same tactic the Shadow Guild had used to send

Homura and Momichi on a mission in the north, with their partners under threat. They would not have known about the bodyguard's situation, except for Homura's warning.

"We owe him," Bren said, "But—"

"Nevertheless," Tano said. "Nevertheless. One cannot argue for him or anyone else. That is what they want. We do not know who is pressured, and how, and from what direction. But my sense says there was a turn in Homura's expression. Algini says it was a pretense designed to break off the interview. I think it was real. But I could be too trusting."

Algini had come close, leaning, arms folded, against the woodwork of the car.

"He may be an asset," Algini said. "But things clearly are chancy up here. We have tried to warn Lord Topari's guard, but I have no idea whether they understand what they may be up against."

"I still think Homura has not turned," Tano said. "I cannot believe he would, if he is free. He has least reason in the world to trust the Shadow Guild's word. And a strong grudge against them if their partners are dead."

"You two have opposite readings of the man," Bren said. "And I must make certain decisions based on your combined advice. How did he find us? Have we ever discovered that? We expected him in Najida. Remotely, possibly he might have gotten word to us in Shejidan. Nobody who is not now on this train had any warning we were going to Hasjuran. Except Tabini-aiji and persons he would have told. Or the Guild itself."

"It is a question," Tano said. "We are not beyond the possibility of sleeper agents still in the Guild."

"We asked him where he had come from," Algini said, "and he went on to answer another question we had not asked. He evaded it entirely."

"He might," Tano said, "have left from Koperna. He *might* actually have come up with the Red Train when it brought Bregani. It would take cold weather gear and determination, with nothing like the cold suits the Guild now has. But it would explain how he knows Momichi is in Koperna, and how he managed to arrive here."

"That," Algini said, "is one theory we both share."

"It would explain a good many things," Bren said. "And it would be his one means of getting a warning directly to us. But surely the Guild is on guard against such things."

"It is the only train that has come up here. And *he* is Guild, and still alive after resigning a Shadow Guild mission."

The scenario made sense. It certainly made sense. And if he had indeed braved that cold to get up here, solely to warn them against a security breach whose target might well have been the dowager's offer—or the dowager herself . . .

"Do you suppose, Tano-ji, that he is aboard now—so to speak?"

"One would not entirely rule it out, Bren-ji. Security is designed to prevent it, and with the possibility that he came up that way, which we did discuss with Cenedi, we are doubly alert."

It was a very cold and snowy thought. A troubling one. The train was going at a steady clip now, headed for the notorious grade and the subsequent switchbacks.

It was a way to die, if something went wrong out there. But Homura had *not* asked to come aboard.

Things still were not right in the world. Cajeiri was sure of that as the rest of the world waked. And adding to the questions that troubled his morning, the four seniors of his bodyguard had reported themselves as not requiring breakfast.

Staff did not always tell him things. He knew that. His own staff did not have seniority enough to keep him informed, because their clearance was not high enough to know what his high-level senior guard knew. His domestic staff, including the oldest, Eisi and Liedi, did not have seniority enough to be told where his high-level senior guard was, or what they were doing.

But his younger bodyguard had left their own breakfast unfinished to find answers.

Cajeiri had an unappreciated piece of toast and another cup of tea, and waited.

The tea had gotten cold in the pot by the time Antaro and others—Jegari, Veijico and Lucasi—came back into the apartment, by the front door.

"Couriers came in from the Guild," Antaro said, resuming her seat, while Liedi put on a new pot of tea. "Early this morning, before the sun was up. We have found that out. We think—that they may have come from Headquarters. They met with your father's guard."

"Did they come on their own, or were they sent for?" He was a little shocked that he had not heard any coming and going.

But something besides worry might have awakened him. Something entering the premises stealthy enough not to wake Boji was hard to imagine, because the doors made noise, but then—they were Guild.

"We have asked senior domestic staff," Veijico said, meaning, likely, Father's major d'. "And there is no refusal to answer. Only a claim not to know what the business was. By that, we assume your father has ordered extreme secrecy."

That was understandable, and such comings and goings were not that remarkable by day, though most inquiries were to Father's downstairs office.

But major movements in the house, in the dark of night?

"Where are the seniors?" he asked. "Talking with Father's guard?"

"They have left the Bujavid. One believes they may have gone to Headquarters."

That was scary. He was half of a mind to put on his

better coat and go to Father personally. He kept trying to think of other reasons somebody might come in secret, things to do with the legislature, or some investigation, or an emergency somewhere—Father *had* no hours when it came to matters he could solve from the top faster than it could climb up the chain of responsibility. Those were the orders for all the Guilds, were they not? If it needs to be solved at the top, start at the top.

But the greatest problem right now was off in Hasjuran.

And his own source of restricted information was out of the Bujavid and across town, possibly talking to the Guild Council.

"I shall want to know," he said, "when Rieni and the rest are back."

"Shall we attempt to contact them?"

"No, we shall wait." Inquiries distracted people who needed to be doing important things; and they told staff he was upset, which became gossip.

And suggested to Father that he was apt to do something he should not. He had *tried* to mend the impression people had of him. He had been given freedoms, and information.

Only right now information was across town, Father had not called him in, and he knew he should not bother people actually dealing with problems.

He stayed a time, letting his aishid finish their interrupted breakfast, after which he rose from table, at a loss, then finally decided that work, even lessons, offered the only possible distraction. He settled to homework, while staff removed dishes, composed the table to its smaller form. The new servants, Tariko and Dimaji, were understandably quiet. But even Eisi and Liedi went about with hushed voices, and his bodyguard settled to their own reading.

It was quiet. All quiet. Eisi and Liedi clearly knew

something was going on. The other two were not exchanging looks, either, or asking questions.

Things definitely were not right.

Bren sat at his table. He wrote, while the tempo of the rails decreased and the slope of the car increased, not quite to the point that he felt the need to steady his teacup, but he glanced at it with some concern. The Red Train would descend to a flat stretch, its full length accommodated by that length of track, one understood—while intrepid Transportation Guild crew got off the moving train, in the weather, to work the switch as the train then came back toward them. As it passed the switchpoint in this forward-and-back process, it would pick up the switchmen and descend again until it reached another level.

One acquired a new respect for Nomari's simple statement as to his occupation in the Transportation Guild: a switchman on the Marid run.

The grade did not at any point exceed six percent, so one understood. It was all under control. They were a long train for this route, but not that heavy a load. That was good. One should not be nervous. It had been, Algini informed him, four years since they had lost a train on the descent.

Bren tried not to think too closely about that statistic, and meanwhile attend to the inkwell and the teacup, while doing his notes and correspondence. There was no view. He tried to imagine the mountain range beyond the windowless walls—a vista that looked out on a great flat floodplain and salt marsh, hazy in the distance—and *not* to imagine the descent in all its technical details.

He made an addendum to his notes for Tabini, while the train slowed further. There was a metal squeal, and then a much, much slower pace to the clicking of the rails.

His aishid was at the other end of the car, as were

Narani and Jeladi, engaged in a game of poker, a game and a set of cards acquired during their visit to Port Jackson. They were quite good at it. All of them.

And the slow click of the wheels and the low rattle and occasional squeal of brakes continued. One tried not to think about ice on the tracks and the switches. One had no expertise to know whether that was a problem, but it was no good asking and less good to worry about such details. One had to trust the Transportation Guild to solve it.

Bren resisted the temptation to go to the one tiny patch of sky he could see, a remaining little glass-covered vent. Curious as he was about the weather, staff was trying to plan and rest as much as they could manage, and he had no wish to distract them or pose a question. He would, he told himself, manage someday to see the world through ordinary windows, in some year when they would have brought peace to the region. It was certain to be grand, the vistas outside, except the blizzard, if it continued. They were supposed to descend into comparative warmth, sea winds and much kinder weather, about a third of the way down.

He had not asked. It was not relevant to them, except that snow might provide cover. Or problems.

Then . . . the click of the rails grew slower. And slower. His heartbeat correspondingly picked up pace.

They were, Jeladi had informed him, a slightly longer train than usually made this descent, though they were not as heavy. There might be, if one let one's imagination run, a little more risk than usual.

Not to mention the switchbacks and the tunnels, all places where an enemy might arrange problems. The Guild had taken precautions. Certain unfortunate personnel had been set out to camp with winter gear, weapons and equipment precisely to be sure there were no problems, so his aishid assured him . . . a white and quiet vigil, masked today in weather which could be an ally of either side.

If Tiajo and the Shadow Guild continued to be a problem, the realization was quite clear from this precarious perspective, there could *be* no rail link operating safely in this region. The Shadow Guild obeyed no civilized rules. No honor, no limits, no restricted targets. They had made that clear over on the coast.

From that circumstance it became clear the dowager was pushing more than a railroad and more than her trade agreement with Lord Machigi. If this was going to be done, if the Marid *was* to be linked to the rest of the aishidi'tat, the dowager's offer of a sea link had only been a quiet opening of operations, a project some believed was only a cover for the dowager's backing opposition to the Dojisigi—a project, never to be fulfilled, that served to annoy the Dojisigi, and just awaiting a provocation.

Ilisidi's opening move, the trade agreement, the prospect of an Eastern port, had gotten Machigi connections to the north, opened the south to certain of the northern guilds. Now, inevitably with the guilds, *intelligence* flowed, so that the north had a more accurate picture of Marid resources, and alliances. The move to decentralize the various guilds to gain support in the Marid had stirred heat in the north. At the opposite end of the map, the move to permit the full range of guilds to operate in the Marid had upset certain townships in the south, townships such as Separti, on the west coast, who had, though technically in the aishidi'tat, also refused the Guild system—even including the Transportation Guild, which everyone else on the continent had accepted.

There had been—was still—a quieter way to go about constructing Machigi's rail link with far less provocation to Tiajo's regime: they could have gone the long way around—routing trains in from the west coast with no greater obstacle than getting up and over the plateau that rose midway, the normal and easy route from Najida to Koperna and back. Even once the new rail link was built and operating, the route lying along that plateau was *still* the sane way most freight had to go, on any truly commercial scale. What did descend the mountain wall from Hasjuran was usually Transportation Guild freight, for their own operations in Koperna, or the same guild repositioning empty cars to the lowland routes, or, occasionally, carrying down goods from Hasjuran itself.

In that regard, what Ilisidi was doing by negotiating everything in Hasjuran was making the greatest possible noise about her arrangements. In effect, she was delivering a personal challenge to the Dojisigin, advising them they were going to have to move against her—or stay out of the way while she dealt with their last Marid ally.

The dowager was known for subtle moves. Tiajo was known for doing stupid things.

Ironically—that meant Ilisidi was relying on the Shadow Guild to control Tiajo, possibly goading them to replace Tiajo to calm the situation, but nothing would change the Shadow Guild's character, or reconcile the Guild in Shejidan with the Shadow Guild itself.

The prospect of conflict was the worst kind of action—Guild taking the field against former Guild, the ultimate violence atevi practiced. Generally atevi left conflict to those with the disposition to lead, to professionals, and to technology. There would be deaths. There were quarrels that could not be reconciled, but civilians had to find a way to make peace, or at very least, the Guild had to take down the party least willing to abide by a directed solution. And for renegade Guild, who had murdered, and threatened, and planted bombs on public roads, there was no negotiated peace.

But one sincerely hoped the Shadow Guild in Senjin, beset by a Guild force inserted into the capital, and with a second force about to arrive, would decide discretion was the better part of valor, and retreat to the Dojisigin. Not that it would eliminate them, but it would keep their damage contained, where time, mortality and slow degradation of supply and information might do the work of a pitched battle.

Slower and slower. The first part of the descent was the steepest grade in the whole system, before they hit the switchbacks. The weather might be both an ally masking them—and an enemy masking other movements.

If—

"Bren-ji." Banichi was back, having gone out into the passageway for a moment. "The dowager wishes a conference. She has asked Machigi and Lord Bregani to come and wishes your attendance immediately."

So, well, Bren thought, they would be hours on this slow, difficult stretch of track. The dowager might even have caught up on her own interrupted sleep, even if no one else had, considering the prospects before them. And now the dowager would be nailing down specifics, where it came to performance and her agreements.

She would also want to locate some common interests between two men who, a few days ago, would never have sat in each other's company. How the dowager would get a light and social conversation out of Machigi was a question.

So . . . someone had to fill the potential silences, while it was very possible there was death and damage still threatening in Koperna. They had word that the city was secure, but that there was trouble at the port. And God knew where the train from this morning was, and what it intended.

Geometry did not hold as deep a fascination as one could wish. Cajeiri found himself staring at triangles and polyhedrons and thinking about patterns not described in straight lines.

Then his aishid reacted subtly, a simultaneous slight move from all of them, seated at the table, that said some signal had reached them.

He looked at them. They looked toward him.

"Rieni-nadi is back," Antaro said. "They have answered. They are back from wherever they were."

Cajeiri stood up. "Call them. And guard the inner door."

Which was to say, guard against the servant staff, even Eisi and Liedi, coming within hearing. It was not to say that his young aishid, stationed outside the doors, would not hear the exchange. But they were Guild.

"Yes," Antaro said, and said, to those absent, "Nadiin, nand' Cajeiri, the sitting room, now."

They came in, Rieni and Haniri, Janachi and Onami, gray-haired, extremely senior, large men, dangerous men, and all under his orders, which was a scary responsibility, except, Cajeiri thought, they would surely judge his reasoning and not do anything stupid. He wanted them to trust him with information. He wanted them to take him seriously, as a sensible person; and not to have them have to go to Father when he asked them questions he perhaps was not supposed to ask.

"Tell me no if you should tell me no," Cajeiri said, having thought long and hard on that opening. "But I am very worried and I want to know what is going on. Has there been a courier? Have we news from my great-grandmother or nand' Bren? What is going on in Hasjuran?"

"Nandi." Rieni folded his arms and leaned informally against the door-frame. "We are secure in this room, are we?" This, with a nod at the inner door, on the other side of which Antaro and Jegari had taken up station, with Lucasi and Veijico present and listening.

"As secure as you have made us, nadiin-ji. My other unit is there, but staff is not. And I want to know what you know. I promise I shall not do anything stupid and I shall go nowhere without you. But if there is any news, tell me."

It was on Rieni, Guild senior, to answer or not, and Rieni considered a moment. Then: "What we know, aiji-meni, is not being told to general staff, or at lower levels within several other guilds, notably Transportation and the Messengers. Nor is the lord of Hasjuran informed. We have been advised by indirect means of a plot to assassinate your great-grandmother, and we have very limited means to advise her that will not equally go where we do not want it to go. She has left Hasjuran."

"Coming back?"

"No, aiji-meni. Going down to Koperna, in Senjin, with Lord Machigi."

Lord Machigi was an ally of mani, and an enemy of Senjin. "Why?" was the only question he could think of.

"We have no other information, except that the Shadow Guild may have moved an asset up to Hasjuran. The Shadow Guild has assets both in Koperna and Lusi'ei, but there is also a Guild force in Koperna, and Lord Bregani has authorized it to deploy against the Shadow Guild. There has been fighting."

"Lord Bregani. Of Senjin." He knew. He had memorized imports, exports, lords, agreements, alliances, notables, famous buildings.

"Yes."

"Why?" His tone was sharper than he meant. A lesson was much more vivid than he had ever wanted it to be.

"Information is coded, and limited."

"Because of the Shadow Guild. In the Dojisigin. And not all in the Dojisigin."

"Exactly, aiji-meni. We trust we have cleared the highest levels of the Guild of problems, but we cannot risk lives by trusting too far. Coded messages say prearranged things. We can construe that Lord Bregani is somehow requesting Guild aid in Koperna, and we know of a certainty that your great-grandmother had two trains under her command, the one she is on, and another she had sent ahead of her to test the track. It went down to Koperna, where it appeared to break down. It carried a large number of Guild, with equipment. Lord Bregani's request saw that force deployed in the city. There is a *third* train, which was launched two days after the Red Train left the station."

"Also mani's?"

"The Guild Council will not say. I am telling you the only fact at our disposal. And we must keep this entirely quiet. The situation is still developing, and Guild Council has advised us to minimize all lines of communication especially regarding that region. Your general staff is not to know. You have discriminated correctly in that. We trust you will personally instruct Antaro-nadi and her unit not to discuss it even among themselves. The question involves lives, locations, and critical assets."

He knew that last was code for something more than he understood. Darker than he understood.

"May the others come in?"

"Yes," Rieni said.

"Then they should," Cajeiri said, and Onami went to the door and opened it. Antaro came in, with the rest of them, and they collectively and solemnly made a little nod of acknowledgment.

"You heard," Rieni said.

"Nadi, yes," Antaro said. "We understand the order. Silence, even among ourselves, and with our principal."

"The room is not now under guard," Rieni said. "Stay by the door. Continue to listen. But you may ask. I do not say we will answer."

"Do we know what the dowager's objective is, na-diin," Veijico, asked cautiously, "in going there?"

"We believe it is precisely to secure Bregani," Rieni said. "But all three trains are currently beyond the reach of secure communications. We are having to send messages through the Transportation Guild, aiji-meni, and in Hasjuran, we have no idea whether that office is secure. The lord of Hasjuran does not have a Guild bodyguard. It is local. They have never hosted any presence such as the dowager's."

"Is Father worried?" Cajeiri asked. That was the surest indicator *he* knew.

"He is extremely worried. He says a recall is impossible, and one gathers it is impossible both because of her location, and, forgive the disrespect, given her inclination to defy threat."

"True," Cajeiri said very quietly. Mani when things were going well could not be moved, and when things were going badly, she was not likely to move either.

"The sum of things is that a series of orders have committed units to Koperna and that the dowager is taking the Red Train to that destination. A precautionary Guild presence in Senjin has gone from observer to offensive status, apparently by a request from the lord of Senjin."

"Bregani's man'chi is to Tiajo. He is her cousin. Or uncle. Or something."

"He now is an ally of your great-grandmother, apparently, since he has asked the Guild to move into his capital."

"What is Tiajo saying, then, nadi-ji? Or does she know?"

"We have no information from the Council. But if your great-grandmother truly has moved to take Senjin, the Shadow Guild will act, and Hasjuran has no defenses but its mountains and hunting rifles. The dowager has tended to move quickly and to strike first when threatened. She has now moved herself, as the most attractive target, out of Hasjuran and down toward Koperna, thus protecting Hasjuran, which is an inconvenient target. She is directly threatening the Dojisigin. That is the situation, young gentleman, and it is very serious."

It was unbearable. "We should call her back to Shejidan. Father should call her back."

"Young gentleman," Rieni said, and did not continue.

Politics. And mani. He knew the situation in the northern Marid, *not* just as memorizations. Shadow Guild ran the Dojisigin and he had thought it ran Senjin, too. So, likely, the Shadow Guild had thought it did. He also knew

Lord Machigi was involved with Great-grandmother, which was well and good.

But Machigi was no ally of Senjin. Even if now Senjin was asking for Guild help, which had to mean something huge had changed, Machigi was still dangerous; and the Shadow Guild was going to be unhappy, whether it was a willing change or a forced one Senjin was making. Rieni knew it and he knew it, and there was no way mani would back up.

"I should be with her," Cajeiri said quietly, with this terrible pressure about his heart. "I have always been with her. And do not say, nadiin, that I am a child and stupid. If I were with her—she would be careful. Nand' Bren can argue with her. Cenedi-nadi can. But I have always been with her. And she is more careful when I am there."

"One does not doubt it, aji-meni. But she will have the advice of her Guild senior and of the paidhi and his aishid. This is no light decision she has taken. She has planned this carefully. She ordered uncommon Guild attendance *and* weaponry when she ordered the Guild to precede the train. On the record, aiji-meni, and I am telling you something we know, but you must not share—the train that preceded her was officially destined for Malguri in the records of the Transportation Guild. That destination changed to Hasjuran *after* it was halfway to that junction. It proceeded. It went to Koperna, where it claims to have broken down. Again—here we must ask your discretion, nandi, since a Guild mission was changed en route as a subterfuge—only two entities could order the Guild to take such action involving, ultimately, moving an armed force into the Marid region. One is your great-grandmother."

"The other is Father."

"Exactly. As it is—with the information we now have—we know her intention is well-supported. We are sure she will not back down. Retreat at this point would

have a profound effect. It would weaken the aijinate.
And that would certainly have consequences."

"So if she were *killed* would there be consequences!"

"And she knows it," Rieni said. "We do not know all
of it. What we are telling you now, very few know. The
greatest asset your father would concede to her is the
paidhi-aiji, and for whatever reason, the candidate for
Ajuri. The Guild has not failed to inform your father
along the way and the Council is moving in several directions to support her. She is forcing a confrontation.
She has been moving in this direction for some time, in
the dealings with Lord Machigi. The agreements urging
the establishment of guilds in general in the Taisigin
Marid and its allies—they constitute three fifths of the
Marid. That *is* of consequence. That *will* worry the Dojisigi. They have been venturing very little lately, excepting Lord Tiajo' quarrels, none of which have seemed
coordinated to any end. But we do not think it consti-
tutes a weakening of that organization. We think they
are exploring actions they can take for the future."

His heart raced. He felt as if time had slipped out
from under him. And that he could not at the moment
control any least thing. He was losing his composure,
and with it, the ability to give any reasonable argument.

He asked quietly and as sensibly as he could: "And
one of them threatens my great-grandmother. Can *we*
not warn her of the people trying to attack her?"

"One is certain, aiji-meni, that she and her aishid are
fully expecting it. As for the specific, as yet we can only
confirm that a credible threat has caused a warning to
go through the system. It is very likely Cenedi-nadi will
have heard it, or will hear it soon. Likely she will not
retreat, except as a tactical move. Destabilizing Senjin
was a step beyond which she will surely have calculated
risks and rewards. They have threatened her. She threatens them. The question is the timing."

Mani was playing chess, Cajeiri thought. She had
with her the best Advisor, who was nand' Bren, and the

faithful Consort, who was surely Cenedi. But on this board, the Rider, the crooked-path piece, had to be Machigi, with *no* assurance he would be loyal to anything but his own advantage. Nomari was just one of the People.

And they had no idea what side Lord Bregani might turn to. Was he the Fortress? Or theirs at all?

"Can we tell one person?" he asked carefully. "Can we tell Lord Tatiseigi? He is mani's closest ally. And Nomari-nadi's ally."

"We are not authorized," Rieni said, "to tell any person but you; and we ask you not do it without your father's specific clearance. Your great-grandmother's life may rely on your discretion, aiji-meni. Please respect your promise, even with your staff."

"I shall," he said. He began to realize the extent of what they *had* told him, which was exactly what he had asked—namely everything they could find out. He was *at* the level of clearance of people who stood right next to the Guild Council and Father, on an official level. So was, now, his first aishid, only a few years older than he was. And he began to feel the weight of it.

"I want to continue to know everything that happens," he said to all his bodyguards. "I want to know, even in the middle of the night, if something changes. I want to know where is mani now, and what is happening." Something occurred to him . . . that he might have asked these men to bring him information much beyond their authority to do so. And they might get in trouble. "Shall I pretend not to know, nadiin-ji? I can do that, even with my father."

The seniors looked troubled. "We would not ask that, aiji-meni," Rieni said, "but we take it as a promise of extreme discretion. One is grateful, but in the chain of command, your father must never be uninformed."

"Nadiin-ji," he said. He had had trouble including the four seniors in the address of intimates: but he felt all barriers down, now. They trusted him; he began to trust them, the way he had to trust the people that guarded his life—not just to protect him, but to keep him as well informed as anybody could be.

They nodded, a slight bow, and got up and went back the way they had come, to their quarters in the private, secret places of the Bujavid.

"We are glad you are here," Antaro said quietly, as his younger aishid came close and settled around him. "We are glad you are here and not there, though we wish we could help."

"I want so much to know," he said. "But I think that was all the truth, was it not?"

"They go where we cannot," Jeladi said. "We would never get the answers they can get."

"We cannot tell anyone," Cajeiri said. "We cannot talk about it around staff. Or anywhere."

"We cannot," Veijico agreed. "We cannot act as if we know anything."

"Or look worried," Lucasi said. "We have to act as if we know absolutely nothing."

Boji set up a screech, having seen people come and go with no egg offered. Boji was as spoiled as a parid'ja could be. And he was supposed to be working on a home for him, a place he could be. It had been Cajeiri's distraction, that project, and he could not forget it, but right now Boji was nowhere on the scale of importance with the secrets he had been handed.

He had wanted to go to Uncle Tatiseigi, who was in residence just down the hall, and who had intended to oversee Nomari's nomination for lord of Ajuri, a matter which had been of great importance before the Red Train left. He wanted to tell Uncle that mani was in danger.

Uncle's abandonment by Great-grandmother, his exclusion from her current plans, began to seem not what he had thought an hour ago, pique over Uncle's support for Nomari, and irritation that Mother had taken Great-grandmother's transportation to Uncle's estate and left her stranded . . . all that had seemed a reason, even if

Grandmother had never in his memory let temper get between her and Uncle Tatiseigi.

Now . . .

Things did make sense, even the noise about a quarrel made sense, protecting Uncle, and he was almost certain Uncle, having much more experience with politics, was upset, and regretful, and wishing he were with Great-grandmother right now, too.

But Uncle could not be told. He had intended to visit Uncle, and now if he did, he would have to sit and have tea and pretend what Uncle thought were the reasons . . . were the reasons, which was a level of pretending he did not think he could do.

He had always wanted to know things.

Now he did. And his stomach hurt.

6

Bren exchanged his ordinary coat for his better one. He was wearing the detested vest still, and used the coat that accommodated it. Narani saw to that detail.

He debated the pistol for traversing the passageways, but carrying it in the dowager's own premises was just a little too forward, granted there would be no shortage of bodyguards directly or indirectly under Ilisidi's command and concentrating on her welfare.

"The dowager's guard will take precedence," Banichi said. "Algini and I are requested to take charge of the adjacent Guild car, Jago and Tano to escort you only to her door, Bren-ji. Cenedi and Nawari will attend."

That was to say he was going in alone, an uncommon state of affairs. Ilisidi was issuing his bodyguards' assignment, and keeping the meeting inside her car, allowing only her own bodyguard as audience. Very likely the maneuver was designed to exclude Bregani's Guild-assigned bodyguard and particularly Machigi's domestic one. If the paidhi-aiji's guard was excluded, the other two lords could hardly protest.

"I shall do my best to gather details," Bren said. "And one hopes to learn something substantial, nadiin-ji. This long silence is worrisome. One hopes the dowager has gathered what she needs."

Which was to say he hoped some sort of communication had been going on, an exchange in an extremely restricted code, either with the mission down in Koperna, or with that train that had thundered past them, but, closely as his aishid on occasion worked with Cenedi, Banichi had not been briefed as yet.

"If you need us," Banichi said, and left it unfinished.

"Yes," Bren said, tugged his cuffs into comfortable order, and let Jeladi open the door for them. They all went out, and as far as the adjacent Guild car. Jago and Tano alone attended him past that compartment, and stayed with him as far as the dowager's own door, where Ilisidi's bodyguard let him in.

The bodyguard—it was Casimi, one of the regulars in Ilisidi's company—showed him to the right, where Ilisidi sat, not on a bench, but on one of two carved and upholstered chairs that surely had been shipped aboard for her personal use. She was not tall—was in fact, about Bren's height. She typically used a footstool for comfort, and used her cane for ease getting about. And on such a long journey, one understood it was not vanity, but reasonable provision for endurance.

Bren bowed, and at her impatient gesture, took the other such chair, while for the two other invitees, yet to arrive, the area held two full-scale couches of apparent antiquity, in dull red leather; and two side tables each, which might serve for hospitality . . . if any were to be offered.

He said not a word. Asked no questions. Made no observations.

Ilisidi said: "The signing this morning went without difficulty." It seemed a question. And his question.

"One believes it did, aiji-ma. Lord Topari was very glad to sign and very pleased to be offered such an honor."

A slow nod. A distracted: "Good."

Tension? The dowager never admitted to it. But there were degrees of familiarity he did not wish to invade with pleasantry. Friendship did not apply with any ateva, least of all here, where the dowager accorded him all the respect due a high atevi official in her service. She had a responsibility toward him, in a minor way, considering the relative ranks; and he had the same for her, in a very major way, considering the same. That was the official emotional exchange. But, one of them being human, sentiments existed. One being ateva, it was possible something untranslatable and somewhat emotional existed on her side, and she took comfort in his presence. He suspected so. But it was all too easy to miscalculate in such circumstances and go a step much too far.

"You have had lunch," she said.

"Yes," he said.

"There will be some delay," she said. "Lord Machigi is the first arrival."

The silence went on then, punctuated by the working of the train.

"One is concerned," he said finally, "aiji-ma, to be of the greatest possible use—such as I can be. But I am at a loss as to what I can do."

She glanced directly, sharply, at him. "Is this my grandson's wish?"

"Aiji-ma?"

"In your interview with him, before we left."

"His order was to be of service to you. My wish, aiji-ma, is the same."

"Are you afraid, paidhi?"

"Not since the first cup of tea, aiji-ma." It was a risky, brash answer. "I have drunk every cup since that without question."

It amused her. A touch of it reached her expression and she nodded slowly. "That you have, paidhi, every one, and I have abused your hospitality beyond measure."

That might refer to Najida, or possibly his first meeting with Machigi.

Or the ruin of the garage. There were so many instances.

"Aiji-ma, the windows you provided are the glory of the house."

She gazed at him a lengthy time. She looked, to his eye, tired. But one dared not say so.

"Did my grandson have specific orders?"

"No. He did not. He was concerned. I betrayed nothing of your business, knowing nothing of it at the time. And still—not as much as I might wish."

Ilisidi gave a very, very slight smile, quickly faded. "He does not wish to know the details. Nor should he. Two Shejidani guilds know our immediate business, and we rejoice to say, the leadership of both the Assassins and Transportation is reliable. One can also add the Treasurers' Guild and the Merchants' Guild, the Builders, and the Physicians to those we can trust in most matters. Things being as they are, we are relying on several guilds' integrity, and we have relied uncommonly heavily on Transportation in this matter. We have been gathering the components of this train since your own visit to Mospheira. We were reserving them, we claimed, for the future transport of the Reunioner folk from the spaceport to Cobo."

The surplus of human population coming down from the space station, a principal piece of business in his recent trip to Mospheira. The operation had been granted the unprecedented dispensation of landing on atevi territory and shipping across to Mospheira's Port Jackson— Mospheira having only one shuttle available, and the need for transport being urgent.

So the aishidi'tat had gathered special rail cars for one purpose, and Ilisidi had apparently diverted them to her own use in this venture to Hasjuran. Landings at the spaceport were a problem for the future.

This one . . . was clearly urgent.

"You are puzzled," Ilisidi said.

He was never inclined to go stone-faced with her. It was far better for the aiji-dowager to read him than for her ever to guess.

"Only as to whether you prepared this mission to forestall a move by Lord Machigi, aiji-ma, or whether Bregani was expected to desert Tiajo."

Ilisidi heard that with a slight amusement. "We promised Machigi defense. He never used the word protection, but he has had it. The issue over which Lord Bregani and Tiajo had a falling out was one of those completely trivial things—a collision in Amarja's harbor. But it blossomed into an extravagant demand, as so much Tiajo does is extravagant, often without coherency. But in this—Machigi says, and we think correctly—Tiajo's Shadow Guild advisors arranged that collision and fed Tiajo's reaction. They have maneuvered to bring Senjin under their direct management, in response to Machigi's agreements with us ... and the aiji-consort and Lord Tatiseigi's overthrow of the last vestige of the Shadow Guild in the north has truly excited them."

"That," Bren said in surprise.

"Yes, that. Nomari. Nomari, with a claim on Ajuri and official backing. Geidaro was murdered, and before the smoke of Ajuri had quite cleared from northern skies, lo, Tiajo took issue with Bregani, and Machigi broke with all habit and came personally to Najida to offer us an opportunity disguised as a railroad. The Shadow Guild in the north is in disarray. The Shadow Guild in the Dojisigi intends to move into complete control of Senjin, likely to pressure Machigi from *his* northern border, and it is a moment of vulnerability and opportunity. We shall foreseeably be dealing with Tiajo, too. And we have *so* desired to deal with Tiajo."

"Hence Nomari's inclusion on this venture."

"Hence my interest in knowing whether *he* is Shadow Guild."

"Surely—"

"There is a darkness in that young man," Ilisidi said,

"that we still have not penetrated. But it does not seem to correlate with the Guild. Cenedi has observed him closely, and your own aishid agrees, that there are certain small habits and behaviors that suggest training. Behaviors he has not manifested in major matters. If he is lying, he is doing it very well indeed."

"Do you in any degree favor him for Ajuri?"

Ilisidi hesitated. "Perhaps."

"But not unreservedly."

"The next events will tell."

"And that train this morning, aiji-ma. May one ask?"

A second hesitation. "We are not sure. I believe my grandson, who has thus far stayed out of Marid matters, has moved to protect us."

"Not personally."

"No. We do not commit willingly to the same field. But there is one spot I am not entirely reluctant to have covered."

"The bridge on the approach?"

"That." Ilisidi nodded slightly. "We shall see to it. But most particularly that abandoned rail spur, a siding and a switch point, which could cause problems. There is a siding where they could pull off and hold that, quite helpfully. I do not believe they intend to enter Koperna. But if they stir up trouble from the Dojisigin, and block the track, I am prepared to be outraged."

Surely, Bren thought, she did not intend to launch an attack on Tiajo *while* trying to stabilize Senjin.

But before he could ask another question, someone had opened the passage door, and staff was meeting some arrival behind him. Cenedi moved to that door, with Nawari, firmly dealing with the arrivals. There was a minor issue. Lord Bregani had brought his wife, who was not invited, and Nawari queried it.

"She will be welcome," Ilisidi said, smiled nicely and added a gracious: "She will satisfy the felicity."

Meaning that Cenedi did not need to sit in to solve the infelicity of four—but he would be present. Their

fifth arrived, Machigi himself, who wanted his bodyguard to be present, but did not persist in arguing.

It was, then, five of them in a circle, Bren and Machigi
on one couch and Bregani and Murai on the other, with a
quiet exchange of greetings, and the pouring of tea, as
Ilisidi's acting major d', a staffer from the Bujavid apartment, managed the courtesies. The numbers were favorable, even balanced nicely by the little natural arrangement
of branches and stones that sat in a nook behind the dowager.

There was tea. There must be tea, and light conversation, while the train was clanking and braking its way
downward on the switchback, a process that had become uneasy routine.

"Welcome," Ilisidi said, and smiled pleasantly. "We
are on our way as promised, though a little late. The
descent off the escarpment is not so trying as the inter-
minable descent off the divide in my own province,
though this is claimed to be the worst. It is a rare experience. None of you have used this route before, we
understand."

"I have not," Machigi said.

"The upward route only," Bregani said, with some
irony, "nandi."

"Well, well, we are likely the longest train ever to
take this route, but they assure us we are just within
tolerance, and we did not need to drop a baggage car. It
will only be slow and noisy."

They slipped. Bren swore they slipped a little, not for
the first time. He took a sip of tea, while his heart stead-
ied.

"We do not receive much freight from the north,"
Bregani said. "Certainly nothing of bulk or weight."

"You do have the convenience of two routings for
rail," Ilisidi said, "the lowland and the highland routes.
But we are pleased to see possibilities for Hasjuran, to
their advantage. How did you find Lord Topari, nandi?
One trusts it was a good meeting."

"It was," Bregani said. "I had heard he was a reasonable sort. He seemed so on meeting."

"He was very happy," Bren said, doing his duty, diverting conversation toward the signaled topic, and peaceful, pleasant things. "He was entirely pleased by the agreement. He will certainly abide by it."

It went on in that vein a space, until tea was done.

"So then," Ilisidi said, setting down her cup, signaling a turn toward business. "Regarding sea trade, nandiin. The Dojisigi may extend their displeasure to refusing Senjin's port and its trade. But with Senjin's cooperation with our plan, Senjin need not care. Trade with the Taisigin will expand. Iron will have to come on the lowland rail, but other goods from *my* province can find their way down from Hasjuran, for Senjin to ship south, so Senjin will find it loses nothing substantial at all in a revision of routes. You draw from the south, Lord Machigi. And the Isles and the Dausigin stand to benefit, as well as your capital of Tanaja. In my own region, in the East, nandiin, I am well familiar with the effects of isolation, and having markets nearer than Shejidan and Cobo is a benefit to us. Agreements on trade with us should follow this building of a rail, trade in which Senjin will by no means lose."

"Trade which can begin," Machigi said, "immediately. The fisherfolk southward will consider themselves within our agreement. If your waters seem safe for their fishing boats, you will see them, and they may wish to trade directly for supplies. We would not oppose that trade. You have a harbor, but no ships of your own. We have a shipyard. You have supply we need. We can do business. If no Dojisigin ship visits your port for a hundred years, nandi, you will not want for trade."

It was, for Machigi, a fair flood of persuasive argument. But Bregani distractedly glanced at Cenedi, standing with Nawari, near them, and at Bren and lastly to Ilisidi, in what began to be an emotional state.

"One could wish not to see a Dojisigin ship," Bregani

said, "but I greatly fear we will see them much sooner. Forgive me. This talk of the future is all very well, nand' dowager, nandiin, but we are headed down where I did not want my wife and daughter to be, and thinking on Dojisigin ships—and our port—I have reason for concern. The warehouses clustered there are vulnerable."

"You will be safe, nandi," Bren said. Dealing with emotional moments was not Ilisidi's habit. She could not promise things she could not materialize. It was the paidhi-aiji's function, promising nothing beyond extant agreements. "You are allied, this morning. You are not alone. That is the point of it all."

"I have signed your documents. I have agreed to things I am not sure of. And I fear this morning that I have exposed my district to a long series of troubles, not engaging, but nibbling away at us, in sabotage, in acts nearly impossible to prevent. In my own aishid, men I have known for twenty years, they found a way. It grieves me. I fear it somewhat unnerves me."

"Your bodyguard is safe, nandi," Bren said, "and only asked to stand down. The injured man is attended by the dowager's own physician. And there will be a search made for the man's family." It was a point of anxiety for him, too, since he had shot the man. The man, Tenjin, had been under extreme duress, unwilling to attack his own lord, but Ilisidi—it was unthinkable, what could have happened. The man had been, however briefly and intermittently, in Ilisidi's presence. And had not carried out his mission—terrified, likely; and morally conflicted. "Threatening and kidnapping is the Shadow Guild's last recourse, but it did not make the man turn on you or yours. His man'chi, his instinct, could not turn on you. And that is the flaw in their method, horrible as it is. They are far from the power they once were; they are gone from the north; and if you need reinforcement from the Guild in Shejidan, that will be, one is certain, a possibility. They can pursue this problem. They can find ways to counter it."

"But not immediately," Bregani said. "I have signed your documents. I am part of this, and I can take my own risk. But someone has to succeed me. I want my wife and daughter safe."

Murai protested with a gesture. "I also choose my risks. And I stay. How would it look if I were to go anywhere else? As if I am a hostage, that is how. And that does no good."

"Murai,—"

"No. I shall not sit in Shejidan."

"It will be possible," Ilisidi said, "to interview your security and locate problems. This man of yours has asked Guild help, and he will have it. So will the rest of his unit. We do not take this lightly."

"Nand' dowager, I am willing to go along with your plan. But this has all happened in Hasjuran. You have cornered me, you have trapped me, you have put me in an untenable position and offered me an alliance, and I have let loose the Guild on my own people on your advice. At your urging."

"For your protection, nandi."

"I have told myself that. But since my bodyguard's action, men I have known for twenty years, and with us all bound downward, and no word what is going on in my district. . . . Nand' dowager, I am asking myself now what I have done, and how far this will go. I am allied with strangers. I have given the Guild leave to operate in Senjin—but for how long? And with what cost of life? Something passed us this morning. Is it war, now, with the Dojisigin? How far are you willing to challenge these people—and what will be our terms when there are attacks on ports and nothing is as simple as seemed last night?"

Bren started to reply, but Ilisidi lifted a hand from the table.

"Will we keep our agreements?" Ilisidi said. "Yes. Will the Shejidani Guild hold your capital safe? To the best of their ability, which is considerable. Will the

Dojisigi take offense? Likely. Will the renegades in the Dojisigin choose to fling all they have at Senjin? I do not think so, because they do not wish to die there. Can we protect you if they do? Yes. As for that train this morning, we shall see. It came from the north, in silence, and I strongly suspect *we* are not the ones who should worry about it."

Bregani listened, worried and showing it. But he nodded slowly. "We are anxious to be home. We are anxious about our home, anxious for our people. I hope you will understand."

"That recommends you well, nandi," Bren said, "and you have more allies than you have counted. Tabini-aiji has no wish to see this mission fail. For a number of years the Shejidani Guild has hoped this outlawed splinter of theirs would simply fade away. But the Dojisigin is now against a wall. That is why they are desperate. As of last night they have lost your trade. They have no other in the Marid. They have no access to rail. Sea is their only recourse, and if they persist in causing trouble, they may find the straits no longer welcoming."

"Tiajo," Bregani said, as if that word expressed every sort of doubt.

"Tiajo," Machigi echoed him, in even less cheerfulness. "These renegades backing her may finally decide Tiajo is no longer useful or amusing, in which case we may have another outbreak of problems. But we are now four-fifths of the Marid, with two harbors, with ships, with a railroad connected to the whole of the aishidi'tat, *and* the space station."

That brought a raised brow.

"It is far from remote from us," Machigi said. "It is up there right now. One understands it has telescopes that can see this train moving across the land. It can see storms moving across the sea. It can tell us when to seek harbor, and what sort of wind to expect and when. There will be steel ships, independent of the wind, but using it at convenience. All these things you will participate in."

"One has heard talk," Bregani said. "One has heard fantastical things. One has heard of things hard to believe. But the aiji-dowager and the paidhi . . . have left the world more than once. And it is true. One supposes it is true."

"It is true," Ilisidi said. "As true as humans on Mospheira and as true as the steel station we used to call the Foreign Star. It exists. It acts. The aishidi'tat controls half of it, humans the other half, and we deal fairly with each other. We have learned how to do that. There is no reason that four-fifths of the Marid cannot have the benefits of it. Four fifths of the Marid is with us. The 'counters will tell us that four is an instability, and I say the sooner we mend that vile number to a healthy five, the better. Let us work toward it."

Bregani and Murai sat side by side, worried, afloat in a set of strange concepts involving the space station that Marid folk generally claimed were at best irrelevant and at worst hostile to their lives. Neither of them had seen a human before. Weather was what happened when nature decided, and ships that plied the Marid were dependent on wind, and came to grief at times because of it. Dojisigin and Taisigin vessels sailed the edge of the Southern Ocean and came around to Separti, Jorida, and Cobo, making a few households rich, but not many. It was the way things were. It was the way they had always been for centuries.

"It is a great deal of change," Bregani said. "But clearly—" This with a glance at Bren. And at Ilisidi. And at Machigi, to his left. "Clearly things cannot stay as they are. From hour to hour I think I must be wrong, and then I think I am doing the only thing that possibly makes sense. And clearly I have yet to explain it to my household, my people, my associates . . . why I have loosed the Guild in Koperna and why I have signed what I have signed. It will not please everybody, but we have been afraid of Tiajo. Everything we do, we are afraid of Tiajo. And as long as we have been partners

with the Dojisigin, Senjin interests have never come
first."

"Three is a felicitous number," Ilisidi said. "Associations three by three have built the world. Let us be optimistic about what will have developed by the time we
arrive down there, and share a brandy."

The train had inched its way to a clanking stop, and
then began to move down again. Transportation agents
would have gotten down, guarded the while, whatever
the weather was out there; they had now thrown the
switch, and the Red Train would start on the next
switchback, lower and lower toward the coastal plain.
The railroad itself was a mad, extravagant project, created because the aishidi'tat had hoped to end the wars
within the Marid and gain the northern tier of it as allies
through trade.

The effort had completed the Grand Loop at Koperna. But betrayal by the Dojisigin had been an issue
before the rail was complete—which was why the Dojisigin was left with a stub of a spur, never finished, impass-
able now, and slowly going to ruin.

Glasses went around, five in number, felicitous five.
Bren thought he was never so ready for a brandy, between
the chancy feeling of the descent, Bregani's understandable skittishness, and the uncertainties of a new and un-
tested alliance—to which the dowager was committing
herself so deeply. Recklessly so. Gambling all their lives.
And complicating her own effort with the solution to the
Ajuri problem; and the risk of provoking another war. In
the start of it all he had just thought—let us not fall off the
mountain. And now it was more specific: let us not start
a war down there, with not only the dowager, but all the
high cards we own aboard a single train.

He took several sips. Heaved a sigh.

The door to the passageway opened. A Guildsman
outside passed a note to Nawari, inside, who read it,
frowned, and passed it to Cenedi, who, reading it, instantly handed it to Ilisidi.

She read it, and immediately she said, "Wari-ji, put Casimi on it."

"Yes," was the answer, and Nawari moved immediately to the door, as Ilisidi said, quietly, "Nand' Bregani, Husai-daja is not in your compartment. Is this expected?"

Bregani and Murai both looked alarmed.

"Nand' dowager," Bregani said, rising. Murai was no slower. "No. It is not expected. Where is her guard?"

"They are apparently looking for her," Ilisidi said. "Nand' Bren. Assist."

"Aiji-ma." Bren rose immediately and, together with the parents, exited the compartment. Jago and Tano were in the corridor. So were the two of the regular Guild accompanying Bregani and Murai. "Husai is missing from her compartment," Bren said. "Alert the Guild car forward. We need to find her quickly."

Atevi moving *quickly* did not take a human stride into account. Bren labored to keep the pace, eavesdropping on a one-sided verbal code as Jago messsaged the Guild further up the train.

"They say there is no breach, no alert," Jago translated. "They are checking baggage and storage."

The train was well into its descent as they reached the passage door of the next car. Bren followed Jago and Banichi across the less certain footing between cars, collecting a bruise on his shoulder from the resistant door. He thought of Homura, who *might* have found some means to attach himself to the train, of Guild who should not have left their charge, of Bregani's original, non-Guild bodyguard, in detention, one of them known to be compromised by the Shadow Guild's new tactic of choice.

And Transportation Guild, who were entering and exiting the train as they manned the switch points.

They passed through the Guild car with no sign of Banichi and Algini. They went on into Bren's own car, and Narani stood in the passage to say, "Banichi and Algini are waiting forward, nandi!"

"Yes," he said, and took what Narani handed him, in body contact. He slipped the pistol into his pocket and kept going.

Banichi and Algini were waiting in the adjacent Guild car, with several of the regular Guild, and took up with them as they traversed that car and went on to Machigi's. One of Machigi's personal guard opened the door, hearing the disturbance.

"Nandi!" the challenge was for the person in charge, and Bren quickly realized that was himself.

"A young woman is missing, nadi," Bren said, conscious of the girl's parents behind him. "Daughter of Lord Bregani, from his car. Have you seen her? Have you heard anything?"

"No, nandi." This in an accent stronger than Machigi's. "No such person is here."

This pair was not tapped into regular Guild communications. They had no way to know what was going on, except something was wrong and their lord and two of their team were a number of cars away. Confusion and worry was plain on their faces.

At the same time the farther door of the passage opened, and a regular Guild member came through, saw them, and gave a quick bow.

"Nandiin," the woman said. "There is a delicate situation."

"Our daughter," Lord Bregani said. "Have you found her? Is she all right?"

"One believes so, nandi. Nand' paidhi. Banichi-nadi. We suspect she is in Nomari-nadi's quarters."

God, Bren thought. Nomari's was the next car. "Is his bodyguard present? Is hers?"

"I am assigned to her," the Guildswoman said. "She *said* she felt ill. She *said* it was the change in pressure. And the train moving. She said she wanted us to make a pot of tea. We went to do that. It took a moment. And we thought she was in the accommodation. The door was locked. When she persistently did not answer, we broke the door and she was not there. We never heard her go out. We were engaged in the galley. We had set no alarms."

As if one ought to need to, though the pair would get a mark on their record. The racket of the train had covered the exit, and it was a willful exit, deliberate subterfuge. Bregani and Murai were utterly expressionless.

Nomari's appointment was at extreme risk. So might the signed agreements be.

"You say you suspect she is in Nomari-nadi's car," Bren said. And to the point: "Why do you think so?"

"Because he is not at the meeting, and we have searched the baggage car up and down and even the cases, and my partner has been asking the transportation crew and they have not seen her. The Ajuri's door is locked. I know someone is in there. I know he has a proper bodyguard. But no one is answering."

"*I* will get a response," Bregani said.

"Nandi," Bren said. An irate father, a teenaged daughter, and a young man who had spent years spying on their country for Machigi, also present. God. "Let us manage this quietly. Guild or Transportation can open that door."

"Yes."

"Then, gods below, do it."

"Nandi," Banichi said, and extracted several keys from his jacket pocket. "Come."

"Please stay here, nandiin," Bren said. "Let Guild investigate."

"My daughter," Bregani said, and pushed past him, a move that triggered Jago, but Bren quickly signed to let be. The Guildswoman who had reported the situation went through the passage door to the next car, Banichi followed, then Bregani and Murai, and Jago after that. She held the doors for Bren, one after the other, and Tano and Algini came after, the other pair of Bregani's guard hindmost into the situation. They were set. They were ready.

Stay back, Banichi signaled to Bregani, who seemed to have realized the potential for something other than scandal beyond the locked door. Bregani had a look of dread on his face, and had, rare among atevi, an arm about his wife in public, restraining her from what both of them wanted to do.

Banichi's key turned in the lock. Banichi drew his pistol. Jago said, quietly, into her com: "This is Jago, of nand' Bren's aishid! Open the door. *Any* staff! Open this door immediately!"

There might be movement inside. The sounds of the train covered it. Banichi was the only one in an exposed position, at the door.

"Open the door," Jago repeated.

There was a little confusion, as someone on the other side accidentally relocked the door, then unlocked it, and opened it cautiously. Guild faced each other with drawn weapons.

Bren could not, from his vantage, see much beyond the fact it was uniformed Guild who had opened the door, and that Banichi, who could see inside, exchanged a few words, asked a question, and holstered the pistol.

"Is she there?" Murai wondered aloud, behind him. "Is she all right?"

"I see no indication of threat, nandi. I think we may come ahead."

Jago, beside him, likewise settled her pistol back in her holster, while Tano and Algini, still with weapons in hand, stayed a little to the rear. Guild they recognized was inside the compartment, and now one more uniformed Guild arrived from the far passage door. They were amply defended, Bren decided, from this end of the passage and the other, whatever was going on inside.

"One regrets," the Guild senior said to Banichi. And to Bren: "Nandi."

"What," Banichi asked, "is going on?"

Then Nomari appeared, and behind him, Husai, both, thank God, decently dressed—Bren's first thought.

Nomari looked worried and Husai looked beyond worried, her hand clenched on Nomari's sleeve, not exactly the attitude of a person lately kidnapped.

"I am very sorry, nandiin," Nomari said, and looked it. "Husai-daja came. She was frightened."

"Frightened," Bren said.

"Daughter of mine," Bregani said sternly. "*What* was your concern?"

Husai froze for a moment, looking as if she would gladly sink through the floor.

"The bodyguards," she said then.

"Did they behave improperly?" Bregani asked ominously.

"Not—" Husai began in a small voice, then said, "No, Honored Father."

"Then what?" Bregani asked.

"Daughter," Murai said. "What happened?"

"Nothing," Husai said in a small voice. "I was just . . . scared."

Bregani asked: "And is this compartment less terrifying?"

Husai's gaze darted from one to the other, lips compressed. There was not much space in the doorway. She seemed to want to fade behind Nomari, himself looking distressed.

"I think we may assume," Bren ventured, "that nothing untoward happened here. Nomari-nadi, can you say so?"

"Nandiin, please ask her. We were accompanied by my entire aishid, assigned me by Lord Tatiseigi and the Guild."

Which was to say, high-up Guild, impartial, without man'chi, and no, not lying.

"Daughter," Bregani said. "Did someone do something?"

"No!" Husai said. "No."

"She is scared of the descent," Nomari said quietly. "She is scared of the situation. And the meetings. And of what may be happening in Senjin. I could at least tell her the train is behaving exactly as it should. Her bodyguard scared her. I apologize, nandiin, especially to her parents, for the locked door. And the silence."

"It is not his fault," Husai said. "Honored Father, Honored Mother, I asked him not to let them find me. I was just upset. And the baggage car was dark, and I just—I came to nand' Nomari's car. And I thought—the next car is nand' Machigi's, and his aishid is—is—"

"Scarier," Nomari said, and with a flicker of eyes to his face and away again, Husai nodded.

"So I knocked at nand' Nomari's door, and he was there."

"Nomari-nadi," Nomari said, staring at the floor, "daja-ma."

"Nomari-nadi," Husai corrected herself. "But he *will* be a lord. And he gave me tea. And that is all we were doing."

"Nandiin," Nomari said, looking to Bregani and Murai, "you were in an important meeting. Husai-daja appeared distressed with the guards. I knew you were with the aiji-dowager, nandiin, and I should not interrupt that, but if anything had happened to make her afraid, I should try to find out without disturbing everything. That has happened, and one is deeply sorry."

"I," Bregani said, "am waiting for the story myself. I am waiting to learn in detail. Daughter."

"It was just the train," Husai said. "It was just the train. I keep feeling we might fall. And you had gone to deal with the dowager, and the guards would not tell me anything that was going on, and I wanted to know. But then—then I just panicked. I thought if I found where you were I could stay. And then I realized I had to go past Machigi's guards. And I was afraid to go back. So I knocked on nand'—on this door. And he was here, and not at the meeting either. He said that he had taken this trip before and that the train was not out of control and everybody was safe, and I just—I just wanted to sit and have a cup of tea and have somebody tell me we are not all going to die."

"The guards did not frighten you," Murai said.

"No," Husai said, and looked at the two who had been hunting for her. "No. It was nothing they did. I am so sorry. It was my fault. I will tell anyone, it was not your fault. I lied. And I slipped out. And I upset everyone. Please do not be mad at my parents."

"Your bodyguard," Banichi said, "should not have to overcome *you* in your own protection, Husai-daja. We may have more than one compromised individual aboard, one of whom you know. Please lessen the risk to your guards and yourself."

"I shall," Husai said. "I am so very sorry."

"Forgive our daughter," Bregani said, and to Nomari: "Nadi, you were cautious, and one appreciates the caution. Forgive her parents' concern."

"Nandiin. I hope the meeting was not disrupted."

"I think it went well, nadi," Bregani said. "Though I think we may wish to sit down in our own compartment and take something stronger than tea. Our profoundest apologies to the aiji dowager."

"I shall relay them," Bren said.

"Daughter," Bregani said. "Nadiin." The last to the Guild unit, who could not, Bren thought, look forward to a report on the matter.

Bregani and his family moved on, *with* their assigned bodyguard, while Banichi reported a curt, "Safe. Stand down," to a Guild operation thoroughly set on end.

Nobody had wanted to upset the dowager's meeting. Nomari had doubtless had a quandary of his own, as to his own situation.

And a teenaged girl and a young man with reason not to trust the law had for a number of minutes thrown the dowager's affairs into disorder.

Machigi had a dark sense of humor, rarely glimpsed. Machigi, if he gathered very much of it, might be quite amused.

The dowager—less so. The Guild, less than that. They did not enjoy working as they did now, with unknowns, outsiders, and strangers. They did not favor sudden assignments to individuals who might have immense significance to plans and absolutely no grasp of the tactics that might be brought against them.

"One apologizes profoundly," Nomari said. "To everyone. I am sorry. I am very sorry."

"It was not all the girl's safety that may have concerned you," Bren said. "Be honest with me. It is generally a good idea."

Nomari drew a deep breath. "You are right, nandi. My bodyguard asked emphatically to report. I—was trying to think what to do."

"Trust the Guild," Bren said. "There were years when that was not necessarily the best idea. But trust the unit that protects you to have your best interests at heart."

"Nandi. Should I write to the dowager?"

"I shall take on that matter," Bren said. "And in the spirit of truthfulness, I also had to learn, several times quite painfully. Trust your bodyguard, so that they can trust you."

7

"So," Bren said to the dowager over tea, while the Red Train screeched and groaned its tilted way down the grade, "we now have everybody back in their respective cars, and Nomari-nadi is safely an entire baggage car removed from the young lady."

The dowager loved a scandal almost more than she loved a good wine. Her eyes positively sparkled, but quickly grew more serious. "It is not a bloom we can ever encourage."

"For many reasons," Bren said. "But I do not greatly fault either, aiji-ma. They are young, they are neither one in power over the situation, they are justifiably anxious about their future and the young lady was quite uneasy about the dangers of the route. Neither is stupid, which is to their advantage, but their intelligence keeps a lively fire under their imaginations. For him, there are ghosts in the shadows and motives are suspect. For her, every clank and squeal is overturn and ruin. I confess this descent makes *me* quite anxious. She is only sixteen."

Ilisidi positively smiled. "A questionable number. And a very handsome young man kept looking at her over dinner. Did you mark that, paidhi?"

"Oh, I did. I saw it going both ways, aiji-ma."

"Mmm. How extraordinary that her imagination overwhelmed her with fears only until she found herself outside the young man's door!"

"She said that it was fear of meeting Machigi's bodyguards that stopped her short and sent her to Nomari's door. Which is understandable."

A wicked, wicked smile. "I have been a girl of her age. And I take all this flightiness as seriously as I take ghosts—though, mind you! there is a very reputable ghost in the vicinity of my house at Malguri, and I have myself heard the old bell ringing down on the shore. So we shall halfway believe in her dread of Machigi and simply count ourselves fortunate we had a convenient very handsome young man in the way to prevent *that* meeting."

Appalling thought, that . . . though Nomari's guards were surely not apt to be fools.

"I feel rather sorry for Nomari, however," Bren said. "He was put in a very difficult place, with her parents standing there, with the young lady in no frame of mind to be logical. And his sleeve wrung to ruin in her hand."

Ilisidi almost laughed. "Do you think anything *did* go on?"

"Oh, there may well have been thought of it, aiji-ma, but there were four Guild witnesses with no man'chi to either. I rather imagine Nomari's mind was filled with visions of your wrath and her parents' indignation, and the collapse of the association so carefully assembled, all falling on him."

"With my forces in control of Senjin's capital, far less likelihood of anything falling. But we have had quite enough Marid blood married into the midlands lordships, and one would not like to view that machimi again if at all avoidable. It has no good lines in it." She took a sip of tea. "Well, well, she is the heir of Senjin, and that fixes her in place. He is safe. She cannot go to Ajuri. And if we do confirm that young man, *he* will be fixed in Ajuri, and I would not be surprised to see Tatiseigi push some regional choice in his direction—ill-starred as that link has been for both Ajuri and Atageini clans. I would rather urge that young man to look to Dur or Cobo."

Northwest and west, as the Atageini sat to Ajuri's east. Good choices, both, stable small clans with a strong economy, a strong Transportation Guild, historic links to Ajuri and no history of conspiracy.

"You are then leaning toward approving him."

"I have found no fault in him. And he truly is a handsome fellow."

"That has no relevance at all, aiji-ma."

"No, but there is no fault in it, either, if, as likely, he will be in my sight now and again, under Tatiseigi's roof, not to mention that he has attracted my great-grandson's approval and, my greater worry, might someday attract my great-granddaughter's. If this young man is wise, he will attach very strong man'chi in both directions and learn his statecraft from Tatiseigi, since he comes to us as a blank slate, untutored and unattached. I have seen nothing in his comportment to say he is a fool, a profit-seeker, or in any degree prideful. He has shown himself modest, has not traded on his prospects, has not pushed himself forward even at clear opportunity to do so. If anything, he is a little too reserved and modest to survive court, as he is, and some people would practice on him, but he is no fool, either, or he would not have lived. One would hope he will resort back to Tatiseigi and learn from him how to send off a scoundrel without becoming one. Mind, I am thinking of my great-grandson, now, too. When Cajeiri is twenty and inclined to act the fool, if ever, that young man will be mature, and fully sensible by then, I would hope, if not sage. The fact my grandson's wife will likely be regent for my great-granddaughter when that child inherits Atageini, well, *someone* should have a memory of having his hands in the mud and muck and making a living on his own. There is such a thing as too elevated a living and too little honest work. And the fact this young man is still alive is all his own doing. No one rescued him."

One was surprised . . . and not. The dowager's own home lacked modern conveniences—including, in many areas, electrics. She had been a competitive rider. She tended her mecheiti herself whenever she had the chance, and while she was meticulous and fussy about some things, she could come in mud-spattered from the stables and cheerfully wade a puddle up to her ankles when she had been caught out in the wet—granted it was her loyal staff who would turn her out coiffed, ribboned, and wearing satin and rubies for dinner in the next hour.

Nomari had somehow seemed to have passed her exacting standards. Nomari had *not* been invited to tea with the dowager, in the way Bren had, when he was new, but then—the dowager had been playing rather higher stakes in that long-ago meeting, her grandson Tabini-aiji having made the unprecedented decision to take a human advisor to his personal retreat, and to *converse* with him.

He did not, personally, begrudge Nomari a gentler start in public life. He was quite relieved to hear Ilisidi's assessment overall. Nothing could have gained her personal interest faster than a breath of romantic scandal; and count Bregani's pretty daughter in for Ilisidi's continuing interest in her future. That young woman had now gained Ilisidi's notice, which could be an advantage, if one did not slide into the negative column. Bregani, a relative of Cosadi, who came near the top of the list of people Ilisidi had detested alive and dead, had sired Husai, who had possibly made a play for a person, Nomari, destined to share a boundary with Ilisidi's closest and most favored ally, Lord Tatiseigi, and to advise her great-grandson, Cajeiri. Was she involved? Oh, yes.

And *a darkness* in that young man, Ilisidi had said. It was not all approval.

Bren sipped his tea and felt the train strangely change pitch, the car rocking ever so slightly. He paused, setting the teacup down, a little alarmed, and then felt the train running on the level.

Ilisidi looked completely unruffled.

There was the curious sound then as the train entered a tunnel—as they were to do twice on this descent. It was the first time that he had had a clue where they were.

Probably the view from the switchbacks would be absolutely spectacular.

If there were windows.

Probably it was all absolutely spectacular, depending on which side of the train one stood. If there were windows. One imagined sunlight glancing off the Marid sea, and a vast flat plain all hazy—no winter in the Marid, where snow rarely came. His imagined vision began to look like a map. With place names. He had absolutely no sense of scale, just the dry recollection of his study. With tunnels to pass through, and timber spans to pass over, and thoughts of sabotage, the Dojisigi surely being aware they were on their way.

But there were also Guild units hopefully snug in shelter, camped along the track and watching those key points.

"I should fancy a game of chess," Ilisidi said. "Will you?"

It was not the paidhi's place to refuse. Ilisidi had done what she had done, had arranged what she had arranged, and one would never suppose that the aijidowager had any nervousness about what she had yet to deal with, no, never.

Cenedi, doubtless her regular chess opponent, bestirred himself from his reading and provided the board and the pieces.

"You seem distracted," Ilisidi observed to Bren.

"I would say this is a unique experience."

"We have lost three trains on this descent," Ilisidi said, "but two were sabotage, back in Cosadi's time. And we have taken measures." She set out the pieces as she spoke. "And when we ship such things as Machigi's steel, we shall naturally do it on the lowland route: heavy loads were never the intent for this route. This rail was built, truly, as a pretext, a way into the Marid that fairly hangs over their heads. Its building vastly annoyed the Dojisigi, and enabled Senjin to maintain some independence, which we saw even then as a good thing and which set them up in what liberty they have. So we continue to use this route—for trade to *keep* Senjin somewhat independent, and for statements such as we are making now, and also to help little Hasjuran, which has clung to life and trade since the days when we were actively building the rail. Senjin *is* a good market for them. Trade between those two points makes sense. No air service, nor any likely to come, for various reasons. And the rail will always be mostly the lowland route."

"But you are still serious about Lord Machigi's sea route, aiji-ma."

"Oh, yes." A pawn moved. "I am serious and Lord Geigi is perfectly serious."

Lord Geigi, master of the atevi side of the space station, who talked about weather prediction, and satellites in various positions to observe the world, even submersibles to study the depths of the Great Ocean and travel the far side of the world, was part and parcel of the dowager's plans. There was no limit to Geigi's imagination, and the more details the human archive poured forth—now that they had achieved parity in technology—the more projects Geigi had in the planning stages. The Department of Linguistics on Mospheira was increasingly agitated by Lord Geigi's projects, and proposed this and that law to curtail access to the archive, to no avail, since the human Captains of the ship had to approve the human director up there, and the human director was, lately, quite cooperative and not at all to the liking of Linguistics and its conservative Committee.

So, yes, Lord Geigi was generally serious about his

projects, and likely lay awake nights imagining new satellites to do useful things.

Bren moved a pawn. Ilisidi moved another.

The train exited the tunnel and clanked on its way.

Uncle Tatiseigi had made a hasty trip out to Tirnamardi and back to the capital again since mani had taken the Red Train and left. Cajeiri gathered all of it from staff, who talked to other staff, and he was worried about Uncle.

He had a standing permission to visit anyone on the third floor of the Bujavid, which was, besides Father . . . mani, and nand' Bren, and Uncle, who was actually Great-uncle. And Cajeiri worried about Uncle Tatiseigi. Mother had called on Uncle Tatiseigi and brought the baby to see him just after mani had taken the train and left, which would have cheered Uncle, Cajeiri was sure.

But that was *Mother's* visit, and Mother had not asked him to go visit Uncle with her, so he had not asked or intruded his presence, thinking he would go later.

And then Uncle had left.

But Uncle was back now, having dealt with something at Tirnamardi that took two days; and Uncle had not sent any messages that staff knew of. Uncle was just keeping to himself and seeing no one.

That was what Eisi found out.

So with Rieni's warning in mind, Cajeiri put on a formal coat and took just his younger aishid, that Uncle knew well, and went out and down the hall to the endmost apartment, which was Uncle's. He was determined to be careful with what he knew, but he was determined, too, that Uncle would not feel disregarded.

Madam Saidin answered the door, knowing they were coming, because staff passed word. Madam Saidin was Uncle's major domo and ran Uncle's business in the Bujavid, whenever Uncle was not in residence.

"Is Uncle well?" he asked. "Is he seeing anyone?"

"One is certain he will see you, young gentleman," she said, and let them all in: Veijico and Lucasi *would* have stood outside, in formal manners, with just Antaro and Jegari coming inside, but Cajeiri beckoned them all in, and they all came with him . . . which was just as well: guards standing outside did advertise to staff and everybody who was meeting with whom, and he had just as well not cause any gossip even on this restricted floor, as tense as the situation was. Mani's staff still received mail and messages at *her* apartment across the hall and midway between nand' Bren's and Uncle's.

Uncle was in his study, at his desk, looking grim and busy over his papers.

"Nandi," Saidin-daja said, clearing her throat, and Uncle looked up. It was as if the sun had come up, the welcome in his expression, which made it certain the visit was a good idea.

Cajeiri gave a little bow, and Uncle asked Saidin-daja to bring tea and cakes.

"All of you sit," Uncle said, meaning even his aishid: they were that comfortable with Uncle.

So they did, and Uncle took his own leather chair. "Have you heard from your great-grandmother?" was Uncle's first question.

"No, Uncle. One hoped you had."

Uncle's face showed a little distress. "One understands she is at Hasjuran. With nand' Bren, Lord Machigi, and our associate from Ajuri, all about this railroad business. I have not heard a word else, and I am worried. I am quite worried. There is altitude, there is cold, and it all involves Marid politics."

"Cousin Nomari spied on Lord Bregani for Lord Machigi."

"I have heard that."

There were things Uncle might not know, not having access to Father. And Uncle, despite being left behind, was mani's strongest ally, and smart, besides. There was *nothing* Uncle would do that would put mani at risk. And of all people who was canny about politics and secrets. Uncle had talked to Father. Once. And in company with others.

He had promised his aishid, he had promised strictly not to tell anyone.

But Uncle . . .

Uncle was no fool. And of all things unfortunate, it was unfortunate that Uncle was not with mani right now, to advise her, and to listen.

It was not right. It was not *right* that Uncle was not involved in this. Father was not used to relying on him, but *he* was. And Uncle was not just *anyone.*

"Mani has gone there," Cajeiri said, deliberately, "to talk Lord Bregani into allying with Lord Machigi. She has taken Nomari and nand' Bren with her. And she has the Guild operating in Senjin. In Koperna."

"Gods less fortunate."

He did not recall he had ever heard Uncle swear, not even when Aunt Geidaro had come to his house to provoke him. "She has one Guild force with her. She has gotten Bregani to sign, and the Guild evidently has Koperna under control. And she has been up at Hasjuran. But now there is a third train, and I do not know what it is doing."

They had not had their tea. Servants had started preparing it, but Uncle's first question had started them down this track, and then the servants all stopped and everything froze. They were Uncle's own staff, Atageini clan, Madam Saidin chief among them, and *her* staff was as honest as any anywhere.

"Dojisigin is going to react," Uncle said. "Does anyone think otherwise?"

"My older aishid thinks she wants that," Cajeiri said. "I asked them to find out what it all is, and they are trying. I promised them the greatest secrecy, and telling you, honored Uncle, I know I am bending that, but *I* approve it. And I think you need to know. You know mani better than anyone. I know she is up to something serious. And I know she does not trust Cousin, but she took him. I think she wants to see whether Machigi being there would find out something. Or maybe he knows something about Lord Bregani. Or maybe she is just trying to catch him in a fault."

"Nomari-nadi will not change. I would be astonished if *he* lied in any significant particular. She is *relying* on that pirate, meanwhile."

Uncle meant Lord Machigi.

"Lord Machigi has Dausigi and Sungeni allied to him," Cajeiri said, a little proud of himself that he had thought on the whole situation, and where mani was now, and come up with a sensible reason. "If he allies with Senjin, too, Lord Tiajo will be all alone."

"And dangerous!" Uncle said. "That is a Guild-trained opposition."

"Great-grandmother is dangerous, too."

Uncle unexpectedly laughed, quietly, but he did look more cheerful at that. "I so wish I were there."

"So do I wish I were there, honored Uncle. I hope she will stay on the train. I hope she will take care of herself."

At that Uncle looked less cheerful. "I would never wager on it."

"Nand' Bren will argue with her."

"One of the few," Uncle said, then looked about him at the quiet, waiting servants. "Tea! Tea, Saia-ji, if you will. My grand-nephew, at least, consults me on matters of state."

"I think you could visit Father," Cajeiri said. "I think he would tell you things he would not tell me. And then you can tell me the rest of it."

Uncle arched a brow, very like mani in that expression—smiled and nodded. "My favorite nephew."

"Your only nephew."

"Well, but still my favorite."

"Tell Father you have heard no news," Cajeiri said.

"It is not quite lying, since after he tells you, you will have heard it."

"You have absorbed *her* ways."

"Mani says," Cajeiri said, "you can mend a little lie a lot easier than you can mend a truth."

"So," Bren said, having invited Nomari to tea and explanations. He set his cup down. Nomari did.

"I told the truth," was Nomari's first statement.

"One does not doubt," Bren said. "Do not be anxious. I am constructing an explanation should anyone in Senjin or in Shejidan ask. But one wishes not to err in the facts of the matter. What was the sequence of events?"

"She knocked at my door, encountered my bodyguard and they brought her in, nandi, as she was in distress."

"No one had harmed her. She had no specifics of any apprehension."

"No one had harmed her. She was uneasy about the descent, and equally so about her parents' meeting with the dowager . . . on which I knew nothing. And could tell her nothing. I still know nothing."

"You reassured her. On what terms? Did you make any promises or offers?"

Nomari considered that a moment, and one detected a flicker of understanding, perhaps, of the reason for questions.

"I assured her, nandi, that the train was operating normally. I told this very train has taken this route before and that the train crew is extremely skilled, this being the dowager's train, and I believe that the Red Train when she is aboard always has the same crew, nandi. But I did not say that. I said just that they were very good."

"Your information on that is likely better than mine. And there were no promises or offers?"

"I offered her tea and wafers. I said . . . I said that, given her father had signed into association with the dowager, her parents should be perfectly safe, and that, besides, the aiji-dowager has never, to my knowledge, hurt anyone who came to tea with her."

That required a certain facial control.

"She would never," Bren said, "extend protection to Lord Bregani and then change her mind. You would also be correct to say that because she has promised to return him to Senjin, she will do it, if it takes the Guild to clear the path—which is actually the case, at the moment. Did you express assurance on that matter?"

"One just said—she would never go back on her hospitality."

The tea incident involving him was an anomaly. Had there ever been another? Bren had no knowledge on that score. Likely it had been a moment's inspiration. Or curiosity, since human intolerance for substances atevi relished was a report, not a certain understanding. But then—his taking the cup had put him, in a sense, into the dowager's personal reckoning, whether because she had not believed it would harm him, and found it was not a lie; or that he had passed a test of nerves. He had not thought he ought to refuse. She might have thought his taking it challenged *her* integrity. Whatever it was, he had passed initial scrutiny. Thereafter she had only tried to break his neck on a country ride, before she concluded he had qualities useful to her.

"One does not say she will never test you," Bren said. "But there is no lord more honest or more protective of her allies. One does not say that you may not also meet sharp questions from her grandson, but the dowager will not change course and leave you. The problem is—*your* problem is—you have associated with her chief ally, Lord Tatiseigi, and her great-grandson, in a region which has been repeatedly threatened by Ajuri's actions. So you can surely understand her interest. And understand her watching you closely on this venture."

"One does, nandi. But I could not let the girl wander about the train."

That was not the answer he was looking for. He let the silence remain a moment. Then:

"You do understand your relevance to current issues."

The silence persisted a moment.

"Yes," Nomari said. "Yes, nandi."

"Have you, in prior times, *met* Lord Machigi?"

"I have reported to him."

"Directly to him."

"Yes."

"Have you met Lord Bregani?"

"I have been in his presence. There was no conversation, as such. I was just a person. A witness."

"To?"

"A meeting. In the residency. I was listening to questions of Lord Tiajo's representative, on trade. On warehousing. On personnel."

"Have you met any member of Lord Bregani's family prior to this?"

"No, nandi."

"Nor met his daughter."

"No, nandi. Absolutely I have not. I saw her once. She was a child, maybe twelve years old."

"After Tabini-aiji's return to power, did you continue to spy on Lord Bregani?"

"Yes."

"Is there anything you should tell me about that, nadi?"

Nomari shrugged. "It was the same sort of thing: what was shipped. What was traded. What Dojisigi might be present in Senjin. What reports came out of the Dojisigin. And what was rumored about the north. Nothing changed. But I left, once it was safe to move about. I stayed out of the Marid, generally. I had no wish to attract attention."

"Were you there when the dowager made an agreement with Lord Machigi? Were you present for any of that?"

"I was not, nandi. I knew nothing of it until it was rumored in the north."

It all accorded with his observations of interactions, at least.

"Why did you restrain your aishid from reporting Husai's whereabouts?"

"Until I knew what was going on, nandi, until I knew it was not something more complicated, I had no wish to interrupt the meeting. I thought if something had happened, at least she was safe where she was, and when the meeting was over, then I would have them report."

"Why did she go to your door?"

"Because she was afraid of the bodyguard in her compartment and she was afraid of Lord Machigi."

"But not of you."

"I am not any power in this," Nomari said. "I am just a passenger. Like her."

"She might think that," Bren said. "But you expect greater things for yourself."

"I am still," Nomari said, "only a passenger."

"For now," Bren said. "But you know your circumstances may change. And what I say now is not factfinding, but a sense of where the dowager stands, nadi, so do hear me, and be honest with me if you disagree. Any association with this young lady, she being who she is, would add far too much complication to your situation. Her house has a history of contracts made and offspring produced with the northern houses, which is why, to a certain extent, we now have the prospect of war before us. The Marid is very loosely attached to the aishidi'tat: its five provinces have had their own intrigues for centuries, as has the north, and the East, and they only get worse by combining their problems. Far better you look to Dur or Cobo, even Targai or Kajiminda for a partner—when it becomes appropriate. Forgive a human for conducting this discussion, but I am relaying the dowager's concerns, for your best outcome and the young lady's."

Nomari looked intensely uneasy—embarrassed, one thought. It was certainly mutual.

"I am far from being able to take on the responsibility of a marriage, contract or otherwise," Nomari said. "But I thank you for relaying that."

"I have said fully enough," Bren said. "Will you enjoy a brandy, nadi?"

"I would not impose."

"We are entirely at leisure at the moment. Please accept. Congenial company is welcome, and you need not feel that you are walking on dangerous ground hereafter, nadi, in casual conversation with me. I swear to you I observe discretion with personal matters, aside from matters of state. I have sympathy for your situation, coming to court as an outsider. I have certainly had that experience."

Nomari looked at him uneasily. Nomari had never seen a human until they had met on this train, but Nomari had been courteous, trying hard, one gathered, to find his own path.

"One is grateful, nand' paidhi. I shall appreciate the brandy."

8

One was glad to have visited Uncle Tatiseigi. And one had lined up mentally the things one *could* say and *should* say, and made a decision, one that he had had to make—for mani's sake, for everybody's. Uncle could not be allowed to fall away from mani, all because Great-grandmother had a feud with Mother.

Cajeiri was back in his own suite. Shedding his formal coat into Eisi's hands, trying to assess what he had just done . . . he was not sorry. He was glad, over all, that he had visited Uncle. Uncle had been worried and had gotten no satisfaction from Father, who had been trying to walk a middle, impersonal course between Mother and Great-grandmother. Cajeiri had no trouble picking that out.

They had had a lengthy talk. Uncle had already found out there was a connection between Machigi and Nomari, so that part had not been news to him. He was not quite sure how Uncle had found that out, but Father might have told him.

Uncle had also called Machigi a pirate, which was not exactly true, so far as he knew, but that had always been Uncle's opinion. Machigi certainly gave that kind of impression, even if there was nothing precisely that had ever proved it—and in fact, Lord Machigi's ships had suffered piracy, from back when the Edi people were luring ships onto the rocks, as they now had promised never to do.

What Uncle truly, *truly* resented about Machigi, Cajeiri was sure, was the fact that mani had made an alliance with him in the first place. Uncle, being a northern and a midlands lord, and one of the most important in all the aishidi'tat, was not in favor of the Marid as a whole, and regarded them as enemies . . . which was actually true through most of history. The whole southern half of the aishidi'tat was different, not being Ragi, and in several cases maintaining distance from Shejidan, though cooperating and paying their taxes and all. The absolutely southernmost clans just stood apart and ignored laws at their convenience, but the northern part of the south—which there ought to be a name for—included the Edi people, and nand' Bren's estate, and Lord Geigi's, and the new Maschi lord, who was an associate of Lord Geigi, so they were all truly, truly part of the aishidi'tat, even if there were irregularities. Like nand' Bren. Like all Najida district being Edi. And just admitted to the legislature.

But there had once been another civilization, on the Southern Isle, way early, more than a thousand, maybe two thousand years ago, that *some* said had had all sorts of secrets and inventions, and had outposts clear up as far as Cobo, and in the Marid Sea, and on Mospheira, when Mospheira had belonged to the tribal peoples. They had fairly well had their way in the world, until a huge earthquake had hit offshore of the Southern Island and a tidal wave had wiped out huge cities and ports and ships and everything, and fairly well devastated the whole south coast of the continent while it was about it. And the earthquakes kept coming, all over the south. Only the Marid Sea had been protected by islands and its deep inset into the coast, and the Mospheiran strait was somewhat protected, and the east and the west coast were protected. So the Southern Island became a wasteland,

and the old cities along the southern coast were ruined and some of them sunk. The only place on the whole southern coast that survived were the colonies in the Marid, who had mixed with the mainland folk until they were speaking a sort of Ragi, and mostly lost their own language, except for scholars.

The Marid's southern islands and its deep inset protected it from all the earthquakes and the waves. Ships that were lucky enough to be there survived. And they set the whole Southern Island under a curse, that as long as people stayed away from it, the sea would stop trying to take it. Which was what Marid folk said. They adopted all sorts of ideas as their own, and they also believed in spirits that did not like people, who brought earthquakes and sent the waves. The Marid folk took to the local gods and said if ever ships landed on the shores of the Southern Island they should be sunk and never allowed to reach a port, because if they did, they could bring these hostile spirits with them, and the rest of the world would suffer.

It was in a book Cajeiri had found in Father's library. It was fairly scary, with pictures of these spirits rousing up the waves to take down the wharves and the towers of the Southern Island, which had had a real name, once, but nobody said it.

That was the Marid, that mani had decided should finally really join the aishidi'tat.

Ragi were the gods' creation from before the gods divided themselves, some of them hostile to their creation and some of them not, which were the Gods Fortunate and the Gods Less Fortunate—the latter called that because their real names invited problems. The numbers of the gods were felicitous, so one must never wish ill on one; and the numbers of the world were felicitous if one could truly calculate them the right way. That was what Ragi thought. And the Edi thought another thing, that they had come up out of the ground knowing things that they knew less and less of as generations passed. And the Maschi of the south thought the same as Ragi did, except they believed the numbers were flawed and the Gods Less Fortunate knew how they were flawed, which was why they were hostile, and wanted to take the world down.

It was all fairly scary, with very little to do with Ragi folk. Except Father was aiji for the tribal peoples, and the whole south, including the Maschi, and now mani, who was Eastern, where they were really strict about the numbers, and constantly trying to calculate them, was involved with Machigi, who supposedly claimed descent from another kind of ship-folk than had arrived in the heavens, if he was old aristocracy. *Machigi* claimed to be descended from the Southern Island, where spirits made the world shake.

It was poetical. But the Marid had been nothing but trouble, ever.

Ragi were the inventing sort. Ragi were the ones who took the things the Marid knew and the things they knew and came up with a steam engine. Ragi were the ones who invented railroads, and built the first one, and then got the Padi Valley clans—including Uncle's Atageini—to agree to let the rail through and unite all the clans under one aiji.

The Marid had never had that. The rail had touched them, finally, but never united those clans, because the Marid were still fighting some old war that had started back before the Great Wave, in which, if he remembered right, Machigi's unaccountably ancient ancestor had fought Cosadi's unaccountably ancient ancestor over some stupid thing nobody remembered. Humans landed and humans finally made peace and kept their agreements. The Marid had just gone on fighting each other, until a little old man in Ajuri, Shishogi, Nomari's great-something uncle, had decided to try to bend the Guild to drive out the humans—as if, in that day, they had had anywhere to go.

Shishogi's plan had been to station amenable Guild

units here and there, where someday they could take the aijinate and go to war against the humans. There were marriages into and out of the Marid, with Shishogi's notion of uniting everything and going against humans and against Father's space program.

It had come scarily close to working—except, first, Father was not dead and Great-grandmother was not lost up in space, *he* was not lost, and neither was nand' Bren. And, to pay some credit where it was due, Machigi had not been dead, either. The Shadow Guild, Shishogi's creation, had killed Machigi's father as a step toward their aim, but that had only put Machigi in charge of the Taisigin Marid, and the Shadow Guild and the Dojisigin had certainly regretted that move. Machigi had allied with Great-grandmother, and the Shadow Guild had ended up losing Shishogi and the Guild Council, and a lot else.

So there was a real reason for mani to want to be allied with Machigi. But that was not saying that that would always be true. That was the problem. Machigi was a scary sort of man who was even scarier on the rare occasions when he turned polite.

And now there was Nomari. Who might take over Ajuri, and who seemed a very good choice.

Except he had worked for Machigi, spied for Machigi. Nomari was very quiet, and very easy-going, and one could really feel sorry for him as having seen his whole family killed by the Shadow Guild and having spent his whole life hiding.

But since he had heard about Nomari working for Machigi, Cajeiri had had certain doubts; and now that Uncle had heard, he thought Uncle might have second thoughts, too.

He and Uncle had agreed . . . there were scary things going on. And he thought, and he thought Uncle thought, that there was more to mani leaving Uncle behind than her being upset about Mother.

It was a matter of Nomari and all that Machigi was,

and all the past troubles, all asking to be admitted not just to the aishidi'tat, but to the family. To the household. *Mani's* household.

He *wanted* to believe that Nomari was just that kind boy who had met Mother a long, long time before, and who was just a good boy who had grown up running from Shishogi's hunters, and who had only the purest thoughts of ruling Ajuri well and being a good neighbor to Uncle and ultimately, to Sister, once Seimei grew up and took Uncle's place.

It was just so much more complicated than that. The Marid was a maze of connections and foreignness, and Nomari had navigated it and made his own alliances, notably with a man who could be as great a problem as the Shadow Guild had become, a man who was another survivor of Shishogi's plots.

"Nandi?"

He blinked, realizing Eisi was holding his at-home coat, waiting for him, while connections had blinked into an instant's clarity, a landscape under a lightning-flash, too wide to see all at once. He moved his arms into the sleeves, accepted being fussed over, tidied up, straightened and cared for.

He really, truly hoped Mother was right about Nomari, and that Great-grandmother could find what they had seen, he and Mother and Uncle, and that they *would* work things out and get home safely.

Meanwhile . . . Uncle knew. He felt comforted by that. Father might hold Uncle somewhat at arms' length, but he did not. And he ought to feel a little uneasy, as if he had disobeyed or broken a promise.

But he did not.

A fool would start drinking and drink too much. Nomari was not that.

He did answer polite questions, details on where he had been, and when, and witness to what.

"You were hiding," Bren observed at one point, in their sharing of brandy, "where the Shadow Guild was and is strongest."

A nod. "Indeed, nandi. But *they* were looking for me in the north."

"Did you ever *know* any of that Guild, nadi?"

"No." Nervous laughter. "I did not seek acquaintance. I knew *of* them. I knew *of* certain ones. Serigi. Paina. Pordiri. Laisu. I knew their routes. I am less sure of the faces, since they moved by night. They traveled to and from Cobo and points along the way."

"Najida."

"Najida. Yes."

"They did not enter there."

"I have no knowledge what they did, except that there were those who went as far north as Cobo, but no further. Some went by sea. Some went overland as far as Najida."

By sea was an established route. Overland was only the wide open expanse of Taisigi territory, their hunting range. Machigi's hunting range. But on that road that led toward Najida, there was also access to Kajiminda, neighbor to Najida, Lord Geigi's estate, which had been under his nephew Baiji in those years. Baiji had been lining his pockets with his uncle's priceless porcelain collection during the years the Shadow Guild had been in control of the government, or seeking to get there. Kajiminda as a contact point was a distinct possibility; and along with Baiji, Pairuti, the lord of Targai, co-equal with Lord Geigi in lordship over Maschi clan lands, and whose wife, Lujo, still living, was Senjin clan. Bren had a brief but keen memory of Lord Pairuti, who had shot him, and who had been shot in turn by Bren's bodyguard.

Lujo had been allowed to go back to Senjin, and a subclan had taken the lordship of Maschi clan and Targai, since Geigi had no intention of coming down to deal with the mess Pairuti and Baiji had made. The current lord was Haidiri, one of Bren's own supporters.

"There was once a commerce involving Kajiminda and Targai," Bren said. "Did you have any knowledge of that?"

"I knew they were places in that network," Nomari said. "I do not know how deeply so. Many places cooperated with the regime. They had no real choice."

The regime. Another euphemism for Murini's tenure in the aijinate, otherwise known as the Troubles.

"Those two were a little deeper into the regime than most," Bren said. "At the time. Not now. Do you know of any *other* connections supporting the Dojisigin Guild?"

"I know there were many trains offloading and onloading at Targai. I know that resistance was operating between Najida and Cobo, and there were incidents."

One had heard of those. Targai under Pairuti as a distribution point was no great surprise. One had heard a little more, since, as wit had it, the retired and the dead had come back to take over the Assassins' Guild and take care of the problems in it. A good many records had surfaced. More were being pieced together from the ruin of Shishogi's office. And now from the basement of Ajiden, since the Guild was currently in the Ajuri great house, going through records going back centuries . . . and of specific interest, records from the time period of a conspiracy that had aimed at ending two hundred years of human-atevi peace.

The tide had definitely turned on the rebel regime. Now, overnight, Senjin had allied with the Taisigin and *their* southern allies, isolating the once fearsome Dojisigin province, despite its port and its ships.

It was reasonably brilliant, what Ilisidi had done . . . granted the Shadow Guild did not come up with a counter-measure, while the train they were on, between braking and grueling climbs, was headed for the current situation in Bregani's capital.

"How do you read Lord Bregani?" Bren asked Nomari bluntly. "Do you think he will break the agreement?"

There was a lengthy silence. And by the look of it, some many-layered thought.

"One hesitates to guess, nandi."

"Guess, nadi. I appreciate your unique perspective. And I shall not hold you responsible for any error."

"Lord Bregani is a fair man," Nomari said. "His citizens support him, generally, and his courts are fair, so far as I have heard. One could say the same for Lord Machigi in his own clan. Lord Bregani has not had freedom from the Dojisigin. He has been in fear for his life over *most* of his life, and likewise his wife, whose cousin was assassinated."

"And if Tiajo went down?"

"There would be a good many things shaken loose. Tiajo favors certain people who keep things in balance, and if she goes, they probably will go down, and then the storm breaks in the Dojisigin."

"Who are these certain people?"

"Her chief of security, Maigi. Her chief of household Dasichi."

They were not unknown names, and what one did know was murder, murder, and murder, sometimes by court order, sometimes by poison, sometimes by drowning at sea . . . falling off a boat at midnight left very little evidence, but whispers spread.

"You think," Bren said, "that removing her would leave these people in charge of the Dojisigin."

"I have no important thoughts, nandi."

"Let us pretend for a moment you are lord of Ajuri. And that I am asking for Tabini-aiji. What then would your recommendation be—for Tiajo after her removal?"

A hesitation. But not a long one. "House arrest, in the north, if it could be maintained. Then she and her staff might cooperate in efforts to prevent her assassination, and she might name names. As in Ajuri, the focus should be on finding records, sifting documented lies from undocumented truth. Establish agents of the true Guild in the Dojisigin, and let them work. Set Bregani over both provinces."

Bren nodded slowly. It was, indeed, what was going on in Ajuri, and the Assassins' Guild had a complicated situation to straighten out—finding records, providing safety for witnesses, and being sure over-hasty justice did not wipe out access to someone far more dangerous.

Messy, no question.

Bregani might, however, decline the honor.

"You are not a fool," Bren said, "and you *have* closer experience of such a situation than most will have. Sadly so. But you have come out of it alive. You have gained my attention."

"You, among others took down my uncle Shishogi. For that, I am forever in your debt. And in that of Lord Tatiseigi, and nand' Cajeiri, and the aiji-consort. These are the persons to whom I give allegiance. And to the aiji if he will hear me." A slight hesitation. "I have an agenda, nandi. There are things I want to do for Ajuri. If I am appointed."

"The aiji-consort and the aiji-dowager observe an uneasy but lasting truce. But to your personal sense of obligation, add the aiji-dowager, who principally drove forward the mission to take down Shishogi. And Tabini-aiji himself, who is considering your appointment. Add in the lord of Dur, your neighbor, and Keimi of Taiben, to your south, who will back you at Lord Tatiseigi's request. These will be your attachments, should you win confirmation. You will not be alone."

"I accept what you say," Nomari said soberly. "I am grateful. If in any wise I can assist the dowager now, I will. Even to going into Koperna. I know my way around the city."

"One understands you might. And I do have a request."

"What would that be?"

"Nothing difficult. Sit with my aishid and a city map, and answer their questions."

It was a two-glass session. The train labored and clanked and braked on its slow progress. And Nomari settled himself with Tano and Algini, and a map, while Banichi and Jago were off consulting with other Guild on matters unknown.

"He does have good information," Tano said, when Nomari had gone back up the passages. "And we have specifics on the whereabouts of certain residences, as he reported activity to Machigi."

"Interesting the things he does know," Algini said. "The location of public garages and the location of transportation facilities and warehouses *and* vulnerable fuel and power stations. He was a good spy—or Lord Machigi asked good questions."

Such things might have been Lord Machigi's points of interest—now less useful, one hoped, to Machigi, granted the peace held. A professional, in his way, Bren translated that. Eyes that noted details without seeming to look. And perhaps that in itself accounted for the darkness Ilisidi had sensed.

Bren sat and took notes, and gathered in what Tano and Algini had learned. There was yet no invitation from the dowager for supper, but it was getting near the hour when that question would arise, whether to ask Bindanda, in the galley car, to prepare them their own, or expect to be invited.

Then Banichi and Jago came back with their own report, and they gathered at the little table, with Narani and Jeladi standing by, equally participant.

"The train this morning," Banichi said, "was not only Guild, it is specifically under Tabini-aiji's direction, and Cenedi, with us, has just confirmed that."

"One is not surprised," Bren said. "One hopes Tabini-aiji is not aboard."

"He is not," Banichi said, "we are relatively sure. Tabini-aiji has delegated authority to a representative of the Guild Council—we believe. This comes in code, which is unavoidably lacking in detail."

"Does this train intend to block us?" Bren asked.

"We do not think that is the intent. We think they are going to stop, but that they will pull onto a siding near the abandoned Dojisigi spur to wait for us and possibly to have a word with the dowager, but we have received no clear statement. Again, the difficulty with codes. They may request the dowager not proceed into Koperna—possibly will request for her to change trains. We doubt that the dowager will comply."

"I also doubt it," Bren said.

"Meanwhile Lord Machigi has been told. He has requested to send messages to *his* capital and to Sungeni and Dausigi, and that is being considered, as he can bring in ships, but the dowager has flatly told him he must not intervene in Senjin."

"No," Bren said. "That intervention would not seem helpful. What *do* we understand is the situation in Koperna?"

"Waiting. Waiting. Nothing is happening, which means problems may have gone into hiding. The airwaves are quiet. This train is armored against gunfire, but any train runs on tracks and cannot evade a problem. It has been our worry, all the way down, but the descending track has been inspected and guarded and is hard for the Dojisigin to reach. Not so, what lies ahead of us."

"Do you wish me to argue with the dowager?"

"Cenedi has spoken with her, and says she is determined to go ahead. We shall see what news we have when we have contact with the aiji's forces."

"When will that be?"

"At dusk."

It gave them a little light to see—if ever they were allowed to open a door. Likely someone would go across and messages would be carried, too sensitive to go by a compromised communication system.

"About two hours from now," Banichi added.

He had lost count of the ups and downs of the switchbacks. The train had run on a relative flat now and again. And then not.

"Homura," Bren said. The man's whereabouts had been a question all the way down. They were about to leave the heights into the borderland between the Dojisigin and Senjin, where a furtive presence could leave them . . . or cause problems of unpredictable nature.

"Nothing," Banichi said. "We believe he has indeed stayed in Hasjuran."

"As well if that is so," Bren said. "Then we have only to ask ourselves which side *Momichi* is on, and where *he* is."

"Lying low with the problems in Koperna," Banichi suggested. "All of us would be happier if there were resistance. We know our own tactics. And we see them reflected back to us, Bren-ji. On the one hand we might wish the dowager would hold back and not go into Koperna. But on the other hand—the border of Senjin and the Dojisigin is not where we would wish her to stay, either. She is moving fast, very fast, in the political sense, and she has closeted herself again with her own aishid, in possession of every fact we have been able to gather."

"I am no help to her," Bren said. "You might be."

"I am in contact with Cenedi," Banichi said. "As is Algini, who has a certain expertise. Decisions are not firm yet. He will signal if we are needed."

"Then we should have supper," Narani said, from behind him.

"I think we should," Bren said. "At least we are in control of that certainty."

"It is," Banichi said, "as good an idea as any at this point."

"Advise Bindanda, nadiin-ji, that they might inquire the dowager's pleasure in the matter, and see that the other passengers have their choice. It may be a very long night."

9

It is taking a very long time, Bren wrote in his personal notes, using a predecessor language, Italian, in the Greek alphabet, which was at least not easy for atevi to crack. *We have a signal that the train ahead of us has stopped and wants a meeting. If they are not on the siding and want to precede us into Koperna, we shall not have much choice about it. The dowager has not expressed an opinion. She is consulting with senior Guild, and we are receiving some information.*

Lord Bregani's message had reached the Guild, and thereby the broadcast center, so all of Senjin *and* their enemies gained more information at the same time—but at least it reassured Senjin that their own lord was still claiming control of the situation.

All they could get *from* Koperna was a coded report that conditions one and two had been satisfied, which Jago said meant they were on schedule and they had assured essential services and established an Order of Civilian Protection.

As for what that entailed, Jago provided a printed and fairly well-worn card from her kit, a Guild statement of martial law which, honestly, Bren had never seen even in the re-taking of the capital. It began with a request to clear the streets, shelter in place, and the final, chilling paragraph: *Lethal force may be used in your area. Once in safety, please stay off the streets, and if you have shutters, close them for your own safety. If you hear movement in your area, stay away from windows and keep as far away as possible from outer walls, doors, and inner stairways. There will be an official broadcast by loudspeaker when this shelter order is lifted.*

God, *try* to enforce that on Mospheira. There would be mass panic and people would *be* in the streets.

One would have expected it to be almost as difficult to apply it in the Marid, where lawlessness was endemic, where no one trusted authority, and where the Shejidani Guild did not ordinarily operate. But Senjin, like the Dojisigin, had spent years under the threats of Tiajo and the Shadow Guild, which did *not* compensate civilians for damages or hesitate at lethal force.

An Order of Civilian Protection is in force in Koperna. One hopes civilians in Koperna are following instructions. He continued his notes. *Koperna radio reports quiet in the city. City offices have dismissed all non-essential personnel to go to their own homes. Lord Bregani's residency had previously dismissed all non-essential and non-resident personnel to go to their own homes and lock the doors, a fact reported on broadcast radio. Relatives and other residents of that residency were encouraged to go to country estates or city houses, as services in the residency are suspended and administrative offices are closed. There has been one major disturbance, a fire at a grocery, but Koperna fire crews were able to extinguish it before it spread to adjacent buildings. The cause of the fire is not known.*

Guild units have claimed the broadcast center, water plant, power plant, and the lord's residency.

The broadcast center states that Lord Bregani is in high-level meetings and receiving reports from the Guild, who are authorized to maintain order.

That is true in essence, though they have not mentioned Lord Bregani's departure from the city. All aboard are resting now, and considering next steps.

* * *

It was sandwiches for supper—sensible, and easy to clear, if there had been an emergency.

Now the train was on much longer run-outs, and the descents were gentler and longer. After hours of tension, a strange sense of safety settled in—completely unjustified, since they were reaching the coastal plain, and the borderland of Senjin and the Dojisigin, but the body could only stand so much panic before it began to declare a sort of truce with the situation.

"Is there any word?" Bren asked, as Algini sat down at the table with a cup of tea in hand.

"There is a sense of organization and compliance in Koperna," Algini said, "but in Lusi'ei, no. The Order of Protection there is being violated by foreigners, understandably confused, and by numerous civilians, many of whom are intoxicated."

The port. And the age old response to calamity.

"We shall pass close by it, shall we not?"

"Close enough for some concern. We will not be unsupported, however. We hope that the Shadow Guild and the Dojisigi currently present in Senjin may be more interested in moving and securing assets than engaging us in what is developing into a several-layered assault. Certain records have been exposed in Ajuri that give us names, and we are going after them."

That was a revelation. The basement in Ajiden had produced some information, at least.

"Do we have general intelligence on their operations here?" Bren asked.

"No. But what we find here may shed light on what we already know. We also have an advantage. We know what we have. They do not. But they know what we *could* have, even if we do not. And that may stir some of them to relocate."

Talking to Algini was sometimes like an ongoing conundrum. But after years, in this situation, one understood exactly what he meant. The dowager, somewhere between events in the north and Machigi's approach, had found an instability, as atevi would put it. Too many Shadow Guild had died. Too many Shadow Guild assets had melted away. The Shadow Guild that had once had the aishidi'tat in its power now was having difficulty holding on to the north of the Marid. It had lost half its remaining territory, in the stroke of a pen up in Hasjuran, and Tiajo, the lord it was using for its last shred of legitimacy, was unstable and incapable of any rational help. The very characteristics that had made her a useful figurehead when the organization had been an intricate mountain of secret connections, made her a liability as the mountain turned to sand beneath them.

"We would be extremely fortunate," Algini said, "if we could engage their first tier officers in Senjin, but they protect themselves. They always have. The elite will have run at the first cloud in the heavens. Their second or third tier is not to be despised, one would never say it; but the whole organization is fragmented . . . mosin'man'chi."

Their man'chi was sick, in other words, the lines of who owed whom gone unreliable and unpredictable. Lord Tiajo, who should sit in the middle of it, the central point of all man'chi, the core strength of the organization . . . was herself a prisoner of a security force that would murder her if she threatened them, and a population that would murder her if she gave them any chance.

"So we will not get a chance at them," Bren said.

"Not likely," Algini said. "Not in the next few days at least. Right now they do not know what our force looks like. It keeps evolving, and the latest train is apparently another reinforcement. That, at least, will keep them off balance, and whether this third force joins us or simply holds the line here, Bren-ji, it will be useful. One only worries how many of us Headquarters has pulled in, and whether we have committed too much."

"Let us hope not," Bren said.

The train seemed to be gathering speed. Algini stood up and said, "I shall be in the Guild car. We are receiving nothing as yet from the other train, but we will be picking up speed. One estimates another hour to reach them."

Father had not held a state dinner or even a business dinner since nand' Bren had gone off to Mospheira, or at least, if Father had had one, Cajeiri thought, he had been off with Uncle Tatiseigi at Tirnamardi, and had escaped it.

But then . . . since mani had left, they had not even had family dinners. Mother and Father had taken meals mostly in their own apartments and he had done the same, with his new staff and his larger aishid for company.

Tonight—tonight there *was* a family dinner, excepting baby Seimiro, who was off with nurse in Mother's rooms. It being an ordinary family dinner, one did not need court clothes, but Cajeiri had wanted to be at his best. He was anxious. And one hoped the dinner was an indication things were going well, and that Father in particular was happy.

But neither Father nor Mother looked cheerful when he arrived in the dining room. Father was at one end of the shortened table, Mother was at the other, he was in the middle, and Father and Mother were both quiet, asking each other questions such as "How is Seimiro?" from Father and "How are the appropriations coming?" from Mother. The answer to both was, "Well."

After which there was silence, while servants served a very good soup, but Cajeiri found himself without a great deal of appetite.

"How is your staff working out, son of mine?" Mother asked, and he answered truthfully, "*Very* well, honored Mother." Then, fearfully, he ventured to fill the silence with: "The new rooms make everything easier, and the staff is very happy. The seniors, too. They are happy."

"They are keeping you informed," Father commented. It was a question.

"Yes, honored Father. They are."

"Good," Father said.

"Thank you," Cajeiri said, and the silence seemed deeper.

"Have you," Mother asked, "heard from the park director?"

Change of topic. A rescue. "Yes, honored Mother. The renovations are on schedule." But then carrying it further seemed like unwanted chatter. Soup gave way to a dish of seasonal fish, which made one think of the port and fisheries at Cobo . . . and trains . . . while Mother and Father were talking about the park, and Boji, and he had nothing to say because he was not part of the negotiations with the park director.

Then one of Father's security came from the door and talked to Father. "There is a query," was all Cajeiri could hear. Father laid aside his fork and his napkin and gave a little nod to Mother and then to him.

"A matter of business," Father said. And: "Tell cook I shall ask for a late snack."

"Yes," Mother said, and Cajeri returned Father's polite nod, with two questions in mind, what the business was and were mani and nand' Bren safe? But Father left the table. Left the room. One heard, down the hall, Father's office door shut.

And there were still the questions.

There was a piece of fish growing cold on his fork. He scraped it off and took a drink instead.

"You should not worry," Mother said.

"I have to worry," he said.

"Finish your dinner. Cook worked hard."

Which was true, and Cook had not even gotten his usual thanks for the meal.

"Please call Cook, honored Mother. I do not think I can finish. I have had all my soup."

"Son of mine, you are fretting when you do not even know for what."

"I have been fretting since before mani left, and I know where they are, honored Mother. I am informed. I cannot help worrying. I am sorry for mentioning business at the table. But I am not hungry. I will sit here while you finish. And we can thank Cook."

Mother laid down her fork. And rang for Cook, who appeared in the inner doorway of the dining room.

"The family will gratefully share this excellent meal with staff, with thanks, nadi-ji, and requests, because of urgent business which has interrupted us, that the kitchen prepare a cold snack available at whatever hour."

"One hopes the problem is minor," Cook said.

"We likewise hope so," Mother said, and laid her napkin on the table. "My son and I will take brandy. Advise our aishid."

Cook bowed and went back into the kitchens. Mother rose and Cajeiri did, and Mother had the doors to the sitting room opened—a very large, very formal sitting room with just a little grouping of chairs and small tables that Father used for small conferences.

Two of Mother's bodyguard attended. Antaro and Jegari did.

And Mother herself went to the buffet and poured a brandy with her own hands, and a tiny swirl of brandy into a new glass, and then a large dose of ice water, which she brought back, serving him herself, which she had never done since—

Forever, that he could remember.

And never brandy. That was yet another message she sent him. He sipped it. It recalled a very unpleasant evening when he had sampled abandoned glasses on a state evening. But it was just the flavor of it, and he understood what Mother was saying: it was serious conversation she meant.

Very serious. Adult conversation.

He took just a sip, and she did the same. Brandy was for uncensored conversation, even blunt truth. And he wanted more than the flavor of that. He wanted it and greatly dreaded it, though Mother was not ordinarily the person he would consult about Great-grandmother's doings.

"What is happening with Great-grandmother?" he asked. "Do you know, honored Mother?"

"She is proceeding down to Senjin," Mother said. "Your Father knew she would, as he expressed it, probably before she did."

He sat and held his glass of flavored water and simply listened.

"Many of the Guild aboard the Red Train are in service to their Council," Mother said, "so Guild Headquarters has gotten word, not steadily, but several times during your great-grandmother's expedition. I asked to be informed for Nomari's sake and for Uncle Tatiseigi's, and your father agreed, and he undertook to inform you when we might know something more."

"He did, from the beginning," Cajeiri said. "But not about them going to Senjin. Or *why* mani is doing this!"

"Very plainly," Mother said, "Lord Machigi presented your great-grandmother a situation in which he claimed Lord Bregani of Senjin was losing favor with the Dojisigin lord. To take advantage of this, he proposed a railroad spur from his capital, and proposed it link to the rail in Lord Bregani's territory. Your great-grandmother accordingly invited Machigi to Shejidan, called the Red Train to the Bujavid, took Machigi, the paidhi, *and* cousin Nomari aboard, along with a considerable contingent of Guild from the capital, over all giving the public impression that she was bound for Malguri, but turning toward Hasjuran. She likewise requested a sizeable escort precede her to check the track for problems—disguised as a regular freight. That was not all it did."

"The first train . . ."

"Went down to Senjin, where it developed a sudden mechanical problem and delayed, not unknown for a train just down from Hasjuran. The Red Train meanwhile stopped in Hasjuran, detached all its occupied cars, and the engine, with several Guild units and a vacant sleeper car, descended to Senjin. The Guild delivered your great-grandmother's message by courier, giving Lord Bregani a very short time to agree to come up to Hasjuran to talk—or stay where he was, and explain to Lord Tiajo, who was already upset with him, why he was talking to your great-grandmother at all."

"Which would not go well," Cajeiri said, when Mother paused.

"It was absolutely your great-grandmother's style," Mother said. "Bregani would agree to come up and meet with her, and openly break relations with Tiajo doing it; or he would not agree, and Tiajo, who has been looking for an excuse to take Senjin, would draw her own conclusions as to what was going on, and act accordingly. Either way, Tiajo was bound to react. So Bregani, being no fool, went up to Hasjuran, signed with your great-grandmother, and now finds himself allied with his old enemy Machigi as well as your great-grandmother, while a Guild force sits in his capital. That should give our cousin Nomari an excellent view of your great-grandmother in operation, should he have had *any* doubt how she is."

Mother and Great-grandmother had been at odds all his life. He had been mostly brought up by Great-grandmother, so *he* had no doubt how Great-grandmother worked, and what chances she would take, as well as how Mother felt about Great-grandmother's influence on him. It was not an argument he wanted to hear right now. He made his face blank, carefully blank, to wait through Mother's expressions of disapproval, and her complaints about Great-grandmother's politics and policies.

"She is *good,*" Mother said unexpectedly. "She is quite good. But she has her ideas, and when she is in pursuit of them—please, in life, son of mine, do be careful. Be a moderating influence on your great-grandmother. And learn from your father as well as from her."

It was entirely unexpected, that direction. He felt pressed by the ensuing silence to say something, and had no idea what to say, except, "One tries to do that, honored Mother."

"She has Cenedi and she has the paidhi-aiji to advise her," Mother said. "And I know she and your father have had discussions on the Marid, regarding Machigi, regarding the railroad, and regarding her building an east-coast seaport. Your father, passionate as he is about human inventions, and with Lord Geigi assuring him that there *are* means to make it work, still believes that this port your great-grandmother is building is far more a political maneuver within the Marid than a reality on her coast, at least in the short term. But," Mother said, before he could defend mani's harbor *and* Lord Geigi. "But as much finance as she is pouring into this fantasy of a port, she has invested still more into Lord Machigi and the direction of his ambitions. I am about to trust you, son of mine, with something your father does not want reported to her or to her allies, not even to the paidhi-aiji. Do you understand?"

He did not want that burden. But he thought he had better know it. And he *would* break a promise if he had to. He *would*.

"Yes," he said.

"Know that she has invested a very great deal in Lord Machigi, and in keeping his cooperation—not his man'chi, which he has not given, none of us believe that—but his cooperation for his own reasons. Know too, that my cousin and yours, Nomari, who has gained my recommendation and Lord Tatiseigi's, and stands to inherit the lordship of a major midlands power—may have been in Lord Machigi's employ. He may still be."

"I do not believe that!"

"Nonetheless, he was, and may still be in Lord Machigi's

employ. One can understand why he did it during the Troubles. But if he did it then, he still might. And this matters. Are you following this? Lord Machigi is a safe and truthful ally so long as his concerns are all with the Marid. But if he had anything to do with our cousin showing up at Tirnamardi to ask Uncle's support, it is all different. If Machigi, an ally of your great-grandmother, has extended a finger into *midlands* politics, if he has attempted to insert an agent into *my* clan and yours, a present neighbor to Lord Tatiseigi and a future neighbor to your sister . . ."

His heart began to beat heavily and faster. "Honored Mother, I see what you are saying, but . . ."

"That is why she invited Nomari on this venture, all innocent, with Lord Machigi aboard. She has *everything* invested in Lord Machigi keeping his place in the Marid and doing what she expects. She does not favor anything or anyone who may interfere with that, or who may give Machigi ideas of power outside the Marid. Even if he did not send Nomari north to deal with Uncle Tatiseigi, who actually has Nomari's man'chi? Machigi may effectively have saved his life."

"*We* have it!" Cajeiri said. "Uncle has it, I have it, and you have it. I am sure of it!"

"Are you that sure of it? He was young. He was left alive. He was running. And Machigi, at some point, took him up. Was it when he was young and vulnerable? Or was the transaction of a later date, in fair trade, service for shelter? A great deal rests on that one question."

"He is not Shadow Guild. I am sure of that."

"I agree. They killed his parents and his brother. They hunted him to kill him. All that, I think your great-grandmother accepts. But that he has wandered the country for years unattached—"

"But gaining the man'chi of all the Ajuri that also ran . . ."

"That is the thing, is it not? He gained others. He has

the gift. One is born with it or gains it in life. And Nomari has it. He cannot move *me,* son of mine, nor *you,* being what we are, outside Ajuri, but you saw him meeting the clan, you watched him respond to them, you saw what he roused, yes. He has the gift. He *can* lead. Adversity crushes some, rouses others, and he clearly has it. The question is—and your great-grandmother did not witness him with his own people—in what direction he will take them. It is difficult to explain to your great-grandmother when she did not witness it. You know how she is. Her own eyes see it, or it does not exist. And when she sees clear facts, she will reinterpret them in her own way. You *have* noticed that."

He had. It was true. But he did not want to take Mother's side against mani. It *was* man'chi, it was who he was, and Mother, sadly, did know that.

"She is not all that stubborn," he said.

"You are so like her," Mother said.

"But I am right in this."

"I hope you are. I do hope it," Mother said. "But there are liars that can be anyone. Shishogi was one. Something was missing in him, so he could become whatever he needed to be. I think even my father—to a certain extent—was one."

Grandfather had scared him. He felt a chill, remembering it. But Grandfather had died trying to turn on Shishogi.

They hoped that was what he had been doing.

"It is an Ajuri curse," Mother said. "And the only thing we can do about it, son of mine, is be aware of it, and not to carry it on. I think, in effect, it is a prime reason your great-grandmother has always mistrusted me."

She does not, would be the polite thing to say. But he was too old to say that. "I think her opinion is improving, honored Mother. I think she just has not understood."

"She did not want me in her children's bloodline,"

Mother said. "As she has grave doubts about Nomari. I hope, I personally hope, that he is everything we hope he is, and not what she fears he is."

"She is not superstitious. She says the 'counters are a cheat. She has no care how many red flowers are on a table."

"Oh, but you may wager she has counted them— habit, perhaps. She was brought up in the old way, and more of it governs her than you have ever seen."

"She taught Father, and he has no respect for 'counters. Or superstition."

"And you do not."

His shoulders gave an involuntary twitch. It seemed courting misfortune to say it aloud. "I think Father is right."

"Oh, politic!"

"He is."

"And I think much the same. But, understand, son of mine, I respect your great-grandmother. I simply was not in her plans for her son. She did not trust Ajuri, she did not want Ajuri linked to Uncle Tatiseigi, and certainly not to your father. From that beginning, we were bound to be at odds. And I admit she was entirely right. But had she had her way about Ajuri from the beginning, I would not exist and you would not have been born. I regret I lost you and she brought you up. That was not my choice either. But I see the result in front of me, and I would not choose any other son."

He had never heard her say so. He found his breathing quite stopped, and his mind thinking—what if he had not gone with Great-grandmother?

But if he had not, then they all might have died, and the kyo would have destroyed Reunion, and the mainland might be at war with Mospheira and the ship, which they never could win.

"Honored Mother," he said. "Father chose the best."

She said nothing for a moment, then gave a thankful sort of nod, but face—she maintained it for a lengthy moment, so he knew she was moved, and was not letting it out.

"So," she said. "This morning another train has arrived in the region. Your father is acting. Your father would not have chosen this particular day to move on the Marid, granted two key lordships are vacant and the humans are about to start dropping from the skies at our spaceport, but the Marid has never chosen convenient moments. Your father could not have ignored the Dojisigin making a move to take Senjin under its administration, and your great-grandmother decided Lord Machigi's warning this was increasingly likely made it a choice between contesting it after it had happened, or preventing it entirely. *Her* plan is to get Lord Bregani's cooperation to maintain a force there, wear the Shadow Guild down, taking out their resources, taking out their agents, and reducing the threat to manageable size. Unfortunately *she* has become the Shadow Guild's prime target, and we have word that the threat involves several Shadow Guild moves to assassinate her, and anyone else in her company."

His heart was beating fast. He was moved to say, I know. But that would expose Rieni, and it was not fair. He let his distress show.

"Surely we can warn her."

"We have warned her," Mother said. "She is descending into the Marid and going ahead with her plans, relying on Bregani and Machigi."

"And nand' Bren." His throat felt dry. He finished his flavored water. "So what will Father do, honored Mother?"

"He will put that train between your great-grandmother and the Dojisigin," Mother said, "and he has not told me all of it. But he launched that train just after she left, I do not know what words they may have had, but I know he felt, on the one hand, that they could not ignore Machigi's information, and on the other, that we do not want a war in the Marid. Nonetheless, he is launching a serious effort against Tiajo."

"Tiajo is nothing!"

"Tiajo is their legitimacy. Without her, the administration falls apart, all the offices, all the authorizations, all the supplies in warehouse, all have to be taken over to be made to operate, and the Shadow Guild is short of that sort of agent. A clerk knows how to find and move supplies. The sort of agent they have trained will not have that ability. When things run short, finding more will be a problem. Their agents are foreigners. The Dojisigin will protect their own households first. Supplies will likely disappear. So will weapons, and transport. Foreigners have never fared well in such situations. Tiajo is nothing. But she is key to the system. Shishogi knew that. Many of his key people were clerks. Has your great-grandmother ever mentioned that?"

"I . . . do not believe we have discussed it, honored Mother."

"Tiajo has to go down," Mother said. "Quickly, before they can get her and the official seals away, to settle legitimacy of a successor. But your father has moved the heavens to protect your great-grandmother. That was his word on it. She often deals with areas that he cannot, for one reason and another, one in the field, one in the office dealing with committees and receiving reports. He *cannot* take the field. He would, but I, for one, have begged him not to. And Lord Geigi concurred. This has been going on even before your great-grandmother took it on herself to leave. I do not know everything they said, but certainly your father has been talking to him a great deal about the landings and transport of the humans from the station, and all that, and I know that they have talked about your great-grandmother and her projects, and about Senjin, and Lord Geigi was against your father having anything to do with it, because Dojisigin is all folds and mountains and very, very difficult land to find anybody."

"Lord Geigi could find them."

"I have heard something about that. I think that has

been under discussion. But not for your father to go in, certainly." Mother set down her brandy glass. "I do not want you to worry about it. You should be aware, but you should not worry. Your great-grandmother has been managing moves of her own long before either you *or* I was born, and she has the very best people around her. Cenedi is a very canny fellow. And she listens to him, more than anybody."

"And nand' Bren," Cajeiri said. "Nand' Bren is very smart. And he can even get Lord Machigi to agree."

"That he can." Mother stood up, and he must. He gave a little bow, understanding he was dismissed and he knew as much as Mother was willing to tell him, and, he almost thought, as much as Mother herself could guess, which was a great deal. Father came and went, or had the office door shut, and tonight it was no great surprise that Father missed most of supper.

It was like that, to be aiji. He saw that. And when Father did talk, it seemed, at least in this, and probably because of Nomari, to be with Mother, and not even his aishid, or his own seniors could have gotten more than they had.

"Do not worry too much," Mother said at the last.

But thinking how there *was* a question about Nomari, and that the Shadow Guild was making a serious effort to go after mani—worry seemed what he had to take from what Mother had told him.

10

The train moved on the flat now, after a last braking descent. It had gathered speed for a while during dinner, and in the racket of the faster clip, Bren took the chance to take a little sleep, a court official's kind of nap, at the cleared table, head on arms, carefully not mussing his clothes.

A change in pace waked him. He lifted his head.

"We are approaching the other train," Jago said.

"The dowager," he said, seeing Narani and Jeladi and Banichi, but not Tano or Algini in the compartment.

"We are waiting for a message," Jago said.

The dowager might be doing the same as he had, there being no guarantee of rest anywhere in the future.

"They are waiting on the siding," Bren said.

"Yes," Jago said. "Communication is minimum. We will pull alongside and confer. The dowager is preparing and wishes you to be ready."

"I am," he said. Information had been in extremely short supply. One hoped to have more of it in short order. He stood up, and heard the clicks of the rail becoming less frequent.

"My coat," he said, and waited for assistance, hoping, meanwhile that there might be some sort of news from

Shejidan, possibly some instruction, or information from Koperna.

Narani brought the bulletproof vest. He did not object. There was too much at stake. But he was surprised by Jeladi offering a heavier coat, not the extremely heavy one he had worn up in Hasjuran outdoors, but the middling-heavy one.

He did not ask. It was a coat, it was there, and perhaps they were going to stand a bit and shut down the heating. He had no idea. Perhaps he might be going across to confer with the other train—it might become his job, though he rather expected Guild to have their orders . . .

The question would be whether Ilisidi would be happy with those orders.

He could well be sent across, maybe more than once, if there was to be a dispute in proxy between Ilisidi and Tabini. He did not look forward to that, if such proved to be the case, but go he would, certainly, as many times as he had to enter prickly situations, and he hoped they would manage to coordinate whatever was going on.

At very least, what they were approaching now *was* their mystery train, it was on their side, and, Jago informed him, putting on her own heavier jacket, they would indeed be going outside.

Slower and slower.

"The dowager is going outside," Banichi said. "Everyone is going outside. And when we do, we are asked to look up."

Up, for God's sake . . .

"Why?"

"We do not know," Jago said.

It was the dowager's instruction, from her aishid. One went.

The Red Train was at a standstill. The corridors resounded to movements, and even Narani and Jeladi were putting on coats.

Bren followed Banichi and Jago, expecting that Tano and Algini, wherever they were, would join them. Somewhere a door opened, and as they exited the passage doors the smell of the air was different, fresh. They opened the door to the Guild car, bound toward the Red Car, Bren supposed, and the air that wafted to them was cool without being icy. They passed that car, and the galley, and by now the general opening of passage doors produced a breeze through the length of the train that scoured out the stale air of so many days. By the time they reached the Red Car itself, with other Guild behind them, it was evident that that car's outer door was open, and a cool wind was coming through.

They reached the Red Car itself, behind a few of the cooks, and Bindanda. The Red Car's door opened on night, and a plain stretching as far as the eye could see. And stars. And people outside, on the slope of the railbed, standing and looking at the heavens.

Look up, the advisement was, and the first out— Guild—pointed to a place in the sky. Bren directed his own attention to the steps, which were always too high for his convenience, held to the safety grip and trusted Banichi, whose hand was right there on his landing.

Then, with his feet on safe gravel, he looked up, up from the reedy plain, the endless flat, with people standing outside, and the engine of the second, modern train sitting there to the side of their own steam engine, ghostlike in the clouds that rose around the Red Train's engine.

Further up, where people were pointing, now.

There was indeed something in the heavens, among the dusting of stars and the sliver of moon. It was strange, and vague, like a full moon that failed to shine.

Ilisidi was near him, as his eyes adjusted to the dark. She was wrapped in black furs, limned in the glow from the doorway of the Red Car. Staff was by her. Cenedi, distinguishable by the white in his hair. Nawari, beside him and the dowager . . . all looking skyward and exchanging words with each other. And another distance away stood Bregani and his family, and Nomari, and Machigi, all with their separate guards. Everyone was out and looking up at that dim intruder in the heavens.

Suddenly that disc in the sky flew away as if carried by winds aloft—and a fire flared up where the disc had been, four fires, after the initial flare, at even distance from each other . . . fires that grew closer and closer, not quite overhead, but somewhat out of their plane.

It came lower, not as something wafting on the wind, but something coming with purpose. The light of those fires aloft began to illuminate the entire area, the people outside their train and its engine, staring aloft, as that thing descended from the heavens.

A shuttle? A shuttle landing was not fire and thunder, rather a rolling set-down on a runway. It was something else, something unpredicted, potentially worrisome when more than humans and atevi had recently visited in the heavens—but not likely kyo, either.

No. Whatever it was, it was expected and known to that other train, which indicated they should look to the space station as its origin.

And when he thought that, he immediately knew what he was seeing: one of Lord Geigi's landers, coming down. There had been a number of them placed at strategic points on the mainland during the Troubles—none since.

Until now.

That disc that had blown away was the petal sail—the parachute. The rest was up to the engines. And the craft finished the descent on its own, its rocket boosters providing the light that filled the whole area as it came down. When it touched, out in the flat, it settled gently, twice the bulk of a railroad engine standing on end, and leveled itself, while grass and brush burned in a ring about it and smoke went up around it like a curtain. Lights flared behind that curtain, red and green and blazing blue.

Ilisidi had never seen one land, either: Bren well knew that. But she stood watching, leaning on her cane, and quite as sure as he was what she was seeing, knowing it was Lord Geigi's, and knowing that things at issue had surely just gotten—larger.

A lot larger.

Machigi, Lord Bregani and his family, Nomari—and all the Guild and staff who had never seen the like—had to be appalled.

And with this arrival, the question of who had sent the train this morning suddenly became much wider.

"The fire may become inconvenient," Banichi said quietly, close by. "We are asked to bring everyone back aboard. The wind is blowing the other way, but the smoke is noxious if the wind shifts and the landing may attract notice."

The dowager was likely receiving the same information, and they turned back toward the open door of the Red Car, with its tamer, golden light.

Geigi, Bren thought. Geigi had stepped in. The lander was more than a statement, it was a threat. It was nothing invited or predicted, and, most critically, it was not the dowager's doing—he was certain it was not. Geigi would never send it down to this region of potential conflict without *Tabini's* direct order.

Regardless, there were assurances that had to be given, questions that had to be answered, quickly.

"Nadiin-ji," he said to his aishid, waiting while the dowager reboarded, "very likely we shall be meeting with our fellow passengers. Very likely the dowager will be asking questions."

"We are receiving answers," Banichi said, distracted for a moment. "So is Cenedi. Guild is being asked to attend a conference on the other train. *We* shall not. The order is for *unassigned* Guild."

Meaning Guild not assigned as bodyguards.

"Is there any clue of its intention?" he asked. He was, by accident of placement, ahead of Lord Bregani and his family. Machigi had lingered longest at the sight outside. And the predicted questions began to drift in the air along with the acrid smell of smoke.

"We have no information," Banichi said.

It seemed likely the other train did have information, and that it was about to pass that on, but it was foreseeable that the dowager knew something, or would know in short order, as soon as units from their own train came back from the conference. Jago went up ahead of him, reached down and pulled him up to the first step. Bren took the next, and entered the Red Car, where the dowager waited, with Cenedi and Nawari and two more. He foreknew the question.

"Did you know, paidhi?"

He was unequivocally glad he had not had to hold that knowledge. "I did not, aiji-ma. Clearly—"

"Geigi will *not* have worked directly with the Guild," Ilisidi said shortly, scanting courtesy. "This is my grandson's doing. And his."

"One tends to the same thought, aiji-ma. Lord Geigi has set down a boundary, at very least, between Senjin and the Dojisigin."

"One *supposes* that is the limit of it," Ilisidi said. "Give my grandson credit for a grand machimi, at very least."

"To your good, one thinks, aiji-ma, if it keeps the Dojisigin entertained."

It was always a risk to go lightly when the dowager's temper was engaged, and it won an intense frown, but not an angry one.

"Those metal things," she said, "defile a landscape. The Marid has not been so blessed until now. We apologize for the intrusion."

Bregani had just boarded, Murai and Husai behind him. Machigi came immediately after, and then Nomari, all of them having exited from the Red Car, all of them returning by the same route. Narani and Jeladi, last aboard, were the only staff of any sort present. Jeladi, absolute hindmost, shut the door, and blocked the smell of smoke.

"That is one of the landers," Machigi said, not happily. "Surely. From Lord Geigi. What is it meant to do, nand' dowager?"

"We," Ilisidi said sharply, "were not consulted in this. The other train evidently expected it. I am very sure it is my grandson's notion of assisting us, and I shall have questions myself. Lord Bregani, we assure you we intended no such thing. My grandson and our ally in the space station have evidently decided to define a boundary, and we are not in accord with the need for it. It *is* a fair warning to the Dojisigin to keep to their own territory. *Clearly* Lord Geigi has taken a hand in matters, and with it, he announces to us, and any who might wish us harm, that he does have a very clear idea where we are and what moves out here on the plain. We know something of these devices. There are a number of them scattered across the continent, including in the East, and they sit. They sit where they are placed, thus far, and we do not know what we shall do with them, but there they are—eyes on the land, and able to defend themselves if threatened."

"Surely this is human technology," Lord Bregani said, not with a friendly tone on the word *human.*

"In point of fact, nandi," Ilisidi said, "it is *not.* It is Lord Geigi's own device. His invention, for atevi purposes. During the Troubles, he was sending them down to observe and possibly to threaten the illegitimate authorities. They never were fully used. *We* returned to the world, the paidhi-aiji and I, and my great-grandson. The people of the north and the midlands and the coast rose up in support of my grandson, so Lord Geigi's program to attack the rebels was never set in motion—nor were all the planned landers built or deployed. Clearly—this one was available, and set to a fair purpose, if it protects your eastern buffer, nandi. Do not be troubled by it. In general, they sit quietly and do nothing unless someone attacks them. So we are told."

"You have promised, nand' dowager. You have given your word."

"As has Lord Geigi given his word to me, nandi, and I now to you, with the understanding I have. I shall have a word with my grandson and another with Lord Geigi in the near future. I swear to you and to Lord Machigi, this arrival is a surprise to me *and* my staff, and it may be a regrettable eyesore, but it will be a quiet one toward you and your allies if it stands there a hundred years. Neither my grandson nor Lord Geigi will attack my allies nor assert demands contrary to our agreements. I say it, and I will see it stand. The only threat this issues is to Tiajo and her outlawed helpers, none to you. I do swear it."

Ilisidi was angry, furiously angry, not at present company; and such was her expression and her tone that one really, truly wanted not to tip the balance in any direction. Lord Bregani was frowning, too, and so was Murai, while Husai looked worried. Machigi was another study, far less readable.

"Will this delay us?" Bregani asked—who above all had an immediate concern that had nothing to do with monster machines floating down from the heavens.

"Not much longer," Ilisidi said, dead calm and steady. "My grandson's notions will not affect you, nandi, though we believe we could have dealt with this with just a little less smoke and fire. If Tiajo is fool enough to invade, success against you has just become infinitely more difficult. Lord Geigi now has an excellent view of this whole region. I rather imagine there are some who hope Tiajo and her helpers make such an attempt. The Guild in Shejidan has ached for a chance to discuss matters with her and her supporters, and unless you wish, nandi, to intercede for her . . ."

"In no wise," Bregani said.

"Then she ceases to be our concern." Ilisidi made a dismissive move of her fingers, and seemed, with it, to have dismissed some of her anger. "We in this car, nandiin, we have other business, and our agreement will stand. It was a spectacle. One is glad to have seen it, and one suspects our own ally Lord Geigi, up in the heavens, watched the progress of the Red Train and timed this arrival to a nicety, to give us a show. He is nothing if not whimsical. So here it is, and here it will stand, doing nothing, unless Tiajo makes an effort in your direction. Then it is capable of causing a great deal of inconvenience. Should she invade instead by sea—*we* have that handled. So shall we settle for a brandy, nandiin, until we have done whatever business the Guild intends, and are free to be on our way? One trusts this conference they ask will not be long."

There was acquiescence, at least. It was an uneasy company that settled, with Ilisidi's staff to provide hospitality—the Red Car mostly cleared, with a small table anchored near the seats at the rear and most other seats folded and stowed. Of the large table there was no sign, just the little table, the bench seat at the extreme rear, and the seats provided.

"Find out what all this is," Ilisidi said in low tones, pausing beside Bren. "We want to know."

So did he, when it came to that. He turned back and found only Jago and Tano, Banichi and Algini not having boarded the car.

"What is going on?" he asked. "Whose plan is this?"

"It is Guild Council in charge over there," Jago said. "One of their number, at least, in command, with his own escort. Guild-seniors are called in, they say, to pick up equipment. We are not entirely sure what the situation may be, but we think this other force *is* aimed at the Shadow Guild. We do not think they intend to hold us here."

"Can they?" he asked.

"It depends on their authorization. The aiji can. And might."

"He is *not* aboard."

"He is not," Jago said. "And if it comes to a contest

between their orders and the dowager's will, one is not certain, Bren-ji."

Clearly enough if the dowager's intent was challenged, diplomacy might be the only rescue, that and direct recourse to Tabini-aiji, security issues tossed to the wind. Bregani was in a vise, but Machigi was not, and they could not have one or the other breaking free. Or come to a governmental crisis between the Guilds and the aijinate.

"I am going over there," he said. "Nadiin-ji, go with me."

They looked hesitant. He did not blame them. But he headed for the door, and they were with him, Jago taking the lead, helping him down, and it was a walk forward the whole length of the train, with the smell of smoke and the faint smell of something overheated in the air, and the glow of a field fire in the distance. The hulking shape of the relay showed a few lights, but no other activity.

But before they had gotten to the engine of the Red Train, beyond which they could cross to the other track, a number of their own Guild appeared coming toward them.

It was chill. It was a question what the dowager was going to say about his unasked departure. And they *might* have to go on to query someone aboard the other train if their own returnees had a wrong answer.

He kept walking, and they did. They met halfway, a mingled group of Guild from Headquarters in Shejidan, and Nawari, with two of Ilisidi's bodyguard, and Banichi and Algini.

"Nandi." Banichi used the formality in the presence of others.

"The dowager grew concerned," Bren answered the implied question. It was, as everyone had to know, an understatement; and he immediately turned about to walk with his reunited aishid to get out of the dark and the possibility of watchers. Banichi, he was sure, was not happy to see him out here. "Do we have information?"

"Yes," Banichi said definitively. "The relay is for our use; it is permanent; and they will prevent any incursion at our backs while the dowager's operation continues."

"She will be happy with that," Bren said, thinking that the dowager might not be all that happy with an intervention, but would be considerably happier, if it eliminated a two-way problem. "Who is commanding, aboard?"

"Maipari, of the Guild Council," Banichi said. "The aishidi'tat is not, he states, at war with the Dojisigin. The *Guild* has, on its own, called on its outlawed members to surrender and given them a last chance of limited amnesty, excepting criminal acts."

"None of the leaders can favor that," Algini added. "One does not expect compliance."

"So is this lander setting a boundary?" Bren asked.

"Not in essence," Banichi said. "It functions, with a satellite, as a communications relay, one the Shadow Guild cannot use and *we* can."

Communication. Secure, at least for the time being. The ability to plan and move and know the enemy was not using exactly the same systems and might have access to current codes.

"It is new hardware," Banichi said. "Use is very simple. One would need no additional instruction."

Banichi said that meaningfully, beyond a lord's need to know—it being illegal for a lord to use the Guild communication system.

"Lord Geigi sent the units down on the shuttle," Algini said. "He is aware what the dowager is doing. He hoped to deliver it before we left the capital, but it is here now. There is a satellite, intended for the Southern Ocean navigation, that will relay the signal from the lander to the station. The communications units are the same as the ones used on the station. We will not need the numeric codes, we will not need the train's relay, and we can communicate directly with Headquarters. Tabini-aiji has sent it. We are to continue using the old system and old codes for most purposes, but now units can talk to each other *or* local command *or* Shejidan without restraint, and the Shadow Guild will *not* be able to breach it."

It was rare to get two sentences from Algini. But it was indeed a major move, as radical as Lord Geigi's original plan, to send landers to every district, armed, potentially mobile, and controlled from the space station, a high ground unassailable by the conspirators who had, for a time, set up a government and tried to rule. But when the starship returned, triumphant, with the aiji-dowager and Tabini's heir apparent, validating Tabini's faith in the humans, the people had indeed risen up in support of Tabini. That had been the unexpected answer to Shishogi's plan to roll back the clock two hundred years and be rid of human influence; and the rebel government, after so much blood and terror, had gone down like a paper figure before the wind. So the whole system had never deployed, and Lord Geigi, who had been prepared to declare himself aiji in the heavens if Tabini were dead, had been very happy to go back to administering the atevi side of the space station, and throwing himself into projects far more to his liking, with the atevi starship unbuilt, and with at least one of his landers undistributed, and with a wealth of schemes to explore the world and the moon, for a start—and the solar system and the stars beyond if he ran out of projects. The last thing Geigi wanted to be was aiji in Shejidan.

And this thing—this lovely thing, Bren thought—was going to sit out here in the plain between the dowager's new ally, Bregani, and the dowager's old enemy, Tiajo, and relay messages from the units going into Senjin and the units sitting out here to be sure the Shadow Guild did not send Dojisigin forces across this coastal flat. The grass fire was a small disaster, but the thing itself, that hulking ungainly shadow, was the presence of their ally in the heavens, and a statement, once the Shadow Guild knew how to read it, that their bluff was called. The

Shadow Guild could not muster a fighting force, their damage was contained and their power, as such, was about to lose their last stronghold.

They reached the steps of the Red Car, and that door opened for them, a signal having passed by regular means. Bren made a try for the steps on the sloping rail-bed, a fairly vain try to reach the hand rail beside the door, but Banichi—he was sure it was Banichi—boosted him up to the step so deftly he was no delay at all. He climbed aboard, met the anxiety inside, and the dowager's frown, and saw the looks change to slight puzzlement at cheerful faces.

"Good news," he said to the company, and to the dowager. "The Guild Council has set itself here to define a boundary. And so has Lord Geigi in the heavens. He has set down a fortification the Shadow Guild likely already understands—having met them elsewhere across the continent. Now the Marid has its own sentinel." He had the confidence of his own aishid *and* the Guild that he would not betray technical information or Guild assets, and he did not state what Guild would tell Guild later and in private, but he could at least report the essence of it. "The force that arrived with that train will deal with matters outside Senjin and at our backs. We have assurance that when we go in, we will not have trouble from behind us, and whatever the outcome, Lord Tiajo is not going to be happy to have Lord Geigi's gift watching what comes and goes out there."

"We are then free to get underway," the dowager said.

"Indeed," he said.

11

The steps were taken up, the doors were again sealed and locked, and the Red Train began to roll toward Bregani's capital of Koperna as everyone headed back through the passages to their own cars.

Ilisidi, however, lingered with her guard and her staff. Bren paused as well. That the dowager stayed . . . indicated that she had somewhat to say—and within present company, only the dowager's aishid, only his, and their staff, anything could be said.

"Geigi," Ilisidi said, "has been a busy fellow. Who, I wonder, put him up to this."

"I did not," Bren said, and venturing further: "I seem to be denying a number of things tonight, but I swear to you, aiji-ma, this was entirely unexpected."

She seemed amused rather than annoyed, altogether in a better humor. "Oh, this begins to fit together like a puzzle-box, paidhi-ji. *You* are not here as my grandson's bid to prevent my murdering the Ajuri claimant. You are not even here to prevent me enlarging my associations in the south, which I have done. No. I am convinced now that my grandson saw me approaching the powder storage with a match, was disturbed, and believes me apt to declare war on Tiajo. I am not such a fool as to go at it with thirteen Guild units and our own household guard; but never mind: my grandson is worried and has called on the Guild and the heavens above us to intervene."

"One is certain," Bren began to say.

"No, no, paidhi, we know our grandson. He was alarmed, he appealed to Lord Geigi, who, he is aware, *has* acquired the ability to watch over us from the height of the heavens. His weather satellite has many useful abilities we have not mentioned. Now our grandson has urged Lord Geigi to spend a resource *we* had discussed when we were on the space station—notably the disposition of Lord Geigi's sole fully functional lander. I had wanted it set somewhat south, perhaps down in the Dausigin to be useful for navigation, but this will do—a little extravagant, but this will do. We can communicate directly with Geigi through its services, and apparently whoever has one of those units can communicate with each other as if they were in the same room. The timing of the lander was an exquisite courtly flourish. One can absolutely see Geigi's hand in it. He was watching us every step of the way."

It made sense, Bren thought. *He* had known about the last remaining lander, which, once the dowager and Cajeiri had returned from far space and the people rallied behind Tabini to take down the conspirators, Geigi had not needed to deploy. So it had stayed up where it was made, fairly well in deep freeze, but available—should any such thing ever be needed. Geigi had formed elaborate plans for it, involving the edge of the continent, or the poles, even the other side of the world.

Now it landed on the border between two potential adversaries, and it would be a very bad idea for a hostile agency to try to tamper with it.

"One thing I do not understand," Bren said. "The handheld units. A shuttle, they say, brought them. But— to get them aboard—and to get the train carrying them here ahead of us . . ."

"The Guild has had the units," Cenedi said. "The

Guild has had them for a while . . . since, in fact, you returned from your latest trip to the station. Their deploy-
ment was delayed in controversy, but they have been
here, in the Council's keeping, against need."

The cell phone debate, Bren thought. There had been
a controversy. *Nobody* trusted the Messengers' Guild,
which had a history of corruption spanning centuries.
There had been talk of cell phones, such as Mospheira
was installing, independent of that Guild. *He* had invoked his long-disused authority over such technological
imports—he had vetoed it because it could be culturally
ruinous even limited to the lords, bypassing the Assassins' Guild's intervention, and making direct conflicts far
more likely and far harder to stop.

At least the system had landed securely in Assassins'
Guild hands, and Geigi's landers, distributed here and
there across the continent, would serve the Guild and
only the Guild. And the relay system of those landers,
Geigi had assured him long ago, were utterly incompati-
ble with the Mospheiran system, so even if, *somehow* a
Mospheiran cell phone made it across the straits, it would
do the smuggler no good at all.

Well enough. There were worse outcomes . . . especially now.

"Only Guild-seniors and those on special assignment
are authorized," Banichi said. "Any unit lost must be
recovered, or destroyed remotely, which Lord Geigi can
do, even if the unit is turned off. That is the order. They
also have inbuilt protections against tampering of any
kind. We have an edge against the renegades and we will
not lose it."

"They are completely secure?" Tano said.

"They are promised to be so," Banichi said, "for now.
They can become less so if the technology spreads abroad,
but right now, and for this operation, we have surprise and
we have communication our enemy cannot breach."

"Technology," Ilisidi said dryly, "has its uses. In this
case, we are in favor. Only let this train full of generous

assistance keep out of our program and away from our operations. I do not *wish* to deal with the Dojisigin this season, and it is not convenient for the Guild to stir them up to an all-out effort. Three days is what we ask. Three days and we should have Senjin secure. Then we can consider next steps, whatever they need be. Tell me the Guild Council is not going to war with the Dojisigin."

"Their program is extraction of key elements, aijima," Nawari said. "Technically they are not challenging the Dojisigin."

Ilisidi gave a breath of a laugh. "Not challenging the Dojisigin—who have no defense *but* these outlaws, entirely thanks to these outlaws. One cannot feel sorry for Tiajo." Her brow knit. "Very deeply sorry for the people she has misruled and abused this long. It is time she ended. But well enough, if the Guild wishes to manage that disentanglement, let them. They deserve the satisfaction."

Rapid clicks of the rail advised that they were making rapid, flatland-style progress toward Koperna, deep into Senjin. One wondered what folk resident near the coastal plain would have thought of the lander coming down, had they chanced to look up—the event would have been visible at a distance. And, windowless, on a speeding train, Bren wondered if there were habitations of any sort around them. There was no such thing as hard and fast borders on the mainland, no city limits, no counties, nor any firm agreement who owned the borderlands between two regions. The residents on the edges of shared hunting-ranges could go either way, pay man'chi to one lord one day and, without rancor, go the other way on the next issue. There were no taxes on such regions. They had their problems, and usually the residents were small farmers or hunters or fishermen, or had some craft locally useful—types who generally wanted not to be bothered with the affairs of lords or other people.

One wondered as well how long it would be before they began to enter Senjin proper, which would happen near the port, Lusi'ei, where the trouble might start. They had the comfort of one of the Council's mobile units running alongside the track ahead of them, to be sure of the rail, but it would not go all the way in.

Meanwhile they had a little distance to go, and Bren was sure he ought to nap while he could, but that was not happening: his brain was far too busy on things he could do nothing about, and while brandy might settle that down, brandy was not a state in which to deal with trouble.

The lander had given him a whole new set of concerns. Was Ilisidi truly reconciled with Lord Geigi's intervention, and was Bregani wholly sure that it was not planned from the beginning, to have that massive machine set on his doorstep? One could not be sure it *was* coincidence.

One could not be sure what *Machigi* thought, and what *he* would do about it, because the fact that there was a power that could reach down from the heavens to threaten the northern Marid might be a disturbing revelation, whether his intentions were fair *or* foul. On the cooperation of those two unlikely partners, the dowager's plans—and safety—rested.

One thing was undeniable. It had been damned impressive watching that thing come down . . . an unforgettable kind of impression, bound to live forever in the minds of those who had seen it, with whatever implication their plans put on it. The Space Age had just come calling on the Marid's long illusion of independence. Machigi's steel ships, that many considered impossible, and no more than political exhibitionism, had just taken on far more credibility.

But had it pleased Machigi to witness the disparity

between the technology of the aishidi'tat and that of the Marid? It had to bring a little unease.

In vivid recall, too, was Tabini's tone, when he had said, in the conversation involving Ilisidi's intentions— Keep her safe . . .

Damn it, had Tabini just decided on his own intervention? And why?

Geigi would not have dropped that last lander without Tabini's permission—possibly his direct order. And the organization of this operation would have taken time. Tabini had postponed dealing with the Shadow Guild, postponed it while a great deal else was occupying his attention.

Postponed it while he had no heir named.

Postponed it while the heavens had dealt with two visitations from deep space, and need urgently to send an excess of humans down from orbit.

They had settled those problems, or were in the process of settling them. The Assassins' Guild had solved its internal problem. Ilisidi had opened negotiations with Machigi for the sea trade, pulling his attention from the western coast.

Tick. Tick. Tick. The pieces had fallen into place, problems solved. Decks cleared. And all that time, Tabini had been moving his chess pieces into place, just as Ilisidi had been.

Still, no one could really move on the Shadow Guild until the midlands crisis was settled.

On the surface, Damiri-daja had settled that crisis in two major, unexpected moves, giving Tatiseigi an heir and presenting a viable candidate to the Ajuri lordship.

But they still had the question as to who that candidate was, really.

And Nomari's past . . . and possibly not-so-past . . . candidate connections *had* to be high on the list of Ilisidi's and Tabini's immediate concerns. The vacancy of the Ajuri lordship had to be filled, and soon, for the sake of stability in the entire region. But a midlands lord with strong connections in the Marid was unacceptable.

So, on getting news of this candidate, Ilisidi had moved suddenly to pull Senjin support away from the Dojisigi, an act she well knew could trigger the Shadow Guild to move again.

Ilisidi was angry about Tabini's interference in her plans . . . but one had to wonder . . . what had she done to his timetable?

For all Tabini promoted the notion that his grandmother operated beyond his control—it was plausible deniability that allowed him to wade in and smooth things over. One overturned a situation. The other put it back together.

But this time, instead of waiting, Tabini had hit the Shadow Guild with a spectacular move, apt to force a counter-move, and complicating Ilisidi's dealings with Bregani before Ilisidi had quite finished what she was about. Bren had not expected it, not the lander, not the Guild intervention, and the Guild's *own* real mission in the region still remained in question, because they were to a certain extent an independent player. Were they going to launch an attack on the Shadow Guild simultaneous with Ilisidi's diplomatic efforts?

War complicated a diplomatic effort. Dangerously so, if one were sitting in the middle of the contested map.

It was not a good time for a disagreement in policy at the highest levels.

Was Ilisidi upset? Yes. Before embarking, she had not visited Tatiseigi. She had not talked to Damiri *or* Tabini. She had not consulted Geigi, by all he knew.

Tabini and Tatiseigi had not consulted her on the matter of an heir for Tatiseigi.

So she had consulted Machigi and launched a good section of the Guild's resources to back her operation in a completely separate theater—snatching up Nomari in the process.

It was not pique. It was not, no matter how it looked.

She might be upset, but Ilisidi moved like this when she did not want to be told no, and she moved like this because she could, while Tabini had the legislature to consult unless he could prove an emergency.

Had she made herself the emergency?

It was possible. It was highly possible. But not consulting Tatiseigi—that was—

Possibly protective. Tatiseigi had *been* a target of an assassination attempt in the past, notably when Homura and Momichi had been assigned the job. But now—

Now she was about to annoy the Shadow Guild in their own territory. She had the questionable heir to Ajuri in her possession, and Lord Machigi and his association were committed with her. If it all was going to implode, it would touch Tatiseigi and Tabini only peripherally. They would have to find a new heir for Ajuri. And fight a war with the Dojisigin. But that was minor . . . compared to the consequences of the *wrong* heir for Ajuri and a replay of the whole midlands crisis coupled with Machigi's rise to dominate the southern Marid.

God, when he tried to think like the dowager, it led down damnably dark corridors. Machigi was an ally when he had someone to restrain him. But he *could* lead: he was in fact a very strong leader, and one who was to be feared, if he slipped out of Ilisidi's influence. She managed him. She, in fact, used him in ways Machigi did not mind being used. And his greatest use was gathering the Marid into one basket, stripped of the Shadow Guild.

The northern problems? They were not at issue here. She would forgive Tatiseigi. Baby Seimei as heir was a logical answer to the dilemma. Yes, Ilisidi would have major problems with Damiri being regent of Atageini, should Tatiseigi die before Seimei was of age . . . but Tatiseigi was happily nowhere near dying. There was plenty of time for Seimei to be trained in all she needed to know to be a good administrator.

But Nomari was another matter.

A cypher, the deeper one dug. And Machigi and his plans were the key to that lockbox.

And if it all went wrong?

It would be, in Ilisidi's eyes, Damiri's fault if Ilisidi's carefully orchestrated stabilization of the Marid fell apart. All because *Damiri* blindsided *her* and tried to take control?

No. Because Damiri was looking out for her son, and her clan, and her uncle, who happened to be Ilisidi's closest ally. And defending her cousin, who happened to have worked for Machigi.

So was Ilisidi emotionally engaged? Yes. But Ilisidi was not reacting in fleeting temper. Ilisidi did not favor Damiri, did not favor her, and had fought her influence—not out of spite, but out of deep mistrust of the shifting sand she believed Damiri to be. Reared Ajuri, Damiri had fled to her Atageini uncle at sixteen, then back to the Ajuri, and back to the Atageini again . . . before snaring Ilisidi's precious grandson Tabini—a young man Ilisidi had personally reared and groomed for the aijinate—not in a contract good for an heir or two—Ilisidi could have lived with that. But in a lasting, life-long marriage, as aiji-consort? The same position Ilisidi attained through a political alliance that had welded the East to the aishidi'tat?

A position Ilisidi had used very cannily her entire life—and did not surrender, twice aiji-regent, and finally, surrendering the aijinate to Tabini, being relegated to aiji-dowager—and his chief defender. She refused to trust Damiri, a northerner born and bred, and out of a clan with a record of treason. And Tabini, who could easily have arranged a contract marriage with Damiri and moved on, had instead agreed to what Damiri asked: marriage for life.

That had been the first and only time Damiri had outmaneuvered Ilisidi.

Until Damiri, out of long inaction, had used her

relationships to settle two of the key three lordships in the aishidi'tat. Damiri was *of* the midlands as Ilisidi could never be. Damiri claimed authority in the midlands simply by existing. She backed Nomari to take Ajuri, and pledged her infant daughter as Tatiseigi's heir, to inherit Atageini—at one stroke, outlining the future of two clans essential to the aishidi'tat and cementing their future connection to—and influence on—Ilisidi's cherished *great*-grandson, Cajeiri.

So—Damiri could re-shape the midlands and the north in her own favor?

Ilisidi had, in her own administrations, done a great deal to stabilize the south, so far as stabilization went. Ilisidi as aiji-dowager, had made an inroad into the Marid, understanding a young warlord who had managed to build an alliance against Tiajo. Yes. An unqualified yes. The Marid did not trust Tabini. But Machigi had found an ally in Ilisidi, and the Shadow Guild had found attacking Machigi a very bad idea.

Tabini knew how that worked. Tabini also knew his grandmother, and Tabini was no fool. They had worked the game for years, Tabini the reserved, quiet ruler, Ilisidi the volatile and aggressive former aiji, no stranger to conflict.

And through it all, Ilisidi's opinion of Damiri remained unchanged.

But then, so had Tabini's attachment to his consort remained unchanged, and Tabini was no fool. *He* had agreed to a permanent, not a contract, marriage. *He* had supported Damiri's recent moves in the north.

North *and* south. Both needed stability. The same events had destabilized them both, and related events were moving again. Tabini and Ilisidi needed to work together.

He, Bren Cameron, was officially the peacemaker. He worked with Tabini. He had gotten Ilisidi to trust him. He had gotten Geigi to trust him. He had overcome Tatiseigi's utter distrust of humans. Least likely, he had gotten Machigi to negotiate with Ilisidi . . . and gotten Tabini to assist the landing of humans on atevi soil, to assist the Mospheiran government.

He had brokered a three-way treaty among three intelligent species, for God's sake . . .

But despite all the peace negotiations he had managed, he could not seem to get Damiri and Ilisidi together.

And as years passed, that was getting to be a problem.

Perhaps . . . perhaps it was time he talked . . . actually *talked* . . . to Damiri.

Narani set a tea service at Bren's elbow and served a cup. Bren took a sip. It was Night Tea, a calming sort.

"How are we?" he asked.

"Banichi is talking with Cenedi now, nandi," Narani said. "We are about half an hour from Lusi'ei."

Half an hour from the port, where apparently there were problems. It was not a forecast of a restful hour.

He sipped the tea and tried to encourage its restful qualities. He tried to think about bed. Which meant lifting the table.

Banichi came to the table and sat down, Jago and Algini eased onto the opposing bench as Bren made room.

"The system is working well," Banichi said. "Very well. We held a quiet discussion, and clarity is remarkable. We will be providing them for units in Koperna, and we should take the advantage fairly rapidly after that."

"Is there word from either?"

"The dowager's operations are now unchallenged in the railyard area. There is some significant opposition in Lusi'ei, at the port. We shall deal with that if we have to, but we shall not stop until we get to the railyard."

"What *is* that freight car we have hauled all the way

from Shejidan, nadiin-ji? One assumed it was not wardrobe."

His aishid was amused. "No. It is not," Banichi said. "The Red Car was modified to take that coupling, we understand. For your curiosity, it is the usual: water, shelter, and field rations, a contingency. But the equipment will be useful . . . tactical transports. The first train in carried five. We bring five more."

He had seen them, some time ago, in the action in the south, small, fast-moving, and able to transport five or more in cramped fashion.

"As for Lusi'ei," Algini said, from beside him, "we are encouraging those who wish to escape from Koperna to escape, and we are setting up detention facilities in a warehouse. We want as many as possible of our problems to leave the city, and the first units in have spread emergency evacuation orders in the name of various Dojisigi officials, to encourage compliance—along with, on the compromised network, our own complaints of escapes, with orders to get fictitious units to establish barriers, which for some reason we are not doing."

Algini had a wry sense of humor. And it was engaged.

"We are studying the daylight images Lord Geigi has provided," Banichi said, "and checking with units already deployed, trying to determine who is holding certain locations. We are now communicating freely with Headquarters and their resources—they also have the advanced devices, as, I believe, does Tabini-aiji. The first-in at Koperna do not have that capability, so there is still some worry about leaks. Local enforcement, too, is adding some confusion to the matter, since they are not on either of our systems and are far from secure, but once we get there and get units into the field with communications, the situation should stabilize rapidly."

"We also," Bren said, "have to explain things to Lord Bregani. And to Lord Machigi and, out of courtesy and for good will, also to Nomari. One doubts either is sleeping."

"I will undertake that," Tano said.

Tano was in many respects the diplomat of the unit. One thought of going oneself . . . but one also thought that one's wits were not at their sharpest if one of those individuals wanted more answers than he ought to give, and raised questions they would not tend to raise with a messenger.

"Do, Tano-ji," Bren said. "I would be very grateful. The rest of us should try to sleep. Tano, tell our passengers we are making progress. And we should all be dressed and ready when we reach Koperna. That is all I know."

12

It was not the easiest thing, to settle to rest with the train making steady progress and a war zone not far removed. Resting in interludes was a thing the Guild could manage—was trained to manage; and an out-of-place human tried, but there were only questions to roll over in his mind, and the pace of the joints in the rails to say that they were indeed proceeding more slowly than that brief burst of speed over safe track.

Was it a threat? Bren wondered; and from where? But Jago had dropped off to sleep. She breathed quietly, steadily, beside him, and he concentrated on that comforting rhythm, which did not change.

So . . . cell phones had arrived—as part of Geigi's bid to put down the Shadow Guild. But they had to come. It *would* bring changes, but only so far, one hoped, as restoring the ability the Guild had once had of mediating a quarrel or coordinating responses. The Guild had its voice back. And it was an atevi solution. It was not a bad thing. Unfortunate the situation that had called them into use, but over all, it was not disaster. He could be glad of that.

The Messengers, whose territory Geigi's system would violate, were going to have a strong response to a change in the Assassins' communications, while the Assassins were going to argue that it was no different than the Assassins' regular exemption from the Messengers' authority—God help him, he could see that fuss shaping up. But it would be a joy and a relief, if that was all.

He had a veto, though a thin one when it came to pro-liferation of a technology already proliferated. Tabini had a far more direct one, and he could get the necessary restrictions enshrined in law. The Assassins, being in charge of the exchanges of a hot nature between clans—had to be the answer. The Messengers, long sunk in par-tisan actions, would not be involved, argue as they might. They might try to claim Mogari-nai's big dish as a prec-edent. But it was an outmoded one, outmoded in only a decade or so, and the Messengers could do as they would with it. Conduct tours of it for the curious, of what had used to be the most secretive and sensitive installation on the continent.

So much the world changed. Geigi had had the clear view, from his perch in the heavens. A paidhi in all but name. Speaker to humans. Innovator with an innate at-evi perspective and instinct.

It was comforting, to think of Geigi up there at the moment, sitting at some console, watching an image, tracking them even tonight, on their way.

He wanted to shut his eyes and open them again at the announcement they had made it into Koperna, that they were coming safely into the station, and the pur-view of another Guild force.

But that was not happening.

Banichi had come back, and sat down. Jago waked.

"Where are we?" Bren asked. "We are going fast, by the sound of it."

"Passing Lusi'ei," Banichi said. "Without stopping. Bren-ji, we have a problem."

"A problem." They were in touch with Shejidan. Any-thing was possible.

"We have intelligence that the Shadow Guild has tar-geted the dowager—seriously, and imminently. We find it possible that she was the real target of Lord Bregani's subverted guard—he is in the second half of the unit and as such was not in her presence: we are inquiring with him . . ."

That could cover a great deal.

" . . . and he appears cooperative. He says he had no information about his target. It was to come. And it never came. But we are not taking that as unarguable truth. Or this man as the appointed agent. We are viewing records and double-checking our research for everybody else in this mission. We may have been lucky. We may have eliminated the threat. But the dowager has certainly given them reason to be upset."

"Homura was invited aboard," Jago said, "and declined the invitation, Tano said."

"It is a consideration," Banichi said. "We hope the dowager will keep to the train, and not attempt to go into the city. You are particularly persuasive with her. As is Cenedi."

"I understand," he said. It was nothing new. There were always worries. But they were not in the north, where resources could be trusted. "Does she know?"

"I believe Cenedi is informing her, and attempting to reason with her."

One knew how well that might work. "If he cannot, I will try."

The passageway door opened, and Bindanda came in, unmistakeable in his galley whites, and his girth. Bindanda had been with the dowager's galley team the whole trip, and brought them a tray, now, with the smell of fresh bread and sweet spices.

They were nearing their destination, for good or ill.

It was early for breakfast. And Bren had not had so much as a change of shirt, let alone a night's rest—napping here and there. The smell of sweet rolls roused Narani and Jeladi, and Bren levered himself up from the chair where he had spent the night.

There was no way to predict what the day would be,

but it was about to resolve itself, and he needed his wits about him, something in his stomach, and at least as a precaution, the damned protective vest and his pistol, after a visit to the accommodation and a change of clothes. Any day that started with that requirement was set up as a long one. He was not sure how long he had slept—not nearly enough, a cumulative two to three hours of catnaps if he was lucky. He had been sleeping Guild-style, where and when he could during the descent, and since the lander.

But, merciless, the galley knew when they would arrive, and when they needed breakfast, at the edge of arrival and a call to duty, all of them.

He had to talk to Ilisidi, somewhere before they arrived.

Lights flared up full, blinding, as he reached the galley counter and took the cup of tea Narani pushed into his reach.

"Rani-ji. Thank you."

A spice roll followed, on a small plate. He stood, barefoot on the tile, and ate, still disreputable. Algini was checking over his gear, and Banichi and Tano, fully dressed, were both having their breakfast. Bren took his turn in the accommodation, shed clothes, shaved and washed—then leaned, forehead against the cold metal of the wall and shut his eyes a moment, thinking...one more hour. One more hour of sleep would have set him up.

Not to be, however.

And he had to look presentable. Or fit to be shot at.

He turned on the cold tap, held icewater to his face for a bit, then toweled dry and came out to dress as far as shirt and trousers.

Narani poured a second cup of tea, and Bren drank it, standing at the counter, while Jeladi braided up his queue. Jago, fresh-scrubbed and in a short-sleeved knit, moved in to take a roll and a cup of tea.

"We have advised the force in Koperna that we are

coming in," Jago said. "They are reconfiguring to give us a safe berth and an easy offload of equipment. We also have word that the *navy* is moving in."

The navy. God. The navy did not magically turn up in the Marid sea, halfway across the continent from its usual range.

"Who arranged *that?*" he asked, swallowing a piece of sweet roll.

"One or the other," Jago said with a shrug. "The aiji or the aiji-dowager. They have come here all the way from the strait, so they started from days ago."

Along with everything else, Bren thought.

Along with Ilisidi's determination. And she *could* move ships of the fleet. So at least Tabini would have been warned that was happening.

In all that had ever gone on since the War of the Landing, the navy of the aishidi'tat had never left their centuries-long watch over the Mospheiran straits.

"What is she expecting?" he asked in some disquiet.

"We do not know," Jago said. "Tabini-aiji will have known where they are, and Lord Geigi might know what is out there, but we do not, at this moment. Cenedi may be in touch with him—with the new equipment."

Might know, as to position. And now *might* be talking directly to them. Geigi would have watched it all. Those ships had to have begun moving, given the distance— God, how far was it from the straits to the Marid, and how fast *could* they move?

The ships were there. That was all he needed to know.

And repositioning them made a certain sense. For the first time in the last two hundred years, there was no perceived threat from Mospheira, but definitely there was a potential one here. It was both disturbing that they had moved, and comforting. There was no ship sailing the Marid that could face one of them. They were much more like the ships Ilisidi had promised Machigi—to Tabini's considerable displeasure—steel-sided and independent of the wind.

And possessed of cannons.

Meanwhile, Banichi had the maps in hand. Jeladi had let down the conference table, and Banichi spread out a map of Koperna, and indicated the railyard where they would come in, below the several hills, one hill with the residency and a number of houses and shops, and another hill with the radio station toward the eastern edge of the city. The railyard and a number of industries and warehouses sat near a small river, the Seski. Two bridges united another residential and commercial area on the south side.

It began to be real. Elsewhere on the train, their passengers would be breakfasted, made aware they were coming in, and have their own anticipation of the next number of hours, wherein, if things went as ordinary, things they had not planned would happen, and they would have to deal with them.

Meanwhile—

He stood, watching the conference around a map he had studied, but did not control, and drank a second cup of tea, waiting for a plan to emerge, waiting to know how to dress, whether they would host civic leaders aboard, in style, or whether they would be scrambling about under fire, with the need to be inconspicuous.

"Ladi-ji," he said to Jeladi, his sometime valet being closest. "I should dress. One has no idea in what. Do we have any idea?"

"I shall ask," Jeladi said, and moved off, hoping that the official plan did not involve the dowager taking one of the unshielded transports up the central street to the residency. If it did not—good. He need not disturb her. If it did—

He *wished* he had a window. He *wished* he had any clue where they were at the moment, except that Lusi'ei and Koperna fairly well ran together, by scattered enterprises and houses. The train was still running as if there were absolutely no difference between this run and the placid northern countryside.

Banichi came to him. "Lord Bregani is asking to return to the residency immediately after we arrive at the station. He is adamant that his people realize he is not a prisoner, and that *he* is in control of the situation."

That sort of thing was not his decision to make. "Will the dowager agree?"

"Cenedi is, at the moment, assessing the situation in the railyard and consulting with the dowager. He has asked us to deal with this. In particular, he has asked *me* to deal with this. He is insisting the dowager cannot leave the train until there is security in town."

That was a distinct relief, but not a final one.

"Unfortunately," Banichi said, "I am called on to escort Lord Bregani up and take command, as next-senior to Cenedi. He is reserving Nawari and an elite force here. I am reluctant to leave you to a situation where you cannot be the priority, Bren-ji. But I do not want you with me."

"And go by yourself?" Break up his aishid for the sake of Bregani's, admittedly justifiable, impatience?

"These are my alternatives, Bren-ji. We cannot delay about this once we reach the station."

That was unacceptable. "Well, then, there is an alternative, that Bregani's assigned aishid continue to protect him and you continue to protect me, while I exercise my office as negotiator and go with Bregani *and* Machigi. I am relatively sure Cenedi had rather see Machigi *and* his guard out of the dowager's vicinity."

"In the case Machigi feels threatened, we might have trouble with Taisigi forces deciding to come in . . ."

"But *you* have communications that could reach to the station and back, and Lord Geigi could advise Lord Machigi that intruding arms into Senjin would not be the best move."

Banichi gazed at him soberly across the table. "It is at best an unstable situation up at the residency."

"It will improve with the forces we will bring with us. The residency occupies two city squares. It will require resources to secure. Bregani's bodyguard, mine, Machigi's . . . perhaps even Nomari's, another problem I had as soon have out of the dowager's vicinity . . . will give you ample personnel to deal with any situation, and lessen the number of problems Cenedi has to watch over. Moving Bregani up to the residency, which he wants, at least does not concentrate everyone the Dojisigin would wish to attack into one train in the railyard. We can divide their attention."

"With bait your personal aishid had far rather not use!"

Bren shrugged. "If they are going to attack, it is an even chance which they would attack first, and my odds are even."

Banichi frowned. Deeply. "You would distract me."

Bren shrugged. "Ignore me. Leave *my* defense to the rest of us."

"You know how impossible that is, Bren-ji."

One only *imagined* how impossible it was. Except when he thought of danger to his aishid. Then imagination was out the proverbial window.

"I promise to hear instruction," he said, and drew a desperate and brief laugh from Banichi.

"Bren-ji. This is not a promise with a good history!"

"I am deeply appreciative of the risk to my aishid wherever I stay, but I have my pistol. I *am* able to defend myself at least for a moment, if you are distracted, Nichi-ji. And Cenedi would not let me defend the dowager. If he is deeply concerned, his *only* concern will be for her."

"Bren-ji." Banichi drew a breath. "You have done admirably on several occasions, but these people do not observe Guild rules. And explosives are not observant of rank."

Mines, in other words. He had met them before, during the fighting in the south.

"I am not afraid," he said. "Do as the situation needs you to do. We *do* have Lord Geigi as a resource."

"You are not afraid," Banichi said. It was a challenge. "This is worrisome."

"I am not overconfident," Bren said. "I am terrified. And I am armed."

"We know," Banichi said wryly, who had given him that gun, years ago.

"Lord Geigi will keep us all in contact. The dowager can make her wishes and recommendations known, and I *can* become useful to the effort in being available to give those orders official endorsement. Bregani might well find himself in need of such backup, and for someone to speak for the dowager. Under this plan, leaving Lord Machigi here with the dowager is not an option; but Machigi's presence may worry some of Lord Bregani's associates, and I *can*, in all modesty, have some influence in that regard. I am *useful* to his situation, and certainly of more use there than shadowing the dowager about aboard the train."

Banichi was not entirely happy. But he nodded. "I shall present the idea to Cenedi."

"Good," Bren said. He had a gun. He had shot a man. Arguing to put himself in Bregani's residency, a concern on Banichi's mind, was like that, a decision under dreadful circumstances, and with farther-reaching consequences if he chose wrong. But useless as he might be in a fight, he was a major asset in Bregani's situation, in arguing Bregani's case for alliance with the dowager.

And Bregani had a valid point: acting as if he were a prisoner of the dowager and staying on the train was not the best idea. Bregani had to be seen to be in charge, giving orders, in his own capital.

Second point that had to be made: that Bregani was in fact in charge of the Guild force presently in the city. *Senjin* alone had not been able to deal with Tiajo, but Senjin with the Guild was another matter. It was here, and technically operating under Bregani's orders, *not* the dowager's, a point which Bregani needed to make clear.

Lord Machigi—well, at least his presence would shock the locals, and maybe it could be shown as another indication of change. Taking him was certainly more politic than having Cenedi lock the passageways and seal him at the other end of the train.

Something resounded off the wall. Several such. He looked instinctively toward the outside wall. But there was no sign of a problem.

It had gotten his aishid's attention. Tano and Jago, poring over the map, had looked up.

"The opposition," Algini said dryly, appearing behind him, "is testing our armor. They believe the windows outside are real. And they know the first train brought the Guild in. They are not happy to see another. Our mobile escort has had to leave us. We have put an officer with the advanced communications up with the engineer."

The train had not speeded up or slowed down.

"We expected some sniping," Jago said, likewise joining them, with Tano. "But they do not hold any of the major points. We are near the port, the difficult area. The city is reported to be quieter. The Guild issued a shelter order at the outset of this."

Ordinarily atevi quarrels tended to bring citizens to the streets and to rallying points, and Guild, if engaged, did not endanger them. A shelter order, however, was martial law, everyone ordered home or to the nearest public building. And as long as this had gone on—people in compliance had to be less than comfortable. It could not continue indefinitely.

"Regarding the situation at the railyard," Banichi said. "We have word we are clear to come into the passenger terminal, and that the area is in our hands, but one fears we will draw detritus of the port action into the city with us."

Comforting. More rounds hit the car, harmless.

A tremendous explosion.

"That was ours," Banichi said.

That was good to know.

The train continued at its steady pace. They no longer had the mobile unit to watch for trouble.

Something hit the train with a thunderous impact, possibly striking the Guild car forward. The pace of the engine did not change.

Another explosion rocked the train.

"That was also ours," Algini said.

"The track is obstructed some distance ahead," Banichi said. "Guild units are in process of clearing it."

The train jolted and something scraped past the outer wall, conjuring an impression of metal wreckage. Bren set a hand on the wall. It was not all that violent—but unsettling in the extreme. If someone had damaged the rails, it would strand them at the port, where clearly not everything was settled. His heart beat faster. But there was nothing he personally could do. Further forward in the train, Bregani's car must be closer to whatever was going on up there. He and Machigi and Nomari were certainly getting the full effect of it.

They were now discernibly gathering speed.

He became aware that his aishid had been standing close about him and the table, and that he and the teapot and his papers were currently pent fairly neatly into the dining nook.

"We are not expecting to crash, are we?"

"We hope not," Banichi said. "We trust not. But we are now in the city, and almost anything is possible."

They had gathered ordinary traveling speed and now held it.

"The plow on the front is intended for rural obstructions," Tano said. "We are given a takehold."

Takehold. A word from the space station.

Bren felt his heart rate approach the tempo of the train.

There was a massive jolt, a scrape, a series of scrapes, one that screamed past their own outer wall.

"A city bus," Algini said.

God. "Unoccupied, one hopes."

"We likewise hope," Algini said. "We are now in the city."

They ran for a time more, in what now seemed freedom. Banichi, listening to his earpiece, said, "We are into the city and are approaching the station, Bren-ji."

"Resistance?"

"The regular communications indicate not. A plan is evolving. We still do not assume the railyard is safe—"

Banichi broke off in mid-sentence, listening, and that listening went on for some time, while the train continued its rapid progress, thump, thump and thump on the joints of the track.

Their hold on the situation was certainly not perfect, if someone had gotten a city bus onto the tracks. There still could be problems ahead, if the Shadow Guild was organized—but there was plenty of evidence in the arrival of a second train to persuade the enemy that escape would not be a lasting opportunity.

The Shadow Guild was not given to self-sacrifice. Their training was tactical, theoretically serving command, but with a man'chi to a cause lost once when the regime went down, and with man'chi to this and that commander or unit leader, but with no true lord. Tiajo could inspire no one, Shishogi was dead; and Geidaro, if she had ever been a factor, was lately murdered by that very organization, whether in disgust or the realization extracting her was impossible. After Shishogi, indeed, they seemed down, militarily, to a cabal of discontented commanders, none of them able to field an army, all of them potent enough to be locally dangerous. Banichi had taken down one such personally, when the Kadagidi clan lord was set down. Other leaders had died in various set-tos, all over the map. Geidaro's brief rise was over.

But one never dared say there might not be something more at the heart of it, someone of consequence, and going into the Dojisigin to try to find it was not Ilisidi's plan. It was the dowager's immediate purpose to secure Senjin, not fight a war. Her plan was to concentrate the waning Shadow Guild in the Dojisigin, where they could find themselves cut off from rail and from sea, with their elite membership growing older—or growing no older at all, if they set themselves in regular Guild sights.

It made sense. And *helping* their enemy leave made sense as part of that plan, no matter what the rank of Shadow Guild they had to let slip through the net. There might be persons they indeed could wish to lay hands on. But the longer they could keep them contained, now with Lord Geigi's ability to watch—and strike—from orbit—they would find themselves less and less relevant, and even the Dojisigin's mountains might become less protection, if every truck and every walker could be spotted.

Times indeed were working against the rebels.

The train sounded its horn, three distinct blasts. Warning of collision? Bren wondered, hoping not.

"We are coming into the station," Algini said, "and we are advising our allies. Any enemies in the city must also know a second train has arrived, and that it is not on their side."

Indeed, they began to slow down. The joints of the track came slower and slower. A second set of blasts sounded, as if anyone in the area could have failed to hear the first.

They were stopping. Motion ceased. And it was both a vast relief—they had arrived safely—and a sense of dread for what came next.

"First," Banichi said, "the hindmost car will disgorge its transports, weapons, and supplies with which we can defend the train. We will be looking for local transport we can take to reach the residency. We will initially be sending various of our units out to contact sector officers and get a report, so that we can extend secure communications to the hill, the radio station, but I, going with Lord Bregani, will be doing the same for the residency. This is Cenedi's direction. Are you still determined to go?"

"Unless my aishid has an extremely strong new reason against it."

"We do not. Let us assume we will be there unsupported for a time. We have the place under guard. But operations there may bring trouble to us."

"One understands."

"You should dress plainly," Banichi said, "and do not expect the paidhi's colors will be a protection. The vest—absolutely. At all times."

Historically, and by tradition, white protected the paidhiin. It would only make him a target for the Shadow Guild, and he unfortunately glowed like a candle in atevi company, even in plain clothes.

"I have the vest." He rapped it for proof. "Narani has not let me go about without it. And I shall obey my aishid's instructions. I swear to it."

"They are saying the city is quiet, compliant with the order," Algini said. "And the first-in has several agents out attempting to provoke reaction. We drew a few out of hiding when we came past Lusi'ei, and teams are on the move to find them."

"With one success so far," Tano added.

"So, well," Bren said, "we simply stay ready, one supposes." He in particular had nothing to do, no way to distract himself. His job was to sit still, not distract his staff, and when they did move, to try to stay as inconspicuous as a pale, small, neutral and generally uninformed human could do. The pistol was a last resort.

So he sat, letting Narani and Jeladi choose what to pack in the way of baggage—nothing that was as difficult of access as the baggage car, only the ordinary—for this.

They packed one case for him. And then began collecting their own, for a second case.

"Rani-ji," Bren said, rising. "You are not required."

"Nandi," Narani said. "If you please. Bindanda will not let you eat there, but what he inspects it; and we have a care how you impress these folk. If you will, nandi."

"I would not risk you."

"We would not risk you attempting to press a coat, nandi. And I am taking an iron. Jeladi is taking the signing-kit, in case someone has made off with one. Bindanda is bringing supplies, and *your* tea, *and* for the dowager, if she decides to come."

The dowager was the deciding point. Bindanda between him and mistakes in the kitchen, and between the dowager and deliberate acts.

"Advise Banichi, Rani-ji. Please take things for your comfort. We do not know what the situation up there may be. And pack my medicines. And put all my papers under lock. You know where. I shall be taking my small writing kit."

"Yes," Narani said, much more happily.

Narani and Jeladi had been with him on the riskiest moves, and this might be a soft berth in a governmental residency, or it might be chaos up there. Bindanda's presence was a reasonable, even an essential precaution, though if the dowager did come she would come with staff dedicated to her comfort and her protection.

Still . . . he had started with a party of five, which would fit in one of their transports. Now they were a very infelicitous eight, if any of them were superstitious.

God knew, no risk had ever stopped the dowager.

The train sat.

And there was the sound of footsteps in the passage, and Narani and Jeladi moving suitcases about.

Something thumped. Bren looked up, wondering if something had hit the train.

No one reacted. He sat frowning, wondering.

Jago looked his direction. He threw a glance aft, a question.

"Vehicles," Jago said, "are being offloaded."

"For us?" he asked.

"No," Jago said. "We have located a small bus. It is being moved in. We shall have mobile units for escort all the way, and we will be loading and moving fast, before our enemies have too much time to make decisions. We are taking our essential baggage, food *and* water."

"Is it intact up there?" Bren asked.

"Intact, yes. The residency has been locked down, with only essential personnel, a few residents, and a handful of staff. There are staff and guards at local banks, technical staff and security guards at the water plant, and at the power plant: the Guild has cleared them and provided them communication for direct contact if they have a problem. Local enforcement is taking a stance at shops and taverns. Senjini security stayed at their posts, with their own communications; and the Guild is in cooperative contact with them. Local rumors are hindered by the lockdown, but three are circulated: that Lord Bregani departed on the Red Train and is on his way to Shejidan; that he is with his cousin in the broadcast center; or that he is dead and Tabini-aiji has sent in the Guild force to prevent a Dojisigi takeover. Additionally, the Guild has left the road to the port undefended, encouraging Dojisigin forces to take that route. There are mobile units dealing with any attempt to head into the hills."

At least it was not warfare in the streets, and it was limited, with local forces attempting to do their jobs, and the northern Guild not challenging them. If it had been Mospheira, citizens would have scattered in skirmishes and upheaval—but citizens and civilian property were completely off limits in a regular Guild operation, and when the head of government or clan could not be found, and in the absence of their own orders, they had thousands of years of reasons to stay low and wait for *someone* official to stand up and deal with what was going on. If no one could be found, then—

Then the sun would come up on restored order, all the same, just a different order, and not necessarily one they would have chosen, but one that worked fairly well the same as the old one—with different people. The shopkeepers and the craftsmen would take visual inventory and get back to work. Eventually word would get around the streets—or from the broadcast center—from whoever was in charge, now, and ordinary people, who belonged to a clan but did not govern it, just waited to hear how their clan leadership had come through the crisis. It was a civilized way to deal with an atevi sort of problem, and rare, very rare, that a clan was badly enough done by that new clan leadership could not work something out of the chaos.

Even Ajuri's shopkeepers and tradesmen and the like, in repeated chaos, with lord after lord murdered and the administration in chaos, had generally come through it all. Dojisigi fishermen just kept flinging out their nets. Hasjuran would fix its transformer and hope the new agreement would bring more traffic, but meanwhile the hunters and the tanners and the leatherworkers would keep at their trade, and the Transportation Guild would go on wondering what else would come through.

Clan lord was a fine honor in peaceful areas.

The problem that Bregani and the Senjini had—the unenviable problem—was sitting between two powers, the Taisigi and the Dojisigi, one of which was allied to the aiji-dowager and the other of which was her bitter enemy—while nothing so law-conscious and careful as the Assassins' Guild enforced the rules the Dojisigin lord managed to set.

But the Assassins' Guild was involved now, and the local constabulary, untrained citizens, and the local security, hired to watch doors and boxes, was no more inclined, apparently, to quarrel with the original Shejidani Guild than with Tiajo's Shadow Guild.

That was not all of it, however. There was sentiment, and a lord who could not muster it one way or the other was on shaky ground. The next salient question was whether Bregani would retain the man'chi of his people, going into a new alignment with regional powers—or whether Tiajo could cause him enough problems to make everything fall apart. The Guild and the lords might win conflicts; but it took the people's will to keep the peace.

And if it cost too much, if Tiajo was too scary—Bregani could lose. And well knew it.

"We are ready, nandi," Narani said. They were packed. Bindanda would join them from the galley, bringing essentials. Presumably their passengers were similarly preparing to move out, and doubtless in both trepidation and determination, with man'chi driving him to protect and hold, Bregani was preparing to bring his family home.

13

A quiet had settled, after the racket of the train.

Then there was the faint sound of an engine, and the higher, more strident sound of several lighter vehicles.

"The bus is moving in, with the escort," Tano reported. "We shall board from the other side of the station building. We shall debark from the Red Car. The galley will be sending supplies over first."

That was as expected. The body of the train would stay locked tight. And Ilisidi would remain in command aboard. They had heard nothing to the contrary—but likely there had been strong discussion two cars away.

Algini and Jago got up as he did, gathering up rifles in the process. Bren had his pistol, and with that weight went an unsettled stomach. Peace in the streets was one thing. The ability of opposing forces to lurk and snipe at other forces was entirely another.

They made their way through the passages, through Cenedi's car, and Ilisidi's, and the galley, as far the Red Car, where Bindanda waited beside a stack of boxes. A number of galley staff and Ilisidi's own bodyguard were actively moving out boxes.

"The others are coming," Tano said. "We should go on. Guild will board first."

The passage door of the Red Car had shut and the side door was open, with the supplies being moved out. The open door let in the first splash of shaded daylight they had had since Hasjuran.

And compared to where they had been, compared even to last night on the coastal plain, the air that came in, fuel-laden and moist, was warm, but not too warm, a temperature that made Bren's middle-weight coat a sensible choice, and the close armor of the usually objectionable vest not that great a trial.

Jago went down first off the single step, and reached up to assist. Bren took her hand and landed on the concrete of Koperna's train platform, facing a last-century style facade, well-kept; and a door of glass panes, through which the box-carriers were moving. Banichi, Tano and Algini followed, with Narani and Jeladi and Bindanda close behind.

The glass-paned door let them into a large waiting room with a number of seats and an unoccupied ticketing booth. Murals adorned the walls, frescoes of people a hundred years ago, stylish and prosperous, ghosts of the Marid that had used to be, in the days when peace with the north had been briefly effective. Renovation had given the place a modern door on the other side, all glass, and at the moment it was propped open for them. Two regular Guild stood by to indicate the way, and they hurried along to another platform, where a bus waited, engine running.

Plain concrete stairs brought them down to its level. The place was entirely deserted except for Guild presence. And for the briefest of exposures, there was a view outward, above low rooftops, in sunlight, glorious, clear, southern sunlight, with wooded hills and the gray haze of the snowy peaks beyond a Marid style of city . . . a sprawl of pale weathered stucco and red tiled roofs. The whole city flowed over several hills in the distance, rising slightly to the north and south, divided by—one knew this from the map—a moderate-sized river to the south. The city bus, sky blue, decorated with an antique sailing ship and a pleasant shore, waited—a sizeable bus, of older vintage than, say, any airport bus in Shejidan, probably half a century old, and noisy in its running. Its cargo compartment stood open, as Guild shifted boxes into it. Its passenger door stood open, offering knee-high steps, typical of every conveyance Bren had faced on the mainland, but without a handrail where he expected it.

Jago quietly and quickly gave Bren a hand up, and he took it, moved back to the second row of seats in the bus, on the right hand, with Jago, leaving the first pair for Banichi and Algini, and two more rows for Tano and staff.

They were in, they were safe, and they waited. The driver, Guild-uniformed, kept the engine running; and in short order Bregani and Murai appeared, with Husai, and their bodyguard, and very little luggage. They boarded, and Bregani paused by Bren's seat.

"Nandi. Our *own* aishid. We have asked, and had no answer. May we have them brought up?"

A fraught question. A challenge, right on the threshold of the whole operation, and a question of autonomy.

"Nandi," Bren said. "Let us discuss this once we are in the residency. I am sympathetic, but I must defer to the dowager, and to the Guild. I do assure you I shall represent your request to the dowager."

"They are our citizens. They are Farai and Senjini. They are *not* under central Guild authority. They are mine."

This with Bregani looming above him, and impeding the flow of persons who needed to board. It was not accidental, one thought, that Bregani made the point now.

"I am concerned that if they are left here, there might be pressure on them concerning their kidnapped relatives . . ."

"Who are likely to be killed outright if they have no value," Bregani said.

"One would hope the kidnappers would not would not get that information," Bren said, "but I appreciate there is that threat."

"And the question of morale of my staff, nandi. And a debt of honor."

"I am persuaded," Bren said. "Let us get through the next number of hours and be sure we have a safe place for you to be, nandi, and once we have that, I shall argue for your point and I think I shall win it. And if I fail, you may prevail with the dowager yourself. Meanwhile, if asked, say that you assigned them to stay for a briefing, and, baji-naji, we can hope the Guild operation here in the city can find their families, or learn where they are. It *is* a priority. And it might solve other problems."

Bregani had rested his hand on the front seat's top rail. He released his grip, drew a breath and nodded. "I have confidence in you, paidhi. As in the whole situation, I have no choice. But I have seen you work twice now."

"I shall try not to fail you, nandi. I do mean that. I shot the man, and I wish I had had a choice. I take it as my own debt of honor to try to help him."

"One is grateful," Bregani said, and proceeded to his seat, with Murai and Husai.

In the meanwhile Lord Machigi had been stalled just inside the door, waiting; and Nomari with him, with their respective bodyguards collectively behind them—Machigi with his own Taisigi set; and Nomari with ones the Guild had set to watch him. They came past, Machigi intent on finding his place, and Nomari just looking, as ever, worried and out of place.

One had to remember—the bus had windows. It had vulnerabilities. But outside were other engines starting up. Through his own window, and past Jago's presence next to the window, Bren spied one of the mobile transports with Guild aboard. There was an impressive-looking gun mounted at the rear.

They were all aboard. The door shut, and the bus

began to move, backing and turning, affording a view of a large cobbled area and surrounding stucco buildings, then the opening of a broad street leading into the city. There were parked trucks in the immediate area, and, grim sight, a gun emplacement on the left, with only Guild uniforms in view near it as they passed.

Their own bus had enough firepower to defend itself. But it was not armored, and they were vulnerable on their way up.

Haste in entering the city had some risk, but delay in restoring Bregani might let rumors run and allow trouble to organize. One escort had pulled ahead of them, the other out of view, possibly behind them; and from what Bren could see past the driver as they traveled the street, the shelter order was doing its job: shutters were closed up and down the street. Flags and pennons moved lazily in a light breeze, but there was no sign of life, no parked vehicles at all, just a stray basket rolling gently to the curb.

They gathered speed, keeping the pace of their lead vehicle. There was one open shutter, which drew the attention of their escort. But it was children looking out, nothing more threatening.

Even among the finer buildings, none was taller than three stories, and most looked about the vintage of the station. The building trim had only two colors, yellow, or earthy red, with one defiant blue. Flowers grew in windowboxes, late in the season even in the Marid, but blooming. Here and there on the higher street were massive pots with shrubbery, well-tended. One saw electric lines strung, but surprisingly few. Shejidan had a vast webwork overhead, and a slow spread of neon signage, which Bren personally decried.

Koperna did not seem so unusual or exotic as Bren had imagined it, a city with a train station, and quite ordinary business shutters on the street level, likewise red or yellow, generally with ordinary windows above.

Then, defiant anomaly, outside a little shop with its

shutters thrown, sat a cluster of old folk at a streetside table, watching their passage, in what frame of mind he could not guess, ignored by the escort in front. One old woman lifted a hand and waved at them, whether welcome or irony being entirely up for question. It was their corner, their bar, their street. Guild authority had undoubtedly cautioned them, but there they were.

And the bus rolled past.

Local folk maintaining their privilege, Bren thought, a healthy defiance one could expect in the north. There was definitely gray hair on the several heads, and they had a pitcher of something drinkable and very possibly against the Guild's direct orders. It was a welcome sense of atevi being atevi, in a region where a human felt twice a foreigner.

Electric lines and phone lines became a little more common as they climbed, but the buildings were no finer, and the vacant cobbled streets were, while clean, not innocent of potholes.

Was it one way for the people, a worn-down poverty while the lordly residence was all luxury? One began to wonder if that might be the case. But things did not markedly become more elegant as they ascended. There was a hotel, proclaimed by its sign, and it was shuttered, the varnished woodwork needing a new coat. They reached the height of the hill, and passed along a stucco wall. Pockmarks told a tale of recent violence, the first they had seen anywhere, but the wall, overtopped by trees, proved not a defensive wall at all.

That was their first turn. Tall evergreens rose above that wall, indicating a garden, perhaps: then the wall became a tile-roofed colonnade beside a public walkway. Midway in that frontage, a broad stairway ran down to meet that walk, and a gateless arch above framed a few more steps up into the building. Guild stood guard at that arch.

The escort pulled to the curb and stopped, and the bus pulled up at the base of the steps. It was, apparently,

Lord Bregani's residency, certainly a building of sufficient size. Covering two city squares, the map had said. With the garden and the frontage together, it did seem to be that.

The unit from their first escort went up the steps, spoke to the guards, and went inside.

Checking the place out, Bren thought. One could agree with that. There would be a little delay for credentials from the units in charge, and an agreement on a change of command, and on where in the building they should go.

It was a massive building, larger than the usual country estate houses, counting that garden, though by no means as large as the Bujavid. It had upper floors, but only two. Being a city center, it likely had the lord's residency on one side, and on the other, city offices for a number of departments and utilities.

But as far as ornamentation or an expression of style or wealth, it might have been a bank or an office complex, and here, too, there was a sense of age, and no lordly luxury at the people's expense. Like its city, it seemed somewhat old, plain, lacking ornament, and careful of its expenses.

Granted a long dependency on the Dojisigin, and seeing the plainness of the residency as well as the city itself, one gained a sense of the quality of life for the entire northern Marid. The southern Marid had been prey to weather *and* northern Marid politics, but one recalled a distinct splendor about Machigi's residency in Tanaja, a hint of glories past and perhaps about to dawn again. Building was starting to happen, one heard, even in the Sungeni Isles.

Clearly this half of the north had not been awash in luxury, and to judge by the sparse appearance of electric lines, a good deal else might not have dawned here, either. Hasjuran had lost a portion of the town's electricity when one transformer went out, true, but it was tiny, while Koperna clearly was a fairly populous city, and had all the complexity of one. The drive up had been like stepping back a little in time—not an outrageously long backstep, but certainly a few decades and a few amenities ago. Buildings even on so major an avenue had been drab, utilitarian, with little evidence of recent building.

One hoped to improve that—not to destroy the city's more leisurely pace of life, not to trouble that gathering of old folk out to defy the occupation, but to at least bring improvements, at least bring science, and engineering that might provide more comforts.

And peace. That foremost. Less outlay of regional wealth in arms and defense, and very certainly an end of Tiajo siphoning off a tax from her sole ally, three taxes, actually, which, combined, had run over thirty percent of everything Senjin produced . . . all in the name of defense against, well, in point of fact—Tiajo.

The trip through the city, and the view of the residency answered questions *and* cemented a resolve to see that the dowager's plans had a chance to work, to see that Tiajo's taxes stopped, and likewise that Machigi behaved himself and became a decent neighbor to the south. Of the two, Bregani and Machigi, he was far more disposed, humanly speaking, to *like* Bregani, and to distrust Machigi with every fiber of his human being, but then, long residence among atevi said that human instincts could go far astray and *liking* could lead one into some very difficult places. One did not easily warm to Algini, among other facts of human perception: Algini's cold stare could freeze rain in midfall—but Algini was one who had given up something near Council rank to be with him. It was just one other way an ateva could be, while being a very good ally.

So one tried to equate the two, and to ascribe some sort of virtue to Machigi, while his gut was saying no and his experience with atevi was saying that the dowager had neatly cut off all Machigi's avenues of self-aggrandizement, and rendered the man a hazardously useful ally.

Even to Bregani.

Even to Tabini, which was going some.

Let us get in there, he began thinking. *What are they doing in there? It is surely safer than sitting out here in an unarmored bus.*

But Guild came and went, and talked to the guards outside, and still delayed.

Then Banichi got up, turned to the company on the bus and said quietly, "They are opposed by local security, who have held the building, and who are unwilling to turn it over to Guild. Lord Bregani might resolve this. Nandi?"

"They are my people," Bregani said, also rising, as did Murai, and Husai. "Let us go. They will not refuse me."

"We shall need to move quickly," Banichi said, "as far as the inside foyer. We can work things out from there."

"Yes," Bregani said. "Absolutely. Let us go."

Bren had no question. He rose, and Jago did, then Tano and Algini, Narani, Jeladi, Bindanda, and, quickly, everybody behind them on the bus.

"The baggage, nandi," Narani said.

"We all shall move," he said. "We shall arrange for the baggage once inside." He called out loudly enough for the back rows. "We are about to go up. Move quickly, up the steps and into the foyer. Do not stop."

The driver opened the middle door, on the left side, facing the steps, which gave the middle seats the first exit, Bregani and family, and Machigi, both with their diverse escorts, ironically together. "Go!" Bren said, as his staff tried to give place in the narrow aisle. "No precedence. Just go!"

They moved. Jago took hold of Bren's arm right before the steps, stepped down first and held a hand out for Bren.

He took it, stepped onto the curb and moved, hearing Algini giving their escort orders for the baggage.

It was an exposed position, sheltered by the bus and two transports. Bren took the atevi-scale steps as rapidly as possible, thinking only to get his aishid under cover, glad of the brown coat, but there was not a thing he could do about the rest of him.

Wooden doors gaped wide. They entered a dimly-lit, echoing interior—terrazzo floors in a geometric pattern, light streaming hazily through a tall window at the end of a massive barrel vault, the height of the building itself, with a balcony on the right, chandeliers above, and a series of plain doors—offices, likely. On the left, an intersecting hall and a curving stairway to another, open floor.

It was not a place built for siege. It sprawled, echoing and re-echoing with footsteps and voices. The walls were plaster, with murals—one noted chips and repair plaster, and an electric socket irreverently inserted on a painted figure's foot.

Local uniformed guards met their lord and took orders, not without worried frowns.

"We are back," Bregani said, and: "Saigi!"

"Nandi," an officer responded.

"Is the building secure?"

"To our knowledge, nandi. But we have not let the northern Guild in. We have not let anybody in who left the building, not the servants, not the mayor, not his staff, and not even the town guard."

"It was well done. Well done. I am back, with allies. Who *is* here?"

"The clan lords, on their own, with a few of their servants. The kitchen staff. Some of the maintenance staff. Some of the cleaning staff. We have a list. All the offices had closed and all the officials and staff had gone home, when the northern Guild started through the city, and told everyone to go home and lock their doors and close their shutters. Officials have phoned, but we told them not to try to come in. Are we indeed accepting the northern Guild operating in the city? They claim, they claim, nandi, that you authorized them. We would not open the doors to them. And they said keep the doors shut, and they went away, that was all."

"Well done in that, Saigi-ji. You have done everything you should have done and nothing that you should not. These are indeed allies, and *now* they may come in. We are done with the Dojisigin, Saigi-ji. We have been threatened for the last time. They and their businesses may go elsewhere, and we are done with them. That is what this is about. We are allying with the south."

Saigi's eyes shifted toward the company, apprehensive, and not approving. The stare lingered on Bren, as if the whole Landing had just arrived; and very possibly he had an idea who the young lord with the raking scar on the chin might be. He said nothing, however, just ducked his head respectfully and said, "Shall they come in at will, then?"

"No," Banichi said unexpectedly, and heads turned. "Refer all Guild attempting to enter directly to me. My name is Banichi, Guild-senior in this operation. My second in command is Algini, here beside me. Our unit protects the paidhi-aiji, here present; but at the moment we are seconded to the aiji-dowager's service, in command of Guild operations in the city. One or the other of us must see and approve any Guild entering this building. In the matter of building staff, nadi, you have the expertise, and we ask you to make that decision, subject to your lord's orders. But like you, we know our own, and we are on the hunt for Tiajo's Guild that may be here in the city. If they are ours, they are admitted; once admitted, they are cleared. Anyone else—we shall deal with as the situation demands. Our respects, nadi. With your lord, the Guild commends your decisions."

Not the northern Guild, *the* Guild. Banichi was precise on that score. And Bregani's officer, thus respected, looked a little less desperate.

Luggage was, meanwhile, piling up outside the doors. And Saigi gave an order to his own men to bring it in and get kitchen staff to bring it upstairs.

Then Saigi asked, quietly, "Where is Adsumi?"

That was the senior of Bregani's own bodyguard. And one knew exactly what was under question.

"My guard," Bregani said, "will be with me, Saigi-ji. Trust me."

Bregani did not explain, did not say there had been a problem, did not say anything of the kind here in the hallway, with only his own guards to witness. Bren felt a little prickling of concern at that, and a need to divert the matter.

"Meanwhile," Bren said, "I will be speaking for the aiji-dowager, and mediating any difficulties of state. But if there are other issues that worry anyone, in her name, I will answer questions." They were not admitting the dowager's presence in the city, not to locals. "She has signed a trade agreement with your lord and with Lord Machigi, which will agitate your eastern neighbor, and she has lent your lord the protection of the Guild so long as he feels it useful. There is no political attachment, but you are now at peace with the Taisigin Marid, and with Lord Machigi's Southern Association. The dowager is aware that Lord Tiajo may be upset to hear it, and that she may continue to try to claim fees and taxes from Senjin. The dowager supports Lord Bregani's contention that these fees are illegal, and have been illegal from the start. It is her understanding that the Guild demands the surrender of fugitives from its own authority, and she calls on Lord Tiajo to comply. Meanwhile she has lent Guild forces to her ally Lord Bregani, to provide security—should your neighbor take exception."

Saigi and his unit listened soberly and stone-faced to that, and Bregani said:

"That is the situation, Saigi-ji. We will have some anxious days ahead, but we will be dissociating from the Dojisigin in all respects. The details are yet to work out, but the Taisigin will trade, and the East *will* ship, and so will the southern Marid, so we shall not be any the worse off in commerce, since the Taisigin will supply the Cobo route; not to mention we shall no longer be paying into the Dojisigi defense fund. I can promise *that* will no longer be a deduction from your salary. Gather the staff, advise them, and let us put things to rights."

No longer a deduction drew sharp attention. Faces betrayed it.

"Nandi-ma." Saigi drew a deep breath and gave a sober, short bow. "What you will."

Banichi asked: "Saigi-nadi. There has been a problem with kidnapping. Relatives of key personnel held hostage. Are there any such cases current?"

"None that I know," Saigi said.

"They exist," Banichi said. "Do not trust where you can avoid it."

"Nandi," Saigi said, with an apprehensive glance at Bregani.

"Say," Bregani said, and Saigi:

"There was a case. The man is dead."

"We have to be alert to the possibility of hostages," Banichi said, "in any Taisigin property we enter. We need to find them, where they exist. That will be a priority. If you have information, we will put it high on the list. Meanwhile we have to secure this building. Is there anyone to your knowledge that might have relatives at issue?"

"No," Saigi said uncertainly, and cast a look around at his own. "Everyone here is trusted. We have inspected and locked all the city offices—" This with a nod to the righthand corridor. "Those are shut. Your residence, nandi-ma—" This with a second look at Bregani and his family. "The assembly room, the great hall, the family residence, all those areas we have sealed off and guarded. The archive, the exhibit hall, all of it—we have held. The northern Guild has moved into the utilities, the broadcast center, the banks, and closed the port road. We have undertaken a control on the residency, the museums, the schools, the library, and our own precinct stations."

"We are very content," Banichi said, "to be a backstop to an efficient local force. If you need reinforcement we will make adjustments, but our first concern now is to see your lord to safety in his own premises. One assumes, nandi, there is a place where we can set up a perimeter, and where you can receive reports and make decisions at leisure."

"Upstairs," Bregani said. "Upstairs and to the left. Our people, our household."

"This is secret," Father said, and laid out a gray oval thing that Cajeiri somewhat recognized, at least that it was somewhat like the communicators on the station, the sort of thing Lord Geigi used.

Cajeiri did not venture to touch it. "This is from Lord Geigi," he said. "Is it about my associates?"

"It is from Lord Geigi," Father said, "but it regards your great-grandmother."

One thing had seemed evident, which he cared about, but now the other was in question, which immediately worried him.

"How?" he asked.

"Lord Geigi has dropped one of his relay stations," Father said. "Sit down, son of mine."

They were in Father's upstairs office, across from his own suite, where meetings happened and things were discussed that were not discussed elsewhere. It was both a familiar place, and a scary place, when Father took that tone. It was rare, nowadays, that he was called in here. But he had been.

Cajeiri sat down. "Is she all right?"

"She is in Koperna. Thus far she is still aboard the train, surrounded by numerous Guild units, possessed of several mortars and various equipment the Guild does not talk about, but say that nothing will approach that train. She is safe enough so long as she stays where she is."

"What are they doing? What is the Guild doing?"

"Protecting her, as ever. That foremost. But that is

not all of it. I have promised to keep you informed. Grandmother has brought Lord Bregani back to his capital, and they have entered with a fair amount of noise and notice. Lord Geigi is now advising us moment to moment what is going on in the region. He claims to be able to see a man walking to market while carrying a basket. This may be exaggeration. It may not."

"One does not think, honored Father, that Geigi would exaggerate that. He can do so many unexpected things."

"And does not need to shock us with his brilliance," Father said. "Fortunately he is on your great-grandmother's side."

"And on ours," Cajeiri said. "Are you able to speak to him directly with this? What does he say?"

"He says that the relay has activated and is performing well, and that no one has approached it, hardly surprising, since there is a train sitting in the vicinity that would discourage all but the most determined. He says that an amphibious unit from Amarja has ventured into the salt marsh that the Dojisigin shares with Senjin, and has attempted to reach a causeway that leads to a hunting lodge. I have asked the Guild to have a look at that."

"And mani," Cajeiri said. "Is there shooting near her? Is she safe?"

"As yet Koperna is quiet as the tombs in winter. We have had to divert a number of passenger trains and strand a handful of passengers in Shejidan, but we are sending sufficient supply by both routes to Koperna, in the case Grandmother might have need of it. And we have stolen back a navy ship that she borrowed. We think one is sufficent to deal with the harbor at Koperna, and we anticipate no difficulty of any sort for Lord Machigi's port at Tanaja, though we will be watching. One *can*, with this, speak directly with Lord Machigi *without* the Messengers' Guild listening in. Or anyone else. I will be speaking directly to your great-grandmother, relayed from the heavens, without a need for the great dish at Mogari-nai, or its keepers. I shall be speaking to her, if she is speaking to me at the moment. Things are fairly much in transition there. And your great-grandmother, will you believe, has put the paidhi-aiji in charge of Koperna, while she does whatever she is minded to do."

"But—" That was astonishing. "Nand' Bren never even manages Najida. Ramaso does that for him."

It was out before he thought, but Father seemed, if anything, amused. "Ah. But he has Banichi, who can talk to Cenedi, who can talk to your great-grandmother, so I am certain they will manage."

That was something, truthfully.

And they could talk, apparently, as directly as they did on the space station, when Lord Geigi would just call somebody and tell them to do something, or one of the techs could report directly, and show Lord Geigi a picture of what was happening.

It was just different.

But it was wrong for Shejidan, nand' Bren said.

And now there was a lander in the Marid. One of Lord Geigi's creatures. It was very, very different than anything that ought to exist on earth. Lord Geigi had made it to help the Guild drive out the Shadow Guild, by relaying messages just like this. They were scary things. And they *would* change the world.

Except Father was in charge of it, giving orders with a thing like those phones, but Geigi had never wanted that to happen.

Once things got loose, Bren had said more than once, once technology was loose, it just kept on growing.

It was a big change.

As scary as the lander itself.

And the Shadow Guild. Wait, he wanted to say. Wait until I am aiji, and I can say what *I* want done.

But that day was, he hoped, far, far in the future, and meanwhile it was all on Father.

"What are we going to do about them?" he asked,

meaning the Shadow Guild, and Father answered, "The phones? We have restricted them to the Assassins' Guild."

Not the Messengers, he thought. The Messengers would not be happy with that idea. They would have a fit. But the Assassins' Guild had their own system, and if it was in *their* hands it was not going to go proliferating—that was a word he had learned from nand' Bren—*proliferating* through everybody's lives.

Meanwhile Lord Geigi was watching over the Marid. Nand' Bren was in charge of Koperna. And mani was safe, with Cenedi, he was sure, surrounded by Guild. It was not as bad as it could be. But—

"Where are you sending the ship?" he asked.

Father gave him a strangely approving look, as if he had solved some strange sort of puzzle.

"You are not sending it back to the straits," Cajeiri said. "Are you?"

"We are sending it to Amarja's harbor," Father said. "And the Dojisigin will just have to consider whether they want to meet it or talk to us."

14

People were waiting in the upstairs of the residency, clan folk and relatives and a few staff, all relieved to see Bregani and his family come up the stairs, a little too forward a crowd for security's liking, and Guild fended off well-wishers who pressed too close. Guild could do nothing about the stares, the misgiving countenances—but Guild predominated here. These folk, in the southern version of court dress, included gray-haired people and younger, a mix of ages, about twenty or so of them, with a scattering of brown-uniformed servants, staring wide-eyed at what arrived, and nobody posing an immediate threat. Saigi's second-in-command had come up with them. Banichi and Algini had stayed downstairs, with the whole city as their immediate concern.

"Nandiin," Saigi called out, lifting his hands for attention. "Your questions in a moment. Lord Bregani is here. Listen to him!"

People had made a little space, jostling one another and trying to see as Bregani lifted his hand high to be seen. "A little quiet!" Bregani said. "We are in good case, here. I trust my cousin Biathi has kept you informed."

"Are the Dojisigi here, nandi?" someone shouted from the back. "Are they coming in?"

"They are not, nandi! If you have heard Biathi's broadcasts, outside of the fact I have *not* been in the city these
last hours—you have heard that I have met with the aiji-
dowager. That is true. You have heard that I have authorized the northern Guild to assist in keeping order. That
is true. You will have heard that we have concluded a
peace with the Taisigin, and *that* is true!"

There were no cheers about it—more a gradual descent to stunned silence.

"Cousins and allies, we shall talk about the details
very soon, but the situation is actually quite simple, and
this is my word on it. No more Dojisigin fees. No more
charges. We shall never again pay the Dojisigin for the
mere privilege of doing business with them, and from
this day forward—actually since last night—we are in a
mutually beneficial trade partnership with the East, and
with the three lordships of the southern Marid, as well
as Hasjuran atop the escarpment, and, potentially, with
the entire aishidi'tat *without* fees—in short, with the
whole world *except* the Dojisigin."

That produced a little undertone of voices, which
Bregani did not allow to continue.

"We stand to be freer, safer, and better off economically with the new arrangement. I have signed documents
we shall discuss in detail, which lay out the barest framework of a continuation of rail to the south, *excluding* the
Dojisigin, which will not make them happy. Not that they
will feel excluded: they have historically rejected a rail
link—but because I intend to keep northern Guild forces
in the city for the interim and tell the lord of the Dojisigin
to go look for other markets. This is not a decision I have
made lightly, but Tiajo's demands have made it clear
there is no satisfying her until she has picked Senjin bare,
and we have no ships but her ships and no trade but her
trade. Dojisigin rejected a railroad years ago, now we
have it, and Tiajo sees our use of it as a trade she would
like to stop, or to tax, or to *own*. We have had to accept
her agents operating openly in the port and here in the

capital, her trade offices are beds of spies, and the number of her citizens who go where they like among us is an intimidation we no longer have to bear. As of the hour I authorized the northern Guild to move into the city, those elements have been made to feel unwelcome. We are permitting them the port, for now. But we cannot say this will continue. There is another large Guild presence between us and the Dojisigin, a living wall to prevent her expressing her displeasure."

That caused a stir, and a general open stare at Bregani's northern Guild bodyguard.

"If Lord Tiajo wants to talk," Bregani said loudly, "she has a telephone. And there is little at this point that she can say that we need regard, nandiin. She no longer has power over us. We are safe. For the first time in two generations, we are our own people. We have a *far* better bargain with our new allies than with the perpetual state of terror the Dojisigin have inflicted on us. With me, guarantee of the dowager's good will, and the firmness of our agreement . . . are the lord of Najida, Bren, paidhi-aiji, negotiator for the aiji-dowager. And Machigi, lord of the Taisigin, head of the Association of the Southern Marid. Also with us is another esteemed guest, the candidate for Ajuri, Nomari-nadi, of the Padi Valley Association of the aishidi'tat."

There was a scattering of verbal applause, a thin one at first, and then a little more enthusiastic, as Bregani seemed to have said all he had to say. But then Bregani claimed the floor again and said, "We are to go into the audience chamber, where we are requested to stay while security makes a general sweep of the building and premises, which may take some time. Security discourages us from moving about the building or going anywhere alone until we can be sure. There are tables, there are chairs. I note that, at the side of the hall, we have a number of staff to help us, and I think we can manage tea and brandy, if no scoundrel has made off with it."

That levity produced both motion from the servants

and a little lightness in mood. "Come," Bregani said, and led a general movement from the huge, carpeted assembly area into an adjacent, still very large chamber, with blown-glass chandeliers, all of which had electric light, and frescoed walls, medallions showing sea, and ships, and painted processions of people doubtless important in the history of the house and of Senjin. There was a scatter of white chairs and a couple of tables at the far side of the assembly area, and those began to be brought in and made available to whoever claimed them.

"Two corridors," Jago noted under her breath, using the new communicator, "left and right of a low speaker's platform." She paused, and said. "Lord Bregani's family apartment is the end of the righthand corridor. Several others, family, have residences to the left.—Rani-ji," she said to Narani, who was close at hand, "I shall stand here. Can we arrange chairs and one table for nand' Bren?"

Mild confusion was the state of affairs, with servants rolling in two large circular tables and setting them up at apparent random. Bregani and his family claimed one, with several of the older officials. Chairs proliferated, more than enough.

"We have three significant exposures in this area," Jago said to the communicator, "the doors we can close and the two hallways we cannot. We are putting the hallways off-limits, and stationing a man in each."

Tano said, at Bren's elbow, "Word is on the other channel that there are six residencies, all cleared, the servants' passages all locked from this side." Guild had been moving through those two halls fairly actively, while the tables were being brought in. "We have two public accommodations off this room, over there—" Tano indicated twin doors disguised in the mural of a hedge on the far side. "Which should be sufficient. There is a foyer to each, a water source which we will test and clear. The righthand hall has two doors, both opening into Bregani's official residence, and we will clear that. Lords of the subclans hold the lefthand hall, and they have been in continuous occupancy, but it is a situation which we do not trust without searching those rooms, and we will include Lord Bregani's rooms unless you have other orders."

"I do not."

"We have two units with equipment to do a proper clearance, and they are both working downstairs and in the basements in an order Banichi has set. He says the lower levels are extensive and the lords' comfort is secondary to safety. They have no security of their own. Building security is not established." Tano paused. Then; "The local guard, with some argument, has agreed to stand down and bed down for a rest in the Office of Public Works, a watch on each other, if nothing else. Their commander has confided to Banichi several names he himself questions. *Only* Guild is providing security in the rest of the building, as we set up electronic perimeters. We are relying on our own food and water in this room. We have enough."

"Good," Bren said.

"They argue," Jago said, with a motion of the eyes toward the cluster of minor lords around Bregani. "But these people are scared. Justifiably. There are those who do business with the Dojisigi, but as Lord Bregani indicated, the Dojisigi have done fairly well as they please, freer here than in their own capital. They thrive on illegal fees and charges. Lord Bregani's power has been very little where it comes to shoring up security. Shadow Guild agents have not been frequent or public visitors, but when they have come, they have fairly well gotten access where they want, taken whom they want, and answered no questions. Murder has silenced complaint. All this, from the general briefing, on our way in."

Compliance, while the threat was present, or possible. And they themselves were the threatening strangers now.

"One understands." One also had a troubling insight

into Bregani's compliance with the dowager's proposal, and yes, it was in pattern, though Bregani had made his own conditions and negotiated fairly well, caught as he had been between two demanding forces and the dowager's own plan. And now Bregani was at one table with Murai and his daughter and the people who made the decisions—and the trade-offs—in his district, and had to explain to them how the northern Guild was going to change their lives, and what moves they had to make next to stay alive.

One wondered if *trust* and *stable economy* were words these people would understand in the northern sense, not just now, but somewhere in the future of all this maneuvering of powers.

Meanwhile they had their table, the one perquisite of rank he felt he did need for the writing he might have to do and for a space they could clear of listeners when they were communicating with Banichi. Jeladi moved it in, with Tano's help. Bren set his teacup down and Jago moved a chair in. Tano brought two more. They were set up in state.

And in the relief with which people received their lord, the way Lord Bregani dealt with them, insisting on no protocol, one began to get the temperature of the place, much more than Bregani had given it to them in his negotiating with the dowager. Machigi had not exaggerated the situation in Senjin, and the extremity of Lord Bregani's situation. But the straightforwardness of the man was an unexpected asset.

"Tell Banichi we have the doors shut now, everyone settled, and we shall hold here. Is there any word from Cenedi?"

"None yet," Jago said. "We should have hot water soon. We have brought the means to heat it. We have a month's supply of tea, and sandwiches at least for tonight."

"I shall stay right here," he said, "out of trouble."

Jago went off to talk to Narani. Bindanda arrived and

leaned on the chair she had left. "Nandi. A considerable number of staff are reported in the kitchens and halls downstairs, and Guild is interviewing them. I have some expertise with that. Narani will stay at your call. Jeladi and I will look over the situation and see if we can provide a certified kitchen, sort out the servants, and tap into staff knowledge of the situation."

Servants saw things. Undoubtedly. And Bindanda, Narani, Jeladi, all ranking civilian staff, were plainclothes Guild, not the combative sort, but very, very good at what they did as staff, and also very good at the less common things they did.

"Go," he said. "Do. And take care down there."

Bindanda laid a hand on his midriff. Not at all soft, Bindanda's bulk. "I shall stay in touch."

With that, Bindanda moved off to talk to Narani and Jeladi, and things proceeded.

He was, thank God, well-served, but set in charge of the operation? He regularly depended on his aishid to tell him where to walk, when to duck and when to breathe. The dowager wanted this place not to be a murder scene before morning.

He tracked things. That he could do. He watched the indications in Bregani's family, in his converse with other clans, assertive and meeting their assertiveness with a frown, but not yielding; Murai was of the same stamp, and teenaged Husai, at the same table, was watching everything, eyes moving from one speaker to the other as she followed what was said while remaining remarkably unreadable. There was a mind in that one.

Machigi was holding a quieter, head lowered discussion with his Taisigi bodyguard, while he pretended to be interested in a lowly water bottle, turning and turning before him. Few clues from that one, or his four rough-looking bodyguards, men that would look at home on the docks of Tanaja. And Nomari—

Nomari could have sat down. There were chairs enough. Instead he stood, looking generally uncomfort-

able, against a square pillar that met the wall, midway in
the room. His aishid was with him, and there were chairs,
but his aishid did not sit while he stood. He leaned there
watching the organization of chaos, perhaps uneasy, perhaps watching someone or something. It was an untidy
position, and an uncomfortable one. His attention
seemed most often in Bregani's direction.

Or was it Husai?

Invite Nomari to sit with him—when his table was the
local center of sensitive information? It would call unwanted attention to Nomari, and in truth, Nomari had
no place here . . . or none that he could assert.

Narani brought a cup of tea, among the first made.
Bren took it, a simple paper cup, nothing elegant, and
sipped it in relief. Servants—there were several, locals—
began to move about, preparing service for those in
their care. One served Nomari, and his guards, and he
drank it standing. So must they.

Tano sat down with a cup. "Banichi reports the port
situation. There are two Dojisigin freighters, one in the
process of lading, which is now stopped. Both are taking
aboard a number of passengers. The Guild is watching,
but not preventing their boarding. Whether the ships
will be permitted to leave is under consideration."

It was Cenedi's problem.

"The more Dojisigin folk we can get out of Senjin,"
Bren said, "the better for us, I think."

"We think so," Tano said. "Banichi says there are calls
from various officials wanting to inquire about conditions
here. The mayor has wanted to come in, and there are a
number of spouses and relatives of the several subclans
wanting to return. Banichi intends to admit them with
some questions."

Jago came over and sat down. "We are receiving
reports from various regions of the city. Things are relatively quiet—some instance of theft from several grocers,
but nothing beyond it. An isolated instance of people
fortifying a street with public vehicles, but nothing threat-

ening us. Their motive seems to be defense. One fire, apparently someone attempting to destroy records, in an import shop, under investigation. Several drunk and disorderly, confined to one apartment building, not on the street, but notable in the general quiet. In various places, we have complaints from windows that they are in need of various things. We are beginning to let grocers and goods shops open in two districts, to make deliveries to apartment blocks and individual dwellings. We are allowing alcohol as one of the goods, but limiting the quantity of it."

"No sign of Shadow Guild."

"None thus far. The port road is wide open, despite published advisement otherwise—which we have hoped would discourage the honest and let the desperate grow desperate enough, but we are not making arrests, no matter the status of the person wanting to reach the port. There is also general street by street clearance going on, starting with the north and the water plant, and then on into residential areas. We are getting, apparently, general compliance."

"No violence."

"Not to speak of," Jago said. "A few accidents, a few burns, nine arrests, a number of cautions, but general compliance. These people are afraid. They are mortally afraid. We have had vehicles up and down the streets advising people to remain calm, and informing them that if they have an emergency that they may get emergency services. The phone system is functioning, and we have set a guard on them. The city has five babies born in the last number of hours, one of them in a hardware storeroom, now in hospital. And regrettably two people have died since the shelter order went into effect, but in a city this size, that is actually less than ordinary. This is not our management reporting the details: this is the commander of the original Guild force. And the people have been remarkably restrained."

"One wishes them well," Bren murmured, the usual

thing one said, but it was a small, weak thing to say when one was in some measure responsible.

At least, to his observation, and in this room, a number of local officials and clan lords who attended Bregani were huddled together, talking quietly and apparently constructively. There was a double, even a triple ring of chairs of persons trying to hear or participate in the discussion.

And finally, to his relief, Nomari had found a chair and sat down, with his aishid, exchanging a few words.

They all were tired. Tension ebbed, and energy went with it.

"The district is getting messages," Jago relayed from Banichi, in a periodic report, "communications from officials in the towns and villages downcoast. We have assured them the Taisigi are not invading, and they should continue to rely on the broadcast center for information. Some city folk who have run to the country are calling the information services, and getting the same message. We are still holding firm on the shelter order, but we will be giving a neighborhood by neighborhood release once the situation in the port is quieted."

"At least it gives people a foreseeable release," Bren said.

"Even so," Jago said. "There is an identification card system, which may be of some use, though forgery is likely. There are no photographs."

"Lord Bregani's cousin is continuing broadcasts," Tano said. "Repeating the same message, that Bregani is in charge."

"Which now is true," Bren said.

"We have to see," Jago said. "Either he is or not. He alone signed the agreement. He knew what it would take."

Meaning his ability to lead, his position as lord of Senjin, rested on his personality, his leadership, his record, and the character of the people who upheld him. He was asserting that, over there at that table, with people who were considering the risk of their own lives in the process.

It said something, that that discussion was quiet, respectful and attentive. People were afraid. The Shadow Guild had made a name for itself. It was feared. Having uniformed northern Guild let loose on them had to have terrified people, but the broadcast from Bregani's cousin had kept saying trust Bregani.

Clearly these people had that or Tiajo for their choice.

The hierarchy had to hold in order for Senjin to stay together, the whole order of man'chi was potentially challenged, larger authority to smaller, all the way down to the households. Clans had subclans, subclans knew their houses, and houses knew their households. Everyone belonged, all the way up, everyone moved together or it all broke down, starting with a fracture somewhere, and a faithless breach.

That was what the Shadow Guild's tactic was aimed at, finding a way to break that most basic of bonds . . . as in Murai-daja's bodyguard, when a man named Tenjin had known his family had been taken hostage, their lives for his cooperation. Tenjin might not have shot Murai, to whom he had man'chi. But being expected to spend his life to disrupt what was going on, even to sabotage or assassinate someone dealing with Bregani . . . that might have satisfied the Shadow Guild. That was the intent behind the tactic.

Had Tenjin been so enterprising as to get off a warning to his controllers that they were being taken north, to Hasjuran? Had he possibly told them it was a call from the aiji-dowager?

Had he been handed a target?

Possibly not. Possibly he had simply reached a desperate stage in his situation, divorced even from his unit, having to think how Bregani's return as Ilisidi's ally would affect his family being held hostage . . .

And that was the unit Bregani had trusted instead of taking, say, Saigi . . . with him.

"Bregani took Tenjin's unit with him as absolutely trusted," he said to Tano. "He took a Farai unit. Did he leave a Senjin unit that routinely guarded him? A human cannot quite judge that. Do we assume that the unit he left in place is Saigi's?"

Tano took a moment answering. "Your aishid has discussed that. Certainly he wanted reliable people to hold the residency safe. And reliable people to guard his cousin and maintain control of the broadcast center. He put his own guard on duty here, and a second unit with his cousin at the broadcast center. Both held man'chi, and still do. But it is a question . . . again involving the Farai."

"Dare we ask him—politely?"

"You might. Banichi might."

"I do not think a human can."

Tano considered that a moment. "Perhaps not."

"I think it a question we should ask," he said.

"I shall relay that."

"Good," he said. He was not used to operating with his aishid in two places, but it was what it needed to be. And it was going fairly well, counting that the assembly hall was a large gathering of black uniforms, with himself in one place and Bregani's knot of concerned officials in another.

They looked in his direction now and again, furtively, none of these local folk ever having seen a human, none of them ever expecting, surely, to see either him or Machigi, who drew his own share of stares. It was his job to look absolutely neutral, absolutely involved with his own group. That was all. It was all up to Bregani, who could not look coerced or dependent.

Eventually Algini called to say they had messages from a group of staffers and family members, located, some of them apparently, at a hotel, and that they were sending letters upstairs, as directed to various people in the residency.

A collection—a quite large collection of rolled or

folded papers—was brought up in a message basket, and handed to Tano, who, being Tano, began to distribute them himself, seeking out names, which, being Tano, he was very likely remembering, face by face—to an anxious reception. Some were for servants, and several of those were sent down to the kitchens. The rest were for the lesser lords and their staffs, who were beyond anxious to read them, and anxious to reply.

And anxious to reply.

"These people will want paper, Ladi-ji," Bren said, "and writing supplies. I do not suppose we have an office of the Messengers."

Being in the Marid, they did not.

But, with minor inquiry, there was a similar office headquartered in the other side of the residency, and since that office was also in charge of the phone system and the broadcast center, it was one of the few offices on premises that was open, however understaffed at present.

Asking the broadcast center to request all staff of the communications center in the residency to report to work was the matter of a phone call, getting the message delivery personnel reporting to their office was a series of phone calls, and getting a list of persons safe and present in the residency broadcast to the city at large was the matter of a sheet of paper being circulated in the assembly hall and another in the kitchens.

Providing a message exchange was not necessarily the Guild's driving priority, but the aiji-dowager had put the paidhi in charge, and relieving people of worry seemed a good forward step.

The broadcast center had already, as a matter of Koperna's own preparedness, been broadcasting places to call to report elderly or sick persons who might need help. Fire and medical personnel, exempt from the shelter order, were handling those calls. That was good.

And shortly after, perhaps inspired by the exchange of information, perhaps requested by Bregani or Murai, a number of servants came up from the kitchens with trays of sandwiches and teacakes and sealed bottles of wine.

So there was, unexpectedly, a sort of lunch. Along with the sandwiches and water meant for Guild personnel and for Bren, Bindanda sent Jeladi up to report that the kitchens were in decent order, staff was at work and beginning, through the phone system, to recall absent personnel.

Bren was relieved. Finally. They all were tired, all who had been on the train. Sleep last night had been a case of moments caught when they could get them. With only minor movement in the hall, with many of the Guild taking the opportunity to rest now, some in chairs, some quite unapologetically stretched out on the floor, he tried to catch a very small nap—sitting upright.

A shadow crossed the light. He blinked. A Senjini servant had come near, bowed, asked, nervously: "Lord Bregani asks will you join him, nand' paidhi?"

Join him. That was the table with all the chairs, where not only Bregani and family were seated, but the subclans, and the elderly heads of Senjin and Farai, the latter of whom Bren had engaged in two fairly heated—though polite—exchanges of letters, in the matter of his estate, and most recently, of his Bujavid apartment.

The lord's name was Agahi, a withered little fellow with a greatly receded hairline.

Bren went to that table, bowed politely to Bregani and his family. "Nandi. Daji. Nandiin."

"Nandi," the general reply was, dispassionate and careful. It was Agahi who had reason to worry in the encounter, under the circumstances, Bren said to himself. And he was not going to give cause for unpleasantness.

Bren took the provided chair, facing Bregani, Murai, Husai, and Madisu, Bregani's grandfather, and Agahi, among others.

Machigi, not given to sociality, but apparently invited, also came over and took a seat, typically not smiling, but not frowning either.

There was tea. That was the social cue. There was to be tea. Polite discourse.

Senjini servants set up cups and went about with teapots, while the rest of the room was all black uniforms and conspicuous weaponry, and the majority of non-black dress was collected about this one table, servants, lords, and staff, green and blues and a murky red.

Tea went the rounds only of those actually at the table, those of highest rank, and the talk was, perforce, thank you, oh, indeed, and not much more.

Bren pretended a sip, unassured, when at the mercy of another staff's preparation, but the smell was proper, a blend he knew; and others were drinking. If no one fell over, Bren decided, the tea must be safe enough from additives. He let Machigi take a sip, and failing reaction, he took a sip of his own, then added four heaping spoons of sugar, not without the notice of the other side of the table. If it was a southern test of endurance, he was not ashamed to fail.

There were introductions, himself, and Machigi, both of rank, and then of the subclans. Agahi of Farai was one. Madisu. The minor clans of Juni, Lusi, Prsegi presented themselves, along with some minor clans Bren had never seen on the maps.

"There were worrisome moments," Bregani said, setting down his cup, and with a look toward Juni and the others, on his right: "You have asked, Juni, why our guard is Shejidani. I left my principal guard to protect the residency, another unit to protect the broadcast center; and Murai's guard to go with us, for what it could do, did it come to that. And now with nand' Bren to witness, I will say we had a very sad security issue. One of Murai's guard is under duress, and we have withdrawn them all from duty. I cannot complain of the courtesy and attention of the aiji-dowager's guard, or the service of the unit we were provided. Nand' Bren, I have told them that the aiji-dowager is here, in the city."

It was not information they had advertised, and a servant was, at that moment, within earshot. So, well, the news was out.

But whatever Bregani had chosen to spread through the city had been Bregani's choice, since they had not restricted him in the least, and possibly—knowing Bregani's nerve—it was one important choice he had made in presenting the news of their agreement. It *might* make the agreement more palatable, that the dowager had come to Koperna in person. It *might* make Machigi's presence a little more welcome, if welcome could describe that situation. *All* the signers of the new association had come down, none returning to safety and none working from a distance.

"I have also told my people," Bregani continued, "that the northern Guild has taken measures to protect this capital and the port, at *my* invitation, as a resource mentioned in the new agreement. The northern Guild, the parent guild, is the *only* force that could authoritatively counter the Dojisigi Guild, and that we have not seen any overt action from them . . . the fact that they are demonstrably *running* from the Shejidani Guild and avoiding encounter, is evidence we have chosen the better side. I have enquired as to the situation in the city, and I am glad to say the streets are quiet, there has been no gunfire in the city. The port is another story, but that is where we have two Dojisigi ships and a concentration of Dojisigi interests to concentrate the problem. We are also assured that the shelter order will be released sometime tomorrow, and normalcy can return. Change is happening, nandiin, at this moment, it is happening. And it will continue until Senjin and all our territories are secure. At this moment we are declaring the hunting range we share with the Dojisigin will be divided, and no Dojisigi presence will be tolerated this side of the river Haugi. We may negotiate a more liberal view later, but until further notice, our people will not cross the river and Dojisigi calling themselves hunters or any other thing will not be tolerated on our side of it. Nand' Bren, paidhi-aiji, will you kindly explain in full the terms of the agreement?"

There were nods, slight frowns, nervous looks. A triple layer of chairs was about the table. Tano and Jago were there, within reach, certainly within their ability to act. But it was not the Guild who had to settle two centuries of distrust of humans.

"Your lord has agreed to the building of a spur of the rail down to Tanaja, using materials supplied by the aiji-dowager, and he has committed to maintain a defensive organization around that operation. The aiji-dowager is within her rights, as a lord of the aishidi'tat, to call on the Assassins' Guild for defense of that agreement against any outside power, and that she has done. Within the interpretation of the agreement, she put a Guild force in position and verbally extended to Lord Bregani the option to deploy the Guild in Koperna, for its protection for as long as Lord Bregani sees fit. Had Lord Bregani declined, be it clear, they would not have deployed. Should Lord Bregani request them to withdraw at this point, they will withdraw. Beyond that, the Guild has no office in Koperna, nor has any authorization to establish one. If you desire one, you would need to negotiate that with the Guild office in Shejidan. There are provisions in the agreement for defense of the project; there are provisions for the dowager to supply and protect the railroad. Beyond that, I yield to Lord Machigi."

"Simple," Machigi said. "We are henceforth trading partners, and two harbors in want of ships. We present ourselves as allies. And with us come the Dausigin and the Sungeni. The Dojisigin have no allies left in the Marid. We can trade with the aishidi'tat by ship and by rail, as convenient. We have a shipyard. We are preparing to build steel trading ships, with options for engines and sail, and we have the advantage of weather information gathered on the space station and passed directly to our ships."

That produced a stir of doubt.

"True," Bren said. "Peaceful commerce and mutual cooperation is to everyone's advantage . . . often in unexpected ways. The dowager has the full cooperation of both sides of the space station. And from their high vantage, detecting a squall line is easy. Your countryside as well as your ships at sea will have the benefit of eyes on the weather."

"We shall be navigating the Southern Ocean," Machigi said. "And ask the Dausigin or the Sungeni whether the Taisigin is a fair partner in trade and whether their ships are free of our port. Yours will be welcome."

"You are four-fifths of the Marid," Bren said as Machigi finished. "You have been paying nearly a third of your trade in fees of one kind and another. The use of rail in the whole aishidi'tat is a reasonable fee based on distance, should you decide to trade as a member state, which, counting the size of the whole network, is a considerable market . . . and your responsibility for maintenance is on your own rail. My own district of Najida finds it a fair bargain."

"This is too good," a lord said. "They will not do this."

"We will do it," Bren said, "and the size of your commitment right now, nandiin, nadiin, is simply Lord Machigi's link to your railyard. Expanding in steps toward the larger system will be perfectly acceptable, at your own discretion. I know the lord of Hasjuran is excited at the thought of direct trade with the northern Marid, on his own. But there is nothing in the agreement about that. You would negotiate it with him; and to negotiate trade with the whole system, you would negotiate with the aiji in Shejidan, and specifically with the Transportation Guild."

The lords were looking now at Bregani, who nodded.

"This is my understanding," Bregani said.

"Fees," one said.

"It adds about ten percent for Najida's goods to reach, say, the midlands," Bren said. "That is the example I can give you. One understands you have been paying more to trade with the Dojisigin."

"A lot more," Lusi said. "But is this in writing?"

"Agreements can be had," Bren said. "We are certainly not short of wax or ribbon."

"All this is ahead of the fact," Lusi said, "that Tiajo is going to send everything she has onto us. And in no short time, either."

"They have to get here," Bren said, "and there is one more Guild force poised on their border, and the aiji's navy is now in the Marid, prepared to defend you against such a move."

"Navy ships!"

"They moved from the straits," Bren said, "anticipating the trouble that might result from negotiations with Senjin. They are a precaution."

"What *is* this?" the head of Prsegi asked. "A northern invasion?"

"I am sure the dowager will not remain against your will. But she does not move without force sufficient for the operation."

"You understand," Bregani said, toying with his cup, "how it is to deal with her. But the situation is that simple, and I am not willing to die or to see Senjin annexed to the Dojisigin. We have hobbled along for years as Cosadi's buffer against the Taisigin and Cosadi's buffer against the aishidi'tat, and the Dojisigin have perched on the iron and the tin and a number of other resources we have to beg for, and the wrath of Amarja if we attempt to buy any of these goods elsewhere. With the rail proposed, and with this agreement, we have access to the whole continent's goods. This is not a disadvantageous bargain. The disadvantageous bargain is continuing to stand by our uncousinly cousin in Amarja, who has imprisoned her own father and her uncle and assassinates anyone in her government who appears to have a shred of common sense. Northerner intruders, the worst kind of northerners, have propped her up as their sole claim on legitimacy, and I am done with it. Will I break kinship with Tiajo, a murderer of her own household? Gladly. Will I risk you, my true cousins, whether by blood or service? I will protect you by using the northern Guild's services until we can arm ourselves. I have done what we should have done long ago had we ever had a chance. I *thank* Lord Machigi for his part in arranging this."

It probably surprised Machigi, who was not accustomed to gratitude, nor indeed, had earned that much of it.

"I thank Lord Bregani," Machigi said in a low voice, "for being outstandingly reasonable."

God, the irony therein encompassed, with a feud that had spanned *over* two hundred bloody years. Machigi had everything he wanted, and Bregani had a chance at a longer life than Tiajo was apt to afford him. The aishidi'tat *had* to commit the Guild down here, with Lord Geigi's watchfulness and the advantage of modern technology, to the hilt. Bren resolved that, if he had any power to persuade.

Pity was that Ilisidi had not had the pleasure of hearing it. But the pleasure of hearing it went with a risk they were not willing for her to run; and there was danger in too much good will up here in the residency, too much agreement from these people nodding acceptance of what Bregani said, too much agreement from people lifelong accustomed to nodding acceptance of Tiajo or anybody else who had force available. It was not a safe or necessarily truthful place. And would not be until Tiajo was out of the question.

Then . . . then they had to worry about Machigi keeping his end of the bargains. All of them. Senjin needed time. It needed the iron substance of rail traffic, bringing in prosperity, doing what they promised.

"Our internal associations," Lusi said, "will not be disturbed by the agreement."

"We do not join the aishidi'tat," Juni said.

"That is not a requirement," Bren said. "Nandiin, I have read the documents. In point of fact I can *provide* the documents. You will find nothing in them to your disadvantage, and no rights in Senjin claimed by the aiji-dowager or by the aishidi'tat. The provisions are simply for the building of rail to Tanaja, and mutual defense of it."

"What does the dowager get?" Juni asked bluntly.

"The favor of the guilds," Bren said, the Shejidani guilds being fairly far removed from the interest of the Marid, excepting Transportation, excepting occasionally the Physicians or the Treasurers. "The Assassins bluntly want the outlaws removed. That issue is between the Guild and the Dojisigin. It *is* their objective, ultimately, to remove that force from Lord Tiajo's support, after which, unless you employ the Guild and File Intent, Tiajo will not be a Guild concern. Your welfare will be, however, so long as you remain within the agreement with the dowager, and it is a matter relevant to the railroad."

"If Tiajo falls," Bregani said, "so much the better. Even if the lordship has to pass out of Cosadi's bloodline, so be it."

That brought its own silence. The people at the table, these lords of the subclans, heard the ruling lord of Senjin, say that in the presence of the senior lord of Senjin, who, silent through the entire conversation, now said:

"It may indeed have to go out of the house of Cosadi. I would not wish the rule of the Dojisigin on Husai."

Eyes all shifted to the girl, the teenaged girl, who was the heir of Senjin. "Great-grandfather," Husai said. "No. *I* could not. I would not."

"Nor should you," the old man said. "Nor should Tiajo have taken it. But it is a thought we shall need to have, if she goes down. The clans should choose—from the full range of choices that are *left* inside the Dojisigin."

Canny, Bren thought. If not Cosadi's bloodline, or

even Senjin clan, if there was no candidate of age, it would be somebody of one of the clans, several of which spanned the border. Farai was one. Juni, Lusi, Prsegi, the lot of them. There was power to be had. And Cosadi's lineage was down to Husai, whose parents did not want her in that position.

"It is to consider," Bregani said. "I certainly do not support it for our daughter."

"Tiajo will not step down," Lusi said.

"Doubtful," Juni said. "She is bound to die."

"I am not engaged with this discussion," Bren said. "I am not qualified, and the dowager I represent has not provided me a position on the question. I ask you excuse me."

"Likewise," Machigi said.

"Nandiin," Bregani said by way of acknowledgment, and they both left the table, with their respective bodyguards.

"It will be interesting," Machigi said to him as they moved away.

"My thanks, nandi," Bren said. "My deepest thanks for your assistance."

"We should not be seen to converse," Machigi said in a low voice, and gave him a bow as well.

Machigi was right. There was ink on paper, and wax and ribbons enough, but now the senior clan, the name-clan of Senjin and the house of Cosadi, of ill fame in the north, now had to deal with the subclans inconveniently strewn on both sides of that salt marsh, in two clans' territories, and satisfy them. That process could not be helped by seeing an infelicity of two, the dowager's representative in private conversation with a new ally who had been Senjin's lifelong enemy.

They separated, Machigi with his escort to the middle of the large hall, Bren with Jago and Tano further toward the doors. Bren sought his chair at the table, which no one else had claimed, and felt as if he had run a race for his life—exhausted, absolutely exhausted in the rush of choosing arguments through a field of broken glass.

They had not lost the agreement.

The subclans were now considering their advantages.

And already planning how they might be rid of Tiajo.

A servant came near, carrying a tray with a decanter and glasses.

"Brandy, nand' paidhi?"

He was tempted. Mortally. But there was business to do and the man was not his servant, not Jeladi, not Narani, nor sent by Bindanda.

"No, nadi, thank you."

He sat still and shut his eyes a moment, and all he could see was his compartment on the train, the fairly comfortable bed there, which was not accessible from here. The city streets, deserted. The high-walled residency.

Geigi's lander coming down, a monster from the skies, supposed to guarantee peace, or at least open a conversation their enemies could not hear.

He wished he could have a lengthy private conversation with Tabini at the moment.

And he could actually do that—but Ilisidi would not take it kindly, and would close him off, which would end his usefulness.

No, he wanted just to sit with his aishid, with people he absolutely trusted, and talk over the situation, but in view of the recent conference, and people who might be observing him to see how independent he was, they would not even take a chair beside him. They were right. In public, in a strange place, with diplomatic rules now in place, they were on duty and on guard. Jago and Tano would not have let him take that brandy, had he not refused it himself.

Nomari, still over there near his pillar in relative seclusion, was likewise protected, though not likely a specific target. He sat, they sat; and he was among people, at least his aishid, that he might have begun to trust.

He was no part of the business at Bregani's table, and was here only because, Bren suspected, Cenedi had wanted nobody left aboard the Red Train who was not either under arrest—like Murai's aishid—or entirely trusted, as were Guild or known staff.

One could not blame Cenedi for handing him Nomari. But it was a tedious long wait for a young man fairly well forgotten in the deals that were being made.

And tedium was not only Nomari's lot. It was all a matter of waiting, now—waiting for the Guild to have done its work, waiting for night to come down on the city, and things to get perhaps a little chancier, since Bregani's defection from Tiajo was no longer in doubt, the number of Guild in the city had doubled, and tonight might be the last chance for any Dojisigi still in Koperna to get out.

15

There was a family dinner, just Father, and Mother, and Cajeiri, and it was quiet and cheerful—Great-grandmother had gotten safely to Koperna, and there was fighting, but not where mani was.

Cook had worked hard, perhaps because Father had been working into the night, on sandwiches and tea. There were spicy dishes and sweet, all in the first course, and there were five, counting the custard dessert that was one of Father's favorites.

Cajeiri had to think to holidays to remember such a supper, and no one had been angry, that was the best thing. Father had *not* gotten a phone call, and that was another.

And Mother told Father what a good conversation they had had, which might have been embarrassing—well, it was embarrassing, but it was what Cajeiri hoped Father would hear. He was fed full and could not have eaten another helping of custard. He would have been happy to be dismissed to bed as usual, and he might have slept better than usual since things were going so well.

But then Mother and Father, who usually retired for brandy, motioned for him to come, and took him into the sitting room with them.

"He may have a drop," Mother said, and the servant, who was Dima, and one that Father favored, prepared a brandy glass mostly of icewater and a little flavor, and served it as he served Father's and Mother's brandy.

"The news," Father said, after they had all had a sip, "from Lord Topari is that they have found a body they cannot identify, frozen solid—they have had weather."

That was a fairly gruesome start.

"An outsider, then," Mother said.

"There was a paper pinned to the man. It said, *He will not be missed in Hasjuran.* That was all."

"Seeming to say," Mother said, "that he is foreign."

"It would seem," Father said. "It is not Grandmother's way of doing things. She would have dropped him on Topari's steps and phoned him to say so. No. The handwriting, I am told, was excellent. And had some northern quirks. We also know nand' Bren did have a contact from a person you may recall, son of mine. One Homura."

That was scary. "He was the Assassin the Shadow Guild sent after Uncle."

"A very good memory."

"One is not likely to forget. Do you think he is the man who would not be missed in Hasjuran?"

"No, one rather thinks he is the one who left the note."

The custard was not sitting very well at the moment. "There is Homura, and there is Momichi. They hid in Uncle's basement, and they were supposed to assassinate him. They came over from the Kadagidi estate, through the hedge, and they were supposed to kill Uncle, but I was there, with my associates; and nand' Bren, and Great-grandmother, and they turned themselves in. The Shadow Guild was holding their partners hostage. They said they were sorry and Great-grandmother and nand' Bren let them go. They swore man'chi to nand' Bren."

"And one may have been true to that," Father said. "The dead man was not Dojisigi. And he was not Homura. We are trying to identify him—or the Guild is. He may have been who sabotaged the transformer."

"And Homura killed him." Mani was fond of saying there were no coincidences in politics, just reasons that stood close together. There was too much here trying to stand on the same paving-stone. "Why was *he* there?"

"A good question," Mother said. "But a lot of very strange things have come out of the Ajuri basement. People are related who might not seem to be related, and people were maneuvered into positions they might not want known. Blackmail and threat go far, far back, before your grandfather's time."

That was his Ajuri grandfather, who had been clan lord for a time, before he was assassinated.

"Son of mine," Mother said, "for more than a hundred years, even before Shishogi took office, there was a problem in Ajuri, much the same as took your grandfather. *And* my mother."

There was a gentle rap at the door. Father's major domo interrupted, saying, "Aiji-ma, there is a call wanting you."

That was how things always ended.

But Father said, "Take the message. I shall deal with it."

And Father stayed, saying, "Son of mine, your mother has a thing to say tonight, and we should both hear it."

"This," Mother said. "Ajuri has a great deal to make up for and needs a leader who will take that as a personal charge. Nomari may become that leader, but he will need help, and advice. He cannot be left alone to deal with Ajuri's problems, and he will need experienced protection. Trouble will try its best, and he cannot be handed that office and left to survive on his own. He needs Uncle's advice, which he seems disposed to take. He will need your father's. And he will need your great- grandmother's."

"I hope he is all right with Great-grandmother. I hope she is not too hard on him."

"She will question him and she will push him hard, I have no doubt. And I am glad she is testing him."

That was not what he expected from Mother, not at all. "You do believe him."

"I believe who he is. Yes. But she will not. She will show him what he is getting into until he shows her what he is. Listen, son of mine. When I was young, like you, I had a fair sense for things not as they should be. And when I was growing up, like you, I stood on the outside of doors that I dared not open. I sat in rooms where people cast looks at each other that I could not read. I know how it is when threat invades the sitting room, when you cannot name what it is that people are talking about, but you have the sense that things are very wrong. I was absolutely excluded from that basement when I was there. But I knew, I knew that answers to my life lay on the other side of that door. And I am learning things now that make sense of those years. I know that my mother, your grandmother, Uncle's sister, was indeed murdered. That my father was complicit in bringing her to the spot where she died. Oh, I think he knew what he was doing. He regretted it, but he did it. He stole me, a new-born, and took me to Ajuri. He told me lies about Uncle, which I now disbelieve. I have, I know, a reputation as, to say the least, as weak, flighty, light-minded . . . no, do not interrupt me, son of mine. I was back and forth between Ajiden and Tirnamardi, once I could ride . . ."

"You can ride?" It burst out. He had had no idea.

"In those days . . . it was freedom. Ajiden or Tirnamardi, I could *not* be at peace. Everybody wanted me to be what *they* wanted. I quarreled with Father, I quarreled with Uncle, I detested Aunt Geidaro, but who did not?—and finally, at the winter festival here in Shejidan, I was being pressured to enter contract marriage with a Kadagidi, and promised freedom if I did. It did not look like freedom to me. So I ran again. In a snowstorm. I saw Uncle's banner above his festival tent, right ahead of me, all lit up from below in the night, and I decided then and forever that Uncle was the best choice. In those days he was all strict starch and tradition, oh, you would not believe how strict, but there were no looks in his sitting room, no silences when I would walk in. I came to winter court with him, my first chance to wear Atageini colors, and I met your father ..."

"She was a vision," Father said. "We talked. I will tell you, son of mine, we could not stop talking. Politics. Art. The aishidi'tat. And technology ..."

"We ran off," Mother said.

"Lord Tatiseigi was going to have a fit. And we were not through ... talking."

"It was a scandal."

"It could have been," Father said, "had I not proposed marriage. But she rejected me."

"I held out," Mother said.

"Grandmother was upset. She was giving a little ground *before* your mother insisted on a life-marriage ..."

"And outraged when you agreed."

"I was in fear for my life," Father said.

"He is not serious," Mother said. "Mine, however, might have been in jeopardy."

"She would not have," Father said.

"You underestimate your grandmother," Mother said.

"No, now, no, the truth. I upset her."

"Well, and I ran home to Uncle the next month," Mother said. "Which absolutely confirmed everything she thought."

"You told her she was wrong," Father said. "You said that a contract marriage would give Ajuri a foothold in the aijinate, once you and your child were back in their control. Grandmother insisted that you would be protected, and you stood there and told her ... told her things I never thought anyone would dare say to her. And told me the same, afterward, when I told her we could renegotiate the contract later, if we just agreed with Grandmother for a start ..."

"The point needed to be made. I was through being anyone's pawn. Not my father's, not my uncle's, and not your grandmother's."

"Considering what we have found in that basement, you had ample reason. But at the time, son of mine, permanent marriage seemed a very big step, until your mother began packing to leave Shejidan. Then—I drew up the papers. *We* drew them up—which set everything off. Then Lord Tatiseigi told Grandmother she was wrong and *they* did not speak for a month."

"Uncle detested technology," Mother said. "He absolutely detested television. And airplanes. And Wilson-paidhi. When your father began to deal with nand' Bren, Uncle was furious. Even more so after your great-grandmother had decided he was acceptable."

It was a world he had not lived in. Clearly.

Then Father turned completely serious. "Understand always," Father said, "that despite the quarrel with your great-grandmother, your mother values her good judgment. They respect each other. They just do not express it well."

He was not sure whether it was a joke. He was not sure why they were telling him this.

"Understand your mother," Father said. "And your great- grandmother. I know you admire her. This situation which Grandmother has taken in hand, this young man from Ajuri, is still under investigation. She often operates afield, which I cannot do, asks questions I cannot ask. But this time . . . she and I are not in agreement on Ajuri, and we are not in agreement on her timing in this move south. She is not taking advice from her usual sources. Lord Tatiseigi is worried. Even Cenedi advised her against this venture."

"Nand' Bren will tell her the truth."

"As she lets him see it. She is making a major move on *Machigi's* advice. The recent situation on the human side of the space station, and the problems with the refugees . . . all this has worried her. The refugees have to be moved down as soon as possible, which *she* sees as apt to cause instability in Mospheira's government—and if human affairs are soon to claim my attention, all the momentum we have gained against the Shadow Guild could be lost, and it has become *her* problem. *That* is what is driving this. She believes if we do not stop the Shadow Guild now, the aishidi'tat is in danger. Most of all, she feels *she* is running out of time."

"She is not sick, is she?"

"She is old, that is all. And things she thought she had settled keep rising up again and again, to her personal frustration. Understand, son of mine, she is the great architect of the aishidi'tat as it is today. While I may have had something to do with the peace we have— I take pride in that—I would never have had the chance without her. And the south of the continent, even more than her native east, is her great concern—that it *will* not settle, and that its unrest and its trafficking with the Marid comes back time and again to unsettle the whole continent. The south was her focus both times she was regent, but she could never gain the support of the legislature, whose attitude was to let the south and the Marid fight it out amongst themselves. And what do we get from that neglect? A widening of the problem, now that the Shadow Guild has exploited it."

"But was she not right?"

"Absolutely she was right. I have supported her actions with very few exceptions. She knows it. She expects it. At times she has taken ruthless advantage of that support. She was initially against Lord Geigi's appointment to the space station because it left a gaping vacancy in the center of the west coast, and there was a Marid lordship—the Farai—trying to claim Najida. Nand' Bren's appointment to Najida settled that matter. Getting Lord Geigi's larcenous nephew out of *his* estate and nand' Bren involved in stabilizing it helped, but the southwest coast, Ashidama Bay, lordless and resistent, remains a problem. We do not even mention the tangle that is the Marid. And here is where the Ajuri basement comes into it."

"The records, honored Father?"

"The records of cargoes. Maritime cargoes to the southwest coast. And records of Guild appointments in various areas, including the appointment of failed or allegedly deceased Guild as plainclothes guard services on the southwest coast, and others in eastern Senjin and in the Dojisigin."

"The Shadow Guild."

"Exactly. Their very foundation. They *are* connected to the Marid, and to the Kadagidi in the north, while the Kadagidi have married into the Marid. When Shishogi went down, in the Guild, when his office and his records system literally went up in flames, we suspected that there might exist such a treasure-trove of dealings off the books, so to speak, things that had to be remembered, but that he did not want sitting in Guild Headquarters. And yes, the Ajuri basement has given us a wealth of information. Your great-grandmother is aware of much of it. *She* believes that the Shadow Guild in the Dojisigin can be isolated, deprived of vital materials until enough pressure on them and a strong association of the rest of the Marid can bring Tiajo's regime down. But the records we have found indicate otherwise, and we fear that they are prepared to melt away again, destroying records, this time, so that we will be years finding them. The fact that the Shadow Guild has taken to a new tactic, kidnapping of family members, threatening and controlling otherwise honorable officials, guards, records- keepers . . ."

"Homura and Momichi."

"Exactly. Like them. Your great-grandmother feels they will remain hidden and not take the field again; and I agree. In their present condition they cannot. But this is not a battle line we are facing. It is the outbreak of a disease, a way of thinking and operating that has no moral restraint. She has set up in Senjin, assuring the Marid states that we are not going to be heavy-handed about this, but in doing so, she has set the Shadow Guild in motion. They are already moving. I have consulted Lord Geigi. And we are about to go in."

"To go in. To the Dojisigin?"

"We will be looking for the Dojisigi equivalent of the Ajuri basement: to get the records. I will give her all the support I can, but I want you to know, son of mine, we are defying her wishes. We have to. And she will find that out very soon."

"But," Cajeiri said, and then could not find a way to proceed.

"We have a besetting problem in this family," Father said, "that we are not always forthcoming with the right words at the right times. I *have* spoken to her, directly. Our move down there, and Geigi's, protects her, and brings our communication up to a new standard. I have talked to Cenedi, and he has indeed persuaded her to keep out of the city. Nand' Bren, who *is* in the city, is surrounded by a major concentration of Guild, and his aishid will not let him take a breath outside their immediate observation. We *are* taking precautions for their safety. What we may not be able to protect is ourselves, from your great-grandmother's reaction once the Guild moves into the Dojisigin. But that will be as it may. She will be even less happy when we ask her to leave Koperna."

"Do you think she will do it?"

"I hope she will. I do not want her in a war zone. The lander is one assurance of her safety, but I shall feel better to have her departing the Marid entirely. *Without* Machigi."

"So would I, but I do not think she will go."

"Uncle can reason with her, sometimes better than nand' Bren."

"I have not taken Lord Tatiseigi fully into my confidence, unfortunately, and it is late to do it. He is too tightly connected to her."

"I can talk to him. Mother can."

"Not as well," Mother said. "*You* are in a special association with him. But I do not know that you want to involve yourself in this, son of mine. That is a difficult,

long-running issue, Uncle's working with her. His man'chi
is to her, and conflicted, now, with his to you; and your
great-grandmother's temper is unpredictable."

"I can talk to him. And to her."

"Son of mine," Father said, "you have never seen
them fight. If you take a position in this, it will be a question of whether you can claim his man'chi as strongly as
she can; and avoid upsetting her. Your mother cannot
enlist him against Grandmother. And I certainly cannot,
where it comes to a power Grandmother and I have both
had—she, twice, and for longer. I want her to leave this
hunt. I want her to take someone's advice. I want her to
come back and bring a good section of the Guild's special forces back with her—for the good of the aishidi'tat,
since we have the landing of humans imminent and also
needing attention. I know your respect for your great-
grandmother. But if you can influence Lord Tatiseigi to
influence her and call her home from this effort, yes. Do.
If we can lay hands on the records in the Dojisigin, your
great-grandmother can come back and settle down and
let the Guild do its work with the details. She will take it
as disrespect, but I do not. I want her safe. That is not my
only priority—it cannot be. But I do not think we can
totally expunge the Shadow Guild in this decade and
maybe not in the next. I want her to leave this to the
Guild to do, as they should, and come back here. Build a
theater. Design a park. Whatever pleases her, for a long
number of years. But I also do not want you estranged
from Lord Tatiseigi, or feeling that I set you against your
great-grandmother."

He had never been handed such a choice. He sat for
a long moment looking at his hands. He had a scar, from
the time he and mani and nand' Bren had crossed the
straits, coming home from space, to go fight the Shadow
Guild and put Father back in charge. He had been a
child then, really a child. Everything right and wrong
had been absolutely clear.

Now it was not. Nor ever might be again.

"I shall talk to Uncle," he said. "I shall tell him he has to talk to her, no matter what. She will not listen to me. Sometimes not to nand' Bren. But I shall talk to Uncle."

Priority had been given, where it came to opening residential areas, involving apartments whose owners were present in the building. Particularly the two residential halls off the assembly hall had seen the advent of Guild with an impressive cartload of equipment, going from one room to another, searching and testing literally down to the wiring and the light sockets and vents. Residents were allowed back into cleared areas, but with absolutely minimal staff. Bregani could well have set himself as first priority, but he declared that the elderly lords of Senjin and Farai should get their rooms first. He had continued as he was, holding modest court at the table with his wife and daughter, in possession of a plate of Bindanda's special teacakes sent up from the kitchens. His and Bregani's were no longer the only tables. An enterprising senior servant had unlocked a store room and they had now a wealth of tables, from one end of the hall to the other, for the general comfort. There was a place to lean elbows, set teacups, set plates, and write notes.

It was going smoothly, considering the situation. Messages both by phone and paper were getting across the city. People had found one another, and in two cases that had caused some concern, lost children had gotten to their frantic parents. Pharmacies, allowed to open, were delivering medications. Physicians were dealing by phone. A water main break had been repaired. It was not a bad afternoon's work, Bren thought, and, the process of residential clearance finally having concluded in the righthand hallway, he sat and watched as Bregani and Murai and Husai went back with their Guild escort to inspect their own apartment.

It seemed a time for a cup of tea and a sandwich for

supper. Bren took the tea sugared, and with a little or-
angelle, and heaved a sigh as Jago joined him.

"Well done," he said. "Truly well done. Have we
heard anything from the dowager or Cenedi?"

"Cenedi has been busy. The first navy ship is in harbor, moored behind the two Dojisigi vessels, and a deck
cannon has been unshrouded."

"One hopes the display is enough. I would so like to
see this end quietly."

"So would we all."

"Nothing from the dowager herself?"

"Nothing."

"Well, we may take Cenedi for her voice, I suppose. I
hope—I truly hope she is getting some sleep. That may
be her plan. With night coming on, things may get a little livelier, and the more problems we can remove by
daylight, the better. She may intend to put Nawari in
command tonight. But *we* will need relief. Is Algini getting any rest?"

"Not that I am aware," Jago said. "He is delegating
what he can. Banichi—" She shrugged. "Banichi is going through files, in his spare moments. The pace of dis-
tractions is ebbing. He says so, at least. And we are
getting word . . ." Jago held the earpiece close for a moment. "There is a little trouble in the port at the moment. There has been an outburst of gunfire ashore and
a building, a machinists' shop set alight."

"One feared we would get to that," Bren said, and
suddenly realized that not only was his aishid uncommonly split, he had Jago and Tano both paying full attention to him. "Where is Nomari?"

"Behind you, over by the far wall, nandi," Tano
said—formally so, this being fairly public, with traffic
going among the tables. "I am watching him. He has
gone into the accommodation, with one of his aishid."

"Do not let me pose a distraction," he said. "I do not
want him wandering about."

"No," Tano said simply, absolutely.

"So what do we know?" Bren asked. "What is the latest?"

Jago said, "The first naval vessel is within the harbor mouth. They will be station-keeping through the night, and preventing any departures. They are lighted, to be sure the opposition knows they are out there. We are in standard communication with them, but the Red Train will direct them. Cenedi reports the railyard is secure. Units in the city send word the main thoroughfare and intersecting streets are secure, likewise the broadcast station, under the lord's cousin and his family. Some who fled the city for the northern hills are now returning. They pose some problem. We have arrested a few citizens for drunkenness and riot, nothing worse. We have the minor cases housed temporarily in a schoolhouse, cases of suspect activity in the city under guard and interrogation. Generally people have been compliant, likely because they are terrified of us."

It was not how the Guild preferred to be regarded. But there were times it served a purpose.

"If we can only hold the situation this calm until the morning," Bren said.

"It has already been a day under Guild rule," Jago said. "And as with the people here in the residency, they have some fear of us staying—but serious fear of us leaving. Banichi has asked Lord Bregani's cousin to keep broadcasting news in small amounts, and listing names of people who are attempting to contact relatives, in the hope people will stay close to their radios and feel some sense of progress in the situation. Banichi also has mobile units out broadcasting advisements to various neighborhoods, so that people know there is some good—"

She stopped, and her eyes unfocussed. "There," she began to say, and stopped again. Tano pressed his earpiece closer, as some server rattled a tray, but shook his head.

"Cenedi reports . . . the Council Guild force, next to

the lander . . . has picked up movement across the marsh. They have deployed. They are somehow . . . They are in direct communication with the second navy ship, at sea, and it is evidently—changing course. Cenedi is querying their intent. Lord Geigi . . . Lord Geigi's name is being mentioned. But one gathers he *is* in contact with the force near the lander and is relaying information."

In contact and relaying information was a distinct possibility, and communication with the relay *was* in the hands of the Guild in Shejidan. Likewise, one was fairly sure, in the hands of. . . .

"Tabini-aiji," Bren said, knowing the dowager would not be pleased. Nor did he want to spread that speculation to passing servants. "Do we have a simultaneous operation starting here?"

"It is—" Jago began, and broke off again. "Banichi is querying. Algini says Cenedi is querying." And a moment later: "Guild Headquarters is sending verbal communication over the compromised network. They are giving Dojisigin units instructions to cease obeying their command and to stay where they are until contacted. They are demanding Lord Tiajo step down forthwith and surrender."

It was *not* the plan. It was not the dowager's plan.

It was going out over regular communications, so all Guild could hear it. Certainly the dowager would be learning that her own plans had been preempted and that one of her two ships was not doing as she had ordered.

"I need to speak to Lord Bregani," Bren said. There was no time to think about it or plan what he would do or how he would explain it. Lord Bregani was on his feet, speaking with his associates in a casual way. Bregani should not hear the news from some passing servant.

Civilians in the room would not have heard what was transpiring yet, but wherever in the residency and wherever in the city or in the port Guild was operating, within reach of their ordinary relays, they were hearing it. A Guild action was underway, invading the Dojisigin, or at least imminently threatening that action.

Bren stood up, reflexively straightened his coat and his cuffs and headed for Lord Bregani and his appointed bodyguard. Bregani's Guild bodyguard was frowning, aware there was a problem, and suddenly focused on Bren, expectant. Bregani was cheerful, uninformed of all of it as he walked, intent on someone else.

Bren intercepted him with: "Nandi. I am the bearer of news the dowager was *not* expecting, and I am conveying it to you as our ally and associate, directly as I have had it. Guild units near the relay are moving." The Senjini standing near Lord Bregani might or might not have been told there was a hulking great object sitting out on the coastal plain relaying Guild communications back and forth to Shejidan *and* the space station. But everybody who had been on the train knew there was a lander out there. As for what it could do—the fact it was now coordinating events on the ground with Geigi, who could see in the dark, and in detail they could not imagine—no, the subclan lords were not prepared for that. Lord Bregani was not prepared for that.

"Units on the other train are apparently taking an aggressive stance. We do not know whether some specific provocation has happened, but the Guild is calling for the surrender of outlaw units and, specifically, for Lord Tiajo to step down."

"God below," the Juni lord said.

"It was not planned, nandi," Bren said firmly. "But your protection was planned, and the dowager's word on that issue will stand, whatever else is going on. You are her ally and her associate, as is Lord Machigi, whom I have yet to inform. Please be confident of *all* her agreements, and trust your status as her ally prior to *anything* Lord Tiajo may have said or done to provoke this. Your territory will not be threatened by this event."

"We have Guild running our streets," Lusi said. "We

have our current chief trading partner under armed assault and a governing lord under attack. We have a great metal ship in our harbor!"

"Parbi-ji," Lord Bregani said, evidently using Lusi's personal name, "clearly something unexpected is going on. Nand' paidhi. Is the dowager aware of this?"

"I cannot swear to the moment, nandi, but she will protect Senjin, whatever is going on. She does not change direction like this. Nandiin, let me inform Lord Machigi before *he* hears it from some other source, and I will immediately start trying to get your answers in specific. One moment, only one moment, nandi, give me that. Then I will use every contact I have to get a response. I can fairly predict the dowager will be no slower in finding an answer."

"Go," Bregani said, frowning, and Bren turned away, looking to Lord Machigi, who was still unaware, sitting at a table with his non-regulation aishid, drinking something that was not tea, and probably wondering what had the Guild suddenly, massively distracted.

"A human *and* a foreigner," he heard behind him, from what speaker near Bregani was not clear. "What *does* he serve?"

There was no answering it. The ground was shifting under the dowager's promises and they had a city under occupation, with a pile of promises dry as tinder and apt to be set off by a spark. All sorts of possibilities were suddenly in play, and, connected as they might be to Shejidan and the space station, they could not guarantee Lord Bregani's safety or even their own if an enemy bent on revenge decided to trigger clandestine units to act.

"Nandi," Bren said, and took a chair across from Machigi unasked, with Tano and Jago standing behind him. "I have just gotten word there is movement on the western border from *our* side. The Guild has outright told Lord Tiajo to step down and seems to be moving east toward the Dojisigin to enforce it. I have just advised Lord Bregani. I have not yet heard from the dowager, but I do not think she will be pleased."

Machigi stared back, one of his impenetrable stares, giving away little. "In your estimation she did not order it."

"In my estimation, no, she did not. She has made all her arrangements on *this* side of the Marid, nandi, assuring that Tiajo would think twice before bringing force against her. She has Lusi'ei's harbor blocked and she is pushing Dojisigi of whatever degree to leave. If Lord Tiajo has any thought of intervening here, we are prepared to deal with her, and we will leave a force capable of defending Senjin. Not part of her plan, but acceptable, the Guild has considerable force poised on Lord Tiajo's doorstep. But to my knowledge this eastward move by that force was not hers—and I do not need all the fingers of one hand to count the agencies that might move to skirt her orders."

"The legislature. Her grandson."

"The Guild Council, regarding their outlawed members and their rules. *And* Lord Geigi, in the heavens, *if* he saw an impending danger—but one would assume he would have warned us, and he has not. One thing I am sure of is that whatever is happening is not aimed to defy her, is not aimed at you, and is not aimed at Senjin. The demand for Tiajo to step down may be a tactic, opening a way to counter-demand and negotiate. The Guild once committed *will* likely pursue its own outlawed members, but not to your disadvantage. For now, I ask your support of the dowager. She will hold to that agreement. That is a commitment made, and it will stand."

"Are there more surprises?" Machigi asked. "Shall we see another of those descents from the heavens land here? I tell you it will not be welcome."

"There are to my knowledge no more of them in existence, nandi. I sincerely believe the one that landed was the last of them, but they were never devised to be

used against the Marid. They were originally aimed at
the outlaw regime and the last of them, where it stands,
will still be used against them. There is, to my knowledge, one navy ship in this harbor, and another at sea,
diverted by someone's order, possibly headed toward
Amarja, in the interest of closing that harbor. I am keeping no secrets about this. My word on it. It is not aimed
at Senjin *or* the Taisigin or your allies. I suspect she is
gathering information as we are, and one must make the
observation: if Tiajo does go down—it will not be bad for
you."

"Ha. If someone wishes to take down that fool, *I* shall
not object. Take them all down, this Guild of hers, and
their works, and light a fire under them. Let the Marid be
free of them once for all. I can deal with Senjin."

Considering the history of the Marid, that last could
be an ominous statement . . . all the more reason to build
up a healthy relationship.

"But dealing with the Dojisigin will not be not the end
of your Shadow Guild," Machigi said. "And if you wish to
know where else I have told the dowager to look. . . ."
Machigi reached for the bottle, poured a considerable
amount into his cup, then pushed the cup across to Bren,
took another slightly used cup and poured his own,
equally generous.

"I am listening." Bren picked up the cup, hoping Jago
and Tano recognized the liquor and could warn him off
another tea incident. He took a careful sip, tasting herbal
flavors beneath the alcohol, but his tongue did not tingle,
which was one warning he had learned to heed.

"Close to your own holdings," Machigi said. "The
west coast."

The west coast was the direction of old and troublesome *Taisigin* ambitions. Ilisidi had traded Machigi the
sea route and the ship designs *specifically* to pry Machigi
away from his ancestral claim on the southwest coast, a
claim so old it predated the aishidi'tat by a thousand
years and involved mythical figures, or at least mythol-

ogized ones. The claim had never been realized, no settlement had ever existed there, and it was mostly a tale
of war between the scattered clans of the south and the
Marid folk who had materialized following the disaster
of the Southern Island and the whole south coast, clans
that for the last thousand years had warred with each
other when they were not warring with their neighbors.

The dowager had gotten Machigi's signature on an
agreement and promised him trade—in exchange for his
giving up his claim on the west coast, and here they sat,
on the verge of an answer for the Marid, and the west
coast was back on Machigi's lips.

A market road ran north to south along that coast
and marked the boundary Machigi had agreed to. The
vast Taisigin hunting range, one of the largest hunting
ranges of any clan in modern times, ran from the Taisigi
capital, Tanaja, to the edge of that long north-south
road, on the seaward side of which lay the coastal clans
of the aishidi'tat. There were independent townships,
several, the Ashidama peninsula, and the Kajidama and
Najidama peninsulas, one of which was Lord Geigi's domain, and one of which was his own. Najida.

"West," he echoed Machigi. "You are surely not
meaning Lord Geigi, nandi. Or me."

Machigi took down a massive swallow and grimaced.
"I have no quarrel with Lord Geigi. Not even in his giving land to the ship-wreckers."

The ship-wreckers would be the Edi, who now lived
peaceably on Najida and supplied a good many of the
Najida staff. They were currently building a new residency on Kajiminda peninsula, and that might have dis-
pleased Machigi: the Edi were an old problem. But . . .
the Edi 'ship-wreckers' were no longer active.

"Separti?" That and Talidi, market towns for the
whole coast, were the only things left.

"Separti, Talidi . . . Jorida. The whole Ashidama region. Look to them for your next trouble, paidhi, in your
own neighborhood."

He had meant to get up quickly, and not to drink more than a sip of the liquor. He stayed seated, and leaned his arms on the table. "If you have observations, nandi . . ."

"Oh, I have observations aplenty and I have shared them with the aiji-dowager. Jorida Isle, in Ashidama Bay. Jorida has money, the vast majority of which has come from brokering between the Dojisigin and your own law-abiding aishidit'at."

Brokering. Curious choice of words. "Black market? Or what?"

"Regular trade up to Cobo. And, yes, black market. Smuggling."

"Black market . . . in what?"

"Items that never should have left their final resting place."

That sounded like grave-robbing. But there was one vast grave all the Marid respected. Or should respect.

"Are you talking about artifacts?"

"Among other things. Yes."

"Where are they dealing?"

"Oh, Cobo, again. Or northward. Or east. With or without their knowledge, northern lords with more money than they need have helped finance your northern Shadow Guild for decades, and Jorida is the hub of it. Jorida funds the looters. Dojisigi, mostly. The flotsam that washed up last, from the Great Wave, brigands from the outset. And if Tiajo's network shatters, the pieces will follow their usual route and end up right on your doorstep, paidhi. I have warned the dowager, and yes, the ships were late into position. This noisy arrival down from the heights hastened everything into motion, with the ships not yet in position."

"They were to block both harbors. Lusi'ei and Amarja."

"One to block Lusi'ei. One to stand off ready to move if needed."

Machigi had been handed a plan he had not been given. Nor, likely, had Tabini, who commanded the navy.

"What were they to do—the ships? What changed?"

"The one to block Lusi'ei. The other to watch traffic out of Amarja, possibly to defend Tanaja."

Machigi's own capital. Likely the ships were the protection *he* had wanted.

"The second seems to be heading now toward Amarja. And the Guild force is going in."

"I have warned her: starve it out rather than burn it. Hit Amarja with major force and the enemy will move." Machigi made a fist and expanded it, fingers in various directions. "They will not fight. And some will be on the west coast, where they always were."

It was not exactly news that Ashidama, the bay south of his own Najida and Geigi's Kajiminda, was a recalcitrant area that had never quite joined the rest of the aishidi'tat, but it had also not actively supported the coup against Tabini. It had not *actively* done anything during the Troubles but trade with the Marid and trade with Cobo. They were not one of Machigi's own trading partners: Machigi did trade with the west coast, but further north, at Cobo.

Goods from the northern Marid, however, flowed to Ashidama Bay by ship out of the townships. Najida likewise traded most of its produce and fish down to Ashidama townships; and villages all along the coasts bought and sold there, as well, in a village-to-village commerce.

"Can you be more specific, nandi?" Bren asked. "What should I say to the dowager?"

"Say that if she can recall the aiji's forces, it would prevent a problem. You *can* reach her by this new system."

"Yes, nandi. I can."

He pushed back from the table, moved off a few paces and looked at Jago. "Inform Banichi and inform Cenedi."

"Yes," Jago said.

Lord Bregani had left the table. He was talking with Murai, standing a little distance away. Watching him and Machigi, quite possibly.

Bren walked over to them. "Nandi," he said with a little bow, "I have talked with Lord Machigi on the same concern. My aishid is contacting the dowager through channels. Lord Machigi shares your concern about a broader conflict. I am sure she is concerned. I shall be trying to get information."

Bregani drew a long breath, then fixed him with a steady stare. "You are not deceiving us, are you, paidhi?"

"No, nandi. Lord Machigi is naturally concerned with repercussions to his own region, and *his* trade. It is not that a confrontation with Tiajo was not foreseeable, but it was the dowager's wish it come later, possibly across a table, and not this early in the process."

"I foresaw it," Bregani said with a shrug. "I saw Tiajo's move as certain, once I signed the dowager's agreement. Surely she knew."

"She knows it will not succeed. A preemptive move was not in her plan, however, rather to let Tiajo see what she faces, and perhaps take a more cautious approach, while we continue to gather information. Lord Machigi is very much in accord with your concerns, for the same reasons. She will be talking to the aiji in Shejidan. She may be doing that at this moment. Excuse me, nandiin, and I shall try to get more information."

He bowed. He pulled away, Tano staying right with him. Jago, absent the while, rejoined them.

"Cenedi says they are aware," Jago said. "Banichi and Algini are also aware. Cenedi is somewhat concerned about local reaction. He offers a return to the train."

"I cannot," he said. "I cannot desert this situation. I think it best, perhaps, to sit, have our supper, such as it is, if the dowager is aware and dealing with this. I shall have to wait for news. Is *anyone* in contact with the operation to the east?"

"Cenedi is," Jago said. "They are moving fast. The second naval vessel is no longer taking orders from the dowager. It is indeed being diverted, one suspects, toward Amarja."

"Tabini," Bren said. There was no other conclusion. "She is *not* going to be pleased."

"No," Jago said. "She will not."

16

Food continued to arrive, in the form of more sandwiches, and some fruit bars. Bren had half a sandwich. There was an acknowledgment of the message, but no reply from the dowager, and no direct word from Banichi. Bindanda sent Jeladi up to say that word had spread through the staff—no surprise at all; and it had spread to the returning staff and residents as well, but not yet to the city, not yet to the broadcast center. A statement had to be prepared, something that would not provoke panic or become inflated into invasion from the north.

Jago and Tano stayed close by him. Banichi was downstairs, along with Algini, directing operations and keeping the city under martial law. Areas and facilities inside the city were still being cleared, building by building. Shejidani teams were going through the offices on the administrative side of the residency, searching them for security issues.

Bren, with a sandwich beside him, court etiquette and the formalities of dinner all ignored, composed a release for the broadcast center, trying for cautious optimism and accurate information.

The cooperation of the citizens of Koperna is helping speed the lifting of the shutdown order, which Lord Bre-

gani hopes will begin by neighborhoods sometime tomorrow. The Shejidani Guild also wishes to thank the citizens for their cooperation with a measure meant to assure the safety of persons and property during a significant transition in law enforcement.

Lord Bregani is meeting with lords and officials in the residency. The office of Communications is open and operating normally in the interests of public information. Other offices are expected to follow in short order.

Particular thanks go to nand' Biathi, who with his household, has with courage and calm guided Senjin through difficult hours.

This disturbance of the ordinary in Koperna, and indeed throughout Senjin, attends the signing of a construction and trade agreement by the aiji-dowager, Lord Bregani, and Lord Machigi, thus ending tension on Senjin's southern border and promising a new and important relationship, with a strong flow of trade through Koperna, the building of additional warehouses and service facilities, and alignment of Senjin in equal partnership with the Taisigin and the Taisigin's Southern Association, with Sungeni and the Dausigin, all in a framework including the East, under the hand of the aiji-dowager, Lord of Malguri.

Likewise the agreement formally ends Senjin's reliance on the Dojisigin for trade and defense. Fees for defense will no longer be leaving Senjin. Senjin will establish its own defense, under its own law and regulation.

The aiji-dowager wishes to ensure that these operations are carried out smoothly, and she supports Lord Bregani and Lord Machigi in their joint undertaking. She has provided Lord Bregani the service of the Shejidani Guild for whatever time is needed to establish an adequate local defense and constabulary.

Additionally, the aishidi'tat has provided her security, not entering Senjin proper, but situated on the rail line, to make a strong statement regarding the aishidi'tat's determination to protect the dowager and the dowager's cosignatories from any Dojisigin response to this shift in alignment.

—From the hand of the paidhi-aiji, in service in the creation of this agreement.

That, he thought, was possibly a little over the line of what the paidhi should properly say. He sent it to Lord Bregani to approve, before sending it to Lord Machigi, Lord Bregani having most at stake here.

But the question still was, in Ilisidi's silence, what was going on with that force out in the middle of nowhere.

"I have no wish to distract the dowager," he said. "Query Cenedi again. See if he has anything further for us."

Jago moved off not too far, while Tano stayed by him.

"Find time for supper," Bren said. "You and Jago." The sandwich had been hot, and appetizing. Now it was neither. His stomach was upset and he could not tell whether it was lack of food or from the food.

"We shall manage, nandi." There was an increasing traffic of non-Guild in this area so that the balance of black uniforms to civilian dress had become about even. The offices of public safety and public records had been opened, receiving reports and instructing employees. The government was slowly reasserting itself at the edge of night, after hours of shut-down. A number of the city council and regional officers had come in, an increased coming and going made the Guild nervous. Credentials were checked and re-checked. Sentries guarded the two corridors that branched off from this huge room, and servants coming and going upstairs had, with few exceptions, to show a time-noted card from the guard downstairs.

Across the room, Nomari had found a place at a small table, isolated near the half-pillar, his appointed aishid near him at all times, all four of them. No one spoke to him, other than passing exchanges. Over the course of the evening a few of the locals had approached him, curious, no doubt, and he rose deferentially to meet them, but no long conversation ever came of these moments. The locals would move on, and he sat back down, a young man trapped in a room and a situation, without a clear place or purpose or future.

Nothing *inside* the residency had been going wrong. A fire hydrant opened somewhere in the city, flooding a street and several basements. A bar had been broken into, though food was the chief loss. It could signal the whereabouts of elements they wanted to find, or it could be desperate householders who had had nothing in the pantry.

Bregani's cousin—Biathi was his name—was reported still broadcasting essentials and advisories. His family was with him, along with guards who had proven, thank God, reliable. That whole family deserved a commendation, in Bren's thinking. Biathi, and sometimes his wife, even their fourteen-year-old son, had kept up a lively and occasionally light patter of news and information from phone contacts day and night, which certainly had kept people in their homes calmer than might have been.

With the influx of council members, meetings went on at various tables around the room. Bregani and Murai, having dealt with the subclans, were dealing with various department heads, as the regional government tried to get back into operation. Dojisigin policies and orders, all of which were now in suspension, were under review. Husai sat with her parents through all of it, looking proper as an heir should, quiet, hands laced on the tabletop, with nothing she *could* do, but with a need to be seen—a statement of family, of clan, of respect.

Bren could certainly understand that position—not being able to do more than sit as a visible presence. He maintained the same, a visible assurance of contact with the general situation, while God knew what was going on outside his reach.

"Nandi." Jago dropped into a chair beside him. "Banichi reports a problem at the port. The navy ship is in contact. They have been jamming the two Dojisigi freighters, preventing them from communication. The initial force is at the dock, but has made no move to board them. We have promised them they will be eventually allowed to leave, but the navy is not permitting that as yet, probably because of the changing situation to the east of us. Now the freighter farthest out has made an attempt to leave dock, and actions to stop them *may* damage the ship or surrounding property. The dowager is presently asleep and Cenedi is reluctant to wake her. Cenedi asks authorization to prevent this ship."

Asleep? If there was one thing the dowager was not likely to do when there was a quarrel with her grandson in the offing, not to mention an invasion taking place that she had *not* directed, and her plans meddled with . . . going to bed was not her logical reaction.

And hand a developing situation at the port to him? It was insane.

Authorize it? Refer it? Tell Cenedi to wake the dowager anyway? God, was she taken ill?

Lives were at risk either through action or inaction. Property was at risk, the port on which Senjin relied. It was not in the paidhi's range of duties, to authorize any attack—let alone one involving the navy, which moved only to the highest orders. And Ilisidi's health and ability to function was the point on which everything rested.

He could refer it back to Banichi. But that was a source Cenedi himself outranked.

"Tell Cenedi," he said, as if every word were sharp glass, "tell Cenedi use his discretion. Try to minimize damage to Senjini property. But meanwhile let Banichi know what is going on. This is not my expertise, Jago-ji."

"Yes," Jago said, and quietly, withdrawn as they were in the ambient noise of a populated room, relayed what he asked.

Then she said, "Cenedi agrees your word is all he needs."

God. He did not want to have done that. He had no

mental image of what he had just authorized, except Cenedi was that reluctant to wake Ilisidi to get an approval. That was how he read it—that it was not the situation in the port Cenedi might be most worried about.

And if Cenedi was worried about the dowager, *he* was worried. He felt sick at his stomach.

"Jago," he said, "Tano. Ask Cenedi whether he needs me there. I *will* come. If he needs me."

"Yes," Jago said, and relayed that, quietly, listened, and said: "Cenedi offers his thanks and says he has what he needs."

So the story stood. Cenedi said she was asleep. Which left him in charge . . . and his Guild-senior downstairs dealing with what the Guild had to deal with in an occupied city. It was not a situation he had ever remotely anticipated.

One thing he had to do—his actual job, which was to inform Bregani, which he did with a small written message, with the date and time.

Lord Bregani, for your records.

Bren-paidhi, representing the aiji-dowager.

We are informed that one Dojisigi ship is attempting to leave. The naval vessel in harbor is moving to prevent that. Their orders are to minimize damage to the ship-channel and surrounding buildings. That will be a priority, but that ship will not be successful in breaking away. Likely their move is to test our resolve to prevent them. We have been jamming their communication, so we think it unlikely that they have received any order from Amarja, nor will they have been able to communicate the situation here.

Set on paper, the situation seemed far tamer, more matter of fact, even calming. Tano took the message over, and came back with Bregani's thanks for the notification.

At least, with Tabini-aiji's intervention, it had not thrown the ships off that far, and it brought them communications they had not had before—including the ability to reach clear to Shejidan, which made him realize he *or* Cenedi *could* have asked Tabini. He knew why Cenedi hadn't. He still could. He could *tell* Tabini that his grandmother was taking a nap at a god-awful moment of their operation.

So might Cenedi have done. Cenedi could have gone to the Guild Council, or asked Tabini directly what to do. Either one would cast the question outside the arena of current action—to people who would not instantly know where all the pieces were—

And more to the point—outside the range of people who might advise Cenedi without taking over the operation.

Which answered why he was deciding things like this. He was still, one way or the other, operating on Ilisidi's wishes, possibly under her direct orders.

"Tell Banichi," he said, entirely after the fact and unsure what Banichi *would* say. "Ask him was I correct to have done what I did, and keep advising him of whatever we learn about that situation." He added: "I am a little concerned. Ordinarily the dowager would not be bypassed. I cannot think she is asleep."

Jago nodded, and moved off a little, turning her shoulder to him while she relayed that message, while Tano stayed close, and he waited for information, hoping he had not done amiss.

The dowager's trust rested on Cenedi. And this whole operation in Senjin was a hope the dowager was right—thus far validated. Now either Tabini or the Guild Council had second-guessed her and complicated the operation. Even Geigi had put his hand in, bestowing that last precious lander where *somebody* wanted it, and settling the cell phone issue, after all the lengthy debate on the matter, and bypassing his seldom-used veto.

Ilisidi had not expected it. *Somebody* had thrown the new relay system into the game.

All of that added up to Tabini: Geigi would cooperate with no less.

It *was* possible even for him, through that system, to go past Ilisidi herself if he judged things were going wrong.

If *he* judged that to be the case. For that very reason, the ability to bypass the chain of command, and the Guild, and disrupt the whole hierarchy on which the aishidi'tat rested, he had ruled against cell phones in general distribution. They linked channels of communication hitherto separated by time and distance.

So now—was he to think of going past Ilisidi?

Jago turned back toward him, came back and dropped into the adjacent chair, leaning close as she handed him the Guild-owned relay unit. "Banichi wishes to speak to you."

Well, that was not as planned. And there was another Guild rule overridden in this operation. Non-Guild did not use Guild communications. Bren took it carefully, not touching the buttons.

"Push this button," Jago said, indicating the black button. "Hold it down only while you speak."

One understood. "Banichi," he said.

"One hears," the answer came.

"Jago told you. Cenedi asked me to authorize an operation."

"Yes."

"I have concerns," he said, trying to speak obliquely even with security promised to be absolute. "One worries extremely that he referred it to me."

"Understood," Banichi said. *"But you are in a position to observe. Your information is possibly more current than his. I just spoke with him. We are about to close the port road, figuring that everyone we want to have allowed to go there has gone. The port has had its problems . . . an attempt to set fire in a warehouse, and gunfire near the boarding for the Dojisigi freighter. The one freighter has cast off its boarding ramp and left dock. This would have met the second navy ship further out, but that ship has now diverted, and we believe informa-*

tion is being relayed by a light signal from shore—we are jamming other communication. Cenedi needed that authorization. He can stop the freighter, we hope without sinking it, but we also want to prevent them sinking it themselves to obstruct the harbor. If it does go down, we shall make sure it is not in the ship-channel. Things have been very busy in Lusi'ei since sunset."

"Have you had any word from Cenedi about the dowager?"

"She is asleep. That is the only word we have."

She was aboard the train—and the train could move, if things went badly, without imperiling the mission. She had her personal physician, who always traveled with her.

But now with things changing rapidly—toward Amarja—

"I think we shall be settling down here," he said to Banichi.

"That would be a good thing. We shall advise you if we have any communication from Cenedi. We are continuing to open up areas of the residency and we are checking credentials of everyone we are allowing in, but right now your immediate area and the kitchens and mechanical offices are still under very tight restriction. Bindanda has taken charge below, with Narani and Jeladi. Right now they are attempting to feed other personnel that have set up in the Registry, and another group of citizens seeking shelter in the public gardens—people who do not feel safe in their neighborhoods for whatever reason. We are attempting to find where these problem areas are, and to take care of them. I would advise you stay where you are, Bren-ji, and sleep as often as you can. We cannot guarantee anything. Guild will be guarding all access through the night."

"I shall," he said. "I am with Jago and Tano. I am safe."

A small outcry to the right drew his attention, and not his alone. A servant had overset a teacup on a tray and it had upset a good half-cup of tea right over Husai's shoulder.

Far from fatal, and everyone was getting tired.

"A spilled teacup," he said, in the case Banichi had heard the muffled exclamation. "We call that a disaster here. We are entirely well, Nichi-ji. Please get some rest yourself. I assure you I shall not leave this room."

"I am only downstairs from you, Bren-ji. And the people around you are elite. Rely on them. The dowager will wake in the morning and, we hope, find the harbor in good order and a city beginning to return to normal. Tomorrow we plan to relax our hold on a number of neighborhoods and open related stores and businesses."

"One is grateful," he said. "Thank you, Nichi-ji."

He handed the device back to Jago, who communicated with Banichi in a few words, and said, "Done."

To him and to Tano, Jago said: "We should start lowering the lights soon, to give these folk the notion of rest, and to stop all this milling about. Two older residents have retired to their apartments to rest. We are generally advising against that, even where rooms are cleared and sealed. You should sleep here, Bren-ji, whenever you wish. Everything is fairly well in hand."

Except the action of a naval ship, which he had authorized . . . a power only Tabini, only Ilisidi could move. Guild could not. And *he* had. And a ship might be sunk.

But it was the request of a wiser head than his, where it came to operations. Cenedi had only wanted a figurative official stamp, which he had given.

He settled back in the too-large chair and heaved a sigh, thinking he would very much like a large brandy, and that resource was available in this room, sent up from the kitchens.

But if he was to get further calls from Cenedi, he dared not relax. He thought, however, having heard from Banichi, that he should resign the current problems and relax. At least try to think of something besides the port, and cannonfire in the harbor. He let his eyes shut, intending to rest them a moment, then caught himself with the distinct impression of having had a time lapse. And something having changed.

The room was dark, shot through with the white light of flashlights.

A thump. The overhead lights flickered on, and went out again. He stood up. Neither Tano nor Jago had a flashlight in hand: they had their rifles. Jago took his arm and, with Tano, escorted him over toward the wall. All over the large hall, people were on their feet, shadows against others lit in bright light, and the pale gleam of eyes beyond, atevi eyes reflecting the light.

"Where is our daughter?" he heard Bregani ask above the general confusion.

"Banichi!" Jago said. "We have lost the lights up here."

He could not hear the answer, but Jago said, "Yes!" and then, to him and Tano: "It is the entire building."

"Bindanda," Tano said, listening on regular com, "requests assistance."

"Bindanda requests assistance," Jago relayed. Then: "Two units are moving to him from our area," Jago reported, which Tano relayed to Bindanda.

And meanwhile, across the hall, Bregani was demanding his security let him find his daughter.

"Husai . . ." Bren began to say.

"A unit went with her," Tano said. "She was going to change her clothes. Area command is ordering that unit to respond."

And a moment later: "They are not answering."

"I am going to Bregani," Bren said and started that direction. Jago's arm definitively barred the way.

"No," Jago said. "Tano-ji. Stay with Bren."

She faded backward, a shadow among shadows, and Bren stood still beside a support element, wedged in by Tano's armored presence, and watched the shadow that was Jago approach the spotlighted group that was Bregani and Murai and their escort. A human was, compared to atevi, night-blind. Atevi eyes glowed gold in reflected light from flashlights all about the room, and he knew his duty, his imperative, was not to make his pale self a target if things were going sideways. Tano had him tucked into the best vertical cover there was. Jago, meanwhile, could communicate straight to command, and for once Banichi would know the situation faster than—

He thought, then, in a moment of suspicion—if Husai was missing, where was Nomari? Nomari had tended to be against this same wall. He cast a look in that direction and could make out nothing.

"Nomari," he said to Tano.

Tano moved outward slightly and looked. "Nomari is with his aishid, Bren-ji. He has not moved."

The teacup, Bren recalled. The spill. Husai's pale blouse.

"Husai's escort still is not answering," Tano said. "Area Command is sending another team."

Jago was coming back toward them, bringing Bregani and Murai and their escort.

"Our daughter," Murai said, in distress.

"Where did she go?" Bren asked.

"To our apartment. To change clothes. With four Guild our bodyguard sent with her."

"They said the hall was secure." Murai's arm was firmly locked in Bregani's, anguished faces suggested in the reflection of flashlights aimed generally aside. "One believed it was safe."

"I have verbal contact with the search in that hall," Jago said, "The outer door of the apartment is locked. No one is answering inside. We are forcing the door."

"Gods," Mirai said.

One could hear a distant impact, and all across the dark hall motion stopped and voices ceased.

The power failure, Bren thought, was *far* too convenient. "Jago-ji. Is Banichi aware?"

"Yes," Jago said. "Exits are all guarded." She gave

sudden attention to the com plug in her ear, pressing it in. And to them: "Nandiin. The young woman is not there. The escort is down, condition undetermined. One—two— of the search team are reporting ill and confused." She lifted the other communications unit. "Banichi. Escort down, search team reporting drug effects. Area Command is sending a unit to assist."

"Our daughter," Bregani said, desperate question.

"First unit is trying to report. They are in the hall. Two are trying to go back in, orders are to wait. Are there windows? They ask are there windows?"

"Three," Murai said. Bregani was holding her in close embrace, trying to comfort her, and Murai was visibly shivering.

"Three windows," Jago relayed.

"But there is no ledge," Murai said.

A lengthy silence followed.

"Can they not get her?" Murai asked.

"Two are going in with masks," Jago reported, and after another space of time. "All rooms entered. Servant passage under seal and locked. Windows and closets, seals unbroken. Husai is not found."

"Gods," Bregani said. "She cannot—cannot have vanished."

"There is a large wall vent," Jago said. "That seal has been broken. A team with masks has gone in and extracted the others. The vent has been sealed and the fans have been shut down. But the substance appears to dissipate rapidly. They are hoping it will not reach beyond her room, but we are evacuating the two corridors to be sure."

"There are ducts," Bregani said, "in every room on the upper level."

"Where does the ducting lead?" Jago asked.

"Down to the basement," Bregani said. "Lower than the kitchens. To cool the air."

"Gods," Murai said in despair.

"Banichi," Jago said. "Room vent seal was broken.

The ductwork runs through second level and the central shaft goes down to the subterranean."

How long had it been? Bren wondered. How much time had they had?

And who the 'they' might be was no question in his mind. 'They' were operating not like servants trembling their way through a forced act of betrayal—except only—perhaps—

"The tea was no accident," he said.

"Sachibei," Bregani said. "Sachibei." It was a name. A servant, one gathered, the one with the tray. "Find him!"

A servant blackmailed, maybe a sleeper agent activated, who knew the backstairs and the servant passages.

Seal broken. And something in the air, maybe—something general, or something released as a weapon...

"She is not there," Jago said. "She was taken out through the ancient vent system. They may not be out of the building yet."

Banichi would be giving orders to search all rooms with such ducts . . . but whoever it was, of whatever agency, had a head start.

"If you were attempting escape, nandi," Tano asked then, "to exit the building complex anywhere on the lower levels, nandi, where would you go?"

Bregani looked at him, momentarily at a loss. "There are the store rooms, there is the well room, there are doors—There is an escape route to the Justiciary, across the street . . . and the garage there. A stair from the deepest basement on this side. We used it . . . going to the train. It is barred. From inside. And there is another exit to the gardens."

Jago relayed that, too, almost as quickly as Bregani said it.

Then Jago said: "We are stopping all exits, all vehicles exiting the area. We are contacting units across the city to stop all vehicles. All available units will cordon off the residency and the gardens, priority."

A shadowy presence had turned up on the edge of the light, light reflected from habitually sullen eyes, light dimly sketching a scarred face. Machigi was with them. "What is going on?" Machigi asked.

"Husai-daja," Bren said, "went to her room, with an escort. She is now gone and, we fear, taken. Have you heard anything?"

"Nothing," Machigi said, and with a nod to Bregani and Murai: "Nandiin, my old opponents, whatever help I can be, I offer, if only to guard us here, but my aishid are excellent trackers."

"The vent system itself," Jago said. "Nandi, by your grace, we will use them. Go to the righthand hall and assist. Be warned. They are using something in the air, dust, or an aerosol."

"Go as he says," Machigi said. "I shall rely on the paidhi's bodyguard. All of you. Go. Split up as need be."

"Banichi," Jago said, "Machigi's aishid is moving to try to track them in the ventilation system."

Banichi evidently responded. Machigi's entire unit was away. There was movement out across the vast darkened hall, but little of it.

"What do we know?" Bregani asked Jago. "What if anything do we know, nadi?"

"Your daughter's escort was overcome, but they are alive. That, and the fact she was taken indicates she is also alive, and that the motive is what we saw with your aishid, nandi. We suspect Guild-level action, speed and stealth and either a deep concealment in the residency or escape by that network you describe, nandi. We are trying to throw a cordon around a sufficient area, but maps we have do not indicate the understreet tunnel or any garden exit."

"The air system," Bregani said. "Serves only these two halls. The old shaft, I have heard . . . is a straight drop to the lowest basement. But there is a grille. I am sure there is an iron grille."

"Neither would be a barrier," Jago said. "If they do get out of the building, the port road is closed, which the kidnappers may not know, and any vehicle will be stopped, which is a point of risk. We have not picked up any transmissions not our own. *If* we can block the streets and escape routes we may force them to hide close by, which is what we want."

"Records," Bregani said, "records may have. I have no idea. I have no idea if there is a complete map of the old stonework. Security knows. And the building manager. If one can find him. The maintenance office will have his name."

"Gods," Murai said. "Just get her back."

Quiet had set into the hall. Various units had been communicating. Now there came a lull. And it was deathly quiet.

17

It was a primitive system, God only knew how old, not a mechanical system and not on the maps because it just—existed as the stub of a system. A historic feature. An architectural curiosity. Guild doing the clearance had seen the vents, probably looked into them, and put seals on them, with nothing on the map they were given, perhaps, to indicate anything except the sort of anomaly ancient buildings had. Like the dumbwaiters in the Bujavid. There. Not functional since their own tragic incident.

Damn, Bren thought. He had sat there falling asleep. Jago and Tano were under strict orders to stay with *him*, and *he* had not been awake to see Husai go off to the hall. She had taken an escort. What could go wrong with four elite Guild to see her there and back?

An elite Guild unit had gone down and two others were affected, in what condition he had yet to hear.

Hell. Bloody hell. *His* fault. *His* job, and his fault . . . a sixteen-year-old girl kidnapped by cold-blooded killers, Guild injured, a treaty compromised and the dowager's entire map for the Marid in jeopardy. *Brilliant* job he had done.

He felt sick at his stomach.

But—the streets were blocked. The culprits could not

get as far as the port carrying a kidnapped teenager, not that fast; and the only vehicles allowed to be moving out there would be under control of their forces, not of locals.

The situation was not beyond recovery. The best thing he could do now was not issue his own orders to confuse things and just trust his aishid. It was Guild against Guild at the moment, and Banichi had studied the maps they had. So had the rest of them. The problem was—the maps had—likely deliberately—excluded other escape routes. The kidnappers had dark on their side if they had gotten out of the building, but there was a lot of building to search, too, in event they had not left.

He could hear Jago's side of the exchange with Banichi as the downed unit was being treated—Tano had gone to the area to gather information. The four who had been with Husai were still unconscious, from a heavy, possibly lethal dose of something. A field medic was trying to help them. From what he himself could hear from Machigi, near his own position, talking to his own aishid, Machigi's men were in the vent system, and descending a shaft with hand- and footholds.

"We have blocked streets at several removes, nandi, notably routes toward the hills and toward the harbor, likewise the two bridges," Jago informed Lord Bregani, in Bren's hearing. "We have drawn in the other Guild command to assist the search. We have also been made aware of the third basement entry port for city utilities. We are moving out into the utility tunnels."

Tano came up on Bren's left, in some urgency, appearing out of the dark. "Nandi. Nomari is missing."

"How?" It was another elite unit, assigned to Nomari directly from the Guild, at Tatiseigi's request, from before this operation had ever begun. "*When?* Is his aishid with him?"

"No," Tano said. "Their attention went aside to an elderly man having difficulty in the dark. They were briefly distracted. They turned back to Nomari, could

not see him in the vicinity and thought he might have
gone to the hallway where Husai-daja vanished. Two
went there, two went to the accommodation in case it
was that. Aishi-aigure." That had no translation, but
was something like a bodyguard getting too close to his
principal, a loyalty too deep too fast, in this case.

Bren cast a look around and saw, by indirect flashlight—
Machigi's frowning countenance, not the most encouraging sight. Machigi's former spy was missing and now *he*
had dispatched four of Machigi's own out to track Husai.

Could Nomari *be* Shadow Guild, the ultimate deep
plot to remove Geidaro and insert a younger, smarter
lord of Ajuri?

Nomari would not betray himself if that were the
case. Unless the plan had utterly shifted to stopping Ilisidi's association.

Or . . . Damn. Unless his focus was neither. And it
was Husai.

"Advise Banichi," he said, which necessarily entailed
advising Jago, whose whereabouts at the moment *he*
could not find in the dark. There were flashlights, a
black on light kaleidoscope of black-uniformed Guild
moving about lighter-clothed civilians, gold-reflecting
eyes and shadows upon shadows of every scale, among
the tables and chairs, about the walls.

Ordinary com reached Banichi. Tano relayed the
message in verbal code, the edges of which even Bren
could catch, and in that tiny distraction, Bren thought,
if it were only his clothing that was pale enough to notice, he imagined *he* could be out of the light and moving, maybe into the side corridors, maybe out the great
doors at the rear, where there was no light either. If a
young man was bent on disappearing, he could be very
rapidly out of view and gone.

The young man's aishid was likely searching, split up,
going through the room, asking questions, going down
the side corridors, checking doors—checking every clue
Nomari might have given them.

Nomari's Guild-appointed aishid had trusted him too soon, too much, and likely now hoped against all fear to the contrary that the potential lord of Ajuri might just have strayed into the moving shadows, one of them apt to turn around at any moment and say, "One regrets, nadiin—I lost track of *you.*"

Jago turned up right beside him, backlit by glare. "Algini and lord Machigi's aishid are going outside, circling the building in opposite directions, hoping to find some indication. It is full dark. The street is entirely vacant. No vehicle has moved."

"The underground. The escape tunnel."

"Staff is already searching there," Jago said. "Bindanda is leading the search in the basement. He cannot have passed the kitchen."

"No telling what ancient details they may have left off the map," Bren said, and there was a distant thump. The lights came on without warning, flickered as if they would go again, and stayed on. All across the huge space, people, mostly Guild, stopped and looked about, taking stock of the situation, where they were and who was there. Bregani and Murai gazed about them, as if hoping for their daughter to appear after all, but that was not the case.

They had to be told the situation.

"We are searching outside," Bren said, approaching them, "as well as below. Nandi, within the last few moments we have also lost track of Nomari. We do not know how, but violence does not seem to be involved. We are searching for him as well."

"Gods," Bregani said.

"One agrees," Bren said. Ragi had no word for love, let alone love-struck. There were indelicate words. It also had several words for noble intentions gone awry. "It may be a notion of helping the search. We do not know. Is there *any* indication you have, any idea the route this young man could have taken besides the escape tunnel?"

"The garden. The observatory . . . the terrace." The ready quantity of exceptions to security was appalling in itself. "None are easy. But to a young man . . ."

Machigi also joined them, listening. Bregani cast an uneasy glance look toward him. So did Murai.

"I have no idea," Machigi said. "Yes, I know him. Yes, he has been under my orders in the past. But not in this."

"You have no clue," Bren said. "No hint."

"I have made no secret of spying on our host during the last regime. And recently . . . yes. I was the source of the dowager's information on the state of affairs with Tiajo. But I have nothing to do with either disappearance: my guard is out searching for your daughter, nandiin, to the best of their skill. What my former agent has done or where he has gone I have no idea."

"Did he mention Husai at any time?" Bren asked. "Have you any indication of his state of mind?"

Machigi's cold gaze settled on him. "His state of mind? Confused. He is offered everything. He is accustomed to nothing. He has no idea how to talk to *me* on this trip. He is a lord and not a lord, a Ragi who has spent years down in the Marid, making associations and selling some of them to the highest bidder. Is he attracted to your daughter, nandiin? He has never been a fool before. But I cannot read him at all since he has come back from the north. *Guild* appears to have lost him. *I* am impressed. We should all be impressed."

Machigi's humor could not soothe distraught parents. Bren asked sharply: "You do not think he has been working for the other side."

"No. Or if he has, I will be further impressed," Machigi said, and to Bregani and Murai: "Nandiin, I assure you, if I had the least clue as to your daughter's whereabouts in this city, I would say it. But *he* might have an idea."

Transportation Guild. Access to commerce. Trains. Trucks. Ships and fishing boats. Everything that moved, from people to mail.

"Nandi," Jago said, and handed Bren her communications unit, not troubling to hide the transaction.

Banichi, certainly. He held the unit to his ear and walked a few paces away, for privacy. "This is Bren. What do we know?"

"Nothing yet," Banichi said. *"We believe Nomari is acting on his own. We suspect he has been inside this building before, and we suspect he has gotten outside, by what route we still do not know. Once into that warren below the kitchens, there is more than one escape tunnel. Bindanda thought he had that blocked, but we were unaware of the ventilation system."*

"Lord Machigi denies knowing anything of this," he said. "I tend to believe him. Husai is the one we have to find, above all else. Does the dowager know?"

"To my knowledge, no. She has retired for the night and we have not heard otherwise. Cenedi is acting on his own in the matter. We are closing streets and both bridges, and we have sent units northeast of the city in case they attempt to leave by land. But this extensive underground around the residency is proving a problem. Apparently these excavations penetrate ancient foundations, extending about a city block from the modern walls, some used for storage, some filled in. We do not know whether this was the route taken. It might have been. For all we know this interconnection of ancient ruins may connect with some modern excavation going off in its own direction. We are searching, but we deem the most logical direction of flight is toward the port, where nothing is moving; or toward the northern hills. They cannot get out by vehicle. We are preventing so much as the launch of a fishing boat, and the navy has boats out. We are covering everything possible. The speed and means by which this was carried off do not argue for amateurs or haphazard planning. Stay where you are, Bren-ji. Encourage everyone to stay in that area. Do not leave the group."

"Yes," he said. "Without question." He handed the

unit back to Jago, who had come to stand near him. She listened a moment, then said "Yes," and closed the conversation.

Bregani and Murai were looking at him, clearly hoping and dreading at once. "There is no news yet," Bren said. "Roads are blocked. Ships and boats are prevented from moving. We are devoting all our resources to finding your daughter."

"If he is looking for her . . ." Murai said, "if *he* is looking for her. . . ."

"He has been here before," Bregani said. "I am more and more certain he has been inside the residency. Not with that name. But I suspect he knows ways *we* may not."

"Husai-daja is our total concern," Bren said, "we will not stop looking. The dowager's people and the other Guild force will all do their utmost."

And what had laid hands on Husai might cross Nomari's path, he thought. Human feelings said there *was* a connection and that Nomari's action was emotional. It was a mental pitfall to say it was a young man in love, when one had to change mental languages even to express the thought—but—

Throw over the likelihood of a province of the aishidi'-tat—to be on the side of the kidnappers and duck out to join them? Nothing of that made sense. If Nomari were Shadow Guild the last thing that agency would want was to lose him as lord of Ajuri. As a logical choice, that was off the chart.

And for an atevi lad, last heir of a line, to throw over his own heritage, give up the associations that could restore his clan, his inheritance, his identity. . . .

Lovesick fool did not remotely translate, let alone apply. Man'chi certainly would account for anything. But man'chi in Nomari's instance, if it was not to Machigi—where was it now? Possibly to Damiri, maybe to Tatiseigi, possibly to Cajeiri, and most likely, very most likely—to his dead brother and parents. The connections led in circles that did not involve Senjin.

And how did any of those translate to reckless action on behalf of a girl he had only just met?

All those years ago, a young boy had found his family murdered, and fled, helpless to do anything.

Was *that* the real man'chi? A duty unable to be done years ago? A nightmare seen and seen again . . . when he had been far too young to do anything?

Their innocent, bewildered boy might not be an innocent, might never have been an innocent, or helpless, where it came to revenge. Shadow Guild agents within his reach, a knowledge of the premises that even Bregani might not have . . .

And the skills to elude his own bodyguard?

Nomari was not going to be found, he thought. "We have to concentrate all efforts on Husai," he said. "Relay that to Banichi. Let Nomari go. She has to be the priority."

There were, Algini and Machigi's bodyguard reported, no evident signs of egress aboveground. Machigi's aishid was coming back, having run out of traces. Algini was reporting back to Banichi, downstairs. With the lights back on, Bindanda and Narani were investigating and interviewing staff downstairs, while Jeladi assumed the pose of an ordinary servant upstairs. They had totally cleared the tables and brought up food and drink they could be sure of.

All of them were exhausted, and most of them had lost any inclination to sleep.

The various clan heads, Senjin and Farai, and the smaller subclans, had gathered around Bregani and Murai at their large table, quiet, sleep-deprived and grim-faced. Bregani and Murai were in no mood for questions from anyone, and Bren had no answers and no inclination to be diverted with questions. Jago reported what there was to report, audible to all of them, and to certain Guild-seniors who came to stand close in the deathly silence. It was no news of Husai, no news at all for the most part, except the reports of units in the Justiciary and on the street, negative, negative, negative.

The situation at the port, regarding the freighter that had attempted to break out, was static. Persons had boarded the Dojisigi freighter and some aboard had tried to leave. Five people had attempted to swim to the dock, and were now in what the Guild called "precautionary custody" pending further developments. The navy ship now held the center of the harbor and deployed small motor launches along the coast as far as several villages adjacent to Lusi'ei.

There had been one incident: a shot fired deliberately short had sent one fishing boat hastily back to its launch point, to be met by Guild ashore. That crew of fishermen had three whose hands did not show any evidence of physical labor . . . so they were answering questions. But thus far they were providing nothing of interest.

Nothing, meanwhile, was moving in city streets. There had been a few ambulance calls, answered, one elderly person moved to hospital, one fall from a roof, likewise, and a baby currently making its way into the world.

But no word of Nomari. And none of Husai.

Bren envisioned the map, a fair distance of marshland and flat plain that was largely hunting range, lying between the railroad and the first of the Dojisigin villages. There was no road to speak of: commerce between Senjin and the Dojisigin was almost entirely by sea. That was cut off. And any persons moving out of Lusi'ei on foot would be crossing pest-ridden grassland and salt marsh, not speeding along an established route.

Geigi had been alerted regarding the open marshlands, that was Jago's quiet statement, which said far more than the Senjini listening would figure. Heatsensitive eyes were on that region. Bren was glad to know it, but he made no comment. It was a classified ability.

And meanwhile they waited, with the situation in the city uneasy and the situation across the Marid Sea developing further and further from Ilisidi's intentions.

Ilisidi was asleep, Cenedi said. One wondered. One wondered was she taken aback so severely it had affected her health—or was it a story to delay questions and gather information? Was it a delay to use secure communications to have a passionate conversation with her grandson, or with Lord Geigi?

And one had to wonder, critically, who *was* commanding the navy at the moment. Ilisidi had moved two ships here and now had one. Where the ships were concerned, Tabini-aiji had to at least have neglected to object to her moving them out of the straits.

Now one of them had diverted off toward the Dojisigin port, and that cast doubt on the idea it was solely the Assassins' Guild Council in charge of the situation to the east. The Guild had arrived with transport sufficient to move into the Dojisigin—evidently—and one was beginning to suspect they had come with intent and that it was not a response to some change in the Dojisigi stance. *Would* the average Dojisigi take up arms to resist the northern Guild? Civilians were immune from Guild action—unless they attacked Guild members, which was an insane thing to do, at least in the north, where people were assured they and their property would not be at issue.

But the Shadow Guild had not had any such policy. And Assassins' Guild and Shadow Guild wore the same uniform, when the latter chose to wear a uniform. They used the same style of attack and defense. One *was* the other, except where they were not.

And except that the Shadow Guild had deliberately created fear around it. One only hoped that fear of them in the Dojisigi citizenry would serve the same purpose as trust of the Guild in the rest of the aishidi'tat, and that civilians would not fling themselves into harm's way to protect Tiajo.

It was also fairly certain that taking out Tiajo would not force a truce. She was an instrument of the Shadow Guild; she was not in command of it. The commander of the outlaw Guild was a far more obscure figure, and when they took out that commander, there would be another, and another, down to the last isolated units to mop up. Very, very few of that lot would surrender. Very few would have any remote claim of innocence.

And if he himself had imagined they could frighten the Shadow Guild out of Senjin and concentrate them in the Dojisigin—

Their own operation moving into Koperna had been quick and virtually seamless, the citizenry mightily inconvenienced, but only for a few hours before a relief system was in place to offer medical care, food and water, communication through a still-functioning phone and broadcast network, and assistance.

In this case, with Bregani's cooperation, they had occupied the capital and locked everything down with little more distress than a city ordinarily suffered overnight— fewer, perhaps, since the taverns and entertainments were all closed down and the crime rate was nothing.

The likelihood of anything so peaceful happening in the Dojisigin, however, was small. *Their* lord would not be on the airwaves telling them to seek shelter and avoid panic. Tiajo's style was temper, outrage, extravagant claims—threatening assassination of her personal targets. Every official would be at fault. Every householder would be on his own.

And if the Shadow Guild had lost any sense of usefulness in Tiajo, they would be taking every possible means to vacate the province and leave Tiajo and her ministers to face what arrived.

It was going to be noisy, and it was not going to be pretty.

And Ilisidi's intention, to deal with the Shadow Guild by attrition, was evidently not what was happening to the east, and exactly what she had promised Senjin would not happen. It was a risky move in terms of outcome, and certainly risky in terms of Marid attitudes toward northern intervention.

And what was the Shadow Guild's countermove? One kidnapping to threaten another key individual— their new ally. Murai's personal bodyguard under detention, one compromised. The upset of a teacup upstairs and a well-timed blackout downstairs, with one servant now undergoing questioning. It was wholly their style.

No ransom demand would come. That was not the way the Shadow Guild operated. Bregani would know, initially, that he had to cooperate with the dowager and go through with the agreements with Machigi . . . but later, quietly, perhaps a message conveyed by another compromised servant, instruction would come, something to undo everything the dowager had done. His aishid knew it. Cenedi knew it. Bren had no doubt Bregani and Murai at least grasped the outlines of it, and were already making mental reservations about what they dared do, could do, *should* do to try to save their daughter. Instinct was strong. But so was a proper lord's downward responsibility, that response to man'chi that was so deep and so strong.

Time enough now for Nomari to have been completely across the city. Time enough for all sorts of things to have happened. Time enough for Husai's kidnappers, perhaps, to learn that the Dojisigin itself was under attack, and that the tactic they had planned to use might not work in the way they had intended—which would make Husai not as valuable as she might have been.

Kill her? Make a statement? They were fully capable of that. A Guild unit was never utterly dependent on orders. If it was cut off, it took measures to survive. If it found other units, it rapidly sorted out a command structure and formed a hierarchy and a plan.

Time might be measured only in how long it took Husai's kidnappers to realize they were running out of resources and out of time.

"If anything can be done," he said to Jago and Tano, "if there is the remotest chance to negotiate with the people who took Husai, I am willing, personally. If we can make that contact. We have the one servant under arrest. Have we learned anything?"

Servants in fact still were present, though not moving freely, being under the glare of lights, quiet and somber. They had not advertised Husai's kidnapping. The arrest of the servant who had spilled the tea had been quiet, the man invited to the righthand corridor and behind closed doors, for inquiry into the accident—an inquiry that had gone on for a long time and might by now have launched other inquiries in the building.

"Nothing yet," Tano said. "They have names, but none that mean anything. It is the same story . . . a threat, as best we figure, levied against a servant, and not that long ago, by someone the man claims not to know, and the claim has credibility. A parent was under threat, but now under our specific protection, and the man, now willing, still has no names."

Efforts to clear the residence of problems and get Bregani and others into their own quarters before dawn had utterly come to disaster. Any servant could be compromised. Any apartment could become a problem. Bregani's cousin and his family remained at the broadcast center, occasionally running taped messages, occasionally updating with banal chatter. The lords of subclans huddled together at one table, while Bregani and Murai stayed close to Bren as often as he spoke to Tano or Jago, hoping for some word. Arrests had been made throughout the city, persons civilly detained, arrests generally without penalty, but forbidding movement except with Guild escort.

"I wonder whether I might appeal," Bren began.

"No," Jago said.

"—might appeal to these Dojisigi still in the city, in my own name, as negotiator. I would not use the dowager's authority. I would not commit her."

"These people," Tano said, "are not reachable. They have trained for years with a corrupt purpose . . . with the *intention* to betray trust for a corrupt cause. No, Bren-ji. There will be no surrender, no negotiation."

"Some might want out," Bren said.

"Could we take a different assignment?" Jago asked sharply.

"You would not," he said. "But . . ."

"Homura? Momichi? Is that the thought? They were themselves coerced. They said. And we still do not know with any certainty what they serve. No. You cannot make these outlaws good. Guild cannot lay down their knowledge, ever. Absent an honest lord, our word cannot be trusted. And their man'chi is not to honest lords."

"You say man'chi has no choice. But if all the choices you are given—"

"It is still man'chi. It will not change."

Feel it, sense it, know where it could go wrong . . . after all these years he thought he knew. He thought he was understanding the bond now, deeper than species, deeper than kinship, deep as any human attachment, with links to emotions all up and down the range of what atevi felt. No man's land. No human's land, that place. It was not love. It was an orientation. An emotional compass that defined everything.

"They have to die?" he asked.

"Most will," Tano said. And Jago:

"The best of them will."

He thought about that. The differences rarely hit him with that force these days. But what Jago had said settled into place like a last, jagged puzzle piece.

"In their man'chi, *you* are their worst enemy," Jago said. "*Humans* are a particular target. Anyone who makes peace with humans is a target. They can have no peace with Tabini-aiji because of his association with you. They hold the dowager as a particular enemy, Lord Tatiseigi as her ally, Lord Geigi as a betrayer and you as the author of all evil—if you have not guessed that,

Bren-ji. Never talk about approaching them to reason with the Shadow Guild. We would not permit it."

What could one say? The author of all evil.

The catalyst for everything that had happened . . . down to this situation.

"Nothing that has happened would ever have happened with Wilson-paidhi," Tano said. "You *are* responsible for what has happened, for the peace, for the station, for the cooperation of the kyo in the heavens, for the restoration of Tabini-aiji—things for which *our* man'chi is stronger."

"I think the dowager, Lord Tatiseigi and Lord Geigi had most to do with those events."

"There would have *been* no negotiation in the heavens," Jago said. "The kyo might have come all the same, and destroyed us. And Deana Hanks as paidhi could not have stopped it."

Deana Hanks. The paidhi the Mospheiran war party had put in to counter him. It had been a different world, when Gaylord Hanks had gotten elected to the Presidency and the Linguistics Department had sent Hanks' daughter across the straits to deal with atevi.

If the Heritage Party on the one side and the Shadow Guild on the other had their way, there would be no cooperation, no exchange of ideas, no peace, and no sharing of the space station, never mind that the Ship parked up there had its own agenda, and would not negotiate with either side. And the kyo would not have cared.

He had done, at every point, what he had to do. In his own aishid's man'chi, in the value of Tabini-aiji's administration, in the occasionally unsettling events the dowager dragged him into—in all these things he had never doubted he was making choices, crazy as they were in human terms, that picked a way through to some more favorable outcome than the alternative. Whether it delivered them all to the best answer, he had no idea. Where he was now outright terrified him. What was going on, the threat to innocents on this side and the other of the Marid Sea appalled him. He was a linguist. A translator. And he was issuing orders at a level equivalent to the highest power on the planet.

But he did not think his aishid was wrong.

"So," he said, "I do not think I have a better notion than the dowager or Tabini-aiji, regarding how to get peace in the Marid. I do not have an idea that will stop the Shadow Guild. I am uneasy that the dowager is not in charge of this, that it *is* down to the Guild—worse, that the situation in the city is in *my* hands. I feel I should do something or know something, but *not* knowing, I do not feel I should try to direct the Guild in dealing with the situation. More—I do not know whether Cenedi is on his own at the moment, making his own decisions, or carrying out her orders. I rely on Banichi. And Algini. And both of you. I have *no* grasp of our situation in the streets, except to hope we can prevent those people using Husai to break down the agreements."

"There is one worse thing that could happen," Jago said. "And that is for them to find you in their sights. If an offer comes, if you feel the urge to deal with these people—send *us*. And if you feel it would be too dangerous for us—do not go *yourself*."

"One hears. One absolutely understands."

"Because we will follow you," Tano said, "if we cannot get in front of you. So do not surprise us."

"I will not. I swear I will not." He rubbed his eyes, trying to focus his thoughts. "What *are* our assets, nadiin-ji? We have the port blocked. We have the streets blocked. We have the broadcast station safe. Is there anything we can broadcast that might convince these people to spend their one asset to get themselves out of here? Will they take a trade of amnesty? And can I give it?"

"Cenedi would be the sticking-point," Jago said. "Granted the dowager is sleeping, and not in charge, granted she will wake with the sun . . . he will likely not want to make that move without consulting."

That touched on an underlying worry. "You think she *is* sleeping?"

"One would not swear she is not awake," Tano said.

Directing Cenedi, and pretending not to, even to them? A subterfuge to cast it on the paidhi-aiji and forestall demands from the locals? Anything was possible.

Including, his deeper concern, that she had taken ill, or that Tabini had seized command of the situation and she was not acknowledging his orders. They had, damn it, an *invasion* of the Dojisigin in progress. Intervention from orbit. And Ilisidi left the paidhi-aiji in charge of the city while Tabini lit a fuse under it.

He was running on adrenaline at the moment. He had two bereft and anxious parents and a handful of lords including Machigi who were under pressure even to be in the same room, though Machigi, sitting nearby, had his arms folded and his chin down, possibly catching a little sleep.

Machigi had no direct involvement in the situation. Machigi was not in charge.

He, however, was. And he had to find something that would reassure the kidnappers that a deal could be made for a live young woman, unharmed. The sooner he could open that possibility . . . the better. Better to let a handful of scoundrels out of the city if it meant he could get Husai back alive.

He could send a search door to door if they could only have some hint—besides the likelihood the kidnappers had intended to board the freighters in the harbor—where in the city they might have hidden.

Not too far away from the residency, possibly, since the streets were blocked. But he had no way to figure that angle. It was a Guild problem. Dealing with the Shadow Guild in any form was chancy, and his aishid was right. Recklessness now could make matters far worse.

The relay network had reported the kidnapping to the Guild force sitting out there on the borderland, and possibly there was some communication Cenedi had with the navy ship now dominating the harbor. Not even a rowboat would move out there. And their enemy might not realize how fast and far they could communicate, or what they *could* see.

The lingering difficulty was that none of them here at the very center of the trouble had had that much sleep yesterday night and now they were deep into another night. There was tea to lend them energy. Bindanda and Jeladi and a small corps of cleared and verified house staff kept up a supply of safe sandwiches, and meanwhile had done a little examination of the electrical panels—there were several—and reported they had cobbled together a lock on the master switch, the sole key in their possession, and an alarm that would advise them of tampering.

Across the wide hall, exhausted civilians found sleep in chairs or on the floor, and Guild caught naps as they could, a skill Bren greatly envied. Lord Bregani and Musai maintained their own vigil, napping occasionally in sheer exhaustion, but only in snatches, and not many of those.

Quiet continued, low voices of Guild reporting to officers. They had planned to let the lords disperse to their own apartments and to have normalcy restored, but the kidnapping had changed that. No one was permitted into the side halls, and missions to and from the kitchens were all escorted. They had made one grievous mistake. They did not court another.

And still there was no word, with the night deep about the city and utter silence prevailing. Reports came in of scattered arrests, mostly of people trying to check on businesses and shops, detained, interviewed, and escorted home as it became feasible.

Bren finally managed a catnap, and waked to Jago's hand on his arm.

"Nomari is back, Bren-ji."

God. "Of his own accord?"

"He approached a patrol. He claims he can extract Husai."

That brought him fully awake. "Where?"

"He is being escorted in right now. His aishid has been notified. They are coming in from the streets."

18

The big doors opened, admitting Banichi and Algini, and, indeed, Nomari, who looked as if he had taken a fall in the street, or more than one. There was a bleeding scrape on his chin, there was blood on his coat, and his queue was only a memory of a braid: hair hung loose about his shoulders.

Bren gathered himself up, stiff from sitting, and Jago and Tano were right beside him. Murai stood up, and Bregani with her. Machigi rose. So did Machigi's plainclothes aishid. Others across the room roused, one waking another.

Nomari gave a bow to Bren, with Banichi and Algini behind him.

"So?" Bren asked.

"She is still in the city," Nomari said, looking past him to Bregani and Murai. "At least—I know people who have an idea where she is."

"Where?" Bren asked.

"Those people," Nomari said, "do not want to be known. But they see how the tide is running, and they want assurances. I have told them . . . I have said. . . . Nand' paidhi, I have made promises I cannot keep. But I have told certain people . . . assured them . . . that if they can recover your daughter, nandiin, and if they can protect her and bring her here . . . Lord Bregani . . . and the dowager . . . may overlook past problems."

"Who are these people?" Bregani asked.

"Just . . . people. Clanless, some."

"Smugglers. Dare one guess, smugglers, thieves . . ."

"All those things, nandi. But they know the city and the port. Not all are Senjini."

Machigi edged closer and stood listening, arms folded.

"Where is she?" Bregani asked. "Give us a *place,* nadi!"

"They did not tell me. But they know everything that moves in the region. I have promised rewards, nandiin. I took it on myself. I had to. I said there would be amnesty for all crimes . . . for her rescuers. For anything they have done in the past."

Not every lord of the aishidi'tat would bargain with criminals. Not in the north. Not among the Ragi. But this was the south, the Marid, where Guild had meant only the Shadow Guild, and anything went.

"Do it," Murai said faintly, and Bregani clasped her hand.

"Whatever they can do," Bregani said fervently, "let them do. If only they can get her back safely, I will agree."

"Let me go back to them," Nomari said.

Banichi looked at Bren. "Nandi?"

"Yes," Bren said.

"Do not follow me," Nomari said. "Nandi, promise me. They will not take that well. It would be dangerous for everyone."

"Banichi," Bren said. It needed a Guild decision. It was that fine line between civil authority, and Guild expertise.

"We will appoint a place," Banichi said, "where they may bring her, unharmed, and walk away safely."

"Tell them," Bregani said, "if they want to claim that

amnesty, best they walk *here,* tonight, and claim it. They will walk away free."

Banichi nodded solemnly. "A fair proposal. You will have escort to the point you contacted us, nadi, and the escort will wait for you. Go from there and tell them the conditions. The Guild will support Lord Bregani's amnesty."

"So will the dowager," Bren said. Nomari had promised it with no authority. He set the dowager's seal on it by saying so, and took the responsibility, for good or ill.

"Nandiin." Nomari bowed again. "I shall tell them. Thank you."

"Escort him down," Banichi said to Algini, and Algini waved a hand toward the doors. With a small bow, Nomari took a proper leave, escorted by Algini, but Banichi stayed a moment.

"We will meet these people, nandi," Banichi said to Bregani, "and we will honor that promise. Lord Machigi. Your opinion of this man might be of value."

"I am not informed," Machigi said. "I do not know who he is dealing with. I do not know where he went, but I doubt it was to the elite of Koperna; and I would not be surprised if some of his contacts have intimate knowledge of the Shadow Guild." A nod, a courtesy to Bregani and Murai. "But he may well have what he says. One does not believe, nandi, that he would have offered to go again if he had thought there was no good hope. If he had thought that, we would never have seen him again. I do not see him sacrificing himself as bait in a trap, and he does know sources in this city."

"One appreciates your assurance," Bregani said quietly, ignoring any irony in the statement. "Thank you, nandi."

"I shall go down," Banichi said to Bren. "Jago. Notify Cenedi. Ask him to stand fast."

"Yes," Jago said.

Banichi left. Bren turned toward his own table, to

resume waiting, and hope, now, that Nomari was not playing against the peace.

But Machigi was standing in his way. And he asked, very quietly, "Did you urge Nomari to this, nandi?"

"No," Machigi said, likewise low-voiced. "Neither his disappearance nor his choice of allies is my doing."

"I apologize, nandi, but you have had experience of him we have not. And I am not questioning your intentions or your honor, only Nomari's . . . in which you are our only source of information."

"Lord Bregani could answer with more authority regarding criminal elements in Senjin, but if I can guess, likely a man named Paigiti is involved, or will be at some level. If given a clean bill once, and adequately compensated, who knows? The old man might decide to hand his business on and retire. There would be no shortage of takers."

"Shadow Guild?" The logic of the Marid was from time to time distressing. And clearly Machigi knew a name he did not.

"A network for hire," Machigi said. "Local logistics the Shadow Guild could use to facilitate their operation. If those people, the actual kidnappers, have run beyond reach of his network, then finding her will be less easy. But they will know. In fact—they may have supplied information or assistance to the kidnappers themselves, but it may be convenient not to ask that question. In Bregani's redirection of man'chi, even thieves and extortionists have new considerations. They will be seeking their own advantage. They will realize that the relationship of Senjin to the world is changing. An offer of amnesty could be particularly good currency tonight."

He had known about the function of the criminal network in Machigi's own dealings, a factor which had made him uneasy in dealing with Machigi. It seemed increasingly likely he was going to have to rethink the entire notion of criminal, where it concerned the Marid.

Machigi's former agent taking to old routes, old contacts in *this* instance—now projected a situation in which enlisting kidnappers and extortionists became a sane course of action.

A busload of equipment announced its arrival. Bren, trying to rest, was aware of it. In the lengthy watch, in the night, lights were lowered somewhat, and with practicality above protocol, Tano and Jago occupied adjacent chairs, arms folded, heads down. Bregani and Murai rested, similarly, their bodyguard slept. Guild all over the hall rested in a quiet so deep one could hear the bus engine outside the walls. And still there was no word from below, no word from the streets. The city had swallowed up Nomari, and there was no report.

Then Jago moved suddenly, and lifted the new communicator to her ear and unfolded to her feet.

"The *dowager* is here," Jago said, as Tano moved, startling other units to move, and catching Bregani's and Murai's attention.

"She is in the building?" Bren asked.

"She is downstairs, with Cenedi. Cenedi and Casimi are taking command. Nawari is left in charge aboard the train. She is insisting on climbing the stairs. Cenedi is insisting on the freight lift in the kitchens. She will not have it."

God, that was Ilisidi. Alive, upright, and insisting on doing things her way, the old-fashioned way.

"The dowager is here?" Bregani asked, from a little distance away.

"Apparently, nandi. Lord Machigi?"

Machigi also had lifted his head, arms still folded.

"Advise Lord Bregani, nadiin-ji," Bren said. "And the rest of us." They were not the only individuals whom the dowager should not find napping, even in the middle of the night. Not that she would demand it, but that the Guild units would want notice.

The double doors at the rear opened. The lights came

up abruptly to full, someone attending that matter as, all across the hall, Guildsmen were getting to their feet.

A small, dark figure appeared in the doorway, a woman of small stature, cane in hand, with three units for a bodyguard and Cenedi's distinctive silver-haired presence right behind her. Her bodyguards carried rifles, and spread out as they entered, protective surveillance. The precision of that move and the carpet-muffled punctuation of the dreaded cane held the whole room frozen.

Waiting.

For him, Bren realized in the next heartbeat.

For temporary authority to wake up and officially give way to *her* authority. Bren walked into the clear spot they maintained for a ragged center aisle and bowed slightly.

Bregani and Murai came to Bren's left, Machigi on his right. There seemed, in the way of the Guild's communication, no need to explain the situation with Bregani's daughter to the dowager. She certainly knew.

She was immaculate in black lace sparked with rubies, Ragi red and black. Bren was far from immaculate, rumpled, in want of a shave, not at his mental best and not up to absolute current on the city or the search in progress . . . but then, the only one who knew that was not back yet.

Thump went the cane on the carpet. Both hands settled on it.

"Nandiin," she said. "We are appalled. We understand, nand' Bregani, there is some hope of locating your daughter."

"Nand' dowager," Bregani said. "We hoped you brought news."

"We have nothing yet. We have been briefed. We are determined, whatever the outcome of the appeal to local sources, that we will not let anything move out of the city in any direction, nothing out of Lusi'ei either."

The paidhi-aiji's mistake had set this up, Bren could only think. He had had resources. He should have used them better. He prepared himself for the dowager to say so, in front of Bregani and all present. But she did not. She turned and fixed him with a stare, and he bowed slightly, then stood ready for whatever she might say.

"The aishidi'tat will honor the amnesty," she said, "if it produces results. We have followed this situation from a distance. We have also alerted Lord Geigi. We are awaiting word." The cane lifted, and impacted the carpet. "We wish to sit down. Nand' paidhi, nandiin, join us."

Guild moved, in the general scarcity of servants. A table was cleared, chairs were moved, and servants scrambled to fill a new tea service, while the dowager took a chair, and Bregani and Murai and Machigi did. Bren settled in the remaining chair, which Cenedi had held empty at Ilisidi's right, the preferred side, not—he judged—without significance, though he was not sure it was a case of favor.

Banichi still was absent. So was Algini. But Casimi, who was supposed to be with Cenedi, had not appeared as yet, was very likely taking command of the situation downstairs, indeed, of the whole operation.

Tano took station immediately behind Bren, which left Jago free to communicate with downstairs—if that were needed.

Tea made the rounds. Bren sipped his gingerly, his stomach entirely uneasy. It was a strong tea, a stimulant, and his nerves by no means needed the jolt.

The engine sound grew loud and then diminished out on the street. "The bus is going back," Ilisidi said, "so as not to disturb the city. Or to scare off these proposed rescuers."

Moving by night was nothing new for the dowager. Neither was taking over a situation that had spiraled out of control. She wore placidity like a mantle, as if nothing in particular had gone wrong, but that was also an appearance she could assume, while concealing a furious anger—if it served her to conceal it. Cenedi was in charge now, Cenedi who would not leave the dowager's side, and Casimi, who was under his orders, downstairs.

Likely orders from Cenedi had gone out by courier to various units—she had hinted at it—and dictated certain moves that would now be underway in Koperna and relayed over to Lusi'ei. God knew how it related to what was going on over in the Dojisigin. But it was certain that Ilisidi knew what was happening over there.

An audience had gathered at a respectful distance, meanwhile, a knot of lordly onlookers roused out from the fringes, positioned behind Bregani and Murai. The heads of the subclans were backing Bregani still, watching the situation anxiously—their lord, with Machigi, with the aiji-dowager and a force that had effectively taken over their city—while making an enemy of the lord of the Dojisigin in the process. It was not a happy expression on any of those faces. But with the capital in the hands of the northern Guild and the northern Guild now attacking their former ally, their choices were all but gone.

"Aiji-ma," Bren said quietly, "to the left, the lords of the subclans, Lusi, Farai, Juni, Prsegi, who are equally worried." He named them off, one by one, political expediency, although he detected, despite Ilisidi's smiles and nods, that she was not as serene as seemed. There was tension, a great deal of it, and probably there were things to be said about mistakes which Cenedi would say, on unbreachable relay, to Banichi.

Not to mention what judgment Ilisidi might make of the paidhi's management of the situation. It was not Banichi's fault. It was decidedly not Banichi's fault, and not Jago's, that the paidhi-aiji had managed to lose both Husai and Nomari in the same hour.

But the smile persisted as she addressed Bregani and Murai: "We have agents out looking, still. One hopes the candidate for Ajuri can manage this on his own, nandi, but if otherwise, we will take measures. We will keep our promises, and using an agency you yourselves have seen, nandiin, that too is involved in the search, at this moment."

What Bregani and Murai had seen was nothing the other lords could imagine . . . technology descending from the heavens.

"We had rather use the Ajuri's plan," the dowager added, "if possible. Your daughter is our chief concern, and your law rules here, nandiin. Grant amnesty, indeed. To us, too, your daughter's safety is a higher order of concern."

"To us—everything."

"We do have a message," Cenedi said out of silence. "A patrol is reporting from the area of concern. Our patrol is allowing approach."

"Is it the Ajuri?" Murai asked. "Have they found her?"

There was a moment of waiting.

"Nomari-nadi's bodyguard has evidently found *him*, nandi, but not alone. They have called a second unit for backup."

"What does that mean?" Murai asked.

"Nandi, the network has not passed that information. We know where he is. Other units are moving to be sure of the area."

"They must not frighten these people away!"

"We are issuing that caution, nandi," Cenedi said. "We are limited in communication. We do not want to inform our enemies. We understand the Ajuri is approaching. We do not, unhappily, have direct communication with him. I am bidding them let him go or come as he wishes, under observation if possible."

A moment's silence.

"He has retreated. He is with a group of six persons, who are in deep shadow."

"Gods," Bregani said. There was quiet all across the hall, as various units were reading that same information.

Jago listened quietly to her communications, the

same that Cenedi and Banichi had. Her face was grave, intent, but not indicative of bad news.

"Do you have identification?" Cenedi asked someone on the relay system, and listened. Cenedi's face betrayed nothing. Jago, likewise listening, gave a strong positive in her own expression.

"They have her," Cenedi confirmed. "They have her, Nomari-nadi, and six civilians who insist on the provisions of the amnesty. They are coming in."

"Is she all right?" Bregani asked.

"Indeterminate, nandi."

"I am going down," Murai said. "I am going down."

"No," Cenedi said. "We do not know the situation. Be patient. She is effectively in our hands now."

The clan lords had moved within hearing. There was a stir, an outburst of questions, a Guild remonstrance, and then quiet. They waited, listening. The dowager accepted an offered chair, sipped a cup of tea, likewise listening, and a servant hovered, eventually to refill the cup.

Downstairs, the doors opened: the building was so utterly quiet one could hear the entry, and distant voices.

"She is inside," Cenedi said, listening. "She is unconscious. There are six locals with Nomari. He says he promised them an audience with Lord Bregani as well as the amnesty and he asks for a physician."

"Nand' Siegi," Ilisidi said, and her own physician, always near, always with his kit when she was in the field, moved close. "Nand' paidhi!" Ilisidi said.

"Aiji-ma," Bren answered.

"Be our eyes," Ilisidi said. "Find what needs finding. Nandiin, be patient. Let Guild and the paidhi-aiji separate your daughter from those people and see to her welfare. Let us manage things with as little excitement as we can manage. Nand' paidhi. Nand' Siegi. Go."

Bren gave a short bow and went. Siegi was an old

man, and entrained two assistants. Bren had Jago and Tano with him. Narani and Jeladi stayed behind, with unsecure communications; and maintained communication too, with Bindanda down in the kitchens.

"One hears," Jago said to someone as they started down the stairs. "We are coming with the physician."

19

It was a strangely assorted lot in the lower hall: Nomari knelt by Husai, Husai unconscious in his arms. Standing by him, with Banichi, was Ilisidi's man Casimi, with a heavy-armed and determined Guild unit and another, lighter-armed, with a scruffy contingent, five rough-looking types attending a white-haired man who could be a banker or a businessman, by his prosperous dress—and was very likely neither.

Bren walked in with added Guild presence, and stood with Banichi, consciously small, pale, and very foreign to these rough Senjini folk, none of whom would have ever seen a human at close range, and who clearly were not expecting it now. The looks were guarded, resentful—not an uncommon attitude in the Marid—and uneasy. The white-haired man looked him up and down with evident unease.

"Nand' Bren," Banichi said, by way of introduction. "Lord of Najida, paidhi-aiji. And nand' Siegi, the dowager's own physician. Nomari-nadi, if you will."

Nomari stayed as he was, holding Husai, while nand' Siegi checked her pulse, then her eyes, and curiously, her breath.

"Tadja," Nomari said in a low voice, "we think. We hope."

"It is," Siegi said, and gave an instruction to his assistant, who took his kit and selected a vial.

"She should be all right in a few hours," Nomari said, looking up, as if he hoped to believe it himself. "We think she may have been unconscious through all of it."

We included his very dubious companions, it seemed, none of whom said a thing.

The assistant prepared a hypodermic. Siegi moved Husai's sleeve and gave an injection, which did nothing immediate. Siegi took her wrist, afterward, tracking her pulse, and held the edge of his hand near her lips, tracking her breathing.

There was lengthy silence. Husai suddenly moved her arm, brushed at her face as if batting something away.

Her eyes showed a flutter of returning tension, but did not quite open. The hand returned to her midriff.

"A good response," Siegi said to an assistant crouching near. "Take her upstairs, nadiin. I shall follow."

"The matter of a promise," the businessman said, rough voice belying the fine coat, and the five with him took a stance that evoked an answering move from surrounding Guild.

Nand' Siegi's assistants gathered Husai up, and Nomari rose.

"A promise," the businessman insisted, and put out an arm, barring Nomari or Husai going anywhere. The Senjini had not been disarmed. In an instant Guild rifles were in motion. Banichi and Algini stopped that, and everything stopped.

Bren stepped out and lifted his hand in a forbidding gesture.

"Deal," he said sharply, "or lose, nadiin. One assumes you came here in trust. Stand and accept your lord's agreement to an amnesty. But be aware, nadi, and be cautious. The amnesty on which you have acted is for past doings, not current or future ones. On the other hand, you have an excellent opportunity to change your future.

So make a choice. I represent, in this matter, Lord Bregani. In more extensive matters, the aiji-dowager."

Motion had stopped. All motion had stopped.

"We want paper," the businessman said. "Signatures and seals."

"We are willing. Our business is here. The lord's daughter is to be taken up to care. If you have been in any way responsible for the young woman's abduction—"

"I am not!"

"—you would still be forgiven by the terms of the amnesty. If not, if instead you have been the agents of the young woman's rescue, you may benefit."

"We found her," the businessman said. "We took her back. We took out your damned problem."

"Did you take them out?" Banichi asked. "Or chase them off?"

"Out," the businessman said. "Dead. And my merchandise shot up."

"Unfortunate regarding the merchandise," Bren said, not stopping to argue nuances. "Then I ask you stand aside. This is the aiji-dowager's own physician. Do not interfere with him. He will take her up to her family, while we shall see about that paper you want."

There was no argument. Bren motioned. Jago and Tano moved to screen nand' Siegi and his aides, and one of the regular Guild moved in to take Husai, a tall, solid man to whom her weight was very little. Seigi and company completed their withdrawal from the confrontation, toward the side hall, Husai still seeming unaware. Nomari, sooty as well as muddy, as two of the Senjini were, stood watching, not venturing to make himself part of that group.

"Paper," the businessman said.

"Kindly honor me with your name," Bren said, "nadi."

"Paigiti. Owner of Paigiti Shipping."

So Machigi had been right. Absolutely right.

"Not myself, nor any of mine was involved in this," Paigiti said. "None of us. None of it. I want that understood, top to bottom. This has cost me property. Bullets went everywhere. Five pallets of glassware! Drums of lye! Four pallets of salt spilling onto the floor! That's a damned mess!"

"So all of you are innocent, and have no motive for asking amnesty," Bren said. "Just the damage."

There was a moment of quiet. "Everybody has something he needs amnesty for."

Bren absorbed that philosophy with a placid nod. "Indeed. And Nomari-nadi, you were able to contact these people quite handily—as a resource. You knew where they were."

"I knew nand' Paigiti's office," Nomari said.

"And he knew about the kidnapping?"

"I know how to find out." Paigiti's language was rawer, rougher than his clothing. "Anything that moves in this city, in the port, I know it!"

Nand' Paigiti, was it? Was there a lordship involved?

"How," Bren asked, "were you informed of a kidnapping?"

A little light of caution went on in Paigiti's eyes. "The boy came asking. I asked around."

"Your warehouse, however."

The light flickered. "I rent space to a lot of people. I don't ask. And all that is under the amnesty, whatever it is. Right? We got her out. We brought her back. Taisigi-boy says we get to meet with his lordship."

And now they had heavily-armed criminals standing one floor below the aiji-dowager. Disarming the ruffians presented a delicate situation. Getting them out the door was preferable; but rewards had been promised, and Paigiti was clearly not happy to deal with a human, especially one that asked embarrassing questions.

Well, it was not the first time he had met that problem.

"Nomari-nadi," Bren said quietly, nodding with full courtesy. Taisigi-boy, indeed. "We are glad to see you safe. You may go upstairs."

"No," Paigiti said. "No such thing. We know who she

is and what her father owes us. We want this amnesty in writing, signed and sealed with ribbons, and we want it legal!"

"You have it from the representative of the aiji-dowager, nadi," Bren said, "which is better than paper. You have to be patient with the process."

"No talking around it! We want that document."

"Paigiti," a strong voice said from the intersection of the corridor, Paigiti's bandits twitched, triggering a like reaction from the Guild; and Machigi strolled into view from the adjoining hall and stairway, with his own non-conformist bodyguard of four ex-rangers. "Paigiti! My old associate!"

"Machigi!" Paigiti said. "The blaspheming gods' own foot-washer. I heard you were involved."

"I hear you want to be forgiven."

"I hear you got yourself a deal. Too good for your old connections these days, are you?"

"I hear Tiajo has made you a good many deals. I hear a lot of things. I hear that you hid that boy of yours up north. You should move him home. Word is getting around to very dangerous places."

"You!"

"I am not the source," Machigi said. "But if I have heard it, she has. Ask the paidhi. You might make protection for that son of yours part of the deal. It costs a very little ink."

A son, in the north, hidden from Tiajo's increasingly frequent recourse to kidnapping and murder—the same they had just prevented. There was no trouble understanding that, or the value of Machigi's intervention.

"Ink is extraordinarily cheap," Bren said. "As is wax and ribbon. Good will is harder come by. A good relationship with lords other than Tiajo would be a sensible thing to ask, forgiveness for past misdeeds, a reluctance to commit more." One had no illusions that Paigiti was in any sense an honest man. There was every likelihood he had worked *with* the Shadow Guild. The damaged warehouse being his property *and* the place Husai had been held—all that pointed to complicity in everything that had ever crawled in Senjin. "There will be no problem in getting your immunity. Understand me: the Marid is changing. Everything is changing. New commerce is coming here, along with Guild enforcement, in which transactions off the books are a crime. You will have your amnesty, you and yours. The moment the amnesty is signed, *all* past crimes are wiped out. Your hired men will be immune from prosecution for anything done for you or others, as, Paigiti-nadi, you will be immune from prosecution or lawsuit for anything you have done or asked them to do. Absolutely clear and clean and as fresh as a new flower. You will have a document signed, sealed, and ribboned, as you ask. But the text, nadiin. The *text* and the legalities. To gain immunity for crimes, you must *list* the crimes you wish to be forgiven. You must identify—"

"Gods below, no! This is outside the deal!"

"This is the law," Cenedi said quietly. "The Guild will be enforcing law in the Marid, authorized by Lord Bregani, until further notice, and if you wish immunity and protection, the paidhi-aiji is telling you exactly the document you must sign."

"You will be immune to prosecution or Guild action," Bren said. "So you should have no fear for the past."

"Not safe from my enemies!" Pagiti objected.

"Immunity grants you *legal* innocence," Bren said. "Anyone who pursues you cannot cite past crimes. And you seem to have an aishid that you do rely on. I reiterate: to gain immunity, you must identify place, and victim, or area of activity, and approximate date, and you must name accomplices as best you can. For all named crimes, you and these several men will be clear. If you commit crimes after signing—then you will be vulnerable to prosecution. And *if* you wish your son—I take it there is a son in the north—to be given protection and a safe conduct south by the Guild, that can be arranged, so far as his transport here, or to some place of his choosing. Is that what you wish?"

Paigiti was breathing hard, incensed, and Husai was now safely upstairs. Paigiti looked in the direction of that vanished asset, then swung around and pointed at Nomari. "Is *he* innocent?" Paigiti asked, and then pointed at Machigi. "Or shall I name *this* person, and his crimes?"

"Name away," Machigi said, and he and his were provocatively close. "I *am* immune. I have had *my* discussion with the Guild and the dowager. We have a fine understanding. And you could do worse right now than court my patronage and nand' Bregani's. We Taisigi are in a position either to make your operations difficult, or to turn you into the honest businessman you pretend to be. Honest. And an abundantly flowing source of information. *That* is how you play this dice-throw. Ask the paidhi-aiji. He is the only *entirely* honest and disinterested lord in this building!"

One was appalled. Entirely appalled. Likely, if Cenedi's contact was open, Ilisidi might be following everything.

"Dirty human!" Paigiti said. "Thieves and pirates!"

One had to appreciate the irony.

"Honesty," Machigi drawled in his thickest Marid accent, "is a truly frightening power. He has it. Do you dare, Giti-sa? Do you dare deal with a man who will not lie to you? He will tell the truth to you, and he will tell it to me, and to Lord Bregani and to the aiji-dowager. So get your story straight and be very honest in that list-making. You would not want to leave something out that could come back to haunt you."

Machigi had set the proposition. It was there to use, when Paigiti looked in Bren's direction, staring in deep anger at the pale oddity in this place.

Bren said, "I have your best interest at heart. And I assure you that the truth, on that list, will not be used against you. But anything you hide can come back and ruin you."

"Filth!"

"Your chance at an honest life, nadi. One and one only. How much is it worth?"

"My *life,* when Tiajo gets wind of it!"

"Tiajo will not hold her lordship forever. In fact, she may not have it tomorrow morning. Things can change profoundly in the Dojisigin, overnight."

That drew a stare, a long one.

"Trust me," Bren said.

"Damn you," Paigiti said.

"Is that your considered answer? You will reject the amnesty?"

"No!" Paigiti said, scowling. "No. Give me a place to write."

"Make them all comfortable, nadiin," Bren said to the Guild around them. "A table, a writing kit. Tea or winc, absolutely. Vodka. Give them every courtesy. I shall get the form of the document from Lord Bregani, and their pages may be inserts. Be sure we have them in quadruplicate."

"I shall happily sign it as witness myself," Machigi said, "or perhaps as principal, granted the list includes things that may involve *my* interests, do you think, old ally? Two for one. And *I* shall throw in pardons for your enterprise in Sungeni and the Dausigin as well as my own province—if they are on the list."

"Damn you both," was Paigiti's response to that. "Yes. Those too."

"How is she?" was Bren's first question to Banichi on the way up the stairs, with Algini and Tano and Jago behind them. Machigi and his guard had gone up ahead of them. So had Nomari, with his own. Paigiti remained with Casimi, provided a conference room, with a desk, his escort, and as much alcohol as they might wish—in the interests of good memory, as Jago put it.

"Husai is coming out of it, still," Banichi said, who had direct communication with Cenedi. "They have taken her to her own room."

"The Guild unit who was with her . . . ?"

"They will recover, though they had the worst of it and will not be fit for duty. Siegi is sending out to a hospital for supplies. He will transfer that unit down to the train soon, where they can be treated. We think it was the same substance in both instances, but they caught the worst of it. Husai will be increasingly unclear on what happened. Eventually she will simply not remember—characteristic of this drug."

"Tadja."

"That is what they are calling it, whether the historic original or some modern concoction. We have seen it in the north. It is rare, it is expensive, it has some medical benefit, but the Physicians' Guild has restricted it severely. The Guild unit that was overdosed is very fortunate not to be dead. If they had not been in reach of a medic as quickly as they were, they would have been. The kidnappers were far more careful with the daughter. Mind, Bren-ji, if ever you smell bitterfruit in the air, hold your breath and get out."

"One hears," Bren said. "Is it always airborne?"

"It can arrive either in tea," Banichi said, "or airborne—tea is safer. And this is the second time we have seen it used by the Shadow Guild."

They reached the upper floor through a scatter of staff and bystanders, residents as yet lacking a place; and passed the double doorway, where everything was under bright light, with an abundance of black uniforms. Bregani and Murai were nowhere present. One assumed they were with their daughter, and nand' Siegi.

The dowager was likewise absent, as was Cenedi: likely she had retired to some place secure and private, one of the cleared apartments, as soon as they had brought Husai upstairs. Siegi was likely in attendance with one or the other.

Machigi and his bodyguard were at a table, in consultation, doubtless saying interesting things in the privacy of ambient noise.

Then, over by the wall, in a cluster of chairs . . . Nomari sat, arms folded, head down, with his escort. His queue trailed a sad ribbon over one shoulder. His coat was ripped at the shoulder and stained with soot and dirt, as was the rest of him. The young man looked absolutely done.

His own aishid were themselves worn and wind-blown, having been out in the streets searching for him. No discussion was going on in that group. None would be easy. Man'chi, however new and tenuous, had been grossly abused, and there was no good excuse. Cenedi was not going to be pleased with the unit. Banichi likely was not. Neither Tabini nor the dowager nor his aishid nor the Guild Council was apt to be pleased with Nomari.

Bren went to the table he had claimed earlier, with chairs that had still escaped borrowers, a great relief. He leaned on the table, preparatory to pulling his chair back—which Jago did for him.

But he glanced aside at Nomari, who was now staring off at nothing, or everything, but not talking; and against all common sense to let it go the way it would, he saw a troubled man'chi, and a team that could not be happy to have lost a young man in a guarded room.

Narani held a tea service, waiting to set it down until after Bren was seated.

Bren straightened his shoulders and said, quietly, "Take the service to Nomari's group, Rani-ji."

Then he followed Narani to the group by the wall and, there being an unused chair in the vicinity, he pulled it over himself, and sat. Nomari, not totally insensible, half-rose, as did his aishid. Bren signed Nomari to sit down, at which Nomari and his aishid all settled uneasily.

"There are things to be worked out," he said, conscious that Banichi had come over, displacing Jago, who had followed him over.

"One regrets, nadiin," he said to the aishid, "that you had difficulty. But I am sure the candidate has expressed that. One regrets extremely. He clearly has developed certain skills at misdirection I trust he will never use on his own aishid again."

Silence followed. Nomari looked at his hands, and at his own aishid, and never quite at Bren. "One regrets profoundly," Nomari said. "Not the action. But your inconvenience, nadiin."

The Guild-senior of the aishid said nothing. The members of the unit said nothing. Nomari sat in excruciating silence. Something was called for.

"I myself came to the aishidi'tat as a stranger," Bren said. "I taxed the patience and expectations of my aishid extremely. On a certain occasion, out of regard for them, I attempted to protect one of my aishid, who informed me in no uncertain terms that she would shoot me herself if I did that again. I confess I have erred since. But I try to remember my place, and I am immeasurably grateful to them. They do not need *my* protection. And they are patient with me. *Why* did you go after Husai, nadi, without telling your aishid?"

Another lengthy silence. Nomari seemed to have something stuck in his throat.

Bren waited.

"If they had seen Guild, there would have been shooting," Nomari said. "And I could talk to Paigiti—having that history with him. I knew where he would probably be. And I know everything rests on Lord Bregani keeping his word. I know Paigiti deals with the Dojisigi, provides routes, places, information. It is not illegal, in Senjin. It has not been illegal, at least. His dealings through me, with Lord Machigi, generally were. Illegal. All of them."

"So you just walked out," Banichi said, standing, arms folded.

"Nadi—nadiin, nandi, I could. I did. I could *do* something that needed to be done. That is the sum of it."

"Spy," Banichi said.

"Yes, nadi."

"And a live spy, traveled all the way around the aishidi'tat and the Marid at will. A spy who found his way to Lord Tatiseigi, and the Bujavid, and here, out again and back, and is still alive." Banichi's deep voice was low and quiet, for this area alone. "You have an interesting principal, brothers, with very high professional skills, and one suggests you discuss with him the signals that should pass between you. Perhaps my partner's promise to shoot the paidhi-aiji might make the point with the candidate, should you wish to stay with him. *Something* needs to be understood. Something needs to be agreed very seriously and lastingly."

"He has been considerate of us," Guild-senior said. "He has been *too* considerate throughout. And too *little* considerate, in this. We do not know, at this point, whether we have his respect."

"More than respect, Barijo," Nomari said. "My profoundest regret for causing concern and for putting you at risk."

"Did you think we would not follow an order?"

"I have appreciated that your orders come from the aiji-dowager, nadi. I am sorry. I did not think you would regard mine."

Guild-senior, Barijo, nodded slowly. "From Guild Council, actually. Yes, we would have restrained you unless you had an authorization. That is where you fit in the chain of command in this operation, and it might have saved a deal of worry, nadi. We erred in turning our backs for a moment. That is where we were in the process of trusting you. It was our mistake."

Nomari lowered his gaze to his folded arms. And nodded. "I would do it again, to do what I did. But I profoundly apologize. I would ask you to stay, nadi. I would ask all of you to stay."

"Do you need our advice?" Barijo asked. "Or will you manage without?"

"I would say I do need it, absolutely. I was in the wrong, where you are concerned. Not," Nomari said, frowning, still looking down, "*not* in getting Husai out."

Husai, was it, Bren thought, and not *lord Bregani's daughter?*

"We shall discuss how that should have gone," Barijo said.

"Will you stay, nadiin?" Nomari asked.

"Pending," Barijo said.

"We shall leave you to that," Bren said, pushed back from the table and stood up. "Tea, nadiin. While it is hot. Narani has brought you a pot."

Discussion, that was to say. There were nods, respectful, silent. There *was* a good deal of discussion that needed to be had at that table.

For his part, standing up, Bren found the low buzz of conversation in the room surreal, and the room, familiar after so many hours, and not, likewise surreal, as if the world could waver out of reality and back. He made his way back to his table, and a place to sit and lean. Banichi sat down beside him. Tano and Jago remained standing behind him. Jeladi was ready with a cup for him, and a pour of hot tea which he was almost inclined to refuse, having had altogether too much of stimulant and sleepless hours.

But the smell was different. It was the relaxing tea Narani had made for them, herbal flavoring, a little hint of berries and star-grass. He sipped it without sugar, shut his eyes and sighed.

"So will they work it out?" Algini asked, slipping into place across the table.

"One hopes," Banichi said. "The unit was working well with him. And trusted him too soon."

"The lad is professional," Algini said. "Here and not here, in the turn of a head. He learned how to read them. They will have to be careful of that."

"No question," Banichi said. "It is an uncommon set of skills, for a lord of the aishidi'tat. Watch that one, Bren-ji, when he has any interest in what may be going on."

"If we can get him back alive," Tano said, as he and Jago sat down.

"He lived through the Troubles," Algini said. "And likely got paid by every side."

"Oh, perhaps not that," Tano said.

"No," Algini said, "every side. I do not doubt he has contacts inside the Shadow Guild."

"Likely Paigiti is close enough to that description," Jago said. "I have no doubt he has been the Shadow Guild's landlord in Koperna. Small wonder Nomari suspected what property they were in. And that man dares complain about his merchandise."

"How long do you give," Tano asked, "before Paigiti or his organization commits some crime not on his list?"

"And is back on our list of problems?" Banichi said. "I give it a few days after our departure."

"You are ever the optimist," Algini said.

Late, late at night, Cajeiri waked, reached up and dragged pillows into a heap under his head. The apartment was still, extremely still, not even the stir of night staff going about their tasks. It became that way at some hours, poised between last night's settling down and the stir before next morning.

The supper table and the brandy, particularly the brandy, stayed vivid in his mind, an overpowering lot of puzzles. He had heard so many things he had never known. It was, in a strange way, like meeting his father and meeting his mother when he had come back from space, not the son they had sent away; only this was more as if his parents had been away together and never told him about it. They had shared secrets, shared opinions, made plans, and mani was not always on their side.

But really she was, and Father trusted her and Mother mostly did, at least that Mother knew mani never trusted her.

He had to work on that. Mani trusted *him* in most things. He could figure how to do that. Mani had accepted his human associates perfectly well. Why would she not trust Mother?

Maybe it was Father, he thought. Mani had been aiji when Great-grandfather died; and then . . . then she had turned things over to her son. Who was Grandfather. Who had not been a particularly good aiji, but he had generally let mani run things, especially outside the central aishidi'tat, so mani said.

And mani had run things after Grandfather died. He had not been all that old, but he had not been assassinated. He had done it to himself, people said, not intentionally, but because he ignored advice, drank too much and took too many pills.

People said. But there were ways it might not have been an accident. There were all sorts of people who were probably not too sorry.

And mani had been regent for Father for quite a long time, because Father had been just a little boy when Grandfather died; and mani had hidden him away in Malguri for years. Father said he had been happy in those years, a little lonely, but happy, being a boy. Sometimes mani would bring him back to Shejidan, and teach him herself. Sometimes he just had his tutors, several of them, some of them part of Malguri staff. But when he was a little older than Cajeiri was now, he had had Guild to teach him, and various people from various guilds assigned to come and teach him, so he learned a good many things that were traditional, and a good many things that were not. He had machimi—he rarely got to see them, but he read them; he learned kabiu. Father himself could arrange a bouquet, and actually enjoyed doing it, because, Father said, plants cooperated better than people.

He wished he had known Father when he was a boy. He always had thought that.

And tonight, as for some little time since events at Tirnamardi, he wished he had known Mother.

They just had not understood each other, but the more he understood Ajuri and Shishogi, and remembered his Ajuri grandfather, the more he had begun to know why she was so guarded, so private about things.

Do not say this, she would say. Do not tell mention this to your great-grandmother, but . . . He did not enjoy such secrets, and often they were stupid secrets.

But the more he understood Ajuri, and the more he understood that her father, Komaji, had very possibly killed her mother . . .

He had not believed that. Komaji had scared *him* so that it was even possible he had contributed to Komaji being killed. He had told Father Komaji scared him, and Father had banned Komaji from the Bujavid, even from the capital, and Komaji had died, not that it was directly his fault, or Father's, but that it was the chain of events, that Komaji had tried to deal with the Shadow Guild and had decided to betray them, and he had died.

All that was Mother's clan. Ajuri. And Mother had grown up in Ajuri and then been in and out of it, sometimes with Atageini clan, with Uncle, and sometimes angry at him and back in Ajuri for a while.

What he had not known, which he should have realized, given the distance involved, and the situation—was that Mother rode. Mother rode. Children did not ordinarily teach themselves. They had to have a teacher, and there was none better than Uncle unless it was mani.

And if one rode, one understood mecheiti, and knew how to take care with them and knew how to manage them. Getting a mecheita to leave its herd was no small feat. And one doubted she had run to Ajuri with Uncle's whole herd: that would have been a situation.

No. Mother had managed it, Mother had gotten one mecheita away, and through the gate, and she had done it with the whole herd upset and Uncle apt to have to repair the fences, but . . . not pursuing her. He doubted that.

Mother rode, because Uncle had taught her. And that meant there had been times they were close. And then not. And it was not what mani called *flightiness*. He did not read that in Mother, who could be as level as Uncle in a crisis. He had seen that in front of him. Mother did not panic. Mother was decisive with the staff, here, when she wanted something done. And Mother deferred to mani, Mother had deferred to mani even when Mother had lost him, because—

Because it was what made sense. Because he was Father's heir, or would be. And getting an education Mother could not give him. Nobody had consulted Mother when mani took him aboard the starship and they were gone for two years; and nobody had consulted Mother when she and Father had had to deal with the Shadow Guild, either, but Mother knew what they were, even before anybody in the rest of the world knew. Mother had had Grandfather and Aunt Geidaro and all sorts of problems claiming kinship with her, and Uncle on mani's side, and Father trying to settle the midlands . . . it had been a mess. All of it.

Now Grandfather and Aunt Geidaro were dead and Ajuri had no lord. Mother backed Nomari, mani was against it, and Father—Father let mani take him away to question, involving Lord Machigi, who was one of mani's associates, and a scary person, besides that.

But then Mother said—he could hardly believe she had said it—that it was a good thing mani was doing that, because it was important to know.

It left a cold feeling in his heart, because he would have leaned more to his feeling in the matter, but—it was the aishidi'tat at stake. And the heart of the aishidi'tat, at that, in Ajuri. And the safety and peace of a lot of people.

It was Father's kind of decision. He was used to that from Father. From Mother . . .

Mother knew what had to be done. Mother had arrived at Uncle's when so much was going wrong: Mother had taken the train and moved in with Guild to back up Uncle, and she had both backed her cousin Nomari *and* said that mani should question him.

And first Mother had invited him to a sort of pretend-brandy; and then Mother *and* Father had, and they had talked to him as if he were a person with an opinion, and explained things and told him things they might tell an adult, things they would not tell him if they thought he was too young or too stupid.

He had to talk to Uncle tomorrow. Tonight was too late, but he had to get Uncle on his side, and then maybe he could get Uncle to talk to him, and figure how to talk to mani.

It was hard to sleep. It was so hard to sleep. He was worried about mani and nand' Bren, worried about cousin Nomari, and worried, too, about the direction things were going, because there were forces moving, and mani had just learned Tiajo was moving first.

That was scary. That was just scary. In the middle of everything was not the time to have to change plans. It created mistakes. And there had been too many in the Shadow Guild's favor.

20

It was, Jago reported, the faintest edge of dawn—the great hall had no windows. There might have been a room for him, Bren recalled, nursing the ache in his neck, but the great hall was still the center of what they held, Guild came and went here from the operations center downstairs, and it seemed, respecting the commission the dowager had handed to him—to be in charge—that staying visible was the right choice.

He washed, in the accommodation that served the assembly hall. He managed a shave, a vast relief, not to look so odd to atevi eyes. He had Narani rebraid his queue and apply a new ribbon from his luggage. He had two changes of clothing in his personal case, and an indoor coat, however slightly creased. To his surprise, Jeladi turned up slightly out of breath, with the coat freshly pressed, courtesy of Bindanda and the house staff.

His aishid had seen their own hard night, but they had an uncanny ability to catnap, and Guild uniforms were tougher stuff. Banichi had received a couriered message from Casimi, currently in charge downstairs, and sent one back, but there had been nothing from the dowager since she had retired to a small guest arrangement connected to Bregani's expansive residence, with

Cenedi and a segment of her ordinary guard. Ilisidi was resting well, one hoped. If she wanted another hour, that was well and good. On her health and sanity, everything depended.

Bren returned to the table in the assembly hall, which had become their command center, and found a pot of tea and small container of eggs and toast waiting for them. Tano and Algini, under the rule of anything might intervene, had not waited. He did not. He sat down, with Jago.

Banichi's plate was as yet unused.

"Has he gone back downstairs?" he asked the others. Cenedi would not leave Ilisidi; but Casimi might want relief. He should have it from Casimi's partner Siemaji—someone other than Banichi, in his own opinion, and he would say so to Cenedi.

"He has gone down for a briefing," Jago said. "One understands Paigiti-nadi has been at it all night and is now asking for a lawyer."

He took an unsauced egg and a piece of toast. "I have yet to draft that amnesty. One presumes he is getting a lawyer? One might be useful to both sides. This *is* the Marid. And Lord Bregani has enough questions to deal with."

"Banichi," Tano said, looking past them, and Bren turned his head. Indeed, Banichi had just passed the doors. Information was coming. And Banichi had a handful of papers with him.

Bren washed down the egg—and a bite of toast. Banichi reached them and slid into a chair and laid a small stack of papers on the table in front of him. "Paigiti's confession has run ten pages, and involves murders, he says, of rivals threatening him. Persons of no good character."

"He says. But we will keep our word, in hope."

"He is refusing to have his aishid contribute to *his* list. Theirs are collective, and less literate . . . Casimi says they are asking the guards to spell such words as arson. More than once. But his account stands alone, and it is producing information of more than legal significance. I have sent to Records, inquiring after a string of addresses he has rented, disclaiming all responsibility."

"One keeps hoping," Bren said, "that we may find Tenjin's family, or any others we do not know about. The hostages may have been moved out of the city, but I fear worse, if our speed in getting here caused the majority of the Shadow Guild to run."

"We have directly asked Paigiti about places he may know about and separately asked his aishid, one by one, and they claim no knowledge of such hiding places. Paigiti says he may have rented a number of apartments and two garages to them, but he has, he says, no idea what use they made of them. Our inquiry to Records, and they have been open and helpful all through the last watch, is converting the property registration numbers to addresses. We do not know what we shall find. But we hope to learn something."

"One hopes," Bren said, with no good feeling. "It is *something,* at least."

"Paigiti has also asked for a book to be retrieved from his office, under a floor tile."

"Are we retrieving it?"

"It is on its way here. In these pages, Paigiti has also given us information on the Dojisigin he knows, names, most of which will be false, incidents and descriptions, which may be of use. We are sending that to Guild operations to the east. We also propose sending to some of Paigiti's identifiable associates, to extend the same offer: provide us information and stay forever clear of the law."

"I will approve it, if the Guild will accept it and if Lord Bregani will accept it. The dowager need not touch the matter."

"We are giving Lord Bregani a fairly extensive and useful network, if he can handle it without falling into their traps, and he is no fool. He has dodged Tiajo this far, and one doubts the likes of Paigiti can get the better of him."

"Paigiti's character will not improve. He will begin to think his own cleverness has given him another chance to profit, and he will transgress the first chance he sees. Do I understand, or not? I do not see a chance he will change his ways."

"If he truly benefits," Banichi said, "there is a remote chance for him, if he were to *find* his man'chi, and he is uncommonly shaken, but he has a distance to go yet, to admit he is not the better of everyone he deals with. We have moved the ground under him. We shall see who he is when he catches his balance."

One doubted, with that one. But man'chi was an inestimable factor. A chance, Banichi said, a remote chance.

"I do not want to present the idea to Lord Bregani myself. I do not want him to assume I understand. Present it as an idea, not a decision. And tell me his answer. If he agrees, I shall draft much the same language. It will be no problem."

"I shall do that. We are loosening the curfew over sections of the city this morning, and that will be going on through the day. We had rather see the dowager back on the train before we do, but she has declined that request."

She would say no. He was not surprised.

"If you can use your influence, do. The city folk have been pent up and frustrated. The Guild would rather that she go before the crowds move about. We will be using the services of the broadcast center to inform people and give directions—Lord Bregani's cousin deserves great consideration for his service thus far, if you will report that to the dowager, and to Tabini-aiji."

"I shall. The whole family, down to the young ones. They at very least deserve a remembrance."

"Meanwhile," Banichi said, "we are receiving reports

from the other force. The operation is proceeding, one gathers. Two bases are now established. This is standard. They are making no great effort at speed, letting the navy ship move into position to control the harbor, quietly so, possibly without the Shadow Guild being aware they are there. Both ships were likely sighted when passing the Sungeni Isles, and the presence of one in this harbor is noisy enough. The Dojisigi are apt to assume they might receive attention from the second ship, and reports are, they will be certain of it by midmorning and the Guild force will be moving. I am about to go down and relieve Casimi. Is there anything in particular you wish to tell Paigiti, Bren-ji?"

"I shall deal with these papers. Additions and amendments will still be possible. I will send the framing language down when I have it composed. Thank him and his associates, and I will see copies made once I have the thing composed."

"Paigiti may have more this morning, after he recovers from his hangover. You will note the writing deteriorates."

One was amused. "We will do the editing," he said. "Preserving the original, should there be any question of accuracy. How late did they go, one wonders?"

"To the bottom of three bottles," Banichi said with amusement. "It was a cooperative effort, until they overset an inkwell."

One could only imagine.

"I shall deal with these. One wishes you a tranquil day, nadiin-ji. Let me know what that tome of Paigiti's deals with."

Banichi stood up. Algini, seated on the far side of the table, likewise stood up. Jago and Tano were arriving, and Narani and Jeladi brought more eggs and toast and tea.

Over to the east, a ship was moving, and a land assault would also be moving, and if things grew complicated their departure from Koperna might be delayed for an unforeseeable time.

Jago and Tano settled to breakfast. At their table against the wall, by the embedded pillar, Nomari and his aishid were having their breakfast.

A distance away, Lord Machigi had set himself up for breakfast with his aishid.

Well enough, Bren thought. He could have another cup of tea. Paigiti's case was not an emergency.

Then a stir of attention among the Guild breakfasting in the area drew his attention to the room behind him. He thought it might be the dowager making an appearance, but the Guild did not have that sense of urgency in their rising.

Tano and Jago had noticed. Bren turned in his chair and saw Lord Bregani and Murai with Husai—Husai walking on her own, though with Bregani and Murai's hands on her elbows, and scrubbed and well-dressed, a very different appearance than the sooted, bloodied and wilted girl of last night. She seemed weak, quite weak, but she walked where she wished to walk, and her parents were there to help her.

Bren stood up. Machigi and his guard did, and prepared to move their breakfast, but Bregani signaled no, let it be. So Machigi and his guard only stood. Tano and Jago moved to stand at Bren's side. And Nomari and his guard stood up, quietly, unobtrusively.

Except that was Husai's direction. She walked over to Nomari while the whole hall watched, and Nomari gave a deep, prolonged bow, and she gave a little one when he was done.

Something was said. Bren could not hear it, but Bregani added something; and Machigi, watching from a distance away, had an ironical, almost pitying expression, that could have been amusement.

Husai offered her hand. Nomari took it and held it a moment, and let go, then bowed to her and her family. Husai kept standing there, until her parents gently moved her away, and back the way they had come. People remained standing while the family made their way back to the righthand corridor, Husai still walking, but slowly, leaning a little on her father.

Everyone sat again, as they were.

It was a deserved thanks. It was moving. It was *not* the dowager's intention to see an appointee to Ajuri developing one more Ajuri tie to the northern Marid. The lines were old, even ancient, the connections had translated to nothing but trouble, and the paidhi-aiji felt disheartened to have to agree with Ilisidi. It was *not* the best match for the future of either region.

Bren glanced Nomari's way. Nomari was not looking at him. Instead he was looking down, and talking to his aishid, who doubtless had instruction from the dowager by way of Cenedi.

One hated to stand in the way. An association was possible, a connection of alliance. *That* would be valuable—if youth and attraction did not turn it into another generation.

Nomari did look at him, in looking up. It might be chance. It might not. Bren gave him his true face, a worried face, and Nomari looked down again.

It was due, it was proper, it was a good outcome. And they were each heirs of districts inconveniently far apart, each with their history of troubles—while a Guild force was moving even at that moment to deal with the effects of the last such round of unions.

Jago said, arriving at his shoulder: "Cenedi is speaking. The dowager invites you to breakfast. An escort is coming. He assumes that we will remain here."

Another breakfast. And God knew what else. His aishid did not leave him by choice. Jago and Tano were assigned not to leave him. But the dowager sent an escort.

His papers were here, the documents Banichi had left him. His writing kit.

His oversight of the situation here.

"Jago-ji. You have to be in charge. Of communications. Of everything. Refer to Banichi if need be. Tano-ji. Be Jago's guard. Or messenger. Narani and Jeladi will assist. I trust I shall not be that long absent. I do not *think* I am in disfavor. Or that much disfavor."

They were not happy with the situation. He saw that, plainly.

"Gather my papers together. All of it. If anything should happen—guard them."

Nothing could be that certain while they were in the field, as they were now. Nothing was as it usually was.

Nor was his situation with Ilisidi.

It was the Farai lord's personal suite that was lent to Ilisidi for the duration, the Farai lord moving to guest quarters, Bren understood, in Lord Bregani's massive apartment.

It was a generous move on the Farai lord's part, possibly gratitude for Husai's recovery, with perhaps some small odor of advantage-seeking: Bren's own career had crossed their ambition more than once, but in this instance, favor-seeking or not, it was a gallant and convenient gesture which Ilisidi had not demanded or even suggested. They had offered; and Ilisidi had had the luxury of a good bed and, one hoped, a safe and decent breakfast from Bindanda's kitchen.

Bren entered, uneasy in the absence of his own aishid. One of Ilisidi's staff conducted him alone to the fairly luxurious dining room, where a not quite luxurious breakfast was laid on a shortened table.

"Nand' paidhi," Ilisidi greeted him. Cenedi was also seated, at Ilisidi's left. Bren bowed properly and took the right.

The servant provided tea, and there were, again, eggs, and toast. And pickle. It was no great sacrifice to have a small second breakfast in quiet, at a well-laid table, considering the chaos of the night and the prospects of the day. He ate.

Ilisidi finished.

He did.

"So," she said. "The girl is up and about."

"She is, aiji-ma."

"She wished to thank her rescuer."

"She did, aiji-ma. It was a brief thank you."

"The prospective lord of Ajuri has contacts who rent rooms to the Shadow Guild."

"I did note that, aiji-ma."

"And what else did you note?"

"We have an extensive record of Paigiti's misdeeds. I am going through them now, and I am certain Casimi has. If the amnesty sends Paigiti into retirement, he may become a useful contact, worth preserving."

"And Nomari?"

"I have not observed anything in his behavior or manner that I cannot recommend. I cannot call him ignorant for going off as he did, his contacts being what they are. I think he has felt more a prisoner than a guest since coming here. I think he somewhat despairs of your good opinion. But he saw his family murdered, and he has a regard for this girl, who is younger than her years, and protected. I agree with you, aiji-ma, his going after her was foolish. But forgive my poesy, aiji-ma, I think it was the boy he was that sent him after Bregani's daughter, not the young man he is."

Ilisidi stared at him, thinking. Thinking.

"Poesy," she said. "You favor him."

"He has not lost my good opinion."

"Ha. *You* would have gone."

"Had I his knowledge, were I not under *your* orders, aiji-ma, I would have strongly considered it. My aishid, however, knows me. His aishid—excellent men—had only started to trust him and had no idea, as Banichi and Algini have both observed, that he has *professional* skills, when it comes to vanishing."

"Not a skill most young lords display," Ilisidi said. "He shows us obfuscation. Elusion. Modesty, when it serves. Maturity, when it does come, will be interesting."

"You do not dismiss him."

"We do not," Ilisidi said, and attempted a sip of tea. She set it down, tapped the table with her finger, and the servant hastened to pick up the cup and to replace it with a clean one and a new pour of tea. The servant likewise replaced Bren's cup.

"I spoke to Lord Tatiseigi at the edge of dawn—by phone, relayed in quite an amazing way. And very obliquely. We spoke a great deal about his hedge repair. In our own code. Our connection could not be secure."

"You have forgiven him."

"Pish. We were never out. We understand each other. He has an opinion, of course, which he made clear. I have an opinion, which I made clear. But we are not at odds."

"One is glad to hear it."

"About my grandson, now," Ilisidi said. "Have you spoken with him? Or has your aishid?"

"To my knowledge, neither, aiji-ma."

"You did not know about this move he has made."

"I have no perfect knowledge of *what* move he has made."

A sip of tea, remarkably calm. "We have also, and with a good deal more frankness, talked with our grandson. We have expressed our gratitude for the ability to talk to him directly, which we have done. Directly. But we are fairly reconciled at the moment. He says these scoundrels have decided to go after *me*."

"We prevented one such. Did he reference that?"

"And are searching for his family," Ilisidi supplied, "with no success thus far. One such. My staff has my full confidence there are others. And I have confidence in my bodyguard. And in yours. And in those the Guild supplied for Nomari. Even Machigi's ill-favored lot. The Guild in Shejidan is looking very, very deeply into records of everyone assigned aboard the train. I do not believe they will find anything. I do not believe trusted Guild is how they would hope to reach us. But—we do not take our trust to foolish levels. Your staff is preparing our food, and I am leaving the first Guild force I sent in place here, split between berths on the train that brought them, and in the residency, so nothing can reach them all. You have not asked. How does my grandson's concern for my safety and his delivery of this communication system account for his diversion of one of *my* ships and his assault on the Dojisigin? Do not say it was a sudden decision. One does not amass such an expedition overnight."

Wariness was indicated. "One thinks it would be a good question, aiji-ma."

"It is. And we asked it." Sip of tea. It was one of the calmative sort. "It seems that our associate Lord Geigi has been busy. He has populated the sky with robot observers. He has circled the world with them. These metal creatures have eyes and they see even into the Great Ocean. And . . . they send what they see, passing it one to the next, to Lord Geigi. He has shared such observations with the humans. He is making observations that bear on weather and claiming he could have extraordinary accuracy, if, he says, we would provide more information from the ground. He also claims there are islands halfway around the world. Did you know?"

"One had heard of islands, aiji-ma, but not the extent of his observations."

"It seems, so my grandson says, that the space station is maintained to stay in one place, while these creatures go about the world seeing amazing things. And that lander might have come down most anywhere Lord Geigi wanted it. But my grandson asked it to be planted here, now, to give us the ability to communicate—in this war my grandson has launched. You did not know about this in advance."

"Nothing of the lander, or a war, aiji-ma. About the islands, yes, but nothing about this."

"My grandson is fairly put out with me," Ilisidi said. A fingertip circled the rim of the cup. "And believes that I have ill-advisedly placed myself in danger. One appreciates the concern. He feels that I may have stirred the waters in which *he* wished to fish, and the records he hopes to recover may be in danger. This, I shall accept. I am being very frank with you, paidhi-aiji. Did he mention his intention to go to war?"

"No, he did not. He said to keep you safe."

A short, silent laugh. "One does not disparage your ability, paidhi. But now he says he has information from Ajuri's productive basement that makes him extremely anxious to see what Dojisigin may have to offer. The Guild is after records. My grandson wishes to divert our operation here into a second Guild operation, after such records on this side of the Marid, should they exist."

"Paigiti's list may be of some value in that."

"Paigiti himself may be on the Guild's list. And if he is cooperating, he may have saved himself. But for the rest, for the rest, paidhi, my grandson believes that we have been both too early, and a number of days too late. Our arrival in Hasjuran was reported to the Shadow Guild, and the Red Train's arrival in Koperna by night not only launched Bregani northward, it launched Tiajo south and west. We are fairly confident where."

"Tiajo herself has fled?"

"Lord Geigi is relatively certain he is tracking a Dojisigin freighter that has now rounded the cape and is headed north, we think. Our suspicion is it will put in at Ashidama Bay, where most of their shipments go. My grandson is somewhat put out about my move into Senjin. I maintain that if we had not made this venture to save Bregani, we would have had, yes, the Dojisigi somewhat preoccupied in taking Senjin and posing a future threat to our ally Machigi and *his* association, over half the Marid. I consider this significant. My grandson is less concerned to preserve Machigi, and we ask *him*, does he prefer chaos in the south? We think not. Whatever Machigi's future disposition—and my grandson says I will promote him until your Najida becomes an unfortunate tributary to a southern aijinate—I say that

Machigi's concern for the south is a proper and moral concern, a leaderly concern, and if the aishidi'tat has to deal with a prosperous third power in the world, I call it a beneficial change, replacing an immoral regressionist power in the Marid, continually fighting us. I wed my East to the aishidi'tat back at the beginning of my public life because it was an intelligent thing to do. I have enabled Machigi to do the same—without the marriage—and I do not think Machigi is stupid. We have the space station, an asset my grandson has never fully appreciated, and Machigi will *forever* be second to that, which he has never quite appreciated either."

"Humans would not well understand Machigi," Bren said. "I scarcely do."

"He is fairly simple. He would kill us all if he had to, *for* his precious Taisigin. But he has lost all motive for doing so. Ambition has taken hold of him, and a vision of a Marid preserving its ways, but able to deal as a power, not as a poor cousin."

"Not to the good of the north *or* your grandson, aiji-ma."

"Ah, but Machigi does *not* have a wide vision. A part of him remains wedded to a bygone glory, a heritage he cannot restore. That is why my grandson is the greater aiji. It is why my grandson has taken you for an advisor, and why he finds the notion of space attractive. My great-grandson, however—he will know what to do with Machigi *and* the powers in orbit *and* this somewhat dubious lord of Ajuri. I do not build for my grandson. I build for *his* son. And my time to accomplish these things is somewhat less than I would want."

That . . . was worrisome. He was immediately concerned. "Aiji-ma."

She waved a negligent hand. "It will be whatever it can be. I do not count risk to my life as a vastly important matter. I am concerned for my household, and for you, paidhi. I shall count it no affront to me should you, at this point, go back to my grandson. You should consider that, at this point. I do not think there is much negotiation ahead."

"I have amazing uses. Protect you, your grandson said. I would urge you go back to Shejidan and let the Guild manage this. Tiajo, of all people, is not worth your effort. Surely you will not pursue her."

"No, she is not. But the south is. And I am likely to run her down in the process. Indulge me, paidhi. I have argued from my husband's aijinate on, through two turns of my own in office, that the only trouble in the south we should truly worry about is the southwest refusing full participation in the aishidi'tat. They should have been in or they should have been out, from their refusal to accept the Mospheiran compact, their refusal to accept Shejidan's appointments, their refusal to comply with the laws and forms of the aishidi'tat and their refusal to act in concert with us, which has *always* given cover to illicit enterprises. They have been the thorn in the arrangement so long as the aishidi'tat has existed. The Marid could never be the problem it has been without the southwest coast supporting their trade in the background, funding their mischief. Machigi and his associates have generally bypassed them, going on up the coast, in spite of the Edi's unfortunate choice of a livelihood."

The Edi had survived by wrecking ships, luring them onto the rocks, and looting them—besides their trade in fishing.

"Now the Edi have forsworn their wrecking," Ilisidi said, "Machigi has only Ashidama Bay to pass, and *they* try to make matters difficult up in Cobo, so that whoever up there trades with Machigi's association has difficulties with Ashidama Bay. This has gone on subtly. It has worsened, since the Edi have changed their ways. So. That the Shadow Guild would go there, to their own trading partners, now that our attention has turned to the Marid, we are not surprised. And this is why I do not think we shall have to search the Great Ocean for Tiajo, and why I think we are in for far more resistance there than here."

"Well, then, I can hardly go back to Shejidan, can I, as lord of Najida, and an ally of the Edi."

"We would not deny you," Ilisidi said, "if you wish to take that position."

"Unless your grandson forbids me. I have that responsibility."

"So. Do, then."

"May I inform your grandson?"

"Oh, inform away. Tell him I shall be leaving the first Guild force here, to carry out operations and support Lord Bregani. My grandson will do whatever he chooses to do in the Dojisigin. I shall take our Ajuri candidate as far as Najida, where I trust he will be welcome, and from there send him back to my grandson with a tentative approval, but with a warning that we do not know *all* his connections. I also rather expect Machigi will part company with us here. He has already sent for a ship to take him home."

"Does *he* know all this, regarding your plans for the west coast?"

"I have had this conversation with him, yes, to extract what he does know, which is interesting. But he has a new situation on his northern border: he has to explain to his people that they are to regard Senjin as an ally, no matter how difficult in the beginning, until Bregani can convince all his people to be polite as well. That, for Machigi, is more critical at the moment. And I do not wish to *provoke* the Ashidama folk, who have a very poor opinion of him. No, he will go from here down to Tanaja, and explain matters to his association. This train, however, will be departing Koperna for Najida, perhaps as early as tonight. I shall explain to Bregani. I think he will be quite busy for the immediate future."

"I am going with you."

Ilisidi smiled benignly. "Well, I would expect it as far as Najida."

"You well know I am not stopping in Najida, aiji-ma. Unless your grandson orders me otherwise. And he will not. I know just as well that he will not."

Epilogue

People were still few on the streets, but shutters were open, and many shops were open, though the sun was close to setting. The bus passed them, with a mobile unit ahead and one behind, and people stopped and watched. In one place, bystanders waved and cheered, perhaps because some of the northern Guild were headed for the train, and leaving Koperna.

The first-deployed, and the first train in, were not leaving Koperna yet. They were setting up for a stay in the city, and in Lusi'ei, where the situation with the Dojisigin freighters was still not resolved, and needed to be, for one thing, because a Taisigi ship was due in tomorrow morning to take Lord Machigi home. He would spend the night at the residency, with some of the first-in Guild brought in to back up his small bodyguard.

Well and good, Machigi said. He had never been so long absent from his capital, and wanted to be home while the northern Guild sorted out the situation in Amarja, in case any troubles spilled over to the open sea, or tried to flee south out of Senjin.

The Red Train, however, was boarding for Najida, withdrawing several of the mobile units and the entire Guild force that had brought Ilisidi.

It was very little trouble to pack. Bren had not unpacked, to speak of, and the cases had gone back onto the bus. The dowager herself had brought very little compared to the usual, and had withdrawn all her personal aishid except Casimi and Seimaji. They were left to command the twelve specialists she had left to assist Lord Bregani, specialists with equipment to set up, for protection of the residency itself . . . in case the Shadow Guild wanted to make another try.

Records had provided a copy of Paigiti's confession, and the confessions of his bodyguard. Copies were in the hands of local enforcement, and were destined for other places where they might be useful, especially the addresses.

Bren had copies of his own, among his papers. The agreements up in Hasjuran were being sent on, physically, to Shejidan, for the Archive; they carried others in their luggage.

He himself hardly knew whether to draw an easier breath as the bus exited the streets and pulled into the railyard, or to nerve himself for worse, involving his own region, and risk to *his* people. Najida was not able to take on a quarrel with the townships of the southern peninsula. He was familiar with Jorida as a shipping power, and an economic power. That the Shadow Guild was setting up there was not good news.

Nomari, in the aisle seat next to him, had said very little this morning. The plan was for the Red Train to stop at Najida and stay there, on the siding, and Nomari was to go to Najida with the rest of them, then be driven up the coast to the airport, and an easy flight to Shejidan, after which—

After which Nomari and the Ajuri question passed at least temporarily out of their concern. The dowager had no use for him on the next venture, and Ajuri was not to be involved.

As for Najida, it would be. The estate bus had not finished its repair from events at Tirnamardi, but it should be serviceable, and conspicuous.

He wished there were a way around that. He did not want to draw Najida's people into a confrontation with Jorida.

And one feared that this venture was not as well-planned as one could wish. He *hoped* they were not going to invade Jorida Isle. But there was no way to say.

Keep her safe, Tabini had said. His power to do that was limited.

The power of the Guild, in numbers that filled the other seats of this bus, which had made three such runs to the station this evening, was itself limited, where it came to Ilisidi's will.

Tabini-aiji was at least informed, through the Guild, that Ilisidi was headed for Najida. He was likely informed, through the Guild, that a brief stay there was not her ultimate intent.

The bus pulled up at the train station, opened the door and let them file out, with some little delay for Ilisidi. Cenedi assisted her all the way down and up again.

Bren followed, down the steps, up to the platform level, and on into the interior, with its historic mural. He recognized the residency in the painting now. He had had no idea, before.

He had had no idea of a good many things, before.

It was not all Guild in the area. A Transportation agent held the other door, that opened onto the platform, a young man in Transportation gray, with heavy-rimmed glasses.

"Stop," Algini said quietly, and aloud, "Cenedi!"

Gunstraps slid from shoulders. Ilisidi's bodyguard became a wall, and Bren lost sight of the door for a moment, behind that screen. Jago jerked him around and behind her, and he was utterly walled in.

There was no shooting. In a moment the alert was off, and he could see the agent in the glasses pinned against the historic mural, but not so fiercely as might have been. The Guild was letting him stand free, with guns, however, endangering the murals.

"Homura," Tano said, but not in a welcoming way. Ilisidi was ordering her guards to give her a view, and Bren had his own.

"Aiji-ma," the young man said, and took off the glasses, giving Ilisidi a profound bow, and another to Bren. "Nand' paidhi."

Cenedi was still halfway between Homura and Ilisidi. And not moving.

"We hope to join you," Homura said. "Or we can find a way."

We. Momichi, likely.

"Visiting the paidhi-aiji, would it be?" Ilisidi asked. "Are we to have another explosion to inconvenience us? Or what *is* your intention, nadi?"

"One regrets the inconvenience, aiji-ma. I took care of the problem before I left. He will not trouble Hasju-ran."

"And you present yourself to us now—why?"

"The Red Train is going the right direction," Homura said. "We have business on the coast. Nand' paidhi. You sent for us. We came to join you . . . at some difficulty."

"Do you know a man named Paigiti?" Bren asked.

"We know you have him."

"He never mentioned you."

"Not by our proper names," Homura said. "But yes, we know him."

"You are putting yourselves in our hands," Ilisidi said, "and you should not expect courtesy."

"It has been rather a hard trip," Homura said, and for the first time Homura's voice faltered into hoarseness. "For much the same reason. We do not need courtesy. But we may be of service, if you are bent on finishing this."

"Take him," Ilisidi said, with a wave of her hand. "Find his partner. Give them Machigi's car."

"Check their equipment," Cenedi said, which one thought was a good idea. They had been Shadow Guild. They claimed not to be, now. They also had not appeared since vanishing into the Marid and now turned up where the transformer had blown, up in Hasjuran.

Now, hitherto operating alone, and betraying the interests that had betrayed them, they showed up in another guild's uniform, expecting . . . it was unclear what. They surely did not mistake the dowager's sudden departure westward for a holiday trip to Najida.

Cenedi's men escorted Homura on ahead of them, through the station. Another rail worker began to follow them, a man about Momichi's stature. They stopped in the far doorway and went on together.

"Do we trust that?" Algini asked, who, with Tano, had nearly gotten caught in the transformer blast.

"There are trails down from Hasjuran," Jago said, "but to make that trip afoot—one doubts it."

Riding exposed to the elements once—maybe twice—risked one's life. It was a breach of the dowager's security, and that was not easy to do.

But if those two had ever told the truth, the Shadow Guild had been trying to lay hands on them since they had surrendered at Tirnamardi.

The Red Train was puffing steam and waiting for them, as it had been, with several cars empty now. It was a flatlands trip, generally, and it had not shed the excess cars . . . in fact they had reloaded their mobile units, one with a heavy gun, and other armament. They were running as they had been all the way from Shejidan, and the Guild that had come to Hasjuran and Koperna with the dowager was leaving with her, while whatever was going on in the east continued, and while the first of the Guild forces provided security in Koperna.

It was a trip they had never made, but they were headed for familiar territory, passing by the allied territory of the Maschi lord, and on to a welcome in Najida.

There was never a time, coming to Najida, that Bren had felt anything but relief. But this time—he did. It was home. It was peace. It was security. And he was bringing the possibility of war with him, with the dowager. With all it entailed.

Past the west coast, there was only Mospheira, before the ocean went on all the way to the east coast of the continent, a vast stormy nowhere. The west coast was where the atevi world stopped, and they had pushed the Shadow Guild to the edge of it.

There was nowhere left to run.

CJ Cherryh
Complete Classic Novels in Omnibus Editions

www.dawbooks.com

DAW 9

Margaret Fortune

—NOVA—

978-0-7564-1081-0

"*Nova* grabbed me from the first chapter, and never let go. What a ride! Unforgettable, fast-paced and original, this book kept me guessing to the end."

—Amie Kaufman,
New York Times bestselling co-author of *These Broken Stars*

"This book definitely scratched my kick-ass teen heroine itch, and it did it in SPACE. That's a perfect combo if I've seen one."

—Book Riot

And don't miss the thrilling sequel
ARCHANGEL

www.dawbooks.com

DAW 216

C.S. Friedman
The Best in Science Fiction

THIS ALIEN SHORE   978-0-7564-1742-0
A *New York Times* Notable Book of the Year
"Breathlessly plotted, emotionally savvy. A potent
metaphor for the toleration of diversity."
—*The New York Times*

THE MADNESS SEASON   978-0-88677-444-8
"Exceptionally imaginative and compelling."
—*Publishers Weekly*

IN CONQUEST BORN   978-0-7564-0043-9
"Space opera in the best sense: high stakes adventure
with a strong focus on ideas, and characters an
intelligent reader can care about."—*Newsday*

THE WILDING   978-0-7564-0202-6
The long-awaited follow-up to *In Conquest Born.*

www.dawbooks.com

DAW 17

Tanya Huff
The Peacekeeper Novels

"Huff weaves a fast-paced thriller bristling with treachery and intrigue. Fans of military science fiction will enjoy this tense adventure and its intricately constructed setting."
—*Publishers Weekly*

"Anyone who has read any of Huff's previous books featuring Kerr . . . knows of her amazing ability to combine action, plot, and character into a wonderful melange that makes her books a joy to read."
—*Seattle Post-Intelligencer*

AN ANCIENT PEACE
978-0-7564-1130-5

A PEACE DIVIDED
978-0-7564-1151-0

THE PRIVILEGE OF PEACE
978-0-7564-1154-1

www.dawbooks.com

DAW 74

Suzanne Palmer
Finder

"A breakneck-paced and action-packed science-fiction adventure featuring an endearing con artist whose current mission to retrieve a stolen spaceship ignites a war.... A nonstop SF thrill ride until the very last page." —*Kirkus*

"Fergus Ferguson makes an excellent lead in this fast-paced hard-sf repo adventure set in space opera's sweeping scale and balanced on the heart of one very finely wrought character. Suzanne Palmer's writing is delightful."
    —Fran Wilde, author of the Bone Universe trilogy

"Palmer makes short-distance space travel feel as comfortable as riding a bicycle, and concludes this entertaining caper with a clever resolution and a hint of intrigue. Fans of space adventure will find this a fine example of the form."
    —*Publishers Weekly*

"Wicked, fast-paced, and fun. This is a total romp, and I loved it."   —Elizabeth Bear, author of *Ancestral Night*

ISBN: 978-0-7564-1635-5

www.dawbooks.com

DAW 219